Returner's Defiance

Copyright © 2024 by Bruce Sentar

All rights reserved.

No portion of this book may be reproduced in any form without written permission from the publisher or author, except as permitted by U.S. copyright law.

Cover Art by Yanaidraws

Contents

Chapter 1	1
Chapter 2	10
Chapter 3	17
Chapter 4	24
Chapter 5	32
Chapter 6	40
Chapter 7	48
Chapter 8	55
Chapter 9	62
Chapter 10	70
Chapter 11	77
Chapter 12	84
Chapter 13	91
Chapter 14	99
Chapter 15	107
Chapter 16	115
Chapter 17	123
Chapter 18	131
Chapter 19	138

Chapter 20	145
Chapter 21	152
Chapter 22	161
Chapter 23	168
Chapter 24	175
Chapter 25	183
Chapter 26	191
Chapter 27	198
Chapter 28	205
Chapter 29	212
Chapter 30	220
Chapter 31	227
Chapter 32	235
Chapter 33	242
Chapter 34	249
Chapter 35	256
Chapter 36	265
Chapter 37	272
Chapter 38	279
Chapter 39	286
Chapter 40	293
Chapter 41	301
Chapter 42	308
Chapter 43	315
Chapter 44	321

Chapter 45	327
Chapter 46	334
Chapter 47	341
Chapter 48	348
Chapter 49	354
Chapter 50	361
Chapter 51	368
Chapter 52	375
Chapter 53	382
Chapter 54	388
Chapter 55	396
Chapter 56	402
Afterword	411
Also By	413

Chapter 1

The howls of demons echoed in the distance, and I pulled myself through the doors only to slam them shut.

I fumbled with the bar for the door, my hands slick with so much blood that I nearly dropped it.

A part of me had known this would be the end. Bastion was the last human settlement that I knew of in the world. Tonight, it would fall. The fortress protecting it had already been breached and an unmatched demon had shattered our best warriors. With the fortress broken, people scattered, trying to flee. There was no point, we were surrounded. Even if I fought on, I was just one man. It was too late.

Instead, I turned to my room and the backup plan I had hatched on a desperate night.

Candles lit the room as several unique SSS ranked artifacts floated around the complex inscription formation. One of them I had even specially modified for this. I took in a deep breath and aligned my mana with the formation, flowing into it, even as the drums of war pounded in the distance.

The enemy would be upon me soon, and the fight, everything I stood for, would be all gone.

Humanity would be gone with me. There might be a few other survivors, but there were fewer than a dozen humans left on Earth. We had been so unprepared for what had come for us.

It had been over five hundred years of war since the Rapture. There had been bright spots, times of victory and times of peace, but the demons never stopped. Not fully. In so many ways, they had already won before the war even started. Our world had been infected from the beginning.

Too often through the years, we had found ourselves backstabbed by people we had considered allies, only to learn they'd been working for the demons all along.

I watched as the book at the center of the formation lifted into the air, the time-worn pages unfolding before me, telling me the story of my life. I had dug up my old journal to use as a focus for the inscription I was preparing.

I had one last idea, one last method for trying to defeat the demons.

I was going to send my soul back in time, before the Rapture, and before everything had slowly twisted in on itself, leading to the horrors surrounding me today. It was an ability used to gaze into the past, but with several artifacts to strengthen the connection and an ability from a demon to send my soul back.

Prompts appeared in front of me as things activated.

[Time Vision - You may step back in time for one minute.]

There I was, writing in the same journal I had before me, only I knew nothing of what was to come. Eighteen years old and I was about to go through one of the most trying times of my life.

[Possession - Destroy the soul of another and replace it with your own]

I swallowed. Fear at what could happen, what paradox effect or what-have-you might happen filled me.

Yet I was out of options. This was a Hail Mary. A last-ditch effort to fix everything that had gone wrong. With me, maybe we could avoid five hundred years of fighting, only to lose.

The book landed on a page, the last entry, which was in 2019. That was two years before the Rapture.

My vision fish-eyed like I was pushing through some boundary that I shouldn't be able to, and everything was stretching, pulling at me to rip me back to my present time.

[Possession F Rank activated.]

CHAPTER 1

I hadn't used this spell before. Stealing bodies from people was not really my day-to-day life. I had gained it from a demon I had killed, never using it until now.

My past self wasn't even integrated into the System yet; he had no defenses.

Possession activated and I felt my soul from the present-day rip and pull as I pushed back over five hundred years.

Pain ripped through every fiber of my soul as I pushed the limits of what the system would allow. For a moment I thought that it had failed, that the demons would overtake the world and soon storm into my room and kill me.

My body bled from every orifice and my heart exploded with the pressure of trying to shove my soul back in time. Immortal Body SS was taxed to the point that even it couldn't keep up with the damage my body was taking, and I felt myself die.

Yet, combat with demons was more than just physical and several abilities to stabilize my soul as I gave it all one final push, there was no going back.

I felt myself snap back at the same instant that my vision switched to normal, a diary sitting in front of me as I sat in a room that had long ago stopped existing.

Letting out a sigh, I focused on my breathing for a moment, I'd done it.

In preparation for this moment, I had read my diary again. It was largely filled with teenager angst and loss as my mother died. The doctors had suggested I start a journal to cope with her death that would come in forty-eight days. She was terminal. It was an 'atypical' blood disease.

The doctors had never understood what had caused my mother's illness, simply marking it as novel. Later, I would learn it was a type of physique-corroding poison, something that meant it came from someone who was part of the System. My mother wasn't a normal human, and a normal poison would do little to her.

I stood up, tossing the diary aside and waiting for a long minute to see if anything happened because of me breaking what felt like some pretty big laws of the universe.

But nothing came. No heavenly tribulation, no sudden death or excision from the universe. Whatever laws governed time travel didn't appear to wink me out of existence, so... that was good.

I tried to call up the System menu, a sheer force of habit, yet there was just static for a moment, then nothing.

I nodded. I had prepared for this situation. I wasn't initiated with this body. So, this body did not have access to the System.

Flexing my hands, I nearly laughed. They felt so weak. They would be nearly useless until I built up my strength. I really needed to get used to my new limitations.

But at the moment, there was something far more important that I needed to do. I grabbed an old sweatshirt and threw it on as I left the two-bedroom apartment and snagged the keys by the door, making sure to lock it on my way out.

It was always best to be careful, and I had grown far more cautious given the dangers of the world I had just exited.

Caution wasn't being a coward. It was learning to survive in a world far more dangerous than anyone knew about in the present time.

Well, not everyone was unaware. The Clans knew, and there were secret sects hidden throughout the world that would crop up like weeds, growing quickly as soon as the Rapture hit.

I was disconnected from my family with my mother's death and then my disappearance into a gang and eventually the mob.

The facts of the past life didn't hurt. They were just facts. The fact that they did not bother me or fill me with emotion let me know that at least part of my soul power had remained with me.

I chuckled at the idea of my whole soul power still being present. If I could find one of those rare soul attacks before the Rapture, I'd be a god. Hundreds of years of demon hunting built a strong soul.

The families and sects were well above mortals at this point in time, but before the Rapture, there just wasn't the opportunity to grow to the extent I had following the event.

Mrs. Rodgers poked her head out. "Bran, are you okay?"

"I'm fine, Mrs. Rodgers. Go back to sleep." I kept my voice calm as I stepped out of the rundown apartment building and onto the street, turning right and walking forward.

Night had just descended on New Vein. That meant in this part of the city that people started to post up at 'their' corners.

I recognized what they were, even if I didn't know who they were. I'd moved into an area that was contested territory, quickly getting sucked into gang life over the next several months.

"Hey there, young man." A night walker waved me down.

I met her eyes and she shrunk away, pulling two other ladies away from me. I nearly rolled my eyes. I needed to tone down my gaze apparently. Whatever she had seen in my eyes involved a history this body had not experienced.

Turning down a side street, I headed towards the hospital that rose above the rest of the cheap apartments on the bad side of town.

"Don't move." A scrappy man, not much more than skin and bones, pulled a gun on me and looked up and down the dimly lit street. The tweaker fidgeted with something in his pocket.

I stopped, not because he wanted me to, but because he posed an opportunity. "I'd put that down, or better yet, hand it over."

"How about I shoot you if you don't empty your pockets." He jabbed the gun at me and took another step closer.

I met his eyes, but they flitted around too much for him to even focus on me. This guy apparently had never heard not to use the product. It was rule number one.

"You deaf, boy?" the man asked.

"No. I'm just waiting for you to make a move so that I can scatter your teeth along the street in self-defense," I answered calmly.

There were certain principles that I maintained. Killing someone for their things went against them, but if he struck me, then my hands were no longer tied. At some point, principles were something you lived and died by.

He jabbed at me again with that gun.

What happened next was fast by most standards, yet far slower than I expected. I pushed the gun to the side, grabbing his wrist and twisting to point the gun down.

My mind moved faster than my hands and the gun went off. I felt a faint pain in my side before I jerked him out of balance, taking the gun and slamming him down onto the curb.

"I promised to scatter your teeth along the street." I kicked him in the face, hard.

There was the tinkle of a tooth dancing on the curb. Less than I had been aiming to do, but it would have to be enough. I didn't have time for more.

I checked the gun. It felt a little foreign in my hand.

Guns were practically relics after the Rapture. Even if somebody happened to make one that was a ranked piece of equipment, it was prohibitively expensive. People who wasted money on something like that didn't last long.

It had three bullets, no serial number. I put the safety on and stuffed it in my jacket pocket.

"What to do with you?" I murmured, checking up and down the streets to ensure that there were no cameras or people watching. I put my foot on his head, jerking my weight down several times as he started to claw at me to stop. Finally, he stopped moving.

There was no reason to leave a problem behind to crop up later.

The sight of his death didn't even phase me. He was merely a resource for me at that moment. And he had started the fight.

Around this part of town, the cops wouldn't even spend more time than filing the paperwork for his body. Hell, some of them might just ignore him because the paperwork was more trouble than a banger's corpse was worth to them.

I fished through his pockets, finding a wad of cash, a car key, some pills, and a baggie of powder.

The pills and the powder went into the first gutter I saw. There was no reason to try and sell something I didn't have confidence in. The cash and the gun would go far though.

As for the set of keys I found, they might be of use later. I had my mother's car, but in the near future, there might be some tasks that I'd want to do and not have trace back to me. Options were always nice.

I continued down the street and lifted my jacket to see where the bullet had grazed me. A part of me expected to watch it heal over as my regeneration activated, but I had no such luck in my current body. But I was headed to the hospital; I could stitch it up there easily enough. The pain was relatively dull in comparison to other wounds I had experienced. But it was a good reminder that I had to be careful with my body. It was far weaker than I was used to.

Integrating with the System was high on my list of things to do, but one thing was at the very top.

The hospital's bright white lights washed out into the surroundings as I stepped up and waved at the front desk. I was fairly certain they would recognize me, so I headed straight up to the sixth floor. It was quiet at this time of night; the only people left here were those who were morose and mourning.

I moved through the halls until I found my mother's room. Five hundred and some years later, I still remembered the sight as I stepped into the room.

Machines beeped as she lay in bed, completely still in the moonlight. The ventilator pumped as green-lit, little squares reported each and every movement of the machines and her functions.

"Mom," my voice quaked, and I fell to my knees in front of her.

Death had become another part of my life quickly after the Rapture. Loss was frequent, and I rarely had the time to deal with each one as they came up.

Yet my mother held a certain place that would never be out done. Her death had been the starting gun for a harsh life. Only later did I get a better picture of what had happened. Before then, I had not understood how deep inter-Clan politics went, and how much strife and how many knives there were in the dark between the Clans.

I never found out who had come for my mom, but later when the family checked her body, they confirmed a ranked poison had been used. Given she was poisoned before the Rapture, it had to be someone who was integrated with the System.

With her death, my life had taken a dark turn. I never was formally inducted into the Clan. But later when I learned of them and my connection to them, I was brought on as a servant of the Clan. It wasn't bad, but far from what it could have been.

And before that, I'd spent time diving into the mundane underworld of Vein City. Though, the mob had done well after the Rapture. They were quick to adapt to the new, harsher realities of the world.

I paused as there was a soft patter of water on the ground in front of me.

I frowned, touching the bed looking for the source of water, only to touch my face and feel the tears running down my cheeks.

Damnit. There wasn't time for this.

Wiping the tears from my face, I stood and held my mother's hand. "No use crying, because you won't die this time around."

I tried to Inspect her, but all I got was static as the System recognized the request but didn't connect to me.

I sighed. That was fine. I'd need to integrate with the System anyways.

There were several ways to integrate now. But after the Rapture, everyone integrated at puberty.

As of now, the families and sects all held a way to do it for their people. Outside of that, there were rogue players that got their integration from accidentally having an instance spawn on them or having a one-in-a-million chance encounter.

The latter wasn't going to be worth chasing down. Yet stepping into an instance was well within my plans. The System even dropped them on people on purpose to get them cleared.

After the Rapture, the Dags, who I ran with, were swallowed up by the Nester Crime Family. There was a bastard son of the boss who told a story of a dungeon spawning on him one night about a week from the present time.

I stood up, a goal in mind as I dug through the drawers in my mother's room, finding a kit to use to patch myself up.

Sewing up a hole, be it flesh or leather armor, was something I was fairly used to doing.

Now it was just time to track down Bobby Nester and become his man. Then, when he stumbled into the instance on one of the coming nights, I'd be the one at his side.

Plans, plans, plans. I'd need to get them into motion quickly. There were only two years before the whole world went to hell in a handbasket.

Chapter 2

Leaving my mother's hospital bed, I went in search of the vibrant nightlife of the city.

My first step into the underbelly of the world had been a bad loan from an even worse man to keep my mother in the hospital. I had ended up working for the Dags to try and pay that debt off.

The world as we knew it had ended before paying off the debt had ever come close to a reality. Instead, I had just gotten sucked deeper and deeper into the criminal enterprises that scurried about the back alleys of Vein City.

This time, I was going to jump a few rungs and be more than a thug with a baseball bat sent out to collect late payments.

More aware now, I knew that the Nester Crime Family ran a good portion of the city. They had their hands deep in both legitimate and less legal endeavors. They were my current target.

The city sidewalks became more crowded as I continued north. Bright lights started to illuminate the street as I left the poor neighborhoods behind and moved into the lovely areas ruled by young professionals.

Twenty-somethings in nice clothes laughed and stumbled along the street. As I passed, men held their dates closer and moved out of my way. I didn't belong, that much was apparent by my sweatshirt and perhaps the blood on it.

Club music thumped, and I found the right building. The bouncers eyed me in the way that told me no amount of waiting in line would get me inside.

But their hesitancy did not matter. I knew the building well.

CHAPTER 2

Slipping around the side, I walked to the kitchen like I knew where I was going, stepping around the trash bags and heading straight into the stainless-steel-covered kitchen with fragrant steam filling the air.

Several cooks got out of my way, not even bothering to yell at me. My back-alley entrance was not uncommon for this business.

I took a left and went straight up the stairs before heading down the hall. Up here, the music was far more subdued, the walls thick and insulated. So much so that you probably wouldn't hear a gunshot from here out on the dance floor.

Each of the doors in the hall had their own private suite that overlooked one of the dance floors of the night club.

I paused as a scantily clad waitress strut past me, looking me up and down and continuing on.

"Nice to meet you too," I muttered and found the right door, entering without knocking. The man I was visiting would not hear the knock anyway.

"Hey!" The man raised his glass of whiskey in the air as I stepped in, ever in a jubilant mood. "Do I know you?" he shouted over the music and the three ladies pawing at him, while two big muscle heads got out of leather seats to address the new problem in the room.

Me.

I patted down the air, indicating to the men they could settle down. Despite my less fortified body, it appeared I could still intimidate well enough. They both hesitated.

"Your father sent me," I spoke loudly over the music.

Those words sobered the man up quickly. He put his drink down and shooed the ladies off his lap. They didn't stick around, grabbing their things and leaving in a hurry.

Bobby wasn't a small guy, none of the Nesters were. However, he had a trim goatee and dark, slicked-back hair that made him look older than he was.

"My father sent you?" He was appraising me far more seriously now.

I knew that his father rarely contacted him, at least for now.

"After your latest fiasco, he thought it prudent to have someone advise you for the time being." I didn't know what fiasco I was talking about, but Bobby had a penchant for trouble. There was bound to be one in the recent past.

"This is bullshit." Bobby pulled out a phone and called his father.

I waited as the phone rang and he started talking.

"Dad. How could you send someone to watch over me? I told you that the fire wasn't my fault. What? Yeah, one second." Bobby looked confused but handed me the phone.

I stepped to the side, facing the corner to talk. "Hello, Carmen Nester. It's been a while. Are you still enjoying life in that place on twenty-third street disguised as a business-to-business paper sales office?"

"I don't know what you are talking about." The man's voice was hard as steel.

Honestly, I respected the shit out of Carmen. After the Rapture, it was men like him that had the principles, not morals, that became the cornerstone of protecting Vein City.

Yet I needed to push him to get what I needed. "Do you still have that bottle of Lagavulin 25 that you keep on the top shelf in the back? The one you used to drink with Bobby's mother? I know you keep just one shot's worth left of it for the day you need to borrow her strength."

There was a long, tense silence on the other side of the phone. "Do you have a name?"

"Bran," I answered honestly. "Mr. Nester, I respect the hell out of you. Sadly, some things need to be done—you're the kind of man who understands that. I need to follow Bobby around. You have my word that no harm will come to him. I know you distance him because you worry about your legitimate children going after him. Even better, I'll make sure none of them touch him while I'm here."

"Bran, huh. Well, let me make myself perfectly clear, Bran. If something happens to Bobby, you will find yourself wishing you never pulled this stunt. You want to watch over him? Fine. Give the phone back to my son." Carmen didn't lose his cool.

But I knew the man well enough that he was shaken. He knew how to hide it and project confidence, but he was not in the position of power that he was used to owning. I had thrown him off his guard, and he would certainly be trying to dig up everything he could on me soon enough.

In my future life, I drank with the man and had entered his inner circle.

Right now, all he knew was that I knew too much to be nobody, and dismissing me out of hand wouldn't help him. I knew things that only his most trusted should. For that, he'd give me enough rope to hang myself.

"Alright. Yeah. Can do." Bobby nodded with the phone before hanging up and glaring at me. "Guess I'm stuck with you. Come on. The mood's ruined, and I still have some business to deal with tonight."

"Of course." I dipped my head and opened the door for him and waved away the two big guys. They wouldn't be needed.

He gave me a funny stare as he walked out and I followed. "So, what can I use you for?"

"Ask me anything you want and I'll also make sure you stay safe and out of trouble," I answered, following him. It was easy to slip back into the familiar role of hired muscle.

***

Bobby had driven around in a far too nice of a car to check on several dealers that he managed. He would get updates from them and manage any issues.

I stood nearby as he made a call to fix a minor supply issue, and now we were pulling up in front of a hotel that was a front for a brothel.

"Listen. Don't do anything stupid in there. This is Madam Sugar's place, and anything you do here gets back to my father. He respects how she runs the place." Bobby parked the car and got out without waiting for my reply.

That was fine with me. I wasn't a big talker. It was easier to be silent and observe.

The hotel had a normal lobby up front, but Bobby ignored that and walked down the hall to the conference center, taking a short hallway that opened up into a den that smelled of clove cigarettes and cheap perfume.

"Mr. Nester." A woman got up from her seat and flowed over to welcome him. "Can I get you anything to drink?"

I looked the beautiful woman over. She was young enough that I almost thought she was the product. She was downright sexy with a dancer's tight, lithe body and sharp intelligent eyes. Yet there was an air around her that told me she was savvy enough to have survived through a difficult time, and yet not openly dangerous. At least not to a customer.

She turned to glance at me, her emerald eyes were beautiful. Our eyes met for a brief moment, and her smile froze before she went back to Bobby. "He's a new one."

"My father sent a minder. Give me something nice from the top shelf, and is Candy available?"

"Of course." The madam, presumably Madam Sugar, nodded and stepped towards the bar. She waved over a young little thing that giggled as she excused herself from three other ladies and joined Bobby with a hug.

"You can enjoy whatever you want. On me," Bobby offered.

"Thanks." I nodded and stepped up to the bar where the madam quickly poured Bobby a drink and handed it off to a woman to bring it to him, before turning her full attention to me.

The rest of the ladies here were in their prime. Yet the madam wasn't old by my standards. In fact, I'd call her thirty-something years young if it didn't come off tacky.

"So, what can I get for you, Mr. Broody?" she teased playfully. "Perhaps some young girl you could enjoy for the night?"

I glanced around the room. The women were beautiful and in their prime. Yet there wasn't any substance to them. "No thanks. They are a little young for my tastes. Two shots of that Blue Label." I pointed to a vaguely familiar bottle on the second from the top shelf.

"Coming up." The madam turned around, making sure to give me a full view of her ass as she climbed a small ladder to get it.

CHAPTER 2

Once again, I tried to Inspect someone using the System, and it failed. This time, there wasn't so much as a shimmer of static.

"Like the view?" She got the wrong idea and came back around to lay out two shots for me and pour them. "Am I joining you?" she asked.

"If you'd like." I took the first one and slugged it back, wasting the nice whiskey, but enjoying the burn as it raced through my throat. It had been a long time since I had tasted a drink this refined, and even longer since I'd felt the burn.

"Has anyone ever told you that you have an old soul?" she asked, pouring herself a finger of liquor in a ball glass.

My eye twitched, and several ways to kill her and keep her quiet went through my mind before I put the shot glass back down. "I'm older than I look."

"That varsity jacket isn't doing you any favors then." She pointed at my baseball jacket.

"It reminds me of better times," I responded, taking the second shot and sipping it. "Some things just age you more than others."

"Don't I know it." She leaned on the counter, her eyes raking me over again. "I'd almost call you a vet, but no, it's darker."

Well, wasn't she insightful. "Much," I confirmed. "You probably wouldn't have heard of the type of fighting I've done." I tried to get off the topic. "How often does Bobby come here?"

"Two or three times a week. He's sweet on Candy, and she doesn't mind the attention. The girls are here of their own free will, by the way." She felt the need to clarify.

"Not a cop," I chuckled. "How very... organic of you."

"I just pay them what they are worth, and young ladies keep finding their way to me. People could always use a little more money." Madam Sugar watched me carefully. "So, if they are too young, what kind of lady do you like?"

"The offer is nice, but I'm on the clock." I sipped the second shot slowly. When she went to top me off, I put my hand over the glass. "That means no women and only a moderate amount of booze. I have some vices to pay."

She chuckled and instead poured herself some more. "Bobby's a good kid. He's a Nester, so he gets to run the roost, but he doesn't abuse it."

I nodded along with her, searching the mirror and checking every person in the room. None of them were overly watching my charge, and so far, it seemed that he was having fun with the three ladies, but giving Candy most of the attention. He looked like a young man in love.

When I had met Bobby, Candy had been nowhere in the picture. I wondered what happened to her between now and the Rapture. Then again, in the first demon wave, over sixty percent of the world's population died.

"That's good. Bobby's not bad. In a few years, I think he'll surprise everyone. For now, he just needs to stay on the right track."

I didn't want to start creating ripples. Having knowledge of the future was one of my greatest assets, yet if I did too much, I threw all of that off. Working in the dark for a few years would be good. The nail that sticks up the furthest is the first to get hammered down and all that.

"You sound like you know what's going to happen." Madam Sugar swirled her drink and took a small sip.

I knew that she wasn't really drinking; it was all a facade as she tried to get to know me and gain information. She was a smart one. The woman had pegged me as the most dangerous person in her establishment the second I had walked into the room.

Chapter 3

"And that doesn't make you uncomfortable?" Madam Sugar asked me as we chatted in the brothel for the third night in a row.

I had opened up a little to her as she kept me entertained each night, only to step away for customers.

"No. Death is a part of life. Honestly, the morals of killing being 'bad' are just a way to keep the status quo. It's one of the things that keeps..." I didn't have a chance to get on my soapbox and explain that further.

Bobby blew past me with his phone to his ear.

I waved goodbye to the Madam and got up to follow him.

"—I'll be there in a minute." Bobby did a double take over his shoulder at me. "Someone's snooping around one of our factories." He jumped into his car.

"The one in the abandoned industrial park?" I asked.

"Yup." He shifted his car into gear as the engine roared.

I grinned as he shot off. This was it. This was just like the story he'd once told me.

A non-initiated person couldn't enter an instance under any circumstance, but there were times when one spawned literally right on top of a person. It was a chance encounter that couldn't be engineered, unless of course you knew the future.

I sat in Bobby's sports car as he raced far too quickly down the highway. The rubber left tracks as he took the exit ramp like a maniac.

I watched as the industrial park came up and recalled what he'd said before. "That building. Why don't we park there and walk up on whoever it is? Your car is too loud if you drive all the way up there."

He glanced at me and said nothing, but he did what I suggested.

The car died down as he opened the armrest to pull out a gun. "Do you have a weapon?"

"I have what I need." I patted my jacket. I still had the gun from the banger, and reaching back, I grabbed a baseball bat from the backseat.

Bobby rolled his eyes but hopped out of the car and gestured for me to follow with his gun held down. He had clearly watched too many cop dramas as he rushed about.

I walked in slow, measured steps, twirling my baseball bat to be sure I understood its balance. The gun would be useless tonight. This bat was a much better tool.

Bobby flattened against a wall. "I heard someone."

With those words, a blue wall of text appeared in front of me.

[Initializing... Please wait.]
[Error. 5029 conflicts found.]
[Resolving...]

Fuck. I braced for the worst as the System worked through the current situation.

"Bran. Bran, what is this?" Bobby wasn't quiet as he turned his head back and forth, like he was trying to shake something off of him.

"Don't know," I answered calmly. "It says to wait."

"What? No, it says to pick a class. It's like a video game." Bobby waved his gun through the space in front of him. I'd seen the reaction more than a few times.

"Close that. I hear something."

There were groans all around us as something dragged on the ground.

My night vision was shattered as Bobby threw his hands up and started firing less than a few feet from my face. In a panic, he emptied the entire magazine into the figure shambling towards us.

[Conflicts Resolved.]
[Please select a class. 30943 options.]

The number made me raise an eyebrow. It seemed that many parts of my future soul had stuck when I had gone back in time, including a lot of credit towards different classes.

That was good news for me that I had not counted on.

Yet I didn't have time to really sort through. I exited everything and assessed the result of Bobby's gunfire.

[Shambler F
Level 3
Strength: 14
Agility: 5
Vitality: 13
Intelligence: 0
Spirit: 0]

The slow zombie had a few scratches on its face. Bobby was actually a good shot.

More moans filled the air as more shamblers appeared from every direction. Each of them was a little different, but they all had the same dark, dry skin as they shambled towards us so slowly that a toddler could outrun them with ease.

I was thankful for such a low-level instance.

"What's going on? Zombies are supposed to die when you shoot them in the head." Bobby was quickly trying to reload his gun and dropped the bullets, his hands unsteady.

Not that I blamed him—zombies would freak anyone out.

There wasn't time to explain anything to him, so I just acted. Pulling the baseball bat back like I was going to hit a home run, I took a powerful step forward and swung hard at the closest shambler's head.

The monster didn't die, but it stumbled and fell from the blow, struggling to get back up.

"My bat works just fine." I tried to encourage Bobby to try something else.

He pulled a knife from his jacket. "Let's get out of here."

I nodded and stepped up to the oncoming shamblers, taking heavy swings at whichever zombies were leading the pack, while side stepping out of their reach. "They are slow. We got this."

Bobby was bouncing from foot to foot, jumping in and trying to stab one, but dodging back out when they swung a decrepit hand at him. "We should get out of here. I can't do anything." Bobby bounced back.

"Then stick behind me." I was happy to soak up the experience. I left the second half unsaid. "I got a message saying that I couldn't leave until the boss was dead."

"Like a game?!" Bobby gasped. "We can barely take these guys on. How are we going to take on the boss?"

"What about that class you mentioned? Mine finally came up, but I put it away to deal with these," I said, striking another zombie. This one must have been hit before. It disintegrated onto the ground, leaving behind a glittering gold coin and a severed zombie leg.

Juking one of them, I ducked in and grabbed the leg, not bothering to Inspect it. Instead, I used it to smash one of the zombies and killed it in a single blow.

"Hey, this leg is better than the bat. Join me." I tossed him the bat and started to go to town, smashing the shamblers one after another with the severed zombie leg.

Bobby picked up the bat and joined me, but it took him four hits to kill one. This Bobby was not nearly as skilled as future Bobby, but then again, he was just now entering the System.

Quickly, the two of us smashed the groups of zombies that had converged on us. I held back, not showing off too much, but I did enough to ensure that Bobby didn't get hurt.

Bobby panted as he bent over with the bat loose in his hands. "Damn, how are you not even winded?"

"Don't know." I shrugged. "I was on the baseball team, so this felt right at home." I swung the leg around.

I was not surprised that the leg was far more effective than the bat. It was a System generated item, meaning it was at least a F ranked item. That was why the gun did barely anything. In the world of the System, an unranked item was next to useless.

After the Rapture, everyone had quickly learned that the System was very regimented. Ranks of items, abilities, and stats of an attack then played against the defense's items, abilities, and stats.

Something like a gun borrowed zero stats, was unranked, and I'd hazard that Bobby didn't have an ability related to shooting. On the other hand, when I swung the bat, I could feel the System's assistance. That meant I had a related skill, and it was taking my strength into account. Without the skill, it took Bobby nearly double the strikes to take down a shambler.

All of that was to say that ranks of equipment and skills didn't just matter; they were the whole deal. Stats mattered too, but they were multiplied by the ranks in the System's equations.

Bobby held his hand out. "Give me the leg."

"Sure. There's an arm here too." I handed him the leg and took the arm myself. While I was at it, I picked up the gold coins, feeling the slight charge to them as they touched my hand. "We should pause and figure out these menus."

With a thought, mine opened up.

[Name: Bran Heros
Class: -
Status: Healthy
Strength: 13
Agility: 15
Vitality: 12
Intelligence: 10
Spirit: 10956

Skills:
Soul Gaze SSS
Soul Resilience S
Blunt Weapon Proficiency F
Endurance F
Throwing Proficiency F]

I nodded at my stats. It seemed that the strength of my soul had managed to come back with me. Only Soul Gaze—an improved form of Inspect and Soul Resilience—seemed to have stuck though for the rest of my skills. They must have been considered more integral parts of my soul.

The rest of my skills had been stripped. That was within my expectations. In fact, holding onto the strength of my soul in 'spirit' was a welcome surprise.

Most people had stats around 10-12 for a normal person. My physical stats were up due to having played high school baseball. As for intelligence, it wasn't a measure of book smarts, but rather an ability to process information faster and in a controlled manner. Before things went down, I wasn't exactly a paragon of intelligence, that would change though.

It was important for mages to be able to process the information for spell forms on the fly. And spirit was a measure of a player's soul. It functioned for certain types of spells as both a power modifier and also as a resistance.

During the first demon invasion, civilization began to learn that the often-neglected stat of spirit was a vital tool when fighting demons that wanted to possess people and devour their souls.

"None of this makes any sense," Bobby complained, pulling at his hair.

I pointed at my screen. "When you focus on something on this screen, a little pop-up gives you more details." I didn't need to go through all of the basics. Strength, agility and vitality were fairly self-explanatory.

Bobby focused back on his. "Thanks. You are pretty calm."

"Not much we can do but figure this out and work from there," I said, glancing at Bobby and activating Soul Gaze.

His stats came up in their entirety because I completely outstripped him in spirit and my Soul Gaze was far more powerful than any defenses he had.

[Name: Bobby Nester
Class: Sorcerer B
Status: Anxious
Strength: 10
Agility: 11
Vitality: 11
Intelligence: 15

Spirit: 10

Skills:
Driving F
Magic Attunement F
Management F
Acid Splash F
Light F

Bobby was more intelligent than people gave him credit for. Like the Bobby I had known, he had chosen sorcerer, which was a very flexible elemental caster. It was a simple but highly effective class.

"What class are you choosing?" he asked me. "I went with a caster. It's always the best in video games. That and magic is... well, it's fucking magic."

I chuckled and turned to my own list.

[30943 Options...]

My vision flooded as the list expanded and scrolled down for what felt like infinity. Yet with the strength of my soul, I was easily able to read it as it went and slowly parsing out which ones were worth a damn.

Chapter 4

The options for my class were a little overwhelming.

Some options were classes that people strove for like Demon Hunter. That class required a player to kill a hundred demons before selecting their class. Many organizations would help someone obtain this class if they wanted.

After all, humanity was pushed to the brink by demons and constantly fighting them. Demon Hunter was one of the most sought-after classes.

Yet, with all of my options, that class felt almost mundane.

I had ones that didn't suit me at all, like Hero. I shuddered at the thought of people calling me a hero for the rest of my life. When people used my last name, I already wanted to stab them.

No, I was used to doing what needed to be done. And that often meant wading into an army of demons and disposing of them in the most brutal, but efficient manner possible.

Bobby was staring at me expectantly.

"There are too many. I am not sure which one to pick," I told Bobby to stall.

"Well, I don't know you too well, but you have combat experience, yeah? Maybe you'd like something that gets up close and personal?" he guessed.

I was also sure he wanted me to be his tank.

There were a handful of options that focused on spirit like Soul Mage or a Necromancer. That one was tempting as hell. I'd be nearly unstoppable until the second demon wave; at which point, everyone and their mother would have defensive artifacts to protect their souls. Then my job would become infinitely harder.

There were other classes more akin to the melee class of Breaker that I'd had before. And now I had access to even better versions, including half a dozen types of berserkers. It was tempting to pick those up and tread down a path that was familiar.

Yet I knew that ultimately those had a limit. I was just one man. Even at my best, wading into combat with just a single ax could only cut so many people.

These options were all so tempting as I scrolled through the list again, filtering out anything less than S Rank.

But then my eyes stopped on one.

[?? Rank Blood Hegemon]

I had never seen a ?? Rank, nor the class before me. Blood was more powerful than many people would know or understand. At one point after the demon waves, I had delved heavily into inscriptions and curses. Blood was very important. The Clans and sects relied heavily on Bloodlines for strength.

This class also had a domineering name, Hegemon. The System didn't bullshit you. If it called it Hegemon, it was powerful.

"Just pick already." Bobby had snuck up on me while I was wavering in my decision.

I jolted and selected the class, cursing as the System accepted the choice. But in reality, I was probably going to pick it anyway. From what I knew, it seemed powerful.

"What'd you get?" Bobby asked impatiently.

"Don't know exactly," I answered with a bit of truth mixed into the fib. "Just sounded cool."

There were three new skills in my list after selecting the class. That in itself was odd. Normally, a class came with two skills. Blood Boil F and Blood Siphon F, I was familiar with both of those. Blood Boil was a low-grade berserk that could be used on myself or on another, and Blood Siphon was a leaching ability.

"You don't know?" Bobby pressed.

"Blood Warrior," I lied. "Sounded badass."

Bobby nodded excitedly. "I'll bet it is. Do you have any cool spells?"

"Looks like I can boost my strength and agility, as well as leech life." I pretended to read.

Bobby's eyes went wide. "That's perfect! Alright, you'll go in first, and I'll stay back here."

The third skill was my most interesting: Bloodline Collection F 0.

Bloodlines were not to be trifled with. They were the cornerstone of the great families' power. Even the sects highly selected for bloodlines. Hell, the demons hunted hosts for their bloodlines so that they could have powerful bodies.

I knew I would have one eventually, but to collect them? That was very interesting.

Sadly, as far as I knew, Bobby didn't have a bloodline. Once I returned to my family, which I planned to do, this time going through the proper rites, this ability would be very interesting. After all, the Heros family was built on a myriad of bloodlines.

"Ready to do this?" Bobby was all of a sudden ready to plunge head first into battle when a few minutes ago he had been scared and looking for a way out.

I had seen it happen before. People got excited the first time they got to use their abilities and pushed themselves a little too far too quickly.

"Looks like I have a blunt weapon proficiency," I told him. "If you are a caster, then could I get that leg? It has a longer reach than this arm."

[Shambler Arm F:
Will probably fall apart with much use—it's a rotting limb]

I could think of a few alchemy recipes that used things like this leg. It was not an uncommon ingredient, but I'd have to use it as a weapon for now.

"Yeah, sure. This thing is pretty gross anyway." He handed me the leg, and I held it by the ankle for a good grip.

"Follow me." I moved forward into the industrial park.

What I knew that Bobby did not yet was that we weren't really in the industrial park. Instances were pocket dimensions that mirrored the area where they landed. There were often extra things, like a giant pile of unmoving corpses to the side, or a brazier with green fire.

Yet it was like they were overlaid on the existing world. Once the instance was completed, we'd step out of the dimension and into the world again.

As we rounded the corner, the parking lot was filled with shamblers moving in small groups.

"Let me try something." Bobby put his hands out and concentrated for a moment. There was a frown on his face as he faced a spellform for the first time, and then a splash of acid shot out from between his hands onto one of the shamblers.

The shambler's shoulder sizzled as the acid ate away at its body.

"Wow. Magic." I tried and failed to interject some awe into my tone.

Not that Bobby noticed. "Yeah. I have fucking magic." Bobby shot another glob of acid at the same shambler, and then a third to kill it as the other three in that group continued towards us.

"Better than a gun, it seems," I added and took my turn, activating Blood Boil on myself.

My arms bulged slightly, my veins coming to the surface of my skin like thick worms before I swung and smashed a shambler with the leg. The shambler lost a chunk of its hip, falling to the ground and disappearing.

I took the opportunity to step into the next shambler as it swung at me. The leg in my hand didn't have quite the same force this time, so I only knocked it back, taking a small cut for my efforts. But my second swing came around and knocked the head off the shambler.

"Damn. Save some for me." Bobby was working to cast another glob of acid.

I didn't wait for him to figure out the skill. I lifted my hand and activated Blood Siphon.

The spell form was simple, and it only took me a moment before a red strand the thickness of a finger pulled itself from the shambler and drained right into my hand.

My small cut quickly healed.

Bobby's spell landed before I swung the shambler leg again, and killed the final one in this group.

"A self-heal. So absolutely dope. You'll make an incredible tank." Bobby rushed up to look at the loot, picking up one of the gold coins. "We'll split everything fifty-fifty." He took two coins and left me the other two.

I stuffed them in my jacket pockets knowing that we were going to be filling them up by the end of today. Monsters only dropped body parts and coins. If they had weapons, they might drop those too. It wasn't until boss monsters that loot became more interesting.

Wolves didn't drop swords. The system was reasonably logical about what got dropped.

"Come on, let's keep going." Bobby was vibrating with excitement.

I stood up slowly and readied my shambler leg, feeling the Blood Boil pull at my senses and make me want to clobber Bobby. Yet my spirit was strong enough to push on that feeling and wash it away, clearing my head.

I checked the messages waiting for me.

[Level Up!
+1 Strength
+1 Agility
+1 Vitality
+1 Intelligence
+1 Spirit]

Great. I had gotten five stats for a single level. This class qualified as an S Rank class then. I wondered why it had question marks on the screen. Maybe it was some sort of glitch from going back to my previous soul.

I moved forward, putting those questions aside as I turned the shambler leg into a weapon of destruction, smashing through several more of the slow zombie groups with minimal help from Bobby.

At the end of the instance, there was a completion bonus based on a player's participation. The System took many things into account, but my self-healing and dealing most of the damage would give me the majority of what could be gained.

My arms ached as we cleared the parking lot, and I stopped to roll my shoulder and stretch out my muscles.

[Level Two
+1 Strength
+1 Agility
+1 Vitality
+1 Intelligence
+1 Spirit
New Skill: Blood Bolt]

I nodded. A range attack would be nice, even if I focused on melee.

"You're pretty good. Do you do martial arts or something?" Bobby asked, picking through the loot for his share. He was carrying an extra two shambler limbs for me. I'd already broken one, and the new one was looking like it wasn't going to last long either.

"Something like that," I answered, having practiced multiple weapon forms and hand-to-hand combat.

So far the System hadn't recognized my skill at anything other than bludgeoning weapons. I'd fix that later. There were ways to get certain skills through brute force. For others, I'd need to find ability tomes.

"Let me get this group." Bobby jumped forward and shot an Acid Splash. He cast the spell faster than the last several. He managed to hit the pack of shamblers coming around the corner.

I watched as the shamblers gave way to a larger zombie.

[Walker F
Level 5
Strength: 16
Agility: 12
Vitality: 18
Intelligence: 0
Spirit: 0]

The walker moved quickly around the shamblers, rushing towards Bobby.

"I'll handle this one, just keep the shamblers away from me," I growled, stepping in and swinging the shambler leg at the walker.

The rotting limb crumbled with my first strike, but it did enough damage for the walker to turn and focus on me. It struck out as quickly with a punch.

Yet I was prepared and dodged backwards, using my palm to guide its claws away from me before stepping in and giving it the old one-two in the chest. Then I danced back out of reach, managing to only receive a small scratch from the walker in return.

Sadly, my jacket was ruined. An unranked item against the monster's claws might as well be tissue paper.

The walker kept on me as I dodged backwards, getting a feel for its swings. I activated Blood Bolt, feeling my blood roil for a moment before it was spit out of my hand in a sharp arc that cut into the monster and left a little of my blood where it hit.

The residual blood caught my attention. I was sure that it would tie to other abilities down the road.

I dodged back out of reach, my footwork a little rusty without System assistance. And footwork only helped when there was space to maneuver. I was rapidly running out.

The walker, sensing I was almost cornered, ducked into a charge.

A lot of fighters dodged a charge, but I went with a low tackle, taking its feet out from under it and forcing it to slam its head into the ground. Rolling out of the way, I earned a kick for my effort, but the walker's arm was bent slightly out of place.

I got to my feet, activating Blood Siphon to help keep me on my feet as I shifted my weight from foot to foot, readying for the next round with the monster.

But it didn't come.

Blood Siphon stopped as the walker fell over and was reabsorbed by the instance. It was anticlimactic. I was just getting warmed up.

"Huh." I stood up straight and turned to see Bobby running in a large circle, splashing his acid spell on the shamblers over and over. I paused, deciding not to interfere right away. "He could use the practice."

I picked up an arm that had dropped from the walker. It was still an F Rank piece of crap, but it might last a few more swings.

Chapter 5

Bobby leaned against the wall of the building and wiped his brow. "We should have brought food and water."

"We weren't expecting to get stuck here," I lied. Food and water might be nice, but a low-level dungeon like this should not take much longer. "Come on. Maybe we are almost done."

After clearing the parking lot, we cleared one of the nearby factories. Walkers became more common as we moved ahead through the instance. At one point, we had fought a few groups that had been more walkers than shamblers.

But I did not see much of a difference between the two, besides that the walkers had limbs that held up much better. I was still using the same one. Bobby had taken off his belt and was acting as my caddy, carrying around a set of eight limbs now for me to use in case I needed spares.

I was not going to need that many as we continued to clear out packs, but I knew that eventually we would find a boss. I knew better than to go into that fight without multiple spare weapons.

Curious how much experience I was getting, I pulled back up my stats during a lull in fighting.

[Name: Bran Heros
Level: 3
Class: Blood Hegemon ??
Status: Healthy
Strength: 16
Agility: 18
Vitality: 15
Intelligence: 13

Spirit: 10959

Skills:
Soul Gaze SSS
Soul Resilience S
Blunt Weapon Proficiency F
Endurance F
Throwing Proficiency F
Blood Boil F
Blood Siphon F
Blood Bolt F
Bloodline Collection 0]

The bonus to spirit almost made me laugh. I did not particularly need that at the moment, but I was not going to turn down free stats.

Bobby and I turned down the end of the street, finding three more walker and shambler packs. But what really drew my attention was a big guy at the end of the street. I quickly checked the big guy's stats.

[Brute F
Level 8 Boss
Strength: 16
Agility: 12
Vitality: 18
Intelligence: 0
Spirit: 0

Skills:
Tough Skin F
Charge F
Smash F]

"Fuck." The ability of tough skin was not a welcome sight. I was not sure if the limbs we had would survive the fight.

"What is it?" Bobby asked.

"Use Inspect on that guy." I pointed down the street.

Bobby frowned. "It only says it's a Brute and that it's the boss."

"Odd. Mine gives a little more detail. Is your Inspect D?"

"No! All of my skills are F. You have a D for them?" Bobby asked excitedly. This kid was all enthusiasm.

"Just the Inspect," I lied, not used to people with such low-level Inspect. "Well, it says it has Tough Skin, Charge, and Smash. We can probably work around the Charge and Smash, but I'm worried about Tough Skin. We might run out of legs."

I ran through options for my best shot at beating the boss.

I had a throwing proficiency. Sadly, the rocks laying around the instance weren't automatically F Rank. If they were, players would collect them and make items out of them more easily. We both had F ranked ranged spells if we ran out of the limbs.

"Let's do this," Bobby interrupted my thoughts and started attacking the first group in the boss room. This time, he used a new skill. A small square of inch-tall spikes appeared on the ground in front of the group before his Acid Splash hit them. "Alright. Now we're talking."

I moved forward, staying out of his direct line of fire.

The walkers hit Bobby's spikes and stumbled, slowing down significantly. And their slowness meant easy pickings for me.

The leg in my hand once again became a brutal bludgeoning weapon, smashing walkers and shamblers while Bobby's Acid Splash continued to fire out and melt their skin.

I smashed through the next three groups. I used another leg in the process, but I gained two from my kills.

I seriously wondered how Bobby and his guard had managed this instance the last time they had come without a weapon. He recounted the story like it was a breeze for them. I had a feeling now that Bobby's story in my past life was mostly bravado. Without me, he would have come out of this far worse for wear.

"The boss," I said, picking out a new walker leg.

This boss was reddish and stood at about eight feet tall, with trap muscles that swelled up to barely give him a neck. He was at the end of the alley with shipping crates blocking off the other end.

CHAPTER 5

"Just make sure to keep using those spikes. If he moves slowly, we should be fine," I told Bobby.

Bobby cracked his knuckles and waved his hand, creating another strip of the spikes right in front of the boss before starting an Acid Splash. I braced myself to save him, anticipating what was coming from experience.

Sure enough, the boss took the Acid Splash to the chest and immediately activated Charge, barreling right over the patch of spikes towards Bobby at an easy thirty miles an hour.

I grabbed Bobby and jerked him out of the way.

The boss careened past Bobby and slammed into the wall.

"Thanks." Bobby blinked, clearly shaken out of his excitement.

I let go of Bobby, moving quickly as I swung the walker leg back and slammed it into the boss' back.

The limb broke after the fourth wild swing, and the boss finished shaking his head and reoriented. This time, its focus was on me. Its fists came up, and I moved instinctively, getting out of reach just in time before those same fists came crashing back down, shattering the asphalt and sending chunks flying.

One of the chunks of asphalt cut my cheek. I ignored the pain, snatching the chunk out of the air and whipping it like a fast ball right back at the boss.

It cut him too.

Green acid splashed on the boss' shoulder, but the boss didn't even turn to Bobby, instead ambling after me.

Even if the spikes hadn't affected the speed of the boss' charge, it worked better now that he was moving without a System-assisted skill. This time, the boss moved more slowly.

I led him around while I circled over to my stack of limbs and grabbed one with each hand. "Doing good, Bobby. Keep it up," I encouraged him and led the boss back over to the spikes on the floor to keep him slow.

"What would you do without me!" he shouted back, seeming to shake off the earlier attack and regain his glee as he continued to fire acid.

I shook my head. This man was a little less mature than the one I had known, but they had the same wild excitement. And right now, I could use that type of intensity. While I held the boss' attention, Bobby could pound away at the boss with his ranged spell.

The boss tucked his chin and took the first step of his charge before I threw my whole body to the side, sliding on asphalt and taking a beating from the move.

Rolling to my feet, I rushed in again with both limbs and pounded on the boss' back. Both of the legs broke, and I hurried away to fire [Blood Bolt] repeatedly at the boss while running.

The Brute lumbered after me, trying to get into range to smash again.

I glanced, assessing our progress. Bobby's attacks were working. The Acid Splash was repeatedly wearing away at the monster's Thick Skin, and patches of weakness were appearing.

I did my best to fire Blood Bolts at those patches and harry the boss further.

During this fight, I had to keep up appearances with Bobby and put on a show as if I weren't prepared for an instance to drop on us. But next time, I was bringing a goddamn weapon. This would have been over quickly if I'd have more than decaying limbs to use to fight the boss.

The boss stumbled to its knees and fell face first, disappearing into the instance. A prompt popped up, but I dismissed it to the side.

Bobby staggered to the side and leaned on a shipping crate. "My head feels like it's on fire."

"Might be all the magic you used." I was looking around until one of the shipping crates popped open, spilling out light to get our attention. "Looks like a treasure room."

"Oh. What'd the big guy drop?" Bobby stepped up to where the Brute had been and bent down to pick up a thin booklet and a white button-down shirt. "A shirt. Really?" He huffed.

"I'll take it if you don't want it," I offered.

It was F ranked gear, meaning that, like the monsters before, unranked items would barely scratch it. That shirt was bulletproof.

CHAPTER 5   37

"You could use a wardrobe change." He tossed it to me, and I caught it, quickly changing out of my ripped sweatshirt and putting on the nicer shirt. For now, the sweatshirt would serve as a bag as I scooped up some of the gold coins and put it in the pocket.

Bobby was looking over the spellbook and failing to open it.

"If it's like a game, you just learn it rather than read it," I told him, smoothing out the wrinkles on my new shirt. "What's the skill?"

"Firebolt." Bobby played with the book for a second more before it shined and disappeared into his head. "Oh. Interesting."

"Is it D rank?" I asked, pretending to be stupid.

"No. It's F, like the others. Perhaps we have to practice them to level them up." Bobby rubbed at his chin and pointed his hand away from us. A jagged blast of fire roared out of his hand and hit a shipping crate leaving a small scorch mark on the side. "Not bad. A little flashy for my tastes."

"Don't use it to impress Candy," I joked and moved to the open shipping crate that had something glowing inside of it. Most abilities required practice to grow to higher ranks and eventually stronger skills. There were a few exceptions, but those weren't important for now.

"That could go poorly," Bobby agreed. "I'm more curious if there are others like us. There has to be, right? But if there are, how do we find others?"

It was a good question. I hadn't gotten involved until after the Rapture, but afterwards, I found out there were supposedly websites with information.

"Ask your father. He might have more insight." I was fairly sure the Players Alliance was established by now. Those like us who got stuck in an instance started becoming more common these few years leading up to the Rapture. "I'll do my best to snoop around too," I told Bobby.

"This prompt says we can restart this?" Bobby asked.

"Saw that. Please don't." I said. "I need some food and a hot bath to think about everything that just happened before we come back. That, and I need a real weapon."

My eyes landed on a small ax about two feet head to handle. "Like this." I smiled, taking the weapon.

Next, I scanned through the items here for an antidote potion, but my luck wasn't that good. Normally, a player found items somewhat related to the monsters in the instance. I'd have to find an instance with toxic creatures to find a potion for my mother.

My other reason for leaving today was to go use my Soul Gaze on her and get more information about what was causing her illness.

"Alright. We'll come back tomorrow?" Bobby asked hopefully.

"Going to spend the day figuring things out. How about you enjoy Candy tomorrow and we'll go the next day." I was in no rush. The chances of another initiated finding this place were quite low.

I fished among the loot, finally finding what I was looking for as I picked up two rings.

"Huh. You see this?" I pretended to Inspect them. Most first clears offered a storage device. It was one of the big reasons that people hunted for new instances.

[Storage Ring F]

I held it out for Bobby.

"Woah!" He snatched it up and put it on his finger before pulling out gold from his pocket and waving his ring over it, causing it all to disappear. "It's a fucking inventory!"

Something like that.

The F rank ones had about one square yard of storage space. It was more than enough for me to store the ax as well as my share of the loot. It would also be enough for me to bring a few packs of water and some food.

The rest of the loot included gems and gold, as well as a wand that seemed to be captivating Bobby's attention.

"Let's get out of here," I told him and brought the prompt back up before selecting to leave.

The air around me shattered, and we sort of rewound back to the spot we'd come in, right next to the car. It was already bright outside. We'd been in the instance for four or five hours.

"Damn." Bobby shaded his eyes. "Let's get back. Suddenly, I could get some sleep."

That would be the adrenaline wearing off and the excitement fading.

"Get some rest and prepare today. Tomorrow night, we'll go back in," I told Bobby.

"Wonder if I can bring more people." Bobby slid into his car. I got into the passenger seat with him.

"They'd have to be people you absolutely trust. This is a big deal," I reminded him.

Though, I knew if a random person walked up here, they'd walk right through the instance and notice nothing. The System did not make it that easy to bring a small army and initiate them. This was why the Clans relied on artifacts.

"Point." Bobby revved up his sports car. "And we'd have to split the loot another way."

I grinned at him, knowing he wasn't going to tell anyone. "I'm more worried about the experience. Getting stronger like this is a game changer."

Bobby nodded and gripped the wheel tightly as he sped off.

Chapter 6

I had Bobby drop me off a block from the hospital. The very first thing I was going to do after finishing that instance was check back up on my mother.

My stats came up with a thought.

[Name: Bran Heros
Level: 5
Class: Blood Hegemon ??
Status: Healthy
Strength: 18
Agility: 20
Vitality: 17
Intelligence: 15
Spirit: 10961

Skills:
Soul Gaze SSS
Soul Resilience S
Blunt Weapon Proficiency F
Endurance F
Throwing Proficiency F
Blood Boil F
Blood Siphon F
Blood Bolt F
Bloodline Collection 0
Regeneration F]

I'd gotten two levels from the boss fight and the completion bonus. Given the low level of the dungeon, the fast progress was going to be short lived. Yet I'd already stepped into the realm of superhuman with the improvements to my body now that I had been initiated.

Regeneration was a huge win. If I'd known the class would get Regeneration at Level 5, I wouldn't have even hesitated. It was by far my favorite ability in my past life. You could regenerate limbs after it reached A Rank, and I pushed aside the memories of why I knew that.

That skill moved up my plans significantly. With Regeneration, I could start working on my resistances soon. I'd need poison resistance if I was going to find a cure for my mother.

The nurse waved at me as I entered the room, and I habitually Inspected her to find she was an average citizen.

I was anxious. I was finally going to get to see who my mother truly was, and how much she knew about this world.

[Elle Heros
Level: 38
Class: Swordmaster A
Status: Body Rotting Poison D
Strength: 45
Agility: 58
Vitality: 43
Intelligence: 25
Spirit: 19
...]

I ignored her skills, focusing instead on the poison.

As soon as I saw her level, I knew what I was dealing with was not going to be an F ranked poison. That level of poison I could likely have fixed relatively easier.

I'd need a D ranked antidote. This increased the difficulty several magnitudes. D rank instances wouldn't start appearing until higher levels, not to mention that difficulty scaled with both level and rank.

One option was still the Heros Clan. They could resolve the poison in a blink of an eye. Yet I'd be exposing myself to them before I was ready. The Clan believed children were supposed to be raised away from the Clan. I could make a simple excuse that my mother had left some note for me to contact them if I needed it.

No, I really didn't want to wade into that swamp until I was stronger.

The Free Player Alliance might have some access to a D ranked antidote, but it would be expensive.

I bit my thumbnail, working through my options. The final option was to go indebt myself to some alchemist, but that might be the worst option of all of them.

I had a number of the legs still that someone might want, but they would be a far cry from the cost for a D ranked item, even a consumable. All I could really do was explore my options and continue to progress myself. There was still time after all.

"Sir, are you okay?" The cute nurse from the hall came back in, seeing me standing and seemingly staring into space.

"Yes. I just worry about my mother," I lied smoothly as I closed the stats. "Thanks for taking such good care of her."

"About that." The nurse winced. "The administration wanted me to remind you of the bills for her stay."

"Not a problem." I smiled at her. The gold coins I had collected couldn't be sold just anywhere, but my money problems were about to vanish overnight. "Let me have those and take a look."

I took the stack from her and tucked them into my back pocket. The harder part of my plan was going to be figuring out the internet again.

***

I glared angrily at the device in front of me. The beat-up laptop blinked the cursor at me mockingly.

What was my god damned password?! I rubbed my fingers through my hair.

I remembered the ingredients for over eight thousand alchemy recipes, and I could create tens of thousands of inscriptions, but I couldn't remember my password from five hundred years ago.

I wanted to slam my hand down on the keyboard, but I managed to reign in my anger.

Pausing to try to figure out what to do next, I had an idea. I'd never used it on a piece of technology, but it should work the same. It was *my* locked item. So the blood of the owner was easy enough for that particular talisman.

I leafed through the mail to find a piece of mail with enough blank space and tore it apart. Then I bit hard on my thumb, making myself bleed. A few swishes here and a few there with my blood on the paper and I had what I needed.

I slapped the talisman to the back of the laptop and activated it with a touch of mana. It sparked, and the laptop looked like it was about to fry for a moment before the password screen disappeared.

I bent back laughing. "Technology can't fool this old man."

I quickly made another talisman and slapped it to my phone, unlocking the other device as well. Before I went any further, I quickly updated the passwords for both with something I could remember.

I felt quite chipper at my success and began to search in earnest.

I had learned that, before the Rapture, the Free Player Alliance had supposedly operated in the open, disguised as a gaming community. They talked about all of their battles as if they were some popular game.

I pecked at the keyboard trying a few different searches. I got back mostly garbage, but on the fourth try, I got to something interesting.

The website was a pretty bare bones forum, but after reading several of the threads, it was obvious that they were initiated. They were discussing how to level certain passives. The information was slightly off, but enough for me to recognize it.

My stomach rumbled, and I sighed, stopped my search, got up and headed to the pantry. I tried to scrounge up something edible. There was barely anything left in this house. As soon as I solved my money problems, I was going to eat better than this.

I put on a pot of water to boil, and while I was waiting for it to get hot enough, I stuck my hand in the burner's flame.

My flesh immediately turned red and started to darken, but the pain barely bothered me. Regeneration kicked in and healed me as the fire continued to burn me over and over.

I knew that sticking hands into open flames and watching skin peel off was probably not normal, but I was not really interested in doing the self-reflection needed to determine what it really said about me.

In reality, I had done some horrible things in the name of survival. Setting my hand on fire didn't even come close to making the list.

With my other hand, I scrolled on my phone that was filled with social media aps. Damn, it had been a while. Several notifications were people checking up on me after graduation. My baseball coach was reminding me that he still had my back even though I wasn't on the team anymore.

I had to blink out a few tears as my vision went fuzzy against my will.

I wondered what had happened to that coach. My life had gone in a very different direction at this point, and I had lost contact with most of the people I knew in high school. A mix of shame and guilt had kept me away as I had gone deeper and deeper into gangs and drug dealing.

High school felt like an entirely separate life all together.

I pulled my hand from the fire and watched as the black bits fell off and new skin grew underneath as my Regeneration healed the burns. Closing and opening my hand, I smiled at having Regeneration again. This was a skill that had carried me through many hard times.

The fact that I had leveled the ability to SS rank and even upgraded it twice told a bitter story.

Sticking my hand back into the fire, I watched as the pot began to boil, and I poured in the noodles before adding a flavoring pack and stirring with my free hand.

The smell of burning flesh always brought back memories, and they were not pleasant ones. Flashes and images of Vein City burning and demons devouring people flitted through my mind.

I followed those images with my own experiences as I began to slaughter demons one after another.

[Fire Resistance F] popped up in my vision. My hand continued to turn red, but it stopped turning black under the mundane flame. Resistance skills were less about inflicting yourself with the type of damage but recovering from it. That's why having Regeneration at this low of a level was going to make such a difference.

I wiggled my fingers to ensure they were fine before using the hand to scroll on my phone. The social media apps had been closed now, and I was on the Free Player Alliance site, quickly devouring as much information as I could find. It seemed there was a market held every weekend in the city. That would be perfect for me to explore and get several of my to-do's finished.

I added the market to my mental calendar and continued swiping and consuming all the information that I could find on the website.

***

After a pot of noodles, followed by several hours of addictive scrolling, I finally fell asleep and slept until late into the night.

Groaning after a comfortable night on a mattress, I rolled out of bed and stretched before getting ready. The F ranked shirt stayed in my ring until I'd need it. There was no sense wearing it at the moment. With Regeneration, I could take some minor injuries, shaking them off and just moving on.

I left the apartment, casually using Soul Gaze on anyone and everyone. My rapid use of it would leave most dizzy, but my soul was up to the challenge of parsing out the rapid-fire information.

There was no such thing as being too wary. I wanted to know if another initiated player was in my vicinity.

Deciding my next course of action, I started heading towards Madam Sugar's to meet up with Bobby. I needed to make sure that Bobby was staying out of trouble.

I continued walking, pausing when my Soul Gaze picked up another player following me.

[Rodger Stone
Level: 8
Class: Thief E
Status: Stealthed
...]

I chuckled to myself, keeping my pace steady. My ability was going to pierce right through any stealth skills.

I took a left, heading through a bad area of town towards the brothel before taking a few more turns to hopefully make the man catch up. After a few turns, I stopped behind a building and waited.

Sure enough, Rodger came around the corner to meet my fist in his face before I tackled him to the ground and pinned both of his arms.

"Why are you following me, and who sent you?" I pressed down on him.

"Like I'd—" He was cut off as I punched him in the face again and drew the ax out of my spatial ring. I held the ax to his throat. His eyes went wide as he saw the weapon appear out of thin air, knowing what that meant.

"I am going to ask you one more time." The blade kissed his neck and drew a drop of blood.

"You're a player too?" the thief asked.

"Rodger Stone, please don't make me repeat myself." I felt him try to Inspect me and brushed it aside with my soul. If I didn't want him looking, he was not strong enough.

A moment later, it occurred to me who might be behind him following me. "Was it Uncle Nester?"

I was paranoid from my past life, but in this one, I shouldn't have anyone sending players after me. Besides, Rodger was too low level to really be here for a hit. If it was someone from the Clan, I wouldn't have even seen them coming.

His eyes shifted just a little at my question, enough for me to know I hit the bullseye.

CHAPTER 6

"In that case." I lifted him off the pavement and dusted him off. "Why didn't you say so? Uncle Nester is just doing his due diligence. After all, I've become Bobby's right hand."

Rodger was blinking quickly as I took a tissue and wiped his blood off my ax. I put the weapon away. If he did anything in the future, I'd be able to hunt him or curse him across the world by having that bit of blood.

"Oh." He straightened his jacket. "You work with Bobby?"

"Yep." I put on a big, fake smile. "I was going to check on Bobby now actually. I wanted to make sure he was relaxing tonight. Madam Sugar's brothel. You know the place?"

He shook his head. "What level are you?"

"Doesn't matter." I waved away his question. "Come with me, or else you might not be able to get in and keep tabs on me tonight. Wouldn't want Uncle Nester to think I was giving his watcher the slip."

Rodger was still struggling with the change in my mood.

And I loved that he was thrown off his game. It was always best to keep people like Rodger off balance so that they didn't notice the little things.

"Come on. And hurry up. I don't want to leave Bobby alone for too long." I waved over my shoulder and kept moving. "Let me tell you about the time Uncle Nester was pulled, quite literally, from the fire. This was, oh, about three years or so ago..." I started to rattle off some of the stories that Carmen Nester had told me over drinks before.

Chapter 7

Madam Sugar had really outdone herself today, dressing up more than usual. She'd had her hair done, this afternoon if I were to guess. It was freshly dyed a touch blacker and styled into ringlets that cascaded over her shoulders. Tonight's dress was a red so dark that it was nearly black, and it clung to her like a second skin. She was most certainly wearing her biggest pushup bra.

Out of habit, I Inspected her, finding that she wasn't initiated.

[Simone Sweet
Level: -
Class: -
Status: Healthy
Strength: 12
Agility: 12
Vitality: 10
Intelligence: 15
Spirit: 14]

I chuckled slightly at her real name before the information hit me like a punch to the gut.

"See something you like?" she teased.

I stamped down my reaction and grinned at her leaning on the counter. "You are a beauty tonight. What's the occasion?" I flirted to stall for time.

She looked nothing like I remembered, but that was also because when I had met the future Simone Sweet, she was possessed and demonified. In fact, she was world famous. She served as the 5th General of the Demon Lord's Army.

I let out a slow breath. I was shocked to find a fish this big so early. But she was not possessed at the moment, which meant whatever had happened to her had not happened yet.

"Just touching myself up. Even if I'm not working upstairs, it's good for business if I am appealing." She couldn't hide just how much satisfaction she got from my reaction.

"How about some drinks? Bobby promised me he'd on his best behavior tonight so that I might get a chance to relax."

"He came in about an hour ago. Already took Candy upstairs." Simone's fingers danced over the bottles as she tried to pick which one to serve.

My mind was elsewhere. If I somehow stole Simone from the Demon Lord, it would be a huge win. He'd find another general, but a demon possessed a body to steal its potential. That meant I could not only remove a piece from the board, but gain a powerful ally in the process.

Yes, I decided. I'd keep a close eye on her.

I scanned the room with Soul Gaze, but nothing else stuck out. I even swept it over the bottles making sure there wasn't some hidden item that might affect her nearby or on her person. I was not sure what would hold the demon soul that eventually would possess her.

Her eyes caught mine in the reflective backing behind the bar.

"Caught me." I grinned. "Whatever you pick will be fine by me. Tonight you can even get me drunk."

"Drunk? You?" She feigned surprise and picked a squat bottle from the top shelf and came down the step stool to take a sniff. "Well, if it doesn't matter to you, then maybe I'll take something a little different out." She pulled out two snifters and poured the unlabeled liquor into them.

"How about you tell me what it is?" She placed the snifter in front of me.

I swirled the snifter with a dark gold liquid that clung to the glass and took a sniff. "Apples? Brandy?" I took a sip and it was smooth. "Very good brandy."

"When I was younger, I traveled quite a bit. Got a case of this from a small shop in Normandy." She took a sip and reveled not just in it, but in the happy memory. "Anyway,

I thought I ran away with a steal because it was so cheap. I always thought of myself as someone with an eye for talent."

"Can't argue that. You marked me as an old soul the second I stepped inside." I took another sip, hiding a check of my status to be sure there wasn't some ill effect about to clobber me over the head.

Thankfully, nothing came.

"Cautious." She regarded me. "If you are looking for a night to let loose, you can take any of the girls. It's on the house for the entertainment you provide me every night." She was testing me in her own way. Her caution was so evident to me.

I clicked my tongue and gave my best roguish smile. "What if I'm only interested in women, not girls? Like the one right in front of me."

"Come now. You're half my age." She stuck her chest out slightly as she moved around the bar.

"No. I'm twenty-four. I told you, I'm older than I look." Technically, I was five hundred and change. She wasn't even a tenth of my age. But that fact did not matter. If I'd told her the truth that this body was eighteen, I had a feel she'd dismiss me out of hand as some brash youth. So, I went with something on the edge of believable.

I wouldn't touch someone who wasn't mature enough to make their own decisions, but after that point, age did not matter as much as character.

"You're what? Thirty?" I erred on the low side.

"Thirty-four." She playfully batted the counter and topped off my drink. "Thanks for guessing low on purpose." She watched me carefully.

Simone was a smart woman.

I liked smart women. Plural. After the Rapture, I took comfort where I found it. Boundaries, laws, and religious judgment all seemed to evaporate as soon as the demons arrived. That and the bond between people who loved each other was the most secure one you could have when you needed someone to watch your back.

"No, seriously. I'd have thought you were on the menu if you didn't call yourself Madam," I laid the compliments on thick.

Her growing smile was indication enough that she was enjoying my flattery.

"Unless…" I swirled my drink. "Is there a secret menu here?" I asked conspiratorially.

She leaned back from the bar top and laughed hard enough to make her chest dance in the tight dress. "You. You are something. One moment." She stepped away to greet a customer and welcome them inside.

I watched the idiot's eyes slide right off the best woman in the place to all the young ladies giggling and laughing down the hallway. He was sucked into the young ladies a moment later.

"Where were we?" Simone asked, keeping watch over the man and her girls like a protective mother.

"Ah. Talking about how fantastic you look in that new dress. I mean, it is hard for words to do it justice."

"Well try." She grinned, happy for the compliments. "And who said it was a new dress?"

"Beautiful, ravishing, the kind of allure that would turn men into beasts." I went on as she blushed. "As for it being new, just a hunch."

"Yes, and why don't you tell me what changed today? Hmm?" She refilled my drink.

This brandy went down so smoothly I hadn't realized I'd finished my snifter already. This minx was definitely trying to get me drunk.

"I warm up slowly. Trust doesn't come easy to me," I admitted, taking another sip.

She watched me carefully, her green eyes staring at me hauntingly over her glass. "That much is obvious."

"Also, when a woman dresses nicer, I've learned it's best to take notice," I added.

She laughed again and poured herself more of the brandy. "Well. I'm flattered that you noticed. But, sadly, I'm not on the menu. Someone has to keep this place running."

"That's probably for the best. I don't think I'd be able to stay away if you were on the menu. Well, I'm not doing a very good job of staying away as it is. Can you imagine it being worse?" I let out a laugh. I expected a forced laugh, but it felt remarkably good and more genuine than I expected.

Even if my interest had piqued now that I knew her real name, I really did enjoy talking to her night after night.

"Worse? I think that's the wrong word. It would be so much better." She practically purred from behind her glass.

I double checked that there was nothing in the drink, but I was certainly feeling something. "You have me stupefied." I shook my head in defeat and poured myself some more. "I'm going to be glued to this stool tonight. Sadly, the woman I had my eyes on is too busy working."

She clinked her glass to mine. "To old souls."

"To old souls," I echoed, and we took a sip together. "Now, this would normally be the part where I try to make plans. Tonight Nester came early and is staying out of trouble because we have something big the next few days."

"You'll stay safe?" she asked me, not diving into the details. Simone was a smart enough woman to know what the Nesters did, and that questions could get a person in trouble.

"As safe as I can be," I promised. With the ax, I should be able to clear the instance on my own. Bringing Bobby along was about making friends. "Now, what does a lady like you do outside of work?"

"You wouldn't believe it." She smirked.

"Try me," I shot back, not missing a beat.

She swallowed a sip. "Exercise instructor."

My jaw nearly hit the counter. "No way." Then I leaned around the bar. "Though, that does make a few things make more sense."

"This job isn't on the books. I need something believable. Besides, you can't imagine how easy it is to advertise my secondary business on the side there." She shrugged helplessly.

"You little minx," I chastised her. "I think I might be in over my head. Next thing I know, you're going to be on top of me. As my boss," I clarified with a grin.

She ran her tongue along her teeth at my comment. "What do you do besides work?"

"Take care of my family. Work on a few self-improvement projects. I have had surprisingly little downtime until just the other day," I admitted. "In fact, I'm overdue for some shopping. This weekend, I was going to hit up a pop-up mall I heard about."

"Are you asking me to join you?" She wanted me to be direct. Yet I didn't want our little game to end.

"You have a discerning eye, and those places are full of fakes. Can't hurt to have a second set of eyes with me. Especially two as pretty as yours."

She tilted her head and looked away for a moment, smiling. "Fine. I'll help you pick out the true quality goods."

"Takes one to know one." I took another sip.

She was now full-on blushing.

I was going to enjoy stealing one of the Demon Lord's generals.

"Stop," she said playfully enough for me to know that I should keep on going.

"What? You are premium, top-shelf goods. If you don't believe me, then when we go out, watch how many men stare at you. I bet you have to beat men away with a stick when you are teaching exercise classes." I kept going, the liquor helping encourage me.

"I do," she admitted. Simone was a beauty. Here, she was surrounded by twenty-somethings barely wearing anything, and the clients clearly marked her as off limits as soon as she showed up with her air of authority in her establishment.

"Then the other question I have is, are you going to be introducing me to the stick tonight?" I raised an eyebrow, daring her.

She narrowed her eyes at me and smiled as she took another sip. "Only if that's the way you like it," she murmured into her glass while her eyes smoldered.

"I like to experiment," I admitted, making her emerald eyes go wide. She coughed to cover up a small gasp.

"Experimenting is good. Though, I might have more experience than you." It was clear that the age difference between us was a slight sore spot for her, but she wasn't going to back down. We were having fun.

"That sounds like a bet you shouldn't take." I winked and poured both of our glasses full again. "Now, on the topic of travels. I've gotten around quite a bit myself. What's your favorite?"

"I feel like I'm supposed to say Paris, but Switzerland landscapes took my breath away. Charming little villages the whole way, and I swear the water is just bluer there." She smiled wistfully at the memories.

I nodded along. "It is beautiful. There's something about the mountains in the background all the time that just makes it feel... larger than life."

"You've been?" she asked, surprised.

"Appenzell. I had a friend there." I felt a sudden pang of loss at the mention of my friend, but I pushed that aside and perked up. "It's beautiful."

She watched me closely and didn't push, knowing there was something in the memory that wasn't for tonight.

I took a big drink only for a notification to pop up.

[Poison Resistance F]

Fuck you too, System. There wouldn't be high-rank booze to be found after the Rapture. Though, there were a few tricks.

Chapter 8

I was waiting for Bobby at the instance when he pulled up in his sports car.

He popped his head out and looked around. "How'd you get here?"

"Walked," I answered. How else would I have gotten to the location?

"It's a long way." He pointed up the road.

I shrugged. "I'm used to it. Let's get going. You brought food and water?"

"Yep. I even brought a surprise." He went to the trunk of his car and popped it before pulling out a large durable case.

"And what is that?"

"A grenade launcher." Bobby patted the case. "A gun might not have worked, but this puppy will help us go through so much faster."

I rubbed at my forehead. "No it won't." He had magic and he was going to use a grenade launcher?

"Say that after I level a bunch of zombies." Bobby walked up proud of his idea. I couldn't give away how much I knew, so I would just have to let him figure it out the hard way.

In front of us was a portal that only players could see. I stepped through and turned back to see nothing behind me. But then Bobby stepped through out of thin air with his grenade launcher held tightly to his chest like it might otherwise fly away.

"Get that set up and let's give it a try. After the gun failure last time, I'm suspicious at best," I played my part.

"You'll see." Bobby popped the case open and took out the launcher, quickly loading it with ammunition kept in the foam padding around the case. "Watch this." He aimed the launcher at the closest group.

The launcher made a hollow thunk, and we both watched the grenade land just to the right of a shambler group, exploding on contact with the ground.

The explosion was impressive, like a low-ranked Fireball, yet it didn't even knock over the shamblers.

"What? Damn, those guys are sturdy," Bobby reasoned and emptied the other five chambers, dropping five more grenades cleanly within the group.

Yet only one fell down. The other two in the group continued on, looking decently worse for wear.

Bobby's mouth hung open. "Holy crap. This did nothing to them."

"Imagine the kind of mess it would make if they got out," I added.

"They can get out?!" Bobby shrieked.

I cleared my throat. "Don't know. Just a thought."

They could get out. Each instance was like a blister on the reality of the world. We'd come in and clear out the monsters, which were a result of the infection, but they were not the infection itself. Eventually, the instance would close unless certain measures were taken to stabilize the instance.

In the same line of thinking, a player could exhaust an instance, and it would only refill with monsters slowly after that. The world wasn't smart, but it was purposeful. The System that governed it used players to clear monsters while rewarding them until the world was able to heal.

In very rare cases, an instance would remain untouched for too long and the infection would fester. The world would sort of 'pop' the instance and let its monsters spill out in a last-ditch effort to heal itself.

I drew the ax from my spatial ring and charged the remaining shamblers. The ax punched right through their chests, and I killed each of the shamblers in a single blow. I didn't have a passive skill for the ax. Yet. That would come the more I used the weapon and gained experience.

"Damn," Bobby cheered. "You do more damage than a grenade launcher." He put his new toy down and drew out his wand. Then he cast Acid Splash on one of the shamblers.

Two shots later, it collapsed and disappeared. Bobby looked at his wand and then at my ax with a little envy.

"I'm sure at higher levels you'll wipe out half the place with a single spell, and I'll still be swinging around a piece of steel one at a time," I encouraged him. "For now, let me shoulder the bulk of the work, and later you can show off."

Bobby grinned like a loon at the idea. I had a feeling he was satisfied at finding that he was essentially a human grenade launcher.

I didn't bother waiting for him as I hurried forward, putting my new weapon to use as I started to practice an ax art that I'd had in my past life. While often depicted as weapons of brute force, they could be used with a certain finesse. And by finesse, I meant raining heavy overhead blows one after another on something durable until it kicked the bucket.

We pushed quickly through the shamblers. We were even able to split up this time. Each of us took a group at a time before converging on the groups that had walkers. Bobby slowly killed the walkers while I cleaned up the shamblers.

Finally, we reached the boss, and that fight was much easier than the first time. After I gained proficiency with axes, the weapon bit through his Tough Hide while I kept running his Charge into walls to stun him.

"More loot." Bobby jumped into the container, quickly looking for where the rings had been last time, only to find nothing.

The loot was only about half of the first time.

"Aww, is it because it was less of a challenge?" Bobby asked, picking up half the gold coins and looking at a dagger in his hand.

"Possibly. Or maybe the last time was the first time and it included special loot?" I tried to lead him to the correct answer and took my own share. There wasn't a skill book this time, and I was uninterested in an F Rank dagger. Getting close enough to use a dagger was dangerous and more of a last resort. I preferred longer weapons, or perhaps a lightweight long sword.

Swords were, after all, the most versatile weapon. The long sword doubly so because it could be used one-handed or two-handed when the time called for a little extra force.

"At least we're making out like bandits." Bobby made gold rain out of his ring and along his hands.

I was unimpressed by the sight and sat down, pulling out a bottle of water and some deli sandwiches I had picked up along the way. My mouth watered looking at the tuna salad. How long had it been since I had had neatly cut triangle sandwiches? All the preservatives aside, the sandwich was fantastic.

"You look happy," Bobby commented.

"I am happy." I opened my eyes from savoring the sandwich. "This gold is going to solve a lot of my money problems. I'm also now growing stronger quite rapidly." I flexed. With the single level we got from this clear, I had stepped up to 21 strength and could go win some Olympic strength sports if I wanted to.

Bobby nodded along. "With this magic, I'm going to be able to make some waves."

"Going to compete with your half-siblings?" I asked.

Bobby hesitated. "Maybe. Dad really favors them, though. Meanwhile, I got the shit hole part of the city to run."

"I live in that shit hole," I reminded him. "Besides, who wants to run organized crime in the business district?"

"Those guys pay great. Gloria mostly does money laundering for them." Bobby munched on some fancy trail bars and pulled out a sports drink. "So, are we going again?"

"Yup. As much as this weird System will let us," I said. "Oh, and I think I found some things online about our situation. It seems there might be other people like us."

Bobby slowly nodded. "I asked my father. He said they are called players, and whatever I do, don't upset the players."

Carmen Nester probably had a few run-ins with the Clans. They had their fingers in just about every pie.

One of them was even responsible for controlling the total quantity of gold and diamonds in the world. If we sold these coins at a pawn shop, they'd track us down and either kill us or give us a scare so that we didn't disrupt their gold markets.

They had global control of a market, and they ruled with an iron fist.

My own Clan was the weakest of the five. They scraped for power by searching out and adding more powerful bloodlines to the family. Then again, they were barely a cohesive Clan, split into several factions that fought amongst each other.

"Got it. Players. Well, that makes a little sense given we have a character menu. I'm going to scope out what I think is a secret player market this weekend. Madam Sugar is coming with me." I took a bite of my sandwich as he stared at me.

"Candy told me there were rumors about you two. Are you really going for her?" Bobby asked.

"Going? I've already caught her." I smirked at the young mobster. "Your news is old. Besides, she's hot, and smart to boot. If I'm going to go poke around this player market, I need a date so that I can not look too suspicious."

"Your call." Bobby downed the bar and washed it down with more sports drink. "Let's go for round two. I bet you need plenty of these gold coins for the player market, if that's what it really is."

I nodded, knowing that was certainly the truth, and stood up, accepting the prompt to restart the instance. It teleported us back to where we'd started. Bobby's grenade launcher was still there, all of the ammunition used up. It had been abandoned.

Shamblers were already roaming around in front of us. I hefted my ax, spinning the shaft a few times to get a tight grip and rushed back into battle.

***

Three days later, I staggered out of the instance with Bobby. We'd only left one other time to sleep in the back of Bobby's car. Then we woke up and dove back inside to keep fighting.

And our efforts had paid off.

[Name: Bran Heros
Level: 8
Class: Blood Hegemon ??
Status: Healthy
Strength: 21
Agility: 23
Vitality: 20
Intelligence: 18
Spirit: 10964

Skills:
Soul Gaze SSS
Soul Resilience S
Blunt Weapon Proficiency F
Endurance F
Throwing Proficiency F
Blood Boil F
Blood Siphon F
Blood Bolt F
Bloodline Collection 0
Regeneration F
Fire Resistance F
Poison Resistance F
Ax Proficiency F
Charge F]

All of my new skills were still at the F rank. Using them against F ranked monsters would help level them, but it would be incredibly slow. Mundane practice would barely do anything to progress them.

What I really needed were higher ranked monsters to really push myself and my skills.

I sighed, working to try to be patient. This plan would take time, and I still had time before the demons came. Two years and I had only just begun. This was the right path.

I hauled another bundle of zombie limbs to the back of Bobby's trunk.

"Are you sure you don't have more room in your ring? Those things are probably going to start stinking." Bobby wrinkled his nose as I threw them in with the rest we'd gathered.

"They might be worth something, who knows?" I shrugged. "Drop them off somewhere safe if you don't want them in your trunk."

"I'm going to hide them in the hospital morgue. They owe me a few favors, and they can probably keep them from rotting." Bobby got into the car with a grimace as the trunk struggled to close. "Might need to bring a more practical car next time."

"I don't know when it'll work again," I said, glancing at the dungeon portal. My statement was part fact. The dungeon was exhausted and would restore eventually, but I really didn't know the frequency. Based on my best guess, it would now offer about one run a day. "Don't be coming back here without me."

"Make sure to split whatever you get from this market," Bobby shot back and revved his car up. "Help me get these out when we get to the hospital."

I nodded. "Deal." I got in and double checked that my spatial ring was still on my finger.

It was a small fortune, but with the split, I had nine hundred and fifty-two gold coins. About a hundred of those would need to be sold for enough cash to start my plans and pay off my mother's hospital bills.

All I had to do now was explore the pop-up market from the Free Player Alliance. Surely, they had some easy way to sell the coins so that I would not need to venture out and try to do it on my own, exposing myself further.

Bobby's tires squealed as he peeled out of the industrial park, the limbs bumping in his trunk as he shot over the rough road and onto the highway.

Chapter 9

After dropping off the limbs and terrifying the poor morgue technician, I checked on my mother before heading home to clean up. I wanted to get some real rest and get ready for my date with Simone.

When I woke up, I showered and put on my F Rank shirt. If I was going to be around other players, I wanted to be more prepared. I threw on some dress pants too, wanting to put some effort into my appearance for Simone.

My dark hair was combed neatly, and I found a pair of scissors, trimming it myself with practiced cuts. It hadn't been so short in a while, but I'd managed to make it look quite clean.

The weather was warm enough that I didn't need a jacket, so I left in my pants and shirt. I headed towards the park for the market, walking the whole way with my hands in my pockets and Soul Gaze scanning everyone I passed. Blood Boil was active and made my muscles swell slightly, but I was doing it because I wanted to practice the ability.

As I walked up, I found Simone already by the entrance, waiting for me. If it wasn't for her staring at me, I might not have picked her out of the crowd.

I almost didn't recognize her but headed straight for her. "How is it that you are almost unrecognizable, but even more enchanting?" I teased her.

"Who told you to clean up so nicely? I feel underdressed." She was wearing a set of sporty bright blue leggings and a jogger's jacket that hung loose at her waist, despite being tight around her arms and chest. She reached out, taking my arm.

CHAPTER 9   63

"No, this is perfect. Did you just come from one of your classes?" I asked her, leading her into the pop-up market.

Dozens of tents were aligned in rows with a crowd moving orderly through, with plenty of kids and dogs in tow. My Soul Gaze told me that plenty of the people around us were ordinary.

I wondered how the market worked. They had to have some way to indicate the type of merchandise.

"I have one in a few hours. Wasn't sure how long this was going to take and if I'd have time to change after," Simone admitted.

"Well, that means I can't take you back to my place after this. A few hours isn't enough time. Shame. But I should probably call you something else than that other name we use. Unless... Maybe I should call you Suga," I teased her with a hideous pet name.

She rolled her eyes. "Simone."

"Real name or another fake?" I teased.

"Real. Is Bran your real name?"

"Yeah. Though it comes with a last name I hate. Heros."

"Wait, like actual Heroes?" she chuckled. "Funny given your job."

"There's no E, and it's Greek. It's a very old family name," I told her. "My extended family is... prominent."

She raised a manicured eyebrow, but she didn't press any further. "Can't say I come with much family. Practically raised myself."

"So. Simone." I played with her name on my lips. "Lovely name. How much of a bobble and art connoisseur are you?"

"This wasn't exactly what I was expecting," she answered as she looked around.

I shrugged. This place was likely hiding quite a few secrets. It would just take some time to peel back the layers and figure it out.

"First time?" A greeter, a young woman waved at us.

"Yes." I decided to play along, still looking around at the spectacle.

"Wonderful. Please be sure to read the rules and let's keep everyone safe." She made eye contact with both of us, and I brushed aside her Inspect ability.

A quick check with Soul Gaze confirmed that she was a player, and I shifted the ability to the rules.

[Hidden Message - Coin costs are 100x dollar costs. Please do not use abilities within the market.]

I deactivated Blood Boil for the moment and continued in.
"So, what are we shopping for?" Simone asked.
"Well, you see, I just moved, and my place is so bare that it is embarrassing. I doubt I could bring anyone there with it in its current state." I shook my head in fake lament.
Really, I couldn't bring Simone back to the crappy apartment at all. I'd fix that soon.
"Oh. Some decorations?" She looked to the right side that had a number of booths selling paintings and headed that way, pulling me with her.
More than a few men's eyes stopped on her when they scanned the crowd. I felt satisfied that her attention stuck to me like glue.
"So. I should have asked, but you don't have a girlfriend or anything?" Simone asked.
"Nope. I'm very single at present. I used to have a few girls, though," I admitted. Sadly, they were all dead in my past life. Though, there was a slight temptation to go find two of them in this life. It would have to wait until later. Things like that were hard to reignite, and I knew that no matter what I did, it wouldn't be exactly the same.
"At once?" She gave me a scandalized gasp.
I didn't feel the need to hide anything. There was nothing wrong with how we had lived our lives. "Happens. We were all happy."
Simone hummed at that but didn't say anything as we approached the first stall.
I scanned it with Soul Gaze, realizing that some of the paintings were weapons hidden with talismans to disguise them as paintings.
Interesting.
"What about this one?" Simone pointed to a pretty lake landscape that was really a hidden E rank Flail.

It was well out of my price range. "Not quite to my tastes. I'd like something big, a statement piece. The style is nice. And you can never go wrong with a nice landscape."

"You need smaller ones for the bathrooms," she added.

I stared at it and nodded, deciding to try something. "That one, please?" I pointed to the painting in question and pulled out a credit card that I'd found in my wallet.

The man managing the stall got out of his seat and used his phone to accept my card before removing the painting and bringing it around the back of his station for a moment. Then he handed it to me.

It wasn't the same painting. If I had to guess, he had swapped it out with one in a spatial ring to give me one that was mundane.

"It looks great." I tucked it under my arm, and Simone held my other arm daintily as we continued to shop.

Some of the stalls were completely mundane, others hid items as jewelry or overpriced woodworking.

I was shocked at how well they managed to hide the transactions in the open. I had always wondered how players had existed in the world without notice before the Rapture.

The Free Player Alliance was better managed than I had expected. After the Rapture, they had gained popularity and power, but I had always considered them a very minor power before then. Apparently, they just weren't coordinated until a mutual enemy appeared.

"What do you think of those?" I pointed at a cocktail mixer stand that was a front for an alchemist. It never hurts to get to know an alchemist.

My eyes scanned over the bitters and cocktail mixers. Both were secretly potions, mostly common health potions. But there were some fun ones like shape change and even antidotes.

"Those things are always a little iffy. They add too many herbs in a bid to make it fancy." Simone eyed the bitters. "Simplicity is best when it comes to drinks."

"Says a bartender, the one who has to mix them," I teased.

She only grinned.

My eyes landed on a 'Lavender Bitters'.

[Antidote D]

My heart skipped a beat. Right here. Right here was the item that could likely solve my mother's poisoning.

As my heart skipped a beat, I looked at the price and winced. $140. That meant it was fourteen thousand gold coins. It completely blew past any budget I had at the moment.

Yet it was probably a fair price.

Simone checked my face and stepped up to the counter. "I'll take one of these." She pointed to the bitters that I'd just clearly been watching.

"You don't have to do that." I didn't need the mundane version, and she was right, it was wildly overpriced.

"Nonsense. Maybe I wanted to try it too," she dismissed my attempt to stop her and bought it.

The seller obviously reached below the counter and pulled out a mundane version, giving it to Simone. I couldn't help but show a little disappointment.

Simone however was all smiles, and I couldn't be glum for long.

"Let's keep going." I didn't want to wait around by the stall. There would be other alchemists that I could approach about selling the zombie limbs.

Most of the items around the market were F rank, with a decent selection of E rank items and a few D rank. The highest I saw was a single C rank that was selling for an exorbitant amount.

Then again, the ability to easily clear more instances could be considered priceless.

I picked up an F rank dagger with a poison effect to help me train my poison resistance. I wasn't a masochist, but some things needed to be done. If I were to find a poison dungeon, I'd need to be ready.

The exchange was interesting, mostly happening with subtle sleight of hand and spatial rings. Using handing a credit card back and forth as an excuse to bump them together and exchange the coins.

"Oh these are pretty." Simone pointed to a mundane booth that had decorative maps of Vein City and the surrounding area.

I entertained her and went into the booth to look at the maps. They were interesting, and I'd seen plenty of maps.

My vision stopped on one of them, my eyes going wide. If I didn't have knowledge of my past life, I'd have missed piecing together the markers on one of the maps.

This one had different marks than the map I had seen before, but it was very clearly the same type of map. Each of those decorative elements—the hill, the tree, the lake—was an instance. A few of them done in the same style circulated in my past life. Almost as if they somehow knew every instance all over the world.

This map was essentially a treasure map for me!

"How much for this one?" I pointed to it.

"Never figured you for a map guy." Simone leaned on my shoulder.

"I don't know. This one speaks to me. It's a different style than the rest." I turned to the woman running the booth who could clearly smell a sale coming off of me. "Did you make this one?"

"Ah. No," she admitted. "It was a friend's, and I'm selling it for them."

"I'd love more maps like this one if you have any. There's something about the small details." I pointed to the emphasized landmarks. "Three hundred?" I pulled out my credit card to see if she'd suddenly ask for coins. But when I had checked her over, she had not shown up as a player.

My card cleared, and I let out a sigh of relief. There couldn't be much more credit on it at this point. Given my situation in my past life, I was already going to be pushing my limit.

The woman rolled up the map, and I watched her closely with Soul Gaze active on the painting the whole time to make sure she didn't swap it out. When she handed it to me in a little protective tube, I took it with a little excitement and tucked it carefully under my arm.

Simone clicked her tongue. "Maybe I should have gotten you the map instead of the bitters."

"Didn't you get that for yourself?" I teased.

She shrugged with a smile, and we continued on through the market.

My next objective was somewhere to turn coins into money. When I spotted a bank's booth trying to encourage people to open accounts, I headed that way.

Soul Gaze told me the three people working there were all initiated and not weak.

"Hello." I walked up and felt each of them Inspect me, and prevented them from working. I did not want them to see my details; mystery was always for the best.

"What can we do for you?" The one in the center, a Level 12 wizard with inflated stats, stood up excitedly. By pushing off their Inspects, they knew I was a player and one with some ability.

"I have some currency I'd like to exchange. Sadly, a lot of my money isn't in USD." I scratched the back of my head. "Does your bank have good rates?"

The wizard smiled and handed me a sheet from below the table that listed all sorts of currencies and exchange rates. "If you'll sit down, we can discuss details."

"While you do that, I'm going to go look at the jewelry over there," Simone excused herself.

I liked a woman that could respect my privacy when I needed it.

She had picked up on the fact that the wizard and I wanted to transact alone.

"Sir, would you be wanting to exchange gold?" he asked once Simone had left.

I thumbed the spatial ring on my finger and held out my hand to shake it. "I think we can do business."

With the handshake, I transferred over a hundred coins. According to what I could decipher on the exchange sheet, I could get ten thousand per System gold coin. These were things that could be sold, but not often bought. Gold coins were precious to players.

They could be used to improve stats and skills, but I needed mine to stabilize my life for now. Besides, that option would always be there later when I truly needed it.

It got significantly more expensive the more coins were used for stats. I did not need the leveling at the moment, and I definitely needed the gold. Getting myself set up and my mother out of the hospital were too important.

"Perfect. Let me give you some details." The man took out a slip of paper and scribbled down some information. "At the end of today, this account will have all the money." He tapped on it twice.

I had just gained one million dollars. Just like that.

Past me would have broken down crying with relief, but I knew that money came and went. This money had a purpose, and it would serve its purpose.

"Ah. I did have some additional business if you didn't mind?" With Simone away, there were questions I wanted to ask.

Chapter 10

"Of course, sir." The wizard was very polite as I worked with him to exchange my gold at the market. "Here's my business card, by the way. If you have any more business in the future, we are happy to accommodate."

I knew the type at a glance.

Gold coins were the epitome of 'money is power' because players could exchange them for stats in their character menu. This man had barely spent any time fighting. And his stats were disproportionate to his level. There was no shame in the strategy. In fact, one of the players that had held a demon gate during the Rapture was a man with a similar profile.

"I'm a little new to all of this." I let out a sigh and visibly deflated in front of him to play the role of a new, weak player. "There was a weird flash and then I was stuck in an alley with zombies."

"Oh. A brand-new player." The wizard nodded. "Welcome. I'm surprised you found this place."

"Ah. I have been using the Inspect skill on everything and saw the sign out front with a 'hidden message'," I lied. "So, I took my date in here and have been looking around."

"Where was this alley?" the wizard asked, managing to keep any greed from his tone.

Damn, he was good.

"Maybe I shouldn't say?" I scratched my cheek. "That's the only place I can get these gold coins."

The man nodded to himself. "Well. The organization here is called the Free Player Alliance."

"Is your bank owned by them?" I played up the innocent youngster.

CHAPTER 10

"By a former officer. Not many people actually join the organization. We still host events like this and run some services like the bank to facilitate. And of course, we take our cut. It's business after all," he added pointedly.

"Of course. Of course. Can't expect you to do all of this for free." I fidgeted with his card and checked the name. It matched his details. So they were hiding in plain sight.

Interesting.

"Are there other ways to get coins? I don't know, jobs for people like me?" I asked, more curious than anything.

The Free Player Alliance would become strong, but they were also my best resource at present.

"It depends." He tried to Inspect me again.

I batted the Inspect aside. "Stop doing that." If a player that knew enough found out my last name, it could prove troublesome. Someone like the banker might know the names of the five Clans.

"You can feel it?" he asked.

"Yup. It's like when someone stares at your back, and you can feel the hairs on your back standing on end. I just nudge it aside." The ability to stop the Inspect was a small secret that people would figure out eventually.

What I didn't tell him was that it also helped that my spirit power was massive. It was unlikely that someone would be able to brush aside my Soul Gaze. As an improved version of Inspect, it came with several benefits.

"Interesting." He rubbed at his chin. "There are some jobs, and people do post to look for partners for more challenging instances. What rank was yours?"

"F rank." I didn't mind sharing that fact; the low rank would decrease his interest. "What we fought were all really low level too. I think I got lucky."

"You did. Some people get D ranked dungeons for their first. They don't survive. Never mind the higher ranks." He sighed and shook his head. "Without your information, we can't really offer you any jobs," he tried fishing again.

"That's okay." I nodded, wanting to keep my cards close to my chest. "I'll just have to farm the one I found. Eventually, I'll be able to afford things like that D rank sword I saw."

"Your instance will eventually disappear. They last at most a single year." He frowned.

That was one of my biggest problems: even if I knew about ones that would appear in the future at this point in time in my past life, I didn't know much about the player world.

"Oh." I stared down at my hands in disappointment. "That's still a year." I started to count on my fingers. "The money I could get from those coins could carry me for the rest of my life. Oh. That's right. If I have things to sell, I wasn't sure if I could just walk up to the stalls here. Is there another way to sell those?"

The wizard's eyes sparkled with interest for a moment before he professionally suppressed his excitement. "What sort of things?"

I went to pull it out of my ring, but he stopped me.

"Put it in my ring." He shook his head with a good-natured chuckle. "We have to keep everything as secret as possible. Otherwise, some dangerous organizations will try to break us up. This world is deeper than you know."

I smiled on the inside at the reality that our roles were actually reversed, but I covered it by putting a shambler and walker arm in his ring.

"Oh. These have some small value," he downplayed the value. "We can offer them up on our site. It'll be less than selling direct like here."

I shrugged. "Sitting around in a booth doesn't speak to me as much as expedience."

He nodded. "How many do you have?"

"A lot," I answered. "Can I come by the actual bank sometime and deposit them?"

"I'm in the branch at Hinton. All of them have an active player on staff. Your account is flagged for a certain type of account manager. If you ask to see one, they'll send you to the player at the bank."

Damn! This was better than I'd hoped.

"Oh wow." I nodded along, taking that information in. "I'll swing by one tomorrow and sell them all. You said you had a site that you sell on?"

He took his business card back from me and scribbled on it before circling the web address. "Gotta type it in. It won't come up on searches. Honestly, that is enough to keep things a secret on the internet now-a-days. SEO works both ways."

I nodded, not entirely sure what he was referring to. Technology was not my strong suit. After all, it became relatively meaningless in fights against demons where ranked items could do more damage. I could type in a web address though. "Thank you. You've been a big help. This is all just a little overwhelming."

The website would allow me to look up what talismans or inscriptions were selling well. That would be my best way to consistently make money over the next two years.

"Yes, I understand. It happened to me about four years ago. Crazy that there's just suddenly a world hidden from the rest of us with supernatural people and monsters are real." He patted the business card again. "Anything else?"

"Nope. Thank you," I pretended to suddenly realize I was taking up his time and excuse myself.

As soon as I stood and had my back to him, my innocent face faded to a more neutral one, and I headed straight for Simone.

She was poking at some bracelets, but she put them down as soon as I stepped away, clearly still paying attention to me. "Well, what did you weasel out of him?"

"A million dollars," I joked.

She snorted. "Sure. You don't have to tell me. I get the feeling that this whole place has a second layer to it that I can't quite see."

I was honestly surprised at just how damned insightful Simone was time and time again. But it did make sense. There had to be more to her if a demon general chose to possess her.

I wondered if she had a bloodline or some innate ability.

"Anything else you're interested in here?" She linked arms with me and we continued to wind through the path.

I had my cash, a poison dagger, the mysterious map, and some healing potions. There was so much more that I needed, but I didn't think I was going to get it this time around.

"More importantly, is there anything that's caught your eye? Some of that jewelry perhaps?" I focused on her.

Simone gave me a wicked smile. "Not today. I'll help you carry this to your car." My expression made her pause as she tried to decipher what had slowed me down.

"Did you walk here?" She looked at the high rises around the park. "Nice area."

And it was a nice area. If they held the market in the same location, it might even be worth moving closer. But I did not live anywhere near this nice of an area at the moment.

We walked out of the park and Simone guided us down a street that was lined with cars, all parked with their occupants likely walking the market.

"Here we are." She paused at a nice enough to be reliable, but not so nice it was eye-catching, sedan. A practical woman.

"I wanted to give this to you." She held out the bag with the bitters.

I grinned and accepted it, pulling the bottle out and feigning surprise. As a sheer force of habit, I Inspected the bottle.

[Antidote D]

My face went from playfully surprised to shocked and a little horrified. "Simone!"

"You noticed?" She seemed proud of herself. "You clearly wanted the one on display more than the one they gave me. Again, something funny was going on. So, while he was trying to look down my jacket, I swapped them."

I glanced over my shoulder to make sure no one was coming for us. Then I scanned our surroundings to see if anyone was watching.

"Bran?" she asked nervously.

"Get in the car. Just get in the car." I hopped in the backseat, putting my other items in there with me.

"You're worried and you work for the Nesters. Bran, you're scaring me. What did you bring me to?" Simone's normally playful attitude melted away as she closed the car door, muting the sound outside.

"I brought you somewhere completely safe, assuming you didn't steal from people," I hissed.

"He didn't seem dangerous." She watched me closely, her foot tapping a little with anxiety.

"Half the booths are run by people who could kill the entire Nester operation," I groaned.

All a player would need is a full set of F rank clothing and they'd be bulletproof. That's really all a person would need to knock over the current-day Nester. Though, he did have one Level 8 on the payroll, it seemed.

"I see." She nodded in turn, taking my words for facts. "That includes you?"

"Huh? Yeah, I guess so. The Nesters are good people, though," I answered absentmindedly, continuing to scan the park for any sign of commotion. I wondered if the player would suddenly realize that their D rank item was stolen.

"So, how much is that really worth?" she asked.

I lifted up the bottle. "This old thing? Try 140 million. At least that's what they were really trying to sell it for." That was the price of fourteen thousand coins. The prices that people put for dollars in their stores was just part of the façade; anyone selling player equipment didn't care what they actually sold their mundane objects for.

The look on her face was priceless as she realized I was not playing some sort of joke. "Oh."

"Let's get out of here. I'm going to see you home," I told her, determined to ensure no harm came to her.

"I have class to teach. Should I call in?" She was letting me dictate what happened next.

"Actually, no. Class is good. They can't do anything in public," I said, considering the situation. The Free Player Alliance and the Clans had very strict rules. While a D rank potion was certainly valuable to these players, they probably wouldn't risk angering any of the organizations.

"Because you are all some secret society? Are you a vampire, Bran? Are vampires real?" she asked suddenly.

I met her eyes in the rearview. "I have a reflection, don't I?"

"That wasn't an answer." She waited to pull out of the lot.

"No. I'm not a vampire."

"Darn. I was hoping you would say 'yes' and then bite me and make me look young too. You know, these revitalizing creams are expensive, and if you shared your fountain of youth with me, I could save a lot of money." She pulled the car into drive and out of her parking spot.

I snorted. "If I could, I'd share it with you now. Sadly, there's very little that goes around. Next drop I get, though."

"Going to hold you to that promise." She met my eyes again. "Otherwise, you don't have to tell me what you're hiding. Seems it might be a little more dangerous than I can handle. It's probably better that I don't know." There was a long pause. "What's the bottle do?"

"Cures a dangerous poison," I answered honestly.

"For you? Or for a girl?" she asked, a touch of jealousy in her tone.

"For a girl." I watched her reaction closely. There was a slight pinch of her brow.

"You said you were single. I don't like people lying to me." She turned down a street.

I grinned at that reaction. She was just upset that I might be lying. "She's my mother."

There was a dawning of realization on her face. "Oh. Bran, I'm sorry."

"It's fine." I tucked the bottle into my pocket to show her before stashing it in my spatial ring. "Thank you. This will help me and her a lot."

"Of course." Simone went quiet as we drove to a workout studio fifteen minutes away, and she parked. "So what are you going to be doing?"

"Make sure no one is looking for you while you're here," I answered. "Then I'll head out after. Sorry for the cloak and daggers."

"No. It's fine. I knew you worked for the Nesters. Some of this is expected." She messed up her hair a little and pulled at her tight workout clothing to remove any wrinkles. "How do I look?"

"Tempting as hell," I answered without missing a beat. "Now, go do your thing while I make sure you are safe. We can talk after."

She leaned back, and I kissed her on the cheek before she got out. "Besides the scare, it was a great date."

Chapter 11

I sat in the back of the car on my phone to both be inconspicuous and to try and access the website I had been given.

I was typing in what the wizard had written on the card, but nothing was coming up. I took a moment to look up and scan everyone walking past the gym again.

No players were present, and nobody was keeping tabs on Simone.

Going back to my phone, I put the address in several times, but it just kept coming up with a search rather than a website.

He said it wasn't searchable.

Damned technology. Why wasn't this working?

I scanned the surroundings again, only to look in the classroom that Simone had been working in and finding her missing. Bolting up in my seat, I scanned around, ready to hop out.

A moment later, Simone came peeling out of the gym, a phone pressed up against her ear and an unrolled yoga mat flapping under her arm.

She got to the car, throwing the mat inside and still talking to someone on the phone. "I'm on my way right now. Please hold on. Just a few more minutes."

"What's up?" I asked.

"Emergency. One of my girls is having trouble." She threw the car into drive and peeled out of the parking spot in a hurry.

I buckled back in. I luckily got the buckle latched just before my body was thrown to the side as she took a turn without slowing down. "Is there anything I can do to help?"

"Actually... yeah. Sounds like some client rolled up with a few guys, and they are trying to get into her place," Simone answered. "I could use a scary man right now."

"That I can do. Would you like me to just scare them away or make sure they never return?" I asked.

"Wait, are you offering to kill them?" Simone glanced in the mirror.

I gave her a helpless look. "Uh. Yeah."

She blinked and shook her head. "No. Don't kill them."

"Got it." I leaned back in the car. Roughing a few people up was well within my wheelhouse.

"Do you kill people often?" she asked.

"When needed," I answered cryptically. "Not much lately." Despite her participation in the seedier part of the city, it seemed she didn't have much taste for blood.

Too much reluctance would be a bad thing.

"Okay." She nodded. "Well, please don't. If you have to... you know... to protect yourself though, then that'll be that. I'll back you up on a police report."

I blinked. Right, she was pragmatic. And she clearly trusted the hell out of me.

I found myself really starting to like Simone and wondering if she might fit into my life. The fact that she had once become a demon general was less of my reason to spend time with her. I wanted Simone on my team, and I wanted her mind at my side.

Simone slammed on the brakes and swerved expertly into a parallel parking spot. "Let's go." She threw off her seatbelt and marched out of the car towards a nice-looking apartment building.

I was right behind her, my items from the market safely tucked away in my spatial ring. She had been too preoccupied to notice that they were now missing.

Simone stopped at the door and buzzed a random apartment. "Delivery," she said and the door buzzed open.

"Some security," I muttered, following her in as she stormed right past the mail room and started up the stairs like she knew where she was going. Keeping up with her wasn't a problem, I was now superhuman and she was not.

As we neared the third floor, I could already hear some man yelling. Sure enough, Simone stopped at that floor and barged out. Down the hall, two big men flanked a skinny one who was doing the yelling and trying to wedge the door open.

"Can I help you, gentleman?" I stepped around Simone.

My Soul Gaze flicked over the three of them, and I found nothing out of the ordinary.

"Get the fuck out of here, Rick. If I hear about you harassing one of my girls again, I'm going to get the cops so far up you asshole that you'll taste them." Simone barked at the man, clearly recognizing him like she'd had trouble before.

Rick, however, wasn't perturbed at all at Simone's statement. He leaned away from the door he'd just been yelling at as if it had all been an act. His eyes raked over Simone in a way that made me tempted to ignore her earlier request and put him six feet under.

I was the jealous type, and I wasn't afraid to admit it.

"Just him?" Rick turned and looked me up and down too. "Break his legs. It's time she learned a lesson about who rules this business."

The two men advanced on me, and I caught the first punch easily.

"This is unfortunate for both of you. Your boss really set you up for pain. First, he keeps eyeing my date. Second, I have something to prove now." I bent the man's fist back and threw a jab into his gut that would have made any heavyweight boxer proud. I followed the hit up with a hook to the face, and big guy number one went out cold.

Number two tried to grab me, but I twisted and threw him off of me and into the wall. He bounced off, and my fist met his gut half way, bending him in half before I kneed him in the face to drop him next to the other.

"Rick, was it?" I rolled my neck, feeling a satisfying pop. "Let's say you and I have a nice little chat, aye?"

Rick didn't cower. He just sneered. "Who's this, Madam Sugar? I don't recognize him. He your new toy?"

"Shut it, Rick. You can't have my girls. They don't want to work for you. They have a choice," Simone said from behind me.

Rick pulled out a gun and leveled it at me. "Then I'm going to take that choice away." There was a certain madness in his eyes—he'd shoot.

"Bran, step aside." Simone's voice cracked.

"No." I hadn't been treated so carelessly in a long time. This guy really thought he had the upper hand on me. People in the future knew better than to make any such assumptions.

"Step aside, boy. You aren't bulletproof, and I'm not afraid to prove it." He had a steady hand and the gun trained right on my chest.

I took a step forward, and as my foot moved, several things happened at once.

Rick fired a single shot, center mass.

Simone screamed.

And I grunted as the bullet slammed home, flattening against my F rank shirt.

My foot landed on the ground, completing my step. Then I took another towards the asshole, a smirk growing on my face. Damn, if the look on his face wasn't satisfying.

Rick's eyes went wide with confusion and fear before his finger twitched again and again. He emptied the whole magazine into my chest and didn't put a hole in the shirt.

"What?!" He let out a strangled cry as I ripped the gun from his hand and threw him against the door.

"You are lucky that she asked me not to kill you. But you did tell your men to break my legs, so this is only fair." I pulled a baseball bat from my spatial ring and twirled it around.

Rick struggled with everything he had, but I pinned him to the door and swung for his knees. Two wet cracks later, and Rick was sobbing on the floor, barely holding onto his consciousness.

I tapped the bat next to his face to get his attention. "Anything happens to Simone, and I will find you. Do you understand that? If she's not here, then she can't ask me not to kill you next time."

Leaving him alive was the wrong move in my opinion. I had learned that it was easier to take out threats than leave them to fester behind your back. But Simone had asked to leave him alive, and I was going to respect that request. It was her mistake to make.

My best option then was to make this man too afraid to make the bad decision I knew was on his mind. Bullies didn't back down until they got taught a harsh lesson.

"Bran?" Simone rushed up to me and touched my chest, peeling off a bullet. "What?"

"Don't mind that." I pulled out a water bottle from my ring and poured it over the least injured of the goons until he shook himself awake. "Get up, get your buddy and get your boss. If I see you again, you won't wake up next time."

The guy gave me a hard stare before seeing his boss whimpering on the floor. He lumbered over to help his boss, keeping me in his peripheral vision. Suddenly, he seemed a bit more wary of being near me.

"Bran," Simone said again, pulling at my shirt.

I let her undo the top two buttons and see the giant bruises underneath. I hissed a little as she pushed on them. "Be gentle with me, okay? I just pulled off a nice big hero play and I don't want to ruin it."

Simone glared at me and knocked on the door. "Crystal. Everything's okay. Can we talk?"

"Simone?" Crystal asked from the other side and was clearly looking through the porthole. "Come in quick. The cops will be here soon after those gunshots."

A bar clicked on the other side of the door, followed by a chain. A moment later, we were inside.

"Yeah, it's fine. Bran took care of them." Simone gestured at me. "He's a little banged up, though. Got some rubbing alcohol?"

"Yeah. Of course." The pretty young lady hurried off through her nice, but very messy, apartment.

"She does well for herself." I glanced around and sat in her kitchen area. It was a nice apartment. And there were actually walls between the kitchen, living room and bedroom.

"The girls make more money with me than they would elsewhere. I try to tell them it's temporary and to save, but some of them spend too much of it." Simone seemed less impressed as she looked around at all the clothes.

They might have been expensive clothes; I wouldn't know.

"Here." Crystal came back with rubbing alcohol and some cotton swabs. "Simone. Rick said he went after some of the other girls."

"He's lying. You're the only one that called me." Simone motioned for me to take off my shirt. "I'll check on the others in a minute. I can't believe he's getting so aggressive."

"Competition?" I asked.

"Yup. But far more unscrupulous," Simone added. "His girls are either coked out or he's holding their visas. Thanks for the help."

"Not a problem. I'm the jealous type, and he looked at you a little too much for my tastes," I made up an excuse.

Simone gave me a soft smile.

"I'll... uh... leave you two alone. Thanks." Crystal hurried out of the kitchen to give us some space.

"You didn't have to put yourself in that position." Simone worked to unbutton the rest of my shirt, revealing my toned chest and abs. But they were a little less impressive covered in dark purple splotches.

The cotton swab covered in alcohol hovered over my chest for a moment at a loss before Simone just started dabbing randomly.

I figured she needed to help and let her do it. I even played it up and winced as she pressed on a particularly sensitive spot. "Nope. I didn't have to. I wanted to."

"Did you want to kill him?" she asked.

"No. Killing him was irrelevant. Protecting you was what was important. Killing him would have done that better, but I gave you my word that I wouldn't." I crossed my arms over my chest and watched her. "Do you have a problem with that?"

"Bran that's..." She hesitated. "Killing Rick wouldn't have done anything. He isn't the problem. The fact that the whole sex work industry is illegal and thus swept into a societal corner is the problem. Another Rick will always appear. Something that is illegal and supposedly shunned by society has such a high demand that he has to rip girls off the street and drug them up to meet it." She let out a huge sigh.

"A Madam with a conscience? You continue to impress me," I teased.

She shook her head. "You are the bulletproof vampire."

"Not a vampire," I quickly corrected her.

"Sure." She moved up to check my head to see if everything was okay.

I snatched her arm and twisted it, looking at what had caught my eye. "You're bleeding."

"Really? You're concerned about a scratch. You just got shot." Simone rolled her eyes.

"I'm bulletproof," I responded distractedly as my entire being seemed to home in on the drop of blood.

I wanted it.

"Bran?" Simone seemed concerned.

Unable to help myself, I pulled her arm close and licked the cut. The taste of her blood was incredible.

A System menu popped up in front of me before I clutched my chest and fell out of the chair with a scream.

Chapter 12

"Bran. What's wrong? Why did you lick that if it would do this?" Simone held onto me, but all that did was drag her down to the ground as my body slid off where I was sitting.

My muscles spasmed, and my whole body ached with a familiar feeling.

[Bloodline Collection 1
Pink Yuan Bloodline A (Unawakened) - Simone Sweet]
[+10 Strength, +10 Agility, +20 Vitality, +10 Intelligence, +10 Spirit]

Fuck. I cursed as I worked through the changes. I had just doubled my vitality, and the rapid changes were taking me down for a moment.

"I'm fine. Better than fine," I spoke through a clenched jaw.

"You don't seem fine," Simone relaxed. "Really, are you a vampire that's allergic to blood or something?"

I laughed but stopped as the laugh hurt before it itched something fierce. Pushing off the ground, I got back to my feet now that my muscles were responding properly.

Simone's eyes went wide. "Your bruises. Holy shit. My blood healed you."

Rather than respond, I was still absorbing the information I'd just received. I knew what a Yuan was; it was a type of lesser phoenix. I'd only ever heard of a red and a blue Yuan bloodline. Never a pink bloodline.

What I did know was that all Yuan bloodlines could be purified into phoenixes. Those were extremely powerful bloodlines, certainly enough for a demon general to want her body.

"Yeah. Sort of. I actually heal pretty quickly on my own." I stood up and started to button my shirt.

Simone's eyes lingered on my chest as it slowly disappeared until she sighed. "Well, if you are fine, then we should get going. Thanks for coming."

"Not a problem. Listen, if anything strange happens around you, you let me know right away." I stared at her seriously.

"Phone?" She held out her hand.

"That would make it easier," I chuckled and unlocked mine to give to her. It was still on the search page that I'd been struggling with. The screen made me a little embarrassed.

"What? It's not like it's porn," she said, reading my face.

"No, I was struggling with something. The web address the bank gave me wasn't working," I told her.

She tapped on my phone. "Uh. That's because you didn't put www in front of it."

I tilted my head slightly and raised an eyebrow. "He didn't write that on the card."

"It's kind of implied..." She stared back at me. "You really don't act like a 24-year-old. Are you really ancient? That would explain a few things." She tapped at my phone and showed me as the website loaded.

"You were adding your phone number," I reminded her.

"You do know how to answer this thing, right?" she asked, opening my texts and sending herself one before adding her details.

"Yes. I know how to use a phone. It's just been a while," I grumbled.

"If you were older than me, I wouldn't mind." Simone finished tapping in her details and handed me back my phone. "In fact, I'd enjoy it quite a bit. Experience is everything." She licked her lips.

"Are you going to keep probing me?" I raised an eyebrow.

"Until you bite me and make me a vampire too. Or better yet, you get me that promised shot from the fountain of youth." She got to her feet. "Let me drive you back to your place."

The offer was tempting, and I was sure Simone would find her way into my place. Yet I also knew that there was a chance that Simone didn't stay Simone.

Reminding myself of that, I felt the need to not grow too attached. While I'd try to protect her, I couldn't be there 24/7.

"No need." I needed to make a few stops on the way. "This week might be busy for me. I'm not sure when I'll be by your business again."

The map I had gotten, if it was accurate at all, would propel me forward in a much-needed way. I had to go inspect those sites after giving my mother the antidote.

"Thanks for sharing what you did for me," Simone said seriously. "You didn't have to stand in the way of those bullets."

"You spot even one of his men and you tell me. I'm serious." With my shirt on, I led her out of the apartment.

"Will do. Stay safe with whatever it is you do. I'm going to go check on my other girls. Oh, do you need to get your stuff out of the car?"

"Nope. It's already taken care of."

She smiled at the doorway. "Of course it is. I *will* see you later."

"Yeah. Not going far. I'll be back," I promised.

This woman was growing on me almost too quickly.

I'd have to think about how to prepare a few protections for her with the eventuality that a demon would come to try and possess her. That, and I needed to think about how to evolve her Yuan bloodline into a phoenix. It would be an S or an SS rank bloodline.

Most phoenix bloodlines even had a royal grade above that. Hell, she could even hit a SSS rank bloodline. My brain was swirling with possibilities.

But all of that was for later.

I couldn't help her if I couldn't get my own solid footing. Seeing the people of the Free Player Alliance today confirmed that I was still too weak. And they weren't even the major players.

***

CHAPTER 12

After briefly being harassed by an officer on my way out, I found myself walking the streets of Vein City glued to my phone like any other person. But while they were swiping to find their latest hookup, I was swiping through the marketplace that the wizard from earlier had given to me.

There was a lot to scroll through.

It was also where the zombie legs would be sold if I gave them to the bank.

From what I could tell, the bank sold items on consignment. Most of them were simple items, like alchemical ingredients and potions. A few D ranked items floated around, but not much.

The inscriptions were interesting. Most of them were fairly poor. Even some simple ones were selling for twenty coins. A player could use an inscription for many things. A popular way to use them in my past life was on small sheets of paper the size of your hand, called talismans.

They were easy to use in combat or as a quick fix for something like a locked door.

These came in all varieties, though. I even laughed when I saw that one used to change hair color was drawn on a painting canvas. What a waste of ink! The ink for those was precious.

Looking through the ingredients and the inscriptions, I did the math. I could make about three times what I spent if I made some of the better selling inscriptions. Though, I was fairly poor at present.

Slightly frustrated at seeing many things I wanted to buy, but being unable to get them, I put my phone away.

Who sells Bloodroot that cheap? Do they not even know how valuable it is?!

Yet I couldn't take advantage yet.

I found myself standing in front of the hospital a moment later, and quickly hurried inside, excited to get to my mother. I kept my head down as I passed the nursing station, heading straight for my mother's room. This moment felt like I was making a huge shift in the course of the future, even if it was just my own.

Ducking into my mother's room, I checked to make sure no one was coming before closing the door and pulling the antidote from my ring. My hand shook so hard that the liquid sloshed about in the glass jar of Lavender Bitters.

I triple checked the antidote and my mother's poison before tipping the jar past her lips and holding her nose while I massaged her throat to get it down.

I kept my Soul Gaze active, my heart pounding as I waited.

When it had all gone down her throat without issue, my hopes ballooned. I let out a huge sigh of relief when her status changed from Poisoned to Extreme Fatigue.

After a poison had gone that far, even a player would need some time to recover. But that's what would happen now. My mother would recover from this.

I let out a sigh of relief and held my mother's hand as tears fell down on her bedsheets. "I did it."

Well, Simone did it.

Otherwise, I'd be working hard right up until the deadline. I owed that woman, and I'd pay it back by protecting her from the demon that wanted her body.

"Alright, get better, mom. I'll be back soon, and maybe this time, you can tell me yourself who did this to you." There was a dangerous glint in my eye as I stood up and bowed to my mother again before leaving.

If I stayed much longer, someone from billing was going to chase me down. At least, that's what I remembered from the end. I had wanted time with my mother, only to be harassed.

Heading out, I fished the keys from that banger that I had killed a few weeks ago and retraced my steps while clicking the key fob. Eventually, a beat-up gold sedan honked. The car had a tow notice on the front window and a busted passenger side window.

The car was crap, but it would get me out to where I needed to go.

Pulling out the map, I opened up my phone's map and compared the two before picking the water icon. Then I put the rough direction into the GPS and started the car.

My ring was stocked with two cases of water and plenty of granola bars.

I pulled out, following the directions as a call came in from Bobby. I fiddled with the phone a little to get it on speaker, nearly running over an idiot that crossed a green light. "Bobby."

"Bran. I was wondering if you had any information about the legs. The mortician tech called me again today. He's really freaking out." Bobby kept his voice low.

"Yeah. I actually got a line on a place to sell them. Right now, I'm heading just outside the city to track down a few things," I said.

"Oh? Anything interesting?" Bobby asked.

"Might be. I don't want to get your hopes up. Let's just say I got a spotty lead on another potential instance." I dangled the carrot in front of him.

"Hell yeah. Wait, you are bringing me if you go, right?" Bobby insisted.

"Depends on what I find." I was confident in what I could do, but sometimes instances threw in new situations that were tough to prepare to take on. Someone having your back was invaluable.

Chances were high that whatever I found would be high enough level that I could use a hand. Sadly, the person I could trust the most right now was Bobby. If only Simone was initiated, I'd probably try and bring her.

"By the way, I was with Sugar today. Some guy named Rick tried to rough up one of her girls," I told Bobby, knowing that he'd get pissed.

"What?! It wasn't Candy, was it?" he growled.

"No. Another girl. Sounded like he was going to try and do some rounds on all of her girls," I told him, taking a turn according to the GPS and getting on the highway out of the city. "Don't worry, though. He won't be seeing any of the other girls for at least a week."

"Good man," Bobby chuckled. "I'd hate to see what you'd do to a person after seeing you fight monsters."

"She didn't want him dead. That's the only reason he's alive. Just thought you'd want to know. Her place is on your turf after all."

"Damn right. I'll have a few extra boys in that area the rest of the week. Thanks for the heads up." Bobby meant it. He was a straightforward person. "Now, I'll talk to you later. Let me know what you find and we'll meet up on Monday at Sugar's, alright?"

"Yeah. If something doesn't happen, I'll be there. Still figuring this all out and can't make too many promises." I was going to leave myself some wiggle room.

"Cya." Bobby hung up, most likely to try and contact Candy to make sure she was alright. He was a good kid.

I grabbed the steering wheel with both hands and started tuning through the radio. Waves of nostalgia washed over me as different old classics started to race through the car's speakers.

Music had power, and I was going to enjoy it while I drove out to check out some of the instances on the map.

Chapter 13

I checked my stats.

[Name: Bran Heros
Level: 8
Class: Blood Hegemon ??
Status: Healthy
Strength: 31
Agility: 33
Vitality: 40
Intelligence: 28
Spirit: 10974

Skills:
Soul Gaze SSS
Soul Resilience S
Blunt Weapon Proficiency F
Endurance F
Throwing Proficiency F
Blood Boil F
Blood Siphon F
Blood Bolt F
Bloodline Collection 1
Regeneration F
Fire Resistance F
Poison Resistance F
Ax Proficiency F
Charge F]

I shook my head as I got out of the car. Damn, I should really go rob a blood bank or something like a deranged vampire. Maybe I could find a few more bloodlines.

The car door slammed, and a few more flecks of safety glass found their way onto my boots.

All around me was flat land that had been mowed down so that a giant quarry could be built, yet it seemed that the quarry hadn't seen much use lately. It was currently heavily flooded. Work trucks sat idle all around while heavy machinery was put aside in neat, orderly rows.

I had to wonder if demand had dried up or if it was seasonal work. Either way, there was supposed to be an instance nearby.

I activated Soul Gaze and peered around before checking the map again. There was always the chance that this map was old and the dungeons were closed. Yet the one time I'd seen a map in this same style, it had turned out to be accurate. I just couldn't shake the feeling that this one would be too.

Walking around all of the buildings, I slowly spiraled out from where I'd parked the car. Yet the longer I went, the more a deep feeling of unease settled in my gut. Something told me that I knew where the instance was.

After an hour of avoiding it, I walked back to the edge of the quarry and stared down into the water, hoping that my ability would pick up on the dungeon even if it was under water.

Yet no luck.

"It's down there." I trusted my gut, but I did not like what I was going to have to do.

I put my jacket and shoes in my ring before pulling out my phone and calling Bobby. "Hey Bobby, got a pen on you?"

"Yeah. One second."

"Do me a favor and write down this account number." I rattled off a series for him. "Go to North Trust Bank and use it. You should get a manager. Tell him you want to sell the legs. Honestly, you can set up your own account with them too. They'll trade those gold coins for 10k each."

Bobby let out a soft whistle. "There's something you can do with them then." He was smart enough to know you didn't pay that if there wasn't another reason for them.

"Yeah. You can buy stats. Try focusing on your intelligence in the menu," I told him.

"Oh? Oh! Alright, yeah I can see that. I'm betting it gets a lot more expensive."

"I bet it goes up very quickly the more you use it. Yet it doesn't go up if you get stats other ways. For now, I'm not throwing my coins at stats," I told him.

"Wait, you're telling me this. What are you doing?" Bobby asked.

"I'm about to dive and see if I can't find an instance. If I find it, I'll bring you here. I'm just having trouble finding it and I have a feeling... well, just a feeling." I'd learned time and time again to trust my gut. "There's a quarry out on the east side. It looks like work's stopped. If you don't hear from me in a couple days, get some gear to go underwater and come look for the instance."

I took a few of my empty water bottles and recapped them. They'd be for seeing how deep I'd have to go into the quarry.

"Right." Bobby sounded a little disappointed. "I'll see you tomorrow."

I hung up and threw my phone in my ring before getting down to my boxers and climbing down a long ladder to the bottom of the quarry. I felt a little better that the water was decently clear. Nothing was disturbing the dust at the bottom of the pit.

I got down into the frigid water and started swimming. I followed the conveyor belt down, using it to pull myself along and conserve my strength.

As I moved, I disturbed some sediment and made the water murkier, but I was able to make great progress pulling along the conveyor. Light quickly faded the deeper I went.

It was eerily quiet. Quiet enough that thoughts of past events liked to trickle up from the dark recesses of my mind. I shook them off and activated Soul Gaze to focus and scan ahead of me. Despite the dark, Soul Gaze still worked perfectly fine.

There was a thin outline of the shapes ahead of me.

An empty bottle appeared in my hand, and I let out my breath before holding the bottle upside down and uncapping it. I made a seal with my mouth and breathed in deep. The water pressure helped me and I had to stop before I ended up breathing water as part of it.

Putting the cap back on, I continued down. I only had eight of those. So after three, I should probably head back up. I could always pack more for a return trip.

The second bottle went just like the first as I passed several horizontal shafts in the quarry. The third bottle went, and I saw something in the distance. Soul Gaze landed on it.

[Level 22 Instance D 18/12 Charges]

Fuck me.

I paused for a long moment to consider what to do next. Level 22 and D rank was going to be a stretch. Though, collecting Simone's bloodline had given me the stats for ten levels. So I could probably swing it, but it would be rough. I'd need to work on some of my skills quickly.

Crouching on the conveyor, I quickly considered my options, crushing the fourth bottle of air.

Bobby wouldn't be much help even if I brought him. At Level 8, even with some bought stats, he'd fall too far behind. Right now, I regretted not having enough allies.

After this, I needed to start working on expanding.

A second thing occurred to me as well. This instance was fresh, untouched, and growing unstable. But if that was the case, how the hell did someone make a map that contained the instance?

What did that mean for the other instances on this map? Most importantly, who made this map and where could I find them? I'd love to chain them up in my basement and make them produce more of these.

I stared at the instance, knowing it was probably a little too high of a level for me at the moment. The others on the map might be more suitable.

Just then, something moved in my peripheral vision. A faint shimmering outline in my Soul Gaze made me tense up and draw the ax from my spatial ring.

[Gold-Eyed Sloop
Level: 22
Status: Starving, Instance Escapee, Weakened
Strength: 21
Agility: 23
Vitality: 10
Intelligence: 1
Spirit: 30

Skills:
Feast D
Swim D
Dive D]

It darted at me faster than I could make out any more details.

I swung the ax to ward it off, tucking my feet into the bracing of the conveyor belt so that I could use my whole body to swing the ax next time. The metal bit into my feet and I was surely bleeding, but I didn't have many options.

The monster darted away at the sight of my aggression and swam in a long circle, watching me.

I got a look at it this time. Its body line looked more like a seal, only its neck was long with a big head at the end. Something told me its mouth had a whole lot of teeth.

A 'sloop' wasn't something I was familiar with, making this whole situation even stranger. But a monster escaping an instance was rare and a sign that the instance was growing increasingly unstable.

The sloop shot back towards me, propelling itself suddenly in my direction. It was a bit off in its attempt, using its long neck to try and snap at me while keeping its body away.

Luckily, I could see well in the dark and braced my feet to slash at the monster's thin neck. The monster cut my shoulder badly with its teeth, but the surprise of my ax was enough to prevent it from tearing a chunk off.

I could taste the blood in the water, and I knew it wasn't all mine. I lost quite a bit of air in the exchange and crushed my fifth bottle of air.

The ax had bitten deep into its neck and the monster was moving around erratically, rushing back towards the instance portal, only to get sucked up by it.

Damnit.

I crushed my sixth bottle of air and knew I wasn't going to have enough to make the return trip. That left me one option.

Pushing off the conveyor, I shot towards the dungeon. They were made by the world for players to clear, meaning none of them were ever so inhospitable that a human couldn't breathe.

As soon as I got close to the portal, it sucked me inside.

I gasped, coughing as I found myself suddenly in a damp, dimly lit tunnel. Glancing around, I could tell that the instance had formed when the quarry was in operation. Strings of lights were stapled to the ceiling of the square shaft.

Yet the square shaft ended quickly and opened up into a cavern. The string of lights with guards over them continued into the cavern.

Perhaps this was why the quarry had closed. If it had opened on the workers, then they would have been sucked in as well. I couldn't imagine that workers going missing en masse was good for business.

As soon as I stepped inside, there was the corpse of a man with a hardhat and reflective vest. I checked him over and tried to see if he had a flashlight or anything on him. No luck. The guy must not have even chosen his class if his body was still here. The System took your body if it had given you enough stats; usually by Level 20, you disappeared just as fast as a monster in an instance.

There wasn't much else left of him, having been picked clean to the bone by monsters. A corpse like this was likely what had drawn that sloop out of the instance.

I looked around, trying to find the injured sloop.

There was a clear trail of blood that went past the body and further into the dungeon. It was still alive.

Putting on my clothes, I included the F ranked shirt before I crouched low and followed the blood deeper into the cavern. My shoulder was starting to itch as the skin stretched back over, knitting itself back together.

Damn, I loved Regeneration, even if training it was a bitch.

The cavern didn't smell like mold or mildew like would be expected. The instance wasn't quite a perfect replica of the real world.

I heard splashing up ahead that made me hurry. Sure enough, I found the Gold-Eyed Sloop slipping into a waist deep pool of water and splashing about, turning the water a frothy red.

The workers that had made it into the instance hadn't made it far. Over a dozen corpses littered the pool, and the Sloop was currently feasting on one of them.

I watched as the bloody gash in its neck healed over. Then it moved on to another corpse. It seemed that this monster was going to come back ready for round two.

Until it started eating, I didn't realize how gaunt it had been when I had found it.

Its skin swelled and the wrinkles on its dark blue skin retreated as it lifted its head, satisfied from its meal. The thing looked like someone had tried to stuff too many teeth into a shark's head and then put it on a long neck connecting to a large seal's body. Though, I'd compare its body more to the size of a walrus.

As I stared, its gold, beady eyes moved and focused on me.

[Gold-Eyed Sloop D
Level: 22
Status: Healthy
Strength: 48
Agility: 41
Vitality: 52
Intelligence: 1
Spirit: 30

Skills:
Feast D
Swim D
Dive D]

Fuck me.

At least the thing didn't have any defensive skills for me to fight.

I opened my menu and touched my ring to strength and dumped out all of my gold coins, preparing myself to fight and hopefully win.

[Stat Increased]
[Stat Increased]
[Stat Increased]
...

Chapter 14

I quickly checked my stats so that I knew how I compared against the Gold-Eyed Sloop.

[Name: Bran Heros
Level: 8
Class: Blood Hegemon ??
Status: Healthy
Strength: 41
Agility: 33
Vitality: 40
Intelligence: 28
Spirit: 10974

Skills:
Soul Gaze SSS
Soul Resilience S
Blunt Weapon Proficiency F
Endurance F
Throwing Proficiency F
Blood Boil F
Blood Siphon F
Blood Bolt F
Bloodline Collection 1
Regeneration F
Fire Resistance F
Poison Resistance F
Ax Proficiency F
Charge F]

I had only managed to buy ten points of strength with the rest of my gold, but it would have to do. I needed to be able to deal more damage in this dungeon; otherwise, I would have been completely screwed.

The sloop's head wove back and forth mesmerizingly for just a moment to lull me into complacency before that tiny neck produced far more power than I expected.

I reacted, stepping into its strike and swinging my ax with all the strength I could muster. Blood Boil made my body become hot and my muscles swell with extra strength.

Its head slammed into my chest, weaving out of my ax's path at the last moment. Its teeth scraped at my chest taking a good chunk with the partial bite. Thankfully, the F ranked shirt dulled its attack a little.

I kept my swing going despite the injury. My ax bit into its neck, and I continued to ignore the damage I was taking as I swung with all of the power I could muster with one hand. The other held onto the shark nose and tried to squirm my chest back to keep away from its opening and closing maw. I was barely succeeding; it was taking more of my shirt and chest with each move of its head.

The sloop had me pinned against the wall, and I screamed with effort as I slammed the ax home again and again, working to stay alive. The poisoned dagger appeared in my other hand as I punched into the sloop and kicked it with my feet.

Starting to grow more desperate, I bit down on the sloop's head and fought like a maniac. There was no defense. My only goal was killing it before it killed me.

The sloop's golden eyes lost their focus, and its biting slowed, but my ax continued to chop down methodically like an insane metronome that would never end.

Finally, it no longer pinned me to the wall and it sagged down, dissolving into the floor as I gurgled on my own blood.

Reaching into my ring, I found one of the health potions from the market and tried to lift it to my mouth. But my head was shaking so unsteadily that I couldn't even get the cap off the sports bottle.

Staring at the bottle, I focused even as I coughed up another mouthful of blood. My hand moved steadily, mechanically as I took the cap off and lifted it to my mouth and chugged.

As soon as it was empty, I let the bottle fall off to the side. My arm went limp and I laid on the ground with my eyes closed, working to recover.

Whatever fucking hell hole these sloops existed on, it needed to burn. One day, I was going to set it all on fire.

My chest itched as the potion repaired what was likely not a pretty sight. I knew from experience that several of my ribs had been broken during the fight. When they popped back, I had to grit my teeth to stop from biting my tongue.

Alongside the potion, my Regeneration was getting plenty of practice. In my past life, I got Regeneration because I had been hurt so many times and drank so many potions that I eventually learned the skill. This was all an unfortunately familiar experience. The skin growing back was the worst part as the nerves reconnected.

Finally, my Regeneration finished. I took two breaths before I sat up and wiped the blood off my chin.

"Back to work." I picked up my ax and the dagger before checking to see what the sloop had dropped.

The drop was a neatly rolled up piece of leather.

[Sloop Hide D]

I picked it up and unrolled it before a grin split my face. I wrapped the piece of leather around my chest several times until it covered me from under my armpits down to hang like a short skirt. Then I took a roll of duct tape and tightly secured it to myself. You could always find a use for duct tape. I had bought the store out when I had seen it.

Now I had makeshift armor. D rank at that.

Okay, maybe the System didn't entirely hate me.

This would be good. It wasn't exactly the easiest thing to move in, nor was it exactly great coverage, but if I fought another sloop and could lead it into the same sort of situation, this leather would last much better under its attack.

Next I picked up ten gold coins from the sloop's loot and continued forward. The dungeon wasn't going to clear itself, and by the looks of it, anyone else who'd been in here was long gone.

I checked my notifications as I walked.

[Level Up]

I sighed. I had expected more than one level for that fight.

[Endurance E]

That was fair. I had endured something. The D rank dungeon, even if a little harder than I liked, was a good place to start training my skills. All of my F ranked abilities would level well here.

Moving down the cavern slowly, I stalked the next monster. What I found was another sloop sleeping in a pool like the first. This one didn't have a pile of corpses though.

I drew my ax back over my head and moved on the balls of my feet to be quiet and try to take it by surprise.

I lifted my ax, just about to strike as its eyes snapped open. It didn't even hesitate before its neck slithered along the ground and its shark head went for my legs.

Dropping an elbow on its head with my full weight behind it, I kicked my legs out of the way of its sharp teeth.

The sloop barked like a seal at me. I pulled out the poisoned dagger, stabbing into it several times until the poisoned status came up. Then I rolled off its head.

It tried to coil up to strike me again, but I booked it out of there, running in my crude leather and duct tape dress. I moved around a corner and kept going. The sloop splashed behind me, its head snapping around the corner, but I was already well out of its reach.

It continued after me, but I realized that this creature was absolutely terrible at traveling on land. It flopped its big flippers like a clown's oversized shoes as that giant head and neck wobbled low to the ground so that it didn't fall over.

Scanning it with Soul Gaze, I checked again that the F ranked poison was active on it, and hurried through the instance. This cavern was filled with pools. I just had to avoid them and lead this thing on a merry chase long enough that it was weakened from the poison, then I could fight it with much better odds.

The sloop continued to bark at me as I ran away, carefully dodging any harm.

***

[Level up]

That meant I was now at Level 11.

I pulled my ax out of another sloop and picked up the coins, dancing them in the palm of my hand before putting them in my spatial ring.

Eight of the sloops had taken a good chunk of what I assumed was a day.

Instances didn't have day and night cycles; they were fixed. And this one was underground, lit only by the industrial lights that magically had power. I had no idea how they were powered, but I didn't ask questions. I was simply thankful for the light.

I pulled out a sandwich and nibbled on it before washing it down with some water.

Another difficulty was cropping up. Turning the F ranked ax in my hand, I could easily see that the blade was chipped and dull.

[Steel Ax F
Damaged]

The damaged status was going to make it far less effective, and the sloops were already hard enough at my current level. I chewed on what to do next in my mind while my mouth worked on the sandwich.

"Could make one," I muttered.

The sloops had also dropped teeth. Each tooth was about as long as my pointer finger and about three times as thick at the base.

But crafting with the System could be odd at times.

I checked the dagger, thankful that it had held up better. I had limited my uses to just poisoning the sloops; it was my best tool at present.

"No. Not yet. I need to keep moving." I picked up another few teeth that had come from the most recent sloop and moved quickly through the cavern with practiced ease.

After the last sloop pool, I saw an even larger body of water. I wanted to see what I was facing next before I started working on a weapon. What I found was a pool of water that spanned the entire length of the cavern. I'd have to go for a swim. It looked like it quickly dropped off into a deep chasm.

Pulling a piece of my sandwich off, I threw it into the center of the pool.

The piece of bread floated with a single ripple fading away from it.

The pool was silent for just a moment before multiple sharp mouths started fighting over the piece of bread. Blood ran in the water as some of the monsters turned and devoured the one that was bleeding.

[Duggarfin D
Level 22
Strength: 14
Agility: 54
Vitality: 12
Intelligence: 1
Spirit: 1

Skills:
Sharp Teeth D
Swim D
Duggarfin Venom E
Swarm E
Jump F]

The apparently venomous piranha's on steroids settled down and the water went still.

Wonderful. Yet... they presented a very interesting potential.

There was no way that I was going to be able to swim across this without dealing with them. They were simply too quick, and even if I wrapped myself in sloop leather, that Sharp

Teeth skill was going to tear through me like a knife through butter.

While the rest of their stats weren't anything important, that Swarm ability was terrifying. Swarms regenerated by adding members back to the swarm when out of combat.

It meant that I could kill them and they'd come back. Individually, they likely weren't worth much experience.

Yet individually, they *were* D ranked.

I closed my eyes, settling on the plan that I knew was my best chance. Carefully, I extracted myself from my leather armor and stripped down to a pair of boxers.

I placed my spatial ring to the side of the cavern before taking out a potion and setting it down. Then I dipped a toe into the water and created a ripple.

There was a painfully long moment of nothing before the swarm came up, but they didn't come into the shallow water.

I reached out and used Blood Siphon on one of them, only for the whole swarm to shoot down below. My ability broke as they dropped out of my sight.

Taking a deep breath, I took two more steps in and stuck my leg out. At this point, I was thigh deep in the water. And I was not at all comfortable using my own body as bait. But I had done much worse and lived.

The swarm shot back up, and as I expected, the leg sticking out became a tasty morsel for them.

As soon as I felt one clamp onto my calf, I threw my whole body out of the water.

Two Duggarfins came with me. One cut through my calf; the other had latched onto my thigh. Another two tried to jump on to get their share, but missed. But damn, the bites that did hit hurt like a bitch.

I punched the one on my thigh in the face several times before it could take a second chomp and take my quad with it.

My calf was already gone.

Both of them flopped on the ground, and I dragged myself away.

I glanced longingly at the healing potion and thought better of it, gritting my teeth and breathing slowly as Regeneration kicked in. Thankfully, my body started to heal.

I hadn't lost my hands or fingers, which ranked up there with my head. But I had learned in previous battles that it hurt extra if you ever lost your spatial ring. Best to leave it to the side if you might lose a hand. That didn't grow back.

I lay back on the ground as my leg repaired itself, listening to the sound of the two fish flopping back and forth on the ground. One of them had gotten it into its head to try and flop my direction.

"Don't you dare." I kicked it away with my good leg as I turned on my side and threw up my recent meal. "There's the venom. Oh, this is going to suck."

Chapter 15

I wasn't sure how long I spent fading in and out of consciousness before I finally woke up.

Both of the fish I had captured were in a small container I'd made from the hides and filled painstakingly with enough water that they wouldn't die on me.

I'd let them nibble on me enough to get the venom back in my system. Then I would go lay down and let my Regeneration and F rank Poison Resistance get workouts.

The venom was only one rank higher than my resistance. Meaning, I would have a chance of curing it entirely, though a small chance. I just had to weather through it and keep going.

But everything I was going through was not only for Poison Resistance. I had a bigger goal in mind.

The second prompt appeared, and I let out a sigh of relief as my Regeneration picked up.

[Regeneration E]

Sadly, I didn't know a way to give myself tougher skin without a skillbook.

When I reached Level 10, I had gotten another class skill. I wasn't familiar with this class or when I would get certain skills, and this new skill was interesting.

I would have a quality to my blood, likely connected to my collection of bloodlines. More importantly to me, it would be able to act as certain reagents for alchemy or inscriptions.

If I accumulated enough bloodlines, I could make endless talismans. Though, I wouldn't want to sell any with my blood. Those could be used against me too easily.

Now that my Regeneration had increased, I was ready to move on.

I used Blood Bolt repeatedly to kill the two fish I had caught and then took a roll of hide and made it into one large loop.

"Stupid fish," I cursed them as they only dropped a coin each and some of their scales.

They were a valuable resource for me right now, but there were easier ways to level Poison Resistance. Some, I didn't even mind.

A monk had once shown me how to mix high-level poisons with cheap liquor to raise the level of the alcohol to a higher rank poison. Sometimes it tasted like shit, but it was potent, which made dealing with the poison so much better.

I stepped into the water far enough to attract the swarm again, and jumped back, throwing the loop of leather into them and hauling ass out of the water.

It worked like I had hoped. I dragged out five fish that flopped helplessly on the dry land. One managed to nibble at my butt, but I kept the rest away. And I was fairly thankful that it didn't go for my front. I couldn't regrow limbs yet. Even my smallest.

The swarm stared at me angrily in the water for a moment before diving back down into the chasm. It would regenerate its numbers quickly.

Yet that was fine for now.

I lifted my hand and shot Blood Bolt after Blood Bolt into the beached fishes. It was time to keep training.

**

[Name: Bran Heros
Level: 12
Class: Blood Hegemon ??
Status: Healthy
Strength: 45
Agility: 37

Vitality: 44
Intelligence: 32
Spirit: 10978

Skills:
Soul Gaze SSS
Soul Resilience S
Blunt Weapon Proficiency F
Endurance E
Throwing Proficiency F
Blood Boil E
Blood Siphon E
Blood Bolt E
Bloodline Collection 1
Regeneration E
Fire Resistance F
Poison Resistance E
Ax Proficiency E
Charge F
Bloodink Quality -]

Farming the fish had been going well.

I sat cross-legged, overlooking the chasm with my baseball bat across my lap as I worked to fit the sloop teeth into the grooves that I'd made on one side. A Duggarfin tooth was in my hand. They'd dropped their teeth along with their scales.

Using the root of it, I hammered in another sloop tooth. I was also poisoning myself with the tooth. I had passed out a few times from the move, but I'd woken up what I believed was not much later and continued on where I had left off.

God, I loved Regeneration.

Some people had tried training resistances like this before, but it took far too many potions if a player didn't have a heal or something like Regeneration. Healers were decently rare and quite expensive. They didn't survive well on their own, especially not at first.

I tapped my leg, considering that problem. I could try to fix that in the early days of the Rapture. A few dozen healers indebted to me would make a big difference down the line.

I let my mind wander as I worked; it helped me stay sane as I worked alone and partially poisoned myself repeatedly. Bobby would probably consider me crazy, but in reality, I was just hardened from what I had already gone through. This was nothing.

The darkness had crept in a few of the times I'd passed out. The nightmares coming for me of what would happen if I didn't push myself to the absolute limit now.

"There. What do you think, System?" I asked aloud. I wasn't talking to myself.

The System was a thing; it even answered me as I used Soul Gaze.

[Sloop-Tooth Ax - E]

"Huzza! Thank you, System." I kissed the new weapon.

When a player crafted something, there was always a more important part of the weapon. In this case, I was using a D rank 'blade' on a mundane shaft. It chose to lean towards D and give me an E rank weapon.

I swung it around a few times. It felt top heavy, but that was to be expected; I wasn't exactly working with the best tools.

"Alright." I patted my knees and stood up.

The skill grind had taken me several days at the least.

I was not entirely sure, given that I had passed out so many times. But I had eaten eight times, and that was usually a decent tracker of time. I was guessing three days had passed.

Add on the first day of killing sloops, and I'd been here four days.

Bobby hadn't shown up, so I could only guess something had stopped him outside. I didn't remember any big problems in the Nester Family just yet. His older sister Gloria would cause a problem soon, but that still had time.

Even in The Dags, we had felt the ripples from Gloria's attempt at dethroning Carmen. I shuddered at the thought of the man killing his own daughter, but she had tried to kill him.

He was someone that genuinely cared for his children, even if he was rough around the edges. But his principles were ironclad. She crossed one, and he was forced to take action. He'd once admitted to me over drinks just how much it hurt him.

I put that out of my mind for now and readied myself to deal with the swarm of venomous piranha. Really, what world had these and sloops? It really needed to be set afire and burnt to ashes.

As soon as I was deep enough for them to reach me, the swarm shot out of the chasm and rushed me.

This time, I was ready. My legs and hips were wrapped with the sloop leather while I held the neck of a potion in a sports drink bottle with my teeth. Finally, my new ax was ready and waiting to shed blood for the first time.

I fired several Blood Bolts into the group before using my new ax. I smashed it into the water as the swarm found my legs wrapped in sloop leather and bit into them, jerking back and forth trying to rip off the hide. I'd worked pretty damn hard to secure that hide well.

My ax slammed down again and again as they bit.

With E rank on my weapon and with an E rank skill for the ax, it was effective enough against the low vitality D rank fish. Together the two E rank effects and my strength were enough that I could smash them in a single swing. Still, there were still a large number of them swarming me.

A few got frustrated at my leather covered legs and jumped clear of the water, latching onto my chest.

I held tight to the potion with my teeth, a little splashing on my lips as I breathed through my nose and continued to smash the Duggarfins. There was only one chance at finishing this off. They would destroy the leather I had gathered in this fight, and I didn't have much from the start.

Their teeth started to poke through the leather, pricking me. Notifications of being poisoned started scrolling to the side.

My ax kept smashing as the swarm thinned.

A fish took a big enough chunk out of my chest to make me take notice. My vision started swirling a bit, so I decided to tip back my head and swallow the potion before spitting the bottle out and continuing to smash the fish in front of me.

After most of them died, the remaining fish were swimming in quick circles around my ruined leather armor, looking for skin to nibble.

I used Blood Siphon to try and keep my health full as well as stop trying to hit them. My ax was becoming less effective now that there weren't so many that I could hit without aiming.

It was at that point in the fight that they destroyed the two pieces of leather that I'd used, and my Regeneration was working overtime, along with the health potion.

Staying focused and keeping my cool despite the current situation, I worked my way through the entire swarm until none were left. With a wave of my hand, I collected the floating teeth and scales.

Breathing out a sigh of relief, I waded a little deeper, my eyes trained on the chasm. Technically, there was no reason another swarm couldn't come out, but that didn't feel right for the level of this instance.

I got deep enough that I was swimming rather than hopping along the bottom. Preparing myself, I made my move. I kicked as hard as I could, swimming across the chasm to the other side.

Nothing came out for me, and I breathed a sigh of relief, only to pull myself out the other side and look through the cavern for what was next.

Pool after pool lined the path going forward. The path looked just like the sloop area before, and crouching a little forward while doing my best to be quiet, I spotted a sleeping sloop in its pool of water.

[Silver-Eyed Sloop D
Level: 25
Status: Healthy
Strength: 54
Agility: 47
Vitality: 58
Intelligence: 1
Spirit: 30

Skills:

Feast D
Swim D
Dive D
Stretch E]

This one was a little stronger, with the addition of Stretch. I could assume that was likely to work with its neck. It was a trick that might catch someone if they were too used to the ones from earlier.

I pulled out a fistful of Duggarfin teeth and gripped them tightly in one hand as I snuck up on the first sloop.

[New Skill: Stealth F]

A grin spread across my face as I plunged the fistful of teeth into the sleeping sloop and took off running in a different direction.

I chuckled to myself, wondering what somebody from this time period would think if they saw me right now. Naked, save for a pair of boxers missing a hole in one cheek, I had grown a thin beard in the four days and was stabbing monsters with a fistful of poisonous teeth.

Luckily, looking sane was not even on my list of priorities as I ran from the sloop only to rush up to another that snapped at me.

Rolling to the ground, I accepted the scrape from the hard floor over the teeth of the sloop, and stabbed its neck several times before activating Charge and shooting out of its reach for another.

Like the first area of sloops, I had decided to poison them and let the poison do most of the work. Though this time, I was going to move as quickly as possible.

I had brought ten days' worth of food, and I had no idea what was up ahead. What I knew was that there was no reason for me to take longer than this required.

Rather than focus on the sloops and dodging them, I let my instincts take the helm, and I daydreamed of what sort of date I'd take Simone on when I got out of this instance alive.

My fistful of teeth found another sloop, and I ran around like a madman, cackling at my thoughts.

Chapter 16

I continued walking back through the cavern, picking up the loot from the dead sloops. There ended up being seventeen in this section of the instance. Most of them had been alone, but I found four groups of two. I guessed that sloops didn't play well together.

Dancing over to the next pile of loot, I scooped the coins into my ring and tossed the leather over my shoulder with the other rolls.

There was a flicker of worry for those outside the instance: my mother, Simone, Bobby. Yet that worry served no purpose at present. I had learned that it often took letting go of caution and a sliver of sanity in order to survive the harsh world and come out on top.

While I had a big weight on my shoulder to try to save humanity, I knew I would not get there without taking risks. So far, I had always found a way. When the odds were against me, I met the challenge.

"A few more levels on the pile. Thank you, Syssy. I used an old nickname I'd had for The System. You always take such good care of me. I don't think you'd be willing to let this work?" I took some of the D rank scales and a particularly sharp tooth, bending down and trying to etch a talisman on the scale the size of my thumbnail.

It was a D rank material.

Though I didn't have ink, I did have my blood. It wouldn't write this thin, but I could try and etch into the scale before just stamping my blood on it. With D rank material and mundane ink, I could make a certain talisman.

The instance had changed up monsters three times. That was normally a sign that it was about done.

At the end of the sloop cavern was a small tunnel, one I'd have to crawl through. Whatever was on the other side, it was unlikely that I'd be able to crawl back out without losing a leg or both.

I needed an insurance policy.

And hopefully, I was making one at the moment.

"Come on, Syssy. You and I go way back, even if you don't remember all we have had together," I talked to the System as I finished etching the first scale and bit my thumb hard enough to draw blood that I stamped into the scale.

I closed my eyes for a moment before I peeked one open with Soul Gaze active.

"Yes! System, I love you. If you came down here, I'd give you a big smooch. Alright, alright. I'll make some more of these. I promise I won't abuse what you have done for me," I lied.

I did not believe the System was really sentient, at least not the typical definition of sentient. Worlds couldn't talk, and the System for each was filled with rigid rules. Some people professed they believed their luck was some measure of the System's good will.

I was fairly sure that was just the human brain making connections when it was just random chance. Still, it was better to talk to the System than to admit I was talking to myself.

Finding my way over to the small tunnel, I sat down and started to scratch an inscription on all twenty-four scales that I had acquired. Five of them failed before I gained the skill.

[Inscription F]

None of them failed after I had the System's assistance. Then again, I was very knowledgeable with inscription techniques. They had saved me more than a few times.

After finishing, I ate a bite, drank some water, and promptly fell asleep. Only after I woke up did I drink some more water and sit down to meditate. I slowly cleared my mind, one distraction at a time. I might not have come overly prepared, but I did know what it took to stay alive.

There were a lot of thoughts and plans swirling in my head, but I suspected a boss fight was up next. Given what I'd seen so far in the instance, I needed to be at my best to take on this boss.

I needed to put aside everything and focus on the present.

I took several more deep breaths, and my eyes flashed open before I checked my spatial ring to ensure I knew where everything was located.

Not letting myself overthink what I was about to do, I just started crawling. The tunnel was tight, and at one point, I couldn't get any leverage with my arms. I ended up having to kick myself through like some worm.

If there was ever a time I wished I had skipped arm day, I was living it. My damned shoulders were too broad.

I came out the other end of the tunnel and scrambled to my feet to face whatever came next. Right now, I was wearing my shoes, this wasn't the time where I wanted to slip and fall. Other than that, I just had on my worn boxers.

I looked around, quickly assessing the space. The cavern I found myself in wasn't lit by the usual industrial lights. Instead, there was glowing moss on three pillars of earth that dominated the room.

They barely illuminated the creature on the other end.

[Three-Eyed Sloop-sloop D
Level: 35
Status: Healthy
Strength: 74
Agility: 69
Vitality: 72
Intelligence: 20
Spirit: 30

Skills:
Feast D
Swim D
Dive D
Stretch E
Fear D]

I squinted in the dim light. The outline of the sloop-sloop's sleeping form was slightly off. I couldn't quite make it out.

Not that it mattered. Whatever it was, I was about to take it on and hopefully win.

I pulled out a fistful of Duggarfin teeth. The cavern was big enough that I could play hide and seek with the boss for long enough for the poison to do its job. It would just be a very delicate game of hide and seek, where if I was found, I'd die a brutal and horrifying death.

I crouched and could feel the System assistance with my attempts at stealth as I hurried around the room.

When my foot stepped in a puddle that had blended into the dim room and a splash rang out around the cavern, I froze, holding my breath to see if the boss would rouse, but nothing happened.

Letting out a silent sigh of relief, I hurried forward, checking and making sure that I didn't make any other sudden noises as I quickly approached the boss.

It was in its own large pool.

For a moment, I thought there were two of them, but then I figured out that this one had two necks and two heads. There was only one body.

Just as I was about to carefully dip my foot into its pool to sneak up on it, all four eyes opened up and locked onto me. A wave of horror slammed into me. It had been awake the whole time I was sneaking over, setting a trap for me! That fear tried to paralyze me.

My soul pushed back, shattering the Fear ability and allowing me to turn and dodge out of the way as one of the jaws closed down where I had just been.

Both of its mouths made the honking barks of a very angry seal as it got to its flippers and rushed after me.

I just needed to get it poisoned. Then we could play tag.

A rushing sound came from the side of the room, and the splashing of water came from where the sloop-sloop had been laying.

Oh. Oh fuck. The implications of what I was hearing washed over me. If this room filled with water, there was no way I was going to win a game of tag.

CHAPTER 16

The one that had been outside in the quarry had been very fast in the water. I didn't want to find out just how fast this one would be with higher stats and full strength.

The sloop-sloop was hurrying forward on its awkward flippers, both heads searching for me as I came back around the corner, my fistful of Duggarfin teeth tightly clenched in my hands.

The second it saw me, both heads snapped forward, both of them at opposite angles like they were going to try and pinch me between them.

I kicked my body into a slide at the last moment, slamming the teeth into the side of one of the heads. Six different applications of the poison went off at the same time.

[Three-Eyed Sloop-sloop resists Duggarfin Poison]
[Three-Eyed Sloop-sloop resists Duggarfin Poison]
[Three-Eyed Sloop-sloop resists Duggarfin Poison]
[Three-Eyed Sloop-sloop resists Duggarfin Poison]
[Three-Eyed Sloop-sloop resists Duggarfin Poison]

I started cursing as the lines popped up on the screen. If I did not poison it, I was going to be so screwed.

[Three-Eyed Sloop-sloop is poisoned.]

"Thank you, System!" I shouted as I scrambled to my feet, letting Regeneration take care of the cuts on my leg. I hurried around one of the pillars.

Water was rushing out of a hole in the back of the cavern, not unlike the one I had crawled through to get inside.

The sloop-sloop splashed through the water behind me, and I kept running, putting my fistful of teeth away and pulling out the talismans that I'd made. I had thoughts on how to use these before I came in, but with the two headed sloop-sloop, it was going to be more difficult.

I just had to get these on the boss. I had made nineteen of them, but it was better to say that I had made nine pairs and a spare.

Without ranked ink, my options were limited. This was an inscription that cared more about the material it was carved on, though. It was a magnetic inscription. With nine pairs of D ranked items, I was hoping I could create a crushing force on either side of a boss to kill it.

I continued to barely evade the sloop-sloop until I backed up to one of the earthen pillars. The water was up to my thighs, and I knew that soon this thing was going to start swimming.

I couldn't let it freely swim about.

The sloop-sloop charged me, both heads grimacing at me. I waited, watching it grow closer, knowing I needed the right moment. I took a deep breath, stilling myself against the fear coursing through me, waiting.

At the last second, I knew it was time, and I juked right, only to dive left.

Like before, the heads split off trying to pin me in from both sides as I went to run around the back of the pillar, slapping several of the enchantments to the side of the pillar before coming all the way around.

The sloop-sloop had a big, satisfied grin on its heads when I appeared, thinking it had caught me.

And that was exactly what I wanted the damned thing to think.

Both heads stretched out, going for me. I rushed right down the center of both of them to the main body, taking a fistful of the talismans and slapping them opposite of the other, creating paired talismans.

A touch of mana was all it took before they all activated.

The sloop-sloop's walrus body slid sideways to the pillar until it was pinned. The spot with the nine talismans pushed in, like an invisible giant had put one hand on the pillar and the other on the sloop-sloop before squishing them together.

Water continued to pour into the cavern, and I was quickly up to my waist as the sloop-sloop's heads came back around. One of them managed to drag their teeth along my back, taking a good chunk with it before I pulled myself out of reach and hurried over to another pillar.

The two heads snapped at me, its necks stretching remarkably long as it tried to feast on my poor legs.

"Let's just hope that holds." I reached another pillar and sought handholds as the water level kept rising, planning to wait out the poison. My back itched as it healed, but honestly, I barely felt it over the thrill of adrenaline pumping through my veins.

The sloop-sloop kept thrashing, but it was held firmly to the pillar as water rose.

Now I understood the pillars. Each of them had a completely flat surface about ten feet across. They were big enough to fight on top of, but not big enough to hide from the sloop-sloop.

I shuddered at the thought of trying to fight that thing from atop the pillar.

No thanks. I'd much rather cheat.

Rising with the water, I got to the top of one and sat down.

The sloop-sloop thrashed underwater, still pinned. The glowing moss still worked underwater. I could easily make out its form. A check with Soul Gaze confirmed that the poison was still in effect.

I'd just have to wait out the boss' life.

My heart still pounded in my chest. A crazy part of me hoped that it would break free and I'd be pushed to my limit again. My adrenaline was starting to wear off, and a part of me craved to get it back.

What else could I use if it did peel free?

I pulled out the Sloop-tooth Ax and put it over my lap as I sat there ready and waiting for a fight that never came.

Eventually, the sloop-sloop started spamming Fear at me. The ability washed over me like I was pressing my face into a shower faucet. There was little it could do to rattle my soul. My soul was hardened by that point. It took a certain personality to kill hundreds of thousands of demons and outlive all friends and family.

The sloop-sloop was not even close to scary enough to instill fear in me.

Eventually, the boss slumped in the water before disappearing as the water level began to fall. The water was draining out the other side, through the same hole I had crawled through.

[Dungeon Complete.
Would you like to leave? Y/N]

I knew what answer I would be selecting.

But before I could choose, the three pillars cracked and I lost my footing as I slid down a pile of gold coins that flowed out of the pillar I'd been standing on.

The other two were the same, thousands of gold coins spilling into the boss room.

Chapter 17

I rolled in the coins for a moment, enjoying my victory and reward for all the pain I had gone through.

[Completion Bonus 100% Credit]

Power swelled in me as I got five levels from the completion bonus.

Sighing, I let the moment of accomplishment settle across me. After a few deep breaths, I started scooping up all of the gold from this run with a chipper bounce to my step. 3193 gold coins crowded my spatial ring.

After collecting the coins, I realized I was missing any other drops. This was a first clear. There should be...

My eyes landed on the pillars, or where they had been. Sitting in their space were three items.

I moved over and grabbed the two D Rank spatial rings and quickly put them on my hand before taking the third item in hand.

[Bronze Bracer D
Grants wearer: Swim D]

I clasped it around my right wrist.

At the moment, I was naked except for three rings, a bracer, my torn boxers, and a pair of waterlogged shoes. Really, I cut quite the figure. Thankfully, I hadn't worn much clothing during the battles so that I'd have some on my way out.

I put my shoes into my ring and fished about the rubble for where the sloop-sloop's loot should have been.

[Leather Vest D]

There was no skill in that vest, but beggars couldn't be choosers. It was fairly thin and dark leather. I could probably get away with wearing this under a shirt, but I put it in my ring as well. We were about to go for another swim.

There was one last piece of loot that I spotted. I picked up the spellbook.

[Water Cannon]

I'd give it to Bobby. He was probably going to be pissed that I had been gone so long and correctly assume that I did the instance without him.

That, and I knew myself well enough to know that I made a very poor mage. Sitting in the back blasting spells off was not my style. Tried it once and got bored enough to let the demon get close enough that I could bash its head in.

I was much more comfortable running around with a fistful of poisonous teeth, nearly getting a chunk taken out of me by weird shark-headed, snake-necked walruses.

Pulling out all the empty water bottles I had saved up, I made sure I had plenty and hit the prompt to exit the instance.

The world moved, and I found myself back underwater in the quarry. Weapon in hand, I kicked my feet, and Aquaman would have been jealous as I shot through the water. I followed the same path back as I had taken through, using the conveyor as my guide.

My body undulated as I kicked. The water seemed to provide no resistance as I shot along the shaft and up to the surface.

I had been going so quickly that I launched myself out of the water and had to grab onto the ladder a dozen rungs up to keep from falling back down and smacking the water.

I did a quick scan of my surroundings. Everything was the same as I'd left it. No one waited for me, and the quarry was as still as a graveyard.

Then again, it was one. If a dozen workers had suddenly disappeared, it was no surprise that this place got shut down.

I quickly climbed the rest of the ladder and got dressed by the car while I waited for my phone to boot back up. It started dinging repeatedly as missed calls and texts flooded in.

Half a dozen were from the hospital, and I got a bit excited, wondering if my mother was awake yet.

Eighty-seven of the texts were from Bobby. Clearly, something had gone very wrong.

Finally, there were three from Simone.

I looked at Simone's first. Well, that explained why Bobby was freaking out and why he didn't come. I nodded along. The meeting was overdue, and I'd face it head on.

"Back in town. Will swing by for a drink tonight. Feel free to let him know," I talked as I texted Simone before throwing the phone into the car.

I checked the time and date on my phone, the instance had taken most of the week. It was close to noon, and I needed a hot shower and a soft bed before I dealt with the Nester Family problem. But first, I needed to see my mother.

I got into the car, checked my hair in the mirror, and took out a small knife to shave the unruly beard before putting the car into drive and pulling out of the quarry.

The drive into the city was uneventful, giving me a chance to decompress. I could feel the knot between my shoulder blades start to uncoil until I hit traffic. I could stay composed around a deadly monster, but traffic was one thing I didn't miss after the Rapture.

People were just stupid, selfish, or a horrid mix of both on the road.

I parked the car between my place and the hospital before getting out and locking it up. The broken window hampered security, but I would only be put out a little if it was stolen.

I walked inside the hospital. While there was a lot of hustle and bustle, coming from the life and death situation of the D rank instance, it was downright peaceful.

"Ah. Mr. Heros." A nurse looked up as I approached my mother's room. "You're here. Your mother has been asking for you."

A grin split my face as I followed the nurse into the room.

"Mrs. Heros, your son is here," the nurse called into the room while knocking on the door.

I pushed past the nurse to see my mother sitting up in the hospital bed, still connected to several machines and eating a Jello cup.

"Bran." My mother's smile lit up.

It didn't matter. It didn't matter that I was a 500-year-old fighter. I was a son, and she was my mother.

I jumped the remaining space, knocking her food tray off her lap and giving her a giant hug. She grunted with a look of surprise. I hadn't restrained my strength, and she got the full brunt of all 50 points.

"I'll leave you two alone." The nurse closed the door behind her.

"Bran." My mother's tone was sharp. "What happened?"

"What do you mean?" I asked, feeling her try to Inspect me. I brushed the attempt aside.

Her eyes opened even wider. "You've been initiated?"

"Yeah, and you have a few things to explain. Like why you never told me. I was dropped into a damned zombie apocalypse with zero warning," I scolded her, but there was no heat behind it. "Don't worry about the bills. I'm back from my recent trip and I'll handle them."

"They are taken care of," my mother said matter-of-factly.

I raised an eyebrow. "You had no money left."

"Not entirely true." She looked to the side. "Your father gives me money every month. I just put it in a bank account that I don't touch. This once, I decided to use it."

I stared at her. In my last life, I had never known my father, but this meant he was very much alive. "Are you going to tell me about him?"

"Not at all. Now show me your stats. Why can you resist my Inspect?" She tried again, only for me to barely let her see my information.

I only let her see my name and level.

She squinted at Level 17.

"I'm not going to show you the rest." Her seeing my spirit might cause more problems than I needed. "There's an ability that seems to resist Inspection."

She accepted my answer with a skeptical nod. "You're eighteen, and family tradition says I should take you back to have your player status awakened. Yet it seems you've jumped ahead."

I shrugged. "What then?"

"We'll go back and explain the situation. Things should be fine. You'll participate in the rites symbolically with the rest of the young adults of age. The next one should be the fall equinox in four months." She nodded to herself.

My experience in the past life was that the family wasn't quite so understanding. It would be better if I faked it.

I held her hand and kissed the back of it. "That's fine. As long as you get better, it'll be fine. Why aren't you already back on your feet?" I asked.

My mother scowled. "That poison wasn't so simple. Did you cure it?"

"With an antidote. You'd been poisoned for a while," I explained.

"It sapped my stats. Even with the healing potions I have on hand, it isn't restoring. It's coming back slowly." She put her hands in her lap. "You got a D rank antidote?"

"It was lucky on my part. There was a vendor selling them at a Free Player Alliance event." I left out the part where the vial was stolen.

"They aren't cheap." She gave me a measured stare.

"No, they are not," I confirmed and stood up. "I've been through a lot to get here and get you better. So, you best take care of yourself, understand? Also, tell me who poisoned you."

"No." Her expression hardened. "You aren't strong enough to deal with them, not by a long shot. You might have become a player and seen people in the FPA, but you don't understand the depth of this world. Your extended family has players with strength that you can't even imagine."

I held back an eye roll. My imagination when it came to strength would blow her mind. "Understood." I nodded instead like an obedient child. "I'm still going to work on growing stronger with what I can do."

"What's your class?" she asked.

"A type of berserker," I lied.

Still, she nodded. "Decently strong, though everyone will see you as a meathead."

"Let them underestimate me," I growled.

She sighed. "You remind me of him a little. I won't stop you, but I want you to understand that I stepped away from instances and the player scene to raise you." She tossed down a D rank protective amulet.

"Keep it. You're the one who was poisoned and won't accept my help in fixing whatever situation got you poisoned. Will you at least tell this extended family that's so powerful what happened?" I pushed her.

"No. The Clan is full of too much strife and competition to announce that I'm weakened. Our branch is weak as it is."

"Then do something, mother." I was getting angry at her for being so helpless.

"I am. Right now, I need to recover. After that, I'll make my moves. Do not tell me what to do, Bran. You might be a player now, but you're not strong enough to make demands of me." My mother's expression was hard.

"Fine." I threw my hands in the air, remembering just how frustrating she could be. "I'm glad you're better, but now I need to go. Somebody needs me."

"What's her name?" My mother stopped me before I left.

"Don't know what you are talking about," I brushed off her comment.

"Bring her by when you are able. I'd like to meet her." My mother had a smug smile on her face. "There are a few things you should know, though. Don't get anyone pregnant."

I nearly choked on the comment. "Not part of the plan."

"Good. Good. You have a long life ahead of you. Don't let her hold you down with a kid just yet. It feels like my son has matured greatly while I was ill," she said the last sentence offhandedly as I left.

She had said four months.

I had that long to get strong enough to weather the mire that was the Heros family. They dated all the way back to Ancient Greece. The story goes that they received a prophecy of the coming Rapture and were told to prepare in secret for the day it arrived.

My family were quite literally the various heroes of Greek stories, the kind whose strength was attributed to being demigods or some other fanciful tale. Their powerful items were simply System-generated ranked items and abilities.

But in the end, they were just players, many of whom had a serious superiority complex and wanted to be famous. At least, that's what I assumed when they had a bard following them around making ballads of their deeds.

After the prophecy was made, they went into hiding, no longer revealing their power to the world. Instead, they trained in secret, waiting and biding their time until the prophecy would come true.

When it had happened, they and every other clan and secret sect had emerged.

I checked my stats again, heading towards home to prepare for my next meeting.

[Name: Bran Heros
Level: 17
Class: Blood Hegemon ??
Status: Healthy
Strength: 50
Agility: 42
Vitality: 49
Intelligence: 37
Spirit: 10983

Skills:
Soul Gaze SSS
Soul Resilience S
Blunt Weapon Proficiency F
Endurance E
Throwing Proficiency F
Blood Boil E
Blood Siphon E
Blood Bolt E
Bloodline Collection 1
Regeneration E
Fire Resistance F
Poison Resistance E

Ax Proficiency E
Charge F
Bloodink Quality -
Stealth F
Inscription F
Swim D (Bracer)]

Chapter 18

After a shower and a nap, I woke up and got ready.

I wore a simple, white button-down, with the leather vest over the top. It wasn't exactly my style, but I wore it well enough. I added a pair of jeans and worked on thoroughly taming my hair. A few more tweaks later, and I felt ready to see Simone.

The bracer was still on my arm, but I covered it up with my shirt as I headed over to her establishment.

I had given Simone a time for a reason, and sure enough, she had arrived ahead of me. Enforcers from the Nester Family discretely sat around the hotel lobby.

As soon as I entered, I noticed that the bar was full of the enforcers as well.

Simone saw me, her eyes wide. "You actually came."

The sight of her made my lips tick up into a smile. She was once again a lovely vision. She was far better to look at than sloops or floors covered in my own blood.

"Of course I came. Carmen doesn't scare me." I caught Simone's hand and pulled her close to kiss her on the cheek. "It was a rough week. Compared to that, Carmen's just a conversation."

"Let me show you to the room." Simone shook her head. "Are you sure you're okay?"

"I'm more worried about you. He hasn't done anything, has he?" I asked her, giving her a once over.

"No. Carmen isn't like that. He's a tough man, but he takes care of his people." Simone gave me a worried look as we approached the door. "This is it. Last chance to pretend you knocked me out and run for the back door."

"Thanks again." I kissed her cheek. "This will go over well."

I stepped into the room. I had a feeling the room was typically Simone's back office. But at the moment, Carmen Nester was sitting at a table with Bobby standing and reporting to him.

"Well, if it isn't Uncle Nester. It has been a while." I grinned like I was meeting an old friend.

"Bran!" Bobby shot straight up. For a big man like him, the move was quite the gesture of solidarity.

Carmen held many of Bobby's traits, including the thick shoulders and broad chest. Bobby took after him well, though the older man's hair was more of a rusty brown with gray starting to mix its way into it.

"Hi, Bobby. Sorry for the delay. Shit happened, and I got stuck at the bottom of a flooded quarry. I'll tell you about it later. I think your father wants to talk to me." Stepping over to the side, I picked out a nice bottle of whiskey from the cabinet and made myself at home.

"Leave us." Carmen's tone was heavy, and Bobby didn't stay a second longer, rushing out. Like most of the Nesters and half the criminal underworld in Vein City, he had a healthy fear of his father.

"I remember that you had a taste for Japanese Whiskeys. I'll pour you a glass and won't be offended that you don't touch your drink until business is done. Business before pleasure, right?" I poured Carmen a glass of neat whiskey and placed it down in front of him, making sure to put a coaster under the glass. Carmen could be a stickler about the weirdest things.

He stared at the drink for a moment and then fixed his eyes on me, looking me over, checking every inch of me.

If Simone had some sort of passive insight, then Carmen likely had something as well. Even before the Rapture, he had a reputation for being quite keen. Well, except for that blind spot with his daughter Gloria.

"You're not anyone's kid, are you? I don't know you. You seem to know me quite well though," Carmen continued to observe me.

"We go way back, you just won't remember because it hasn't happened yet." I smiled at him and didn't sip my drink either. "I'm guessing you stopped Bobby from coming for me last week?"

"You made him a player." Carmen didn't answer my question. "You are a player."

"Yes and yes. I'd like to take all the credit, but there's some to be had elsewhere. Bobby was destined to become a player either way. I just wanted to make sure that I was there when it happened to protect him."

That was a slight fib, but one I was willing to risk in front of Carmen, because I still meant those words. With my help, Bobby would be stronger than my past life too.

"What do you want?" Carmen asked, getting to the point. His face betrayed no emotions. Even for someone who knew him, it was difficult to get a read on his thoughts.

"That's quite simple actually. I want to work with you. Not for you, but with you. Things are coming that the Nester Family isn't ready to take on at present. Player things are coming," I warned him.

"You speak like you know the future." Carmen had barely moved during the conversation. It was a little unnerving and purposefully slow. I'd seen the mob boss crack people without so much as lifting a finger.

"Maybe I do. Doubt you'd believe that, though." I paused, tapping the armrest of my chair. "In two weeks, Gloria is going to try and strap a bomb to the bottom of your car. Don't worry, you'll survive. And Bobby will be able to get you a healing potion that puts you back on your feet."

Gloria was straining at the confines that Carmen kept her in at this time. She wanted to do more and was growing increasingly frustrated.

Carmen tilted his head slightly. "Why? Why are you doing this?"

"Because we go way back, and I know you are what the world needs in the coming times. You are a dangerous and determined man. Sometimes the world needs dangerous men between them and an even worse danger." I tapped the side of my glass, still not drinking, but the noise was satisfying. "I want to keep working with Bobby. Soon he won't really need a hand protecting himself. He'll be fairly resistant to mundane attempts on his life. Then I will expand my own enterprise."

"To prepare for this other danger?" Carmen surmised.

"Yep. I'd like to be prepared this time," I told him honestly.

His eyes narrowed at those words. "This time," he repeated.

"I only know the future because I've lived it once before." I was telling him a lot, but I also felt a deep sense of gratitude to the man from my past life. Too much to bullshit around with him. He was also the kind of man that could make moves if he knew things were coming.

Surprisingly, Carmen took my statement better than expected. Rather than deny it, he just picked up his phone and called someone, putting it on speaker for me to hear.

"Hi, Daddy!" a chipper woman answered enthusiastically.

"Gloria. How's the east side?"

"Doing well, but you don't normally call for an update. What's going on today?" she cut to the point.

From everything I had heard about Gloria, she was ambitious to a fault. She had basically done all she could with her section of the city, and when she had nowhere else to grow, she tried to take over to make herself room to grow. As a daughter with the blood of the real Nester lineage, people would probably follow her if Carmen was gone.

"I'm sitting with a man here today. Somebody I think you should meet as well." Carmen locked eyes with me as he spoke.

"Oh?" Gloria asked. "Why's that?"

"Because he's your new fiancé," Carmen stated it like an order.

"What?! No. Father!" she shouted over the phone for a moment before she realized that she'd yelled at him and got quiet.

"This is punishment for that plan you have in motion," he said as if he'd known the whole time.

"What plan?" There was a touch of nerves in her tone.

"The one with the bomb you were preparing for my car. You plan things through so thoroughly it gives me time to catch you." Carmen's tone was ice.

The woman on the other end of the line was dead silent for almost a minute. "I... I understand. Where is he so I can meet him?" She sounded defeated. No one went against Carmen and lived.

Carmen's expression flashed with pain, and he closed his eyes for a moment of silence. "Madam Sugar's. Come now."

He hung up and stood up far faster than anybody would expect given his frame. Then he threw his phone against the wall, shattering it. For a man of principle, his own daughter planning to kill him like that was enough to enrage him.

Meanwhile, I sat in shock.

Gloria? I knew the bare minimum about her. She was dead before I joined the organization. All I knew was the story and to avoid bringing her up because it easily set Carmen off.

She wasn't part of the plan at all. She was supposed to be dead. Yet, at the same time, Carmen was tying me to the Nester Family.

"I killed her." Carmen stared at the wall, his shoulders still heaving.

It wasn't a question, but I still answered him, "Yes. And it nearly broke you."

He shook his head and came back to sit in his seat. For being so worked up a moment ago, he was eerily calm. "Then thank you for sparing me and her. I believe you. If you want to make something in Vein City, it seems that my daughter needs additional work to occupy her mind and time. She's always been one to get destructive when she's bored."

It sounded like he was giving me a ticking time bomb!

"Uh. Okay," I said dumbly. "Wasn't part of the plan... but I can work with it. I can make a player side of the business for the Nesters. I'll plug her into some of that and see what she can do. Does she keep the east side?"

"For now." Carmen crossed his arms and sat back, still not taking a drink of his whiskey.

"There's more business to discuss?" I asked. Her living was a decent-sized butterfly flap. I worried about the potential ramifications of what the change would do to future events.

"Are you able to make others into players?" he asked.

I shook my head. "No. It requires a rare chance, one that I just happened to know was coming. Although, it can also be done through priceless artifacts that are under too tight of security for me to steal. You'll become a player in about two years. Everyone will."

"Everyone?" Carmen asked doubtfully. "That would…" He trailed off, seeming to understand some of my earlier words in a new context. "That would create a very dangerous world and quite a bit of chaos."

"You have no idea." I shook my head. "It gets worse, but I won't go into that right now. Don't bother trying to arm up. The weapons you have now won't do anything."

"Bobby told me his gun barely scratched the zombies." Carmen nodded. "You'll make Bobby stronger, and you'll marry Gloria. Together, the two of you will prepare a division to deal with this eventuality. I'll leave that in your hands." He leaned forward and grabbed his drink.

I grabbed mine and lifted it before we both took a sip. "By the way, why do you believe me so easily?"

"Trust. My life is built on trust. Creating it, receiving it, and giving it. The things you mentioned showed that either someone I trusted deeply had given you that information, or somehow you had gotten them. If in another life I had told you those, then I trusted you deeply. That, and I've seen strange situations with players in the past. Living another life isn't outlandish." He took another sip.

"By the way, I already have a woman," I told him.

"Simone?" he guessed correctly. I wondered if he had heard about my run in with Rick and pieced it all together.

"Work it out with Gloria. She doesn't have a choice. I won't give her one. Use that as you wish." He took another deep sip.

I joined him for the sip and took my glass with me as I got up. "Then if you don't mind, I need to talk to Simone before Gloria comes blazing in here."

Everything was about to get a little tricky, and I was hoping to start putting out fires before I got burned. Handling two women at once was a tricky ordeal, especially when one was coming into this less than interested.

Remembering that I hadn't messaged Simone in a week, I grimaced. That was not the best way to start the upcoming conversation.

CHAPTER 18

I got up and left Carmen to his thoughts as I spotted Simone at the bar and walked up. "All of you get lost." I waved away the thugs.

They turned to me questioningly.

"Go ask Carmen. Oh, and Gloria is about to come blazing in here. Make sure she's not armed and she comes in alone." I waved them off with enough authority that they looked at each other and stood.

One went to talk to Carmen while the others stepped to the entrance and waited.

Simone raised a manicured eyebrow. "Dare I ask?"

"Oh. We'll get to it," I groaned. "Give me something from a middle shelf and fill the glass." I grabbed a ball glass from behind the counter and put it in front of my new seat, trying to decide how to approach the conversation with Simone.

Chapter 19

Simone filled my glass. I dropped a Duggarfin tooth into the beverage and started to stir. She only raised an eyebrow at the odd tooth as she poured herself a drink at the abandoned bar.

"Don't drink from my cup. It'll knock you dead," I warned her. "I need some very strong stuff to get really drunk right now."

Mixing System poisons with alcohol could help rank it up so that it would affect me past my Poison Resistance. The old monk's lecherous grin flashed through my mind. He had even leveled up his Poison Resistance twice to Poison Body. The fucker actually got stronger getting drunk on deadly poisons.

"That bad?" she asked. "You walked out of there alive."

"Worse." I checked the glass. It had become an E ranked poison, so I added another tooth and kept stirring. "Carmen just decided to fix two problems by engaging Gloria and me."

Simone choked on her own drink.

"Yep. She's coming here to meet me." I tongued my cheek and blew a breath into the air.

"Are you strong enough to tell Carmen 'no'?" Simone asked.

"Maybe. Actually, yes. I respect the guy. But the issue is that I don't quite disagree with why he's pairing us up. It gives me access to the Nester Family in a way that I need. That's one of the problems he was trying to fix. The other was that Gloria was planning to kill him, so he's making her my problem."

The drink before me changed to a D rank poison, and I held the teeth as I took a sip. The liquid burned and the Duggarfin venom tasted like an unripe lime that was partially rotted.

But with the added poison, I felt the alcohol. I knew from experience that if I did this enough, I'd steadily grow immune to poisons. Though, my drinks would become more expensive as I climbed the ranks.

"Where does that leave... us?" Simone asked, handling the situation better than I had anticipated.

"Complicated." I took another sip. "If I wasn't the jealous type, I'd accept the engagement and completely ignore her to do whatever she wants while I have what Carmen wants on paper."

"But you are the jealous type," Simone spoke with a smile.

"Pretty much." I took another drink. "That, and I want you a lot more than I want Gloria. Thus, the need for a strong drink."

Simone glanced at my cup again. "What would happen to me if I drank that?"

"You'd probably die within a minute." I sipped it while holding eye contact with her. "The teeth are from monsters I was hunting this week. They are a nasty type of fish." I pulled one out of the drink.

"What kind of fish has teeth that big?" She stared at the tooth with a grimace.

"Not the friendly kind." I put it back in my drink and stirred it around. "So. What do you think?" I held my breath.

"About?" She playfully dodged the question. "You just got back. You should ask me to dinner or something before you ask me any complicated questions."

I sighed. "Would you like to go to a park market with me again? I'll even treat you to lunch after."

"Are you concerned about returning?" she asked.

"They won't do anything. Worst case scenario, I'll pay it back." I shrugged and raised my glass to her. "To another wonderful date. Will you wear another incredible outfit for me again?"

"Is that what you like?" she teased.

"I'm a man of *very* diverse tastes," I chuckled to myself. Some of my interests were decidedly not human. The other worlds had some interesting people.

"Somehow, I feel that answer is even broader than my horizons. Are werewolves real too?"

I coughed into my drink. "I'm not a vampire. And no, there are no werewolves but there's a race of dog people. But they look largely human except for ears and a tail. Not big, hairy hulks."

"Really? How drunk do I need to get you to hear about them? Got any more of those teeth? I'll keep a bottle of your stuff back here," she offered.

I played with the tooth. "One of these goes for far more than your most expensive bottle to the right buyer."

She narrowed her eyes. "And you are using them to stiffen your drink?"

"A man needs to have priorities." I shrugged. "Besides, putting in the drink will just take the venom out. I can still sell the tooth, and there's plenty more of these." Some people might even prefer it without the venom. Poison made a lot of people queasy.

"In that case." She fished one of the teeth out of my drink with a spoon and put it in a plastic bag. "This thing can hurt someone like you?"

I glanced at it and shrugged. "Yeah, if for whatever reason someone like me comes at you, use this one." I put a fresh Duggarfin tooth on the counter. "Pick it up with the bag please." I held out my hand for the one she had in a bag.

She quickly swapped them out and looked at the tooth for a moment before she put it under the counter.

"It's sharp. Will go through leather like paper if you try," I told her.

"Got it. I'll be careful. Maybe I will put it in a metal case," She considered her options. "So, where will we be going to eat tomorrow? I need to know how to dress."

I stared at her blankly, not really knowing any place by name. It had been a very long time. That sort of information wasn't something I held onto.

"There's a nice place called Three Little Goats not far from the park," she suggested.

"That's just the place I was thinking of," I took the offered help. "It's a real casual place."

"Dress casual," she corrected me. "You could wear what you had last time, or even this."

I glanced down at my outfit. "Yeah. Maybe this. I'm a little short on clothes recently. That old outfit doesn't exist anymore."

She glanced at the teeth in my drink. "Can't imagine what happened to the clothing."

"Fish. Fish happened," I sighed and took another drink as a commotion stirred outside the door to Simone's place. "Ah look. My bride-to-be is here," I sighed. "Still on for the date tomorrow?"

"Wouldn't miss it. Don't keep her waiting. I hear Gloria is a bit of a handful."

As if to prove her right, the door was thrown open and a woman a few years older than Bobby stormed inside.

Gloria had sharp features and high cheekbones. She made herself look a little mysterious with purple eyeshadow and dark mascara. Her hair was a trendy purplish-silver and pulled back in a bun with enough of it loose that it hung at the sides.

She wore a simple black wrap dress, a coat hanging on her shoulders without her arms in the sleeves, yet she stormed in with authority.

"Where's my father?" she demanded, stopping in front of Simone with her hand on her hip.

Honestly, considering the bulk of her half-brother and father, I was surprised at how attractive she was. She cut a rather envious hourglass figure.

"Ask him." Simone pointed to me. I didn't blame her. Gloria was my problem, not hers.

I turned to give Gloria a once over, Soul Gaze giving me more information.

[Gloria Nester
Level: -
Class: -
Status: Terrified]

She was a normal person. Then again, her father couldn't have gotten rid of her so easily if she'd been a player.

I had to give her credit. She didn't look terrified. She was completely masking it by being painfully authoritative.

"Hello, Gloria," I spoke up, checking the two mooks that came in with her. One of them caught my eye. "Care for a drink? I'm sure Simone can get you something nicer than I drink." I motioned for Simone to pour from a bottle she already had out.

"I don't have time for a drink. My father is going to rip my guts out," Gloria snapped.

"No, he's not. He pawned you off in order to save you," I sighed. "If you took your plan any further, he'd have no choice but to put you six feet under. You know him. He has to stick to his principles. Anyone makes an attempt and he'll end them. Not even his own daughter would be spared."

Gloria's full attention shifted to me. Her body pivoted as she stared at me for a moment, realization dawning on her. "You're him."

"In a moment, dear." I stepped past her in a rush, my fist landing into the gut of her man and bending him in half before I twisted. My other fist flew into his temple, sending him flying across the room and knocking a couch over.

He groaned. He was only semi-conscious after those hits.

"What was that!" Gloria snapped at me. Now there was some fear in her eyes.

"I said in a moment." I stared at her and put her in her place. "You brought trouble with you, and I am going to take care of it before we proceed further." I picked up my drink and strode across the room.

Everything had stopped. All of the ladies and thugs were staring at me, trying to decide what to do next.

That guy should have been down for the count after those hits. They'd been directly to the temple with inhuman strength. His struggling to get back up was actually quite impressive.

[Terrance Biggs
Level: 5
Class: Assassin D
Status: Nervous, Dazed
Strength: 62

Agility: 42
Vitality: 102
Intelligence: 15
Spirit: 12
...]

This guy had spent quite a few coins leveling his stats to get there at Level 5. The only way I'd imagine an assassin would make that much coin would be using his player status for easy hits.

Terrance shook off my punches and drew a dagger on me. He moved far faster than would be expected of a man of his size.

I took his stab to the chest without blinking and grabbed his throat before I shoved my drink down his gullet. He sputtered and choked on it for a second before he pulled his dagger back and stabbed again. Both strikes only hit my vest, and his dagger went nowhere.

I found it interesting that he was using a mundane weapon.

I watched as the rest of my drink had its intended effect. Terrance staggered back, coughing and grabbing his throat as purple veins started to spread over his lips and down his neck.

He grabbed onto a chair to steady himself and started shaking uncontrollably. In just a few seconds, the poison had ripped through his body.

"It's strong stuff, isn't it?" I asked him, crouching slightly so that our faces weren't that far apart. "Here's what's going to happen. You're going to tell me who sent you, and then I'll give you the antidote."

He motioned for me to get closer.

I did so with an abundance of caution.

"Die, bastard," he groaned and tried to slash at my throat with the dagger.

I stepped to the side to dodge his feeble strike and shook my head. "Wrong answer. Now I'm going to let it happen slowly."

It was always going to happen—my version of an antidote involved sharp, pointy objects. Technically, his corpse wouldn't be poisoned.

Terrance fell to the side, struggling under the effects of the D rank poison. He didn't even have F ranked Poison Resistance and quickly passed out, likely to die within the next few minutes.

Simone came around the bar. "Gloria, I hope you know I'm going to bill you for this clean up. Also, Bran, please let everyone know you put something in that; otherwise, they won't trust my drinks. That's not good for business." She walked over to the guards at the door and asked one of them to go flip the sign out front and close the place.

I scratched my cheek. "Sorry about this."

"Not the first time someone has been beat down at my place. Besides, with Carmen here, business was slow anyway. Girls." She clapped her hands. "We are closing. Enjoy the night off and be safe."

"You heard the lady. We are causing trouble." I waved to some of Carmen's men. "Tie this guy up with some chains. Chances are he'll die, but just to be safe, make him very secure. Go overboard." Reaching down, I plucked a ring off the assassin's finger and pocketed it for later. "As for you." I glanced at Gloria. "Let's go talk to Uncle Nester. I never want to see you bring guards to meet me again. You are safe with me, and if you can't trust that, I'll smash in the teeth of anyone you bring with you until I get the point across."

Simone chuckled. "He's the jealous type. Oh, and Bran? I look forward to our date tomorrow. I'll wear something lovely for you."

"Wait. You're dating her?" Gloria scowled as she dismissed her other guard. "I thought my father said I was going to be engaged to you."

"Yeah. Well, I have lots of plans. And I'm not going to upend everything for you. Besides, Simone is fantastic. A complete keeper. I'm not going to let something silly like an engagement to another woman get in the way of keeping her." I continued towards the back, to the same room where I had spoken to Carmen earlier.

Gloria stopped in the middle of the hallway, her mouth opening and closing like a fish out of water.

Chapter 20

Gloria was surprisingly quiet as she followed me into the back room, a far cry from her original state when she had whipped into the establishment. I had a feeling she was still a little shocked as she stood to the side with her head down. And now she was about to face her father, the man she had been planning to try to kill.

Carmen stopped talking to Bobby as we entered, staring at his only daughter.

"Well, now you are here. Seems you met Bran already. What was the commotion outside?" Carmen turned, asking me the question.

"A player assassin. He's been handled," I said simply and sat down. There hadn't been anything in the ring that was incriminating; in fact, there was hardly anything ranked by the System and only a few gold coins.

"Player?" Gloria asked.

Bobby was the one to answer. "People who have supernatural abilities. We have a weird floating menu like in video games. I guess that's why we are called players."

Gloria frowned and glanced at me. "And you're one too?"

"Yup. So is Bobby. We accidentally got sucked into an instance," I told her, glancing back at Carmen who had a thoughtful look on his face.

"Gloria… that man. How long has he been in your employ?" Carmen asked.

"Three weeks." She only had to think for a second. "He was tough as nails, and I promoted him a few days ago to watch my back."

"That's a pretty quick step up," Bobby said and turned to me. "Could he have had an ability to... I don't know... sway my sister?"

"Yeah. That must be it." Gloria latched on for entirely different reasons. "That has to be why father. I'd never..." She froze when he didn't even look at her. His eyes were locked on me.

I'd seen the man's abilities. There were no abilities that would fall into any sort of mental manipulation.

Gloria focused on me now too.

I considered the option of lying. It might help him patch things up with his daughter, and I had seen what the betrayal had done to him. But the man had never led me astray. He deserved the truth.

"He had no such abilities. That's not discounting that he might actually be manipulative, just not supernaturally so," I answered honestly.

Gloria's face fell.

"Thank you." Carmen nodded. "That said, Gloria, you'll be working with Bran to help us expand our business into enterprises revolving around players." He nodded towards me to explain.

"Players largely buy and sell goods from instances. Bobby and I can enter them. Rodger Stone, in your employ, is a player too," I told Carmen.

He nodded along. It seemed he was already aware.

"Right now, the only major place for transactions that I have identified is a weekly market that happens in one of the parks. Players and non-players go to set up stalls. Players are selling items discreetly, using talismans or more mundane means to hide the goods," I explained.

Carmen nodded. "What do they use to pay?"

"These." Bobby flicked out a gold coin charged with mana. "It also comes from instances. Not only is it a currency, but it can be used to directly strengthen a player's stats."

I nodded. "Which was why I could tell that man was getting paid with gold coins and had done a number of jobs already. His stats were way too high for being Level 5."

"That's how you knew he wasn't really on Gloria's payroll." Carmen pieced everything together. "For him to have those stats, someone else was paying him in these gold coins. Thank you." He closed his eyes.

Gloria frowned. "How am I going to start helping then? I'm not a player."

I glanced at her. "Because there's something else they all really want. They want access to instances. Bobby and I know where one is, and I spent the week tracking down another. We can sell access or even let them go in and take a cut of what they find." It would be a start for her, something to get her started on the player world.

"Who's going to enforce it? They could just steamroll right over me and any bouncers I put in place." Gloria crossed her arms.

Bobby and I shared a look. I let him tell her.

"The one we found is a really weak one. It's perfect for someone who's barely above being a normal human. I don't think we'd attract anyone strong. Half a dozen big guys could enforce. What about the other one you were at this week?" Bobby asked.

I shook my head. "Level 22-35 and D rank. Right now, it's too valuable to let anyone know where it is. Besides, it's underwater. Getting people in and out, along with enforcement, would be a nightmare. Instead, I'd recommend going back in with Bobby and maybe Rodger to get them both some levels, as well as farm some more gear."

"D rank." Bobby rubbed his chin. "That's going to be dangerous. How'd you survive?"

I grinned. "Grit. But you are right. It would be dangerous. The first half you could do fine. The monsters are powerful, but slow. There's a middle section that I'd need to prepare for better before we go back in, but I could tank it probably. The last challenge is going to be the boss. The room floods, and it's an aquatic creature."

"Gloria. Find out what you can about the man that Bran killed," Carmen cut in. "Bran, show her around this market and keep her close while you organize and plan with Bobby. She might see some business opportunities that you'd miss."

"I'm going with Simone to the market tomorrow, but maybe the weekend after. I think we can let the zombie instance restock another week." I glanced at Bobby, ignoring that Gloria was trying to stare a hole in the back of my head. "Did you go in by yourself while I was gone?"

"Nope. I'd rather not," he admitted.

"How are you finding these? Maybe I could help identify more." Gloria tried to be useful.

I shook my head. "Secret. Not going to discuss how I'm locating them. Yet I'm willing to share the locations with this group after I've confirmed them."

My map was completely mundane, yet the first one I checked on it had been completely untouched. There were four more, and I wanted to see what they held as well.

"Then what am I doing this week?" Gloria huffed at me.

"Find me a new place to live and perhaps a car," I told her offhandedly.

"I'm not your secretary," she shot back.

"No, you aren't. It would be great if you were. But right now you are only a burden that's been placed on me." I glared at her. "No harm will come to you, but just because your father handed you off, doesn't mean that I suddenly like or care for you. There's a thing called effort."

"Gloria," Carmen stopped her from responding. "You are engaged to Bran. I hope you take that engagement seriously. He has the opportunity for you to expand into the player business. I hope that you can thrive there. Who knows, perhaps in the near future, Bran will have a way to help make you a player too."

"Fine. Where are your funds?" Gloria asked me.

I looked around the room and found a bag in Simone's office, picking it up and holding my hand out over the bag. Gold coins spilled out of one of the rings on my finger until the bag was full, then I placed the bank business card on top.

"This bank exchanges gold coins for money. I need a place close to the big park on the east side, and it needs to be nice enough to impress Simone. As for a car, something that can handle going off-road and can carry a trunk full of equipment." I handed her the bag like it was full of paper not gold.

She grabbed the bag and almost fell over when I let go. "Fuck, that's heavy."

"It's gold, Sis," Bobby chuckled.

He earned a glare for the statement.

"I'll get something done," Gloria added.

I got up to leave. "Oh, and Gloria?"

"Yes? What now?" she huffed as she gave up on carrying the bag and was about to go get some men to take it from her.

"I'm the jealous type. Your father just engaged us. I'd kill any man that touches you," I warned her.

She rolled her eyes. "You think I'm easy? Fine. Do I need to get female security so that you don't punch their teeth out?"

I paused. "Wouldn't hurt."

When she glared at me, I could only shrug. I was aware of my character flaws. She had some work to do. I was not going to let Gloria treat me like I was beneath her, and I certainly was not going to pull around dead weight, even for Carmen.

Until she was ready to be a true partner, I would use her like a gopher to get some tasks done for me.

But I wasn't entirely against the engagement. Having a direct connection to the Nester Family might speed up my plans nicely. Gloria's help buying up what I needed, be it land or recruiting personnel, would make everything a dozen times easier.

She could step into a certain level of business meeting with ease while I would be stuck explaining to a security guard that I in fact did have money. She would be a sound business partner, but beyond that, I was not sure. While I might get jealous and not share her with others, she was abrasive and needy.

All in all, it was more reason why I was not going to give up Simone. I might be stuck with Gloria, but I still would pursue whoever I wanted.

As we walked out, Simone was still behind the bar. The passed-out player assassin was now gone and her furniture was reset.

"Ah. How'd it go?" She asked.

"Much better now." A genuine smile bloomed on my face as I went and sat at the bar with her. "A vision like you always cheers me up."

"Glad I'm not relegated to being a mistress just yet." Simone winked. "I'd offer you a drink, but we're closed." She took a long sip from her own drink.

"Shame." I shook my head regretfully. "But does that mean if you're closed, we can head elsewhere?"

"Not tonight. I need to wait for Carmen to leave before I can close the place down." She nodded in the back where the three Nesters were most certainly having a stern conversation. "So, Mr. Bulletproof Vampire. Tell me what you did this week?"

"Mostly killed fish," I answered vaguely.

"The kind with impossibly sharp, poisonous teeth?" she asked and served me a drink without my prompting.

"Yeah. Not all of them were poisonous. Some were more sharks than fish," I said, taking the drink and not adding any poison to it. It wasn't going to have the punch of alcohol, but it reminded me of a simpler time.

"So. I have to ask about my blood. Do you need more?" She stared at me expectantly.

"Nope. Just the small taste was enough." I enjoyed watching her mind take in the information and quickly try to break it down.

"Does it have to be fresh?" She was getting at something, and I paused to regard her.

"I honestly don't know. Why?" I frowned.

Simone put her drink down. "Come with me." She came around the back of the bar and led me into the little kitchen area that was spotless like it hadn't been used in a while. "You know I run a high-level establishment. That means that we check the girls regularly."

"For diseases?" I asked.

"Yep," she told me. "Which means blood tests."

"Not just any blood does things for me," I told her. "It's actually quite rare."

"So, my blood is special?" she asked.

I paused, still debating what I should tell her. So far, she hadn't directly asked me what was happening; instead, she seemed to enjoy pulling it a thread at a time.

So I'd been letting the dance go on without spoiling the whole thing.

"Your blood is very special. Right now, it's just so-so. Yet it has the potential to completely blow me away," I told her.

"Really?" She drew the word out. "Are you just interested in me for my blood?" She swayed her hips back and forth a bit, teasing me.

"Caught me red-handed. That and your lips, tongue, and brain. Conversation with you is far more fun than it would be with any of your girls, not to mention most of the female population." I slipped my arm around her waist and held her to me as she continued to lead me back until we got to a freezer door.

"You are just too charming." She took a coat that hung on a hook next to the door and disentangled from me for a second to put it on. "Do you need a coat?"

"No. A little cold might be good for me." And my resistances, I thought.

Simone opened the door and stuffed a crate into it to prop it open as she turned on a light. There were several racks of vials stacked one after the other in the freezer.

"I hold onto some of the samples. A nurse comes in to draw all the blood, but we don't use it all for the testing," she explained.

I stared at all the vials of blood. "And you are going to offer them to me?"

"Do you need me to thaw them out?" she asked.

"No clue, let me see..." I activated Soul Gaze and started to scan over the blood in front of me.

Chapter 21

The System screen flashed new information.

[Amanda Carter's Blood
Bloodline of the Two-headed Dog F]

It was the first one I spotted, and I pointed to the vial. Simone took the vial and put it on an empty rack to the side.

I went through and found four different bloodlines among her samples. "Huh. None of them even come close to comparing to yours." We had found three F and one D rank bloodlines among the samples.

"Give me a comparison," she said, picking up the rack and leading me back out.

"All of them together are probably not even half of what yours did for me. That paired with your actual potential, they don't even hold a candle to your blood," I told her honestly. I could only guess at what a SS or SSS bloodline would do to my ability.

"Such a sweet talker." She put the rack on a stainless kitchen counter.

While she worked, I had a thought and took out a sloop tooth and cut my arm.

Simone caught the motion. "What are you doing? Your arm!" She watched as the cut healed over. "Right. Not a vampire," she muttered.

"Not a vampire," I repeated. "Do you want to know what I actually am?"

"Don't ruin the game," she sighed. "But thank you for asking me rather than telling. Maybe once you've given me that fountain of youth shot, we can talk."

"Deal." I grinned. I really liked Simone. I really needed to figure out how to keep her from being possessed. She wasn't going to be safe until I could make something to protect her permanently. That would be a while.

I used Soul Gaze on my own blood.

[Bran Heros' Blood
Heros Bloodline (Dormant)]

I was surprised that the System actually recognized my family's bloodline as its own concept. Interesting. I'd be curious to see what I awoke when I performed the Clan's rites.

Rather than a single bloodline, the Clan focused on continuing to amalgamate many different and potent bloodlines into the family. The family rite would then awaken one of the many bloodlines present in our own. The power of that bloodline would be equal to a player's status in the clan.

In my last attempt at this life, I had forcefully awakened the bloodline of a Dragon-Swallow before joining the Clan. It was a B rank bloodline, and I had managed to upgrade it once to a Dragon-Crane at the A rank. That one had come with many benefits.

This time around, I'd get the full rites and hopefully a stronger bloodline from the start.

Simone unstoppered the vials. "Tell me what we need to do?"

I took the vial and put my nose to it. Simone's blood had created an almost uncontrollable reaction in me. These just sort of gave me the same feeling as being in the room with an open box of cookies. I was tempted, but not overly so.

"Here." She handed me a thin pair of long tweezers.

"You're just prepared for everything." I broke off a chunk of the frozen blood and pulled it out to melt on my fingertip.

"Comes with the gig." She shrugged, watching expectantly.

I put the drop of blood to my tongue.

[Bloodline collected.
Purple Hare D]

I grinned and quickly did the same process with the other three. But I was surprised a moment later.
One of them didn't work.

[Bloodline Collected
Two-headed Dog F
Error...
Unable to connect to bloodline. Host is deceased]

I sighed and shook my head. "This one. She's dead."

"Doesn't work if they are dead?" Simone asked.

I realized I had just inadvertently revealed a potentially dangerous secret. If one day I leaned too heavily on the bonuses from these bloodlines, then the best way to weaken me would be to sever the connections by killing those that held the bloodline.

Apparently, the ability only worked if they were still alive.

That was a complicating factor.

"Yes. Though, that's very important you keep it secret." I stared at her. "Right now, the best way to weaken me would then be to kill you."

Her brows went up and she quickly nodded. "Understood. This one is still in my employ. Should I do anything extra to protect her?" She pointed to the D rank bloodline.

"No. For now, I'm not in a position to start hoarding ladies in a fortress to protect them," I joked.

Simone gave me a look for that. "I don't need to be 'hoarded'."

"No, you don't," I agreed quickly. "In a few years though, things are going to get messy. I'm preparing for that eventuality."

Simone nodded slowly. "I understand. How about everything else?"

"Well, it certainly raised a few questions for me. But nothing bad. I got a little stronger, so I will be able to come back from my activities hopefully faster and less banged up."

I grinned at her in thanks, but words were always better. "Thank you again. This helped."

"Sure. Now, do I need to start knocking over blood banks for you?" she asked with a tone that was far too sweet for the question.

"Uh... no. I think I'd prefer quality over quantity in this particular setting." Both F ranked bloodlines gave me two stats, while the D ranked gave me six.

"Then how do we find quality?" she asked a question I was pondering myself.

I leaned against the counter, playing through the options in my head. "Going to think about that some more. There are some very big organizations. Ones that make the Nester Family look like ants picking up scraps. They'd have quality, but I don't really want to get involved in them just yet."

One of the clans I knew was likely already infiltrated by demons and was likely collecting people of bloodlines for them to use as hosts.

The thought made me shudder.

I could perhaps use that knowledge to my advantage, but I wasn't really sure where to start. Right now, I needed to expand my own foundation. I would up my strength while using Gloria to raise the Nester Family into something that could step into the player world on better footing.

What would help the most would be an artifact that could initiate people.

I glanced at Simone. An artifact that initiated people would be a great way to protect her too.

"Penny for your thoughts?" she asked.

"Thinking about where I can get a fountain of youth shot for you. I can't do everything myself, and I'd really like to get your help."

Simone's eyes opened in shock before they lowered into a smoldering heat as her lips curled slightly at the edges. "You certainly know how to butter a woman up."

"Don't get your hopes up just yet. Those things are heavily sought after and sadly easily identified. I'm not sure where I can get one yet, but I'm going to work on it." I wondered if my mother might have ideas if she was feeling cooperative. "Either way, I'm looking forward to our date tomorrow."

"Is Gloria going to crash it?" Simone asked, putting the blood samples away and closing up the freezer.

"I told her I'm going with you. I'll go with her next week," I answered.

"But she's aware that you are going tomorrow." Simone closed the door and hung up her coat while rubbing her arms.

I came around her back and hugged her for warmth, rubbing her arms. "Yes, she's aware. She's a touch too proud. If she comes tomorrow, I'm going to be a jerk to her."

"Negging doesn't actually work," Simone told me.

"I'm not trying to make her interested in me. She needs to find that on her own. I'm just going to reflect back her behavior until she chills out. Gloria is a smart woman, even if she's a little spoiled." I shrugged.

"She's very pretty." Simone looked into my eyes over her shoulder, gauging my reaction.

"Of course she is." It was the truth.

Simone gasped. "Not going to lie to put me at ease?"

"I'm engaged to her, Simone. Right now, we don't get along, but that's going to be fixed eventually. The Nester Family provides me a leg up if I follow through on this engagement."

"All for this nebulous future and conflicts that I'm not aware of," Simone added.

"One day, you will be. We'll see if I can't get you that fountain of youth shot and bring you entirely up to speed. Gloria knows some of it. Carmen has brushed with this world before in the past."

Simone nodded, holding my hands to her arms as she soaked up a little warmth. "Fine. Should I be a jerk to her as well?"

"Do what you want. I'm the jealous type, not the controlling type." I grinned at her and kissed her cheek. "Besides, how is it fun if I already know what's going to happen?"

She moved and held onto my arm. "Keep me company while I wait for Carmen to leave?"

"My absolute pleasure. Couldn't think of a better way to pass the time." I kissed her cheek and led her back to the bar.

But as we walked, I got a little distracted in my character sheet.

[Name: Bran Heros
Level: 1
Class: Blood Hegemon F
Status: Healthy
Strength: 55
Agility: 43
Vitality: 51
Intelligence: 37
Spirit: 10983

Skills:
Soul Gaze SSS
Soul Resilience S
Blunt Weapon Proficiency F
Endurance E
Throwing Proficiency F
Blood Boil D
Blood Siphon D
Blood Bolt D
Bloodline Collection 4
Regeneration D
Fire Resistance F
Poison Resistance E
Ax Proficiency E
Charge F
Bloodink Quality F
Stealth F
Inscription F
Swim D (Bracer)]

It seemed along with collecting several bloodlines, my class officially had a rank to it. Only, it wasn't what I expected.
F rank.
Well, I wasn't sure that was entirely the case. Something told me that this class's rank was variable. Adding new bloodlines could change the rank of my class.

But what really captured my attention was that my level had reset.

There had been a flash of irritation that was quickly replaced with a spark of joy. If each level gave me stats still, then this was an incredible boon. I'd be able to quickly level back up to twenty or so before I tried to reset it for a free hundred stat points.

Then there were my skills. Each of my class skills had gone up a rank as a result.

Another class in my past life had interesting requirements to level up the skills. Notably, Demon Hunter didn't rank up from practice. Instead, they ranked up based on how many demons a player killed.

Demon Hunters were their own sort of crazy. Thankfully, there were plenty of demons around at the time. If I had gone with that class now, I'd be stuck until I could find some of their hidden organizations. And those organizations had a leg up on me at present.

"You are staring off into that space again," Simone broke me from my thoughts as we reached the bar. "It's like you are staring one or two feet from your face."

Insightful as ever.

"I sort of am. You'll understand eventually." I sat up at the bar. "Do you have a few pieces of thick paper?"

"Do napkins work?" She pushed the stack in front of me. "Otherwise, I'd have to go disturb Carmen."

I glanced at the napkins and shrugged. "So, what are you doing this weekend outside of a lovely date tomorrow?"

Simone shrugged and leaned on the counter. "I was sort of thinking that I might go track down some of the ladies that work for Rick and get some blood samples from them."

I paused in my preparations. The stack of napkins was next to a sloop tooth and I was cleaning off a space in front of me. "Whatever would you do that for?"

"If they have quality blood, they need to be protected, right? Would you steal a few of them from Rick for me if they turned out quality?" she asked.

That was not one of the options I had considered, so I took a moment to think through the potential outcomes. There certainly could be a few that had bloodlines, and if that was true, then I'd be stupid to turn them down.

"And what would I then do with them? You wouldn't perhaps be trying to manipulate me, would you?"

"Darn, I've been caught," she said playfully. "Good thing I'm talking through the plan with you rather than springing it on you later."

I nodded in agreement. "So *if*—and that's a big if—you find one, I'd be interested."

Slavery wasn't really uncommon in the future. Power hierarchies quickly created social ones. Even in the present day, many people were heavily taken advantage of by the wealthy. Their hands just weren't in shackles—their bank accounts were.

I had grown somewhat numb to seeing it around me, and I recognized that. Personally, I had no joy in controlling someone. Yet I had come to realize there was always a hierarchy in society. Humans just couldn't seem to help themselves.

"Good. That's all I need. I'll see what I can do. Those girls are in a poor situation and I'd save one if I could, even if that means using my favorite bullet-proof vampire." She smiled at me. Simone really tried to make lives better for these sex workers.

I grinned back. "I like that you stick to your principles. Now, let's do a few things for your place." I pricked my finger, concentrating on the Blookink ability before using one of the washed-out Duggarfin teeth. They had a hollow channel for their venom that I filled with my blood before I started drawing inscriptions on the napkin in quick order.

Simone washed glasses while she watched me. "What do I do with that?"

"Put a few under the bar and the hostess desk. They are to ward away a certain type of person."

I was giving Simone demon wards. They didn't work if one had a particular goal in mind, but if one was idly looking around, the talisman would push them subtly away.

The more I placed around her place, the stronger the effect. It could even become a thin barrier to buy her a moment to get ready. It was the least I could do to try and keep her safe, especially when I didn't know how she became possessed.

Until I knew she would be safe, my heart towards her would always be a little guarded.

Chapter 22

I was dressed in a different button down, but the same vest, as I showed up to the park market first and waited by the entrance.

The lady at the sign greeting people gave me a hard look during a lull in the flow of traffic, her Inspect sliding off of me as I pushed it aside.

I raised an eyebrow at her. "Must you?"

As I paid attention to her, I studied her even harder. Most of the time, players become complacent. Inspect gave them information, and they often took what they could see as being all they could glean from someone.

Yet the more I looked at this woman, the more I felt the blood that stained her hands. A predator could recognize another. Though, her preferred prey seemed to be other players as she scanned those coming and going.

It might seem like a reach to pick all that up from a look, but my instincts were honed and tested to the point that I trusted them enough to set the bait. I wouldn't kill her out of hand, but if she took the bait, then the gloves could come off.

"You're the first person that's even noticed." She studied me. "How do you do it?"

"Have a really high spirit stat," I answered honestly. "Is there any way to get into a group that does instances?"

"Hard when you won't even show me your stats." She crossed her arms as I checked her stats.

[Amy Smith
Level: 32
Class: Spearwoman C

...]

I grunted. "Try again." This time I let her Inspect see my first name, and then my stat block besides my spirit.

"Won't even show me your class?" she asked.

"Nope. I keep my cards close," I said honestly. "What I showed you should be enough though."

"Yeah. You are decent. Problem is, everyone's trying to find instances." She watched me.

I leaned on the table next to her. "We both know that there are two types of players. Those who are playing it safe, wanting to farm some easy F and E rank low-level instances. Then there's those that want to take on something higher. I'm crazy enough to go solo on a Level 22 D rank instance. There have to be some people trying to go for something higher."

She looked me up and down. "You don't look like the thrill-seeker type."

"Trust me. I turn into a different person in an instance." I grinned while thinking of running around with Duggarfin teeth in nothing but damaged boxers.

"There're some people who do groups. We don't control the instances though," she said. "You try talking to the guys at North Trust?"

"Didn't much like their tone. They really the best option?" I was hoping for more, but I was also throwing out a bit of bait. Talking about doing a D rank dungeon on my own might draw a type that I knew well.

Sometimes killing players could be far more lucrative than farming instances. I wouldn't go hunt down other players, but if my instincts were right, I wouldn't have to.

"Yeah. They are the best option." She glanced behind me.

I stepped back before I turned around.

Simone had a giant smile on her face that was mirrored by Gloria's scowl. Both ladies were a vision, but I only had eyes for Simone.

"Well, this is a surprise," I said to Simone before glancing at Gloria. "You two just happen to meet on your way or something?"

"Oh. I picked her up." Simone's smile was a bit too satisfied. "I know she has a job to do, and I didn't want her to fall behind. As for you." She tapped me in the chest. "We are still on for lunch, but did you know that we were going to look at places after lunch?"

I groaned. "Funny, I asked Gloria to look for some places."

"Well, we need to find a spot for those paintings you bought for your 'new place,'" Simone told me.

"In fairness, I am getting a new place." I shrugged. "It was just a work in progress."

"Uh huh." Simone wasn't really listening to my excuse. "Apparently, you have a huge budget."

I glanced at Gloria. "How can you be so loose-lipped in your line of work?"

"Don't blame her. I'm good at extracting information" Simone patted my shoulder and urged me towards the market.

This Simone was a little scary. It seemed that if I was going to have multiple women, she was going to face it head on and establish herself at the top before I even knew an order was being established.

"She's your woman. There's no reason I should hold back, right? Besides, you didn't tell me that you lied," Gloria said.

"It was a fib. Hardly a lie. My 'new' place was a work in progress. I was simply getting decorations for a new place ahead of time." I juggled the situation.

"Well. We'll go look at the places. I mean, I can't think of a better date than helping you apartment shop." Simone held onto my arm.

Today she was in a cute sweater with a low neckline and a pair of skintight jeans, complete with a pair of heels that she wore even knowing we were going to be walking through a field.

They at least had a strap around the ankle. I felt like that had to help. But it was always hard to tell with women's clothing. Sometimes it was functional, and sometimes it was purely aesthetic.

"Where does that leave Gloria?" I looked at the woman over my shoulder.

"She'll be organizing. We talked." Simone gave her a tight smile.

Damn, I didn't expect Simone to whip Gloria so quickly.

The mob princess gave me a smile without any joy in it. "I lined up a series of places, though I'll disappear during your lunch. This is the place?" She shifted her focus to the market around us.

"Yup. Bet you can't see anything wrong with it," I challenged, curious what she would pick up.

Gloria squinted her eyes.

Simone pointed at a stall. "Those aren't sports drinks. See how they grab them from the back? That way they can control what they are really selling."

"Quiet," I warned her. "We don't talk about it where others can hear."

"What are we looking for today?" Simone asked, holding my arm tight.

I was trying to figure out if she felt threatened by Gloria or if she was just putting in extra effort for another reason. "There's a fish problem where I'm going."

"You had a fish problem last week," Simone studied me.

"Yeah, one I went into unprepared and suffered for it," I grumbled, thinking about how many times I had regenerated my calves. "This time, I want to be better prepared because I'm dragging two other people with me."

"What do you need? Flippers? I don't think we'll find those here." Simone scanned the stalls as we started to wander the market. She seemed incredibly comfortable.

After a moment of thought, I turned to Simone.

"Simone, you don't need to butter me up before you bring me back those blood samples," I told her.

She turned to me mechanically. "I'm just going all in, because I think you're worth it." She grinned. "But, what do you need from here?" She pulled us back to the task at hand.

"Don't need flippers. That's for sure. I could make Olympic swimmers look like toddlers learning to swim. No, what I need is a very sturdy net." If I bought D rank armor, it was going to be chewed through like the leather.

A net would help me farm the Duggarfins, with Bobby and Rodger doing the sloops.

I also needed to see if that decorative map booth was here again and if they had any more information on where they got the map I had bought.

The next thing I'd need was a way to deal with the sloop-sloop, which really meant getting my hands on some ingredients for talismans. On top of that, I was going to pick up extra ingredients so that I could sell talismans for a profit.

The easiest way to get invited to an instance was to be known for something. In my past life, people came to me because I had a reputation. That reputation was for breaking things—bones, demons, and inscription problems.

"People are staring," Gloria said.

"Doesn't bother me," I told her, having long gotten over stares. "That place." I pointed to one disguised as a craft shop.

"Hello." The woman at the counter had a particularly hipster vibe as she stood and Inspected my group.

No doubt she got both of the ladies, yet when she tried me, I met her eyes and pushed it aside. "Looking for a few particular things. This. How much do you have?" I pointed to a stack of paper that had been treated with some sort of mixture to make it F rank.

"That particular one, I have maybe two reams in total," she answered hesitantly.

"I'll take it all." I held out a credit card to her and she took it, bumping her ring to mine and I transferred over the gold.

She 'ran' the credit card and forgot to make me sign. Then she handed me back the card and bumped her ring to mine, dropping a few hundred pieces of F ranked paper into my ring.

"Here's my information." I tore off a piece of mundane paper and scribbled my phone number on it. "As much of that as you make, I'll buy it."

"Ah. Really?" she asked.

"I'm particularly skilled at using it," I answered honestly. "Then I'll take ten of these paints, five of those, and twelve of these." I quickly started buying everything I wanted.

She hurried, and we made another transaction, handing me a few of the mundane items in a bag to make it look real.

Simone and Gloria were watching me carefully enough that the woman felt a little awkward, but she shrugged it off.

"You all have a nice day." She had a big smile after all my purchases.

Truthfully, my purchase had been more aggressive than I had been planning to spend, but it was well worth it.

"So, those are for things like what you did with the napkins at my place?" Simone asked as we moved away.

"Yep. Though the napkins were quick and dirty ones. These can be more permanent and have a far greater variety of uses," I explained.

"Napkins?" Gloria asked.

Simone didn't answer her, waiting for me.

"There's a type of magic called inscriptions. It's a written form that has a specific effect. I put wards against demons in Simone's place," I said, realizing that I hadn't told her about demons yet.

"Demons?" Simone asked suddenly. "Are you worried about demons for a reason?"

I felt suddenly awkward and decided to be honest. "Yes. Think of it this way. You'd be very interesting to them."

"My blood?" she asked.

"Yes." I imagined that her blood was one of the qualities that attracted her such a high-up demon.

"Can I take some of those napkins back to my place?" she asked.

"I'll send you home with more after today," I promised quickly, coming up to one of those stalls that hid the items in paintings.

"More art for your new place?" Simone teased.

"Yep." I stepped into the booth.

They had it set up so that I had to go in to see all of the art. My Soul Gaze swept over the items, but to my disappointment, there was no net. I was starting to suspect finding the net would be difficult. Most people were selling armor and weapons.

"I need to get a few sports drinks." I pointed to another stall on our way out, avoiding the place where Simone had stolen some bitters. "Do you two want any?"

"I'm fine," Gloria said.

"Me too," Simone said. "Though, thank you for offering."

CHAPTER 22

I stopped there and picked up a small armload of potions. Not just for me, but to cover Bobby and Rodger in case they weren't quite as well prepared. I couldn't let either of them suffer under my watch.

"That's more than last time." Simone squinted.

"I'm bringing Bobby. Gotta make sure I can look out for him," I told her.

"You used up the ones from last time," she noticed, squinting slightly at me. "That means you got hurt."

"It's part of the gig. Most of the time, I'm pretty resilient. But sometimes, time is of the essence and I need to get a little hurt to speed through," I tried not to worry her.

"What can you really do?" Gloria asked, curiously.

"He's bulletproof," Simone supplied, causing one of Gloria's brows to rise up high. "Also he's very fast and very strong. I don't know entirely what he is, but I joke that he's a bulletproof vampire."

"You drink blood?" Gloria frowned at me.

"No," I said.

"Yes," Simone countered me. "He drank my blood, saying it was the best."

Well, that told me she was at least a little threatened by Gloria.

"Huh," Gloria just grunted. "If you need blood, we can get you plenty. Just let me know. I own a few blood banks. Easy place to distribute to people on a monthly basis. No one really thinks much of going to give blood."

"Oh really?" Simone's interest was piqued. "That might be interesting, but Bran would have to tell you a few secrets that I'm not sure he's going to share just yet."

"Look, they have some nice paintings. What do you think of looking at them while we stop poking at Gloria?" I pulled Simone with me and whispered, "Stop being so defensive."

She grinned at me. "This way you don't have to be the jerk. You get to be the hero." She kissed me on the side of the cheek as my mouth hung open.

I paused, digesting that bit of information, and also appreciating Simone in a new light. I really needed to figure out how to lock this woman down so that no demon could lay their hands on her.

Chapter 23

"You minx." I nudged Simone as soon as we were free of Gloria and the market.

"You should be thanking me," Simone shot back.

"Well, then thank you." I held her arm as we stepped up to the hip restaurant. The place had chalkboard menus by the sidewalk, and I paused to look it over. "Duck tongue. I didn't know you could eat duck tongue."

"It's a little fatty, but quite tasty. They fry them, and they are like little meaty French fries."

I blinked at her. "We might just have to try those then."

"Just the two of you?" A hostess reclaimed her podium.

"Yep, let's eat outside," I told her. The hostess gathered the menus before we followed along. "So, what did you do to tame Gloria?"

"I haven't the faintest idea of what you mean." Simone put a hand to her chest aghast.

"Fine, keep your secrets." I gave her a smile as we sat down. "What do you want to drink?" I opened the menu as the hostess wandered off. "For the record, I'm buying." I didn't even look up to make sure she acknowledged the statement.

"In that case, I'll do a Goated Punch."

I raised an eyebrow at her.

"It's their special. You should try it."

"It sounds fruity." I made an exaggerated face.

"It most certainly is. It's lunch. I'm not going to drink straight whiskey at lunch." She put her menu down. Clearly, she had been to the restaurant before and knew what she was going to order.

I took a moment longer before putting my menu down as well. "So, you at least seemed to figure things out with Gloria.

Thanks for poking her so that I didn't have to be a jerk today. I'm still going to use her as a gopher for a while. She's actually really good at it."

"She runs a criminal empire. Of course she can fetch you a new house and a new car." Simone waved the waiter that came over.

"I'll do a House Merlot, and she'll do a Goated Punch. For the appetizer, we'll do that fried duck tongue." I nodded to the waiter as a dismissal and turned back to Simone. "I didn't say I thought she was incompetent, just overbearing."

"Enough about her. This is our date." Simone leaned forward. "What about you? Playing with more fish this week?"

"Yes. They are quite lucrative." I pulled out another tooth.

"If you put that in your wine, I'm leaving." Simone narrowed her eyes.

"Just showing off." It disappeared into my ring again as I aborted putting it in my wine. "Yes, quite lucrative. Though it's hard to extract so many teeth, I manage. Bobby and another of Carmen's guys will be going with me."

"Because you need the help?" she asked.

"No. There are other resources in there that they need." I was half-tempted to just explain everything, but based on her questions, she was enjoying piecing the information together.

"Interesting. How long will you be gone?" She got quiet as the waiter came over with our drinks.

I took a long sip of the wine. It had been a very long time since I had tasted wine. It wasn't exactly a high priority to make wine during the last phase of the demon wars. The last time I had had wine was probably over a hundred years ago.

"Like your wine?" she asked, watching me.

"It's been a while." I put the glass down. "We'll probably be gone all week again, but this time, we'll pop up for air every now and then. Maybe every day or so. If you have any dire need, I won't be prompt, but I'll come."

"What do you do in your spare time when you are getting fish teeth?" she asked.

"Paint," I answered quickly. "Puts my mind at ease. Also, painting is easy enough with a wide variety of materials." Including demon blood.

She narrowed her eyes. "There's something you left unsaid."

"Yes, there is. What about you? What's your favorite thing to do in the world?"

"Sex," she answered shamelessly and took a drink from her glass, watching my reaction over the rim. It was a red, sugary looking punch.

She got the reaction she wanted. I coughed into my wine. "Sex?"

"Sex," she repeated. "I really like sex."

"I guess that makes sense." I tried to cover up for my brief bout of coughing. "Is that a hint that I should hurry this up?"

"Heavens no. It's more fun when the tension is so thick that it might just snap and make us both go crazy." She grinned as she took another drink. "Besides, I'm waiting on this shot from the fountain of youth. I'm a little worried I can't keep up with a bulletproof vampire. And no, don't tell me more. Sometimes it is better to stay in the dark until you can do something about it."

I shook my head at how much she impressed me. "Well, then. What do you do with your free time?"

"Hey now. I get the next question. You said you like to paint. Would you show me some of your works?" She leaned on the table.

"Hmm." I pretended to think. "With the move, I don't think I brought any with me. I'd have to make a new one. Then I could show it to you. What's the prettiest place in Vein City." I held up my hand to stop her from answering. "Wait. I know the answer. Any place you are." I gave her my most seductive smile.

Simone laughed. "You are laying it on thick."

"You said you liked it so thick that it might just snap and make us both go crazy. I'm just trying to hurry that along." I played off her earlier words.

"Touché," She laughed. "I enjoy talking to you."

"Me too. Honestly, I just came for your blood. Who knew the person with it all would be so charming."

"Keep it up." She sipped her drink.

I smiled at her. But then my eyes flitted off to the side as Soul Gaze picked up a player that had been watching us since we had sat down. She wasn't someone I'd seen before.

[Georgia Timpleton
Level: 32
Class: Scout C]

She was a decently high level, but didn't have the stats for a sect or clan. If I had to guess, my gamble earlier had paid off and now I just had to let her follow me around.
I'd control when I was in a vulnerable position.

***

Simone and I were a little late to the house showing Gloria had set up because we'd lost track of time.
Simone leaned heavily against me as we showed up to the first place. Gloria stood by the doorway with her arms crossed, waiting for us. The mood was a little tense.
The real estate agent looked like she might shit herself standing next to Gloria, looking around for who the mob princess was waiting to arrive.
"Gloria!" I waved. "Pleasure to see you, darling."
The agent glanced at me, a slight confusion in her brows. I was clearly not what she was expecting.
"This is the first of four places," Gloria said tersely. "You didn't give me any details besides location and budget."
"Yet you've done a fine job regardless." I grinned at her.
The realtor picked up on the relationship between us, and her worry and fear transfixed onto me. "I'll happily show you the place. It's on the twenty-second floor. You would have the whole floor."
"Sounds lovely. Let's go see it." I held Simone closer and followed after the realtor. "All of these are for sale, correct?"
"I was thinking of showing you one for rent," the lady answered.

"Cancel it. I'm only interested in buying." I was going to end up warding the shit out of any place that I lived, so I was not in the mood to deal with some landlord.

"Of course." She nodded dutifully and waved past security in the lobby to bring us to the elevator and up to the twenty-second floor. "This building is about twenty years old. It's getting to the point that they are repairing it and there are building fees."

I glanced at Gloria. "It's within my budget?"

"Well within." She nodded.

"Then don't bother talking about costs," I told the realtor. "Let's just see what merits it has."

She stiffened but continued. "Then the place overlooks the park. I hear you wanted to be close to it."

She stepped out of the elevator and used a fob rather than a key to go through the door. I didn't care about human security very much. A demon kicked through a door whether it had a lock or a fob.

"The place was recently renovated, for a more modern look." She waved, highlighting the area.

The space was all sharp angles and stone features.

"Oh. What do you think?" Simone asked. "I'm not sure if you're more of a mahogany dark wood man or a modern man?"

"Honestly, it's better than a damp cave." I shrugged.

The realtor's face grew confused as she tried to figure out how to sell me on the space.

I walked past the first room over to the next. This one had a pool set into it, with the far edge around the pool being a balcony that overlooked the park. We were a few blocks away, but there weren't any buildings tall enough to block our view.

I glanced at the pool and then at the smaller hot tub attached to one end. The hot tub could be useful for some alchemical baths. As for the pool, I was fairly sure I could find a use for it. Underwater combat was not something I particularly excelled at and perhaps I could use a little training.

"What do you think?" the realtor asked after a long moment of silence.

"He's probably having some thoughts that wouldn't occur to you," Simone laughed. "But I think he likes it."

"Suitable," I said. "Let's see the other rooms."

She showed us over to the kitchen and den area. The areas were nice and open, with ceilings high enough that I could even practice some polearm movements if I moved some of the furniture out of the way. Overall, it took up most of the space.

And the stove had enough burners so that I could prepare quite a few meals at once to stock up my rings. The fireplace didn't quite seem placed in a spot to be functional, which meant it was largely decorative. Why anybody would do something just for visual appeal was beyond me, but I could let that pass.

"Bedrooms?" I asked.

"There are three," she continued. "The two smaller ones are mirror images." She wandered down the hall and showed me the two rooms.

Both of them were larger than the apartment that I was staying in, and staged with furniture that made them look incredibly inviting.

"As for the last one..." She reached the end of the hall and paused between a set of double doors with two big bars for handles.

It was a sturdy door if I put a few inscriptions on it. I would bet it could withstand a few blasts from powerful players.

"The master suite is the best part." She pulled the double doors open with a flourish.

The room beyond was almost as big as the main area. It was split into a lounging area with two couches and a big leather chair. In the corner sat a large desk, a perfect spot to work on some inscriptions. There was a curtain that was half drawn between it and the bedroom, or rather just the bed.

The bed itself was huge, with the frame built right into the room. A pillar on each corner connected to the ceiling.

"If you don't like the bed, well, that's unfortunate. Those pillars are actually functional and needed for the stability of the roof," the woman joked.

"What's above me?" I asked.

"A maintenance floor," the realtor answered. "It's used for things like the pool, as well as hot water. This high up, there's auxiliary pumps on the floor above you as well as a boiler for hot water and more."

I glanced up at the ceiling, my thoughts running along how I could sneak up there and turn part of the maintenance area into a workshop. No one would mind the noise if it was insulated well enough that I wasn't hearing the pump run right now.

"Simone, what do you think of the bed?" I reached over, grabbing her and tossing her onto the mattress.

She bounced playfully. "Very soft. Perfect, I'd say."

"Great. We'll take it and everything that's in it right now." I didn't have time to furniture shop, and it was frankly a waste of Gloria's talent.

"Oh. Oh!" The realtor blinked. "We can do that."

"Just give me three of those fobs." I held out my hand.

"There's some paperwork and..." She hesitated as I held my hand out further.

"I'll take care of that," Gloria promised her. "Please just give the man the keys to his new place."

Chapter 24

The realtor had only brought one fob, so I took it with the promise to give the two ladies theirs soon enough.

Then I made several wards with my own blood and pasted them under cabinets and behind furniture to keep the place safe while I was away. The wards were only F ranked, so they wouldn't do much more than keep out the riff raff, but they were certainly better than nothing.

I watched Simone drive off with her own set of wards in hand and instructions on how to place them in her own home.

Now, it was time for me to play another game.

Taking the jeep that Gloria had bought me, I used the little light remaining in the day to drive off to check on another of the instances marked on the map I had bought.

This time, I was heading off-road towards a large chasm indicated on the map. Part of me was giddy with excitement that there might be four instances around Vein City that I'd have full access to.

That would be just what I needed to progress quickly.

Stopping the jeep after regarding the map again and comparing it to the GPS on my phone, I decided to hoof it the rest of the distance. I also had decided it was time to make myself available for the people following me.

Ever since the market, the scout had stuck to me. And as soon as I had left the apartment, I had spotted her using her phone by my jeep.

She hadn't been able to follow me through the off-roading without being obvious, but as soon as I got out of the car, I checked under it to find a little black box strapped to the frame. In my day, we'd use talismans, but I guess technology could fill the same role now.

I had no idea what would happen if I messed with it, and I didn't care much. I wanted them to come to me. Instead, I would walk from here and let them track me through the woods.

Heading the direction that the instance should be, I anticipated that I was headed towards a chasm. The first one had been depicted as a lake, and this one was marked as a chasm on the map. Based on the first instance, the markers were quite literal.

And a chasm would be perfect for a trap.

As I moved forward, I started pulling out that F ranked paper, and bit my finger to start scribbling out talismans as I went. Picking my way through the forest, I quickly slapped a talisman to the underside of a branch and tore the bottom half off before continuing in the direction of the instance.

I wandered around, continuing to slap talismans high above where the players would likely be looking. People really did not learn to look up until they'd had more training, or just a lot of moments to try to work on survival.

It was a travesty how ill-prepared these players were for what was coming, but that was fine. If they just followed me for the instance's location, I'd hide it. Though, all my instincts told me that they were going to come for me.

Lost in my thoughts, I almost missed the fact that I had hit the chasm. My feet stopped as I kicked a few rocks down a crack in the forest floor. Tree roots struggled to fill the gap, and I walked along it as it grew wider.

My eyes were trained down into the chasm, but the instance surprised me. Rather than being at the bottom, it was at the other edge just below the surface.

[Level 87 B Ranked Forest Instance.
23/12 Charges]

I let out a soft whistle. That level was well outside of my reach. Instances scaled on both level and rank.

There was a group of scholars that had survived the first demon wave and had gone about collecting all the data they could on instances and monster ranks, levels, and stats.

Interestingly, the monsters' stats followed a very linear projection. The monsters had a base amount of about 40 stat points. Then based on rank, they had a certain number of stats per level. For a D rank like the instance I'd been in, it was about 6 stats per level. For an A rank? 50 stats per level. Meaning, an A rank instance was filled with monsters that were about eight times as strong as those in a D rank instance.

Given that this was a little over three times the level as well, something in this instance would be twenty-four times stronger than the D rank that I just suffered in.

Even I knew my limits.

Taking the talismans that I had been working on, I made a quick circle of eight talismans around the portal before activating them at once. The portal shimmered out of existence.

Soul Gaze penetrated my illusion formation well enough that I could find it again later.

Now it was time to play with my guests.

Taking the ripped half of many talismans in my hand, I stuck them to my forehead. My vision split a hundred different ways, fractured like a bee's vision. Yet I was able to parse all of the scenes easily.

Most showed nothing but the forest that I'd traversed, but two views held movement of a group of players moving through the woods.

Sadly, I couldn't use Soul Gaze to get more information on them. But I could tell that Amy was present. And so was the scout who'd been following me. Two more men joined them, and one of them seemed to be in charge.

Body language told me that he was stronger, but not so much so that he could force them to do something. His skin was turning gray. Only classes above S rank caused physical changes. I'd have to be careful of him.

That meant I was being followed by four players, three in the low thirties with approximately D ranking stats. I'd go ahead and knock Mr. Leader up on par with C ranking stats for his level.

There was no reason to fight them outright.

Moving around the chasm, I quickly set up several more elaborate formations with my talismans. My blood, and the paper being Frank, limited what I could set up, but I was able to do what I thought would be enough.

My strategy was to create an elaborate illusion.

Another instance portal appeared at the bottom of the chasm, this one fabricated by me. That scout might be able to pierce my illusion, but I'd just have to deal with her first.

Creating an illusion that interacted with the System was difficult and required several more talismans. But what I had created would read [Level 25 D Rank Instance] when they scanned it.

I grinned like a fool as I worked, occasionally checking the talismans and the group's progress.

***

"This fool," Tom chuckled as Georgia led them through the forest using an ability to follow his tracks. "He actually led us straight to his instance." He rubbed his hands together greedily.

"Maybe we should just clear it," Larry whined.

"That's not how this works, Larry. He could just as easily then go sell the information about this instance to someone else. Hoarding these locations is how we've gotten stronger. If he was like that Level 62, then maybe we'd let him live... for now." Amy narrowed her eyes at the weakest member of their party.

Some days, Tom considered silencing Larry before he made a stupid mistake. Yet the man was a healer, and so far had been critical to their team's success in raiding other player's instances.

"Something is wrong." Georgia put out her hand as they stepped into a clearing with a large cut running through the ground like a giant's ax had fallen there.

"It's in there. I can feel it." Tom stepped forward, ignoring Georgia and spotting the instance down below at the bottom.

"Bet he already went in. What's wrong, Georgia?"

The scout frowned, looking around. "I just feel something. His tracks also disappeared."

"It might be the instance. We've seen them put out tons of mana before." Tom waved off her concern. His Inspect had already told him what he needed to know. This was the same instance the idiot had bragged to Amy about finding.

If it wouldn't have looked completely stupid, he'd have danced.

"Come on. Let's get in there and get him," Tom called out to the rest of them.

"What if he's strong? Amy said she couldn't Inspect him," Larry, ever the pessimist, threw in his useless two cents.

"If he was strong, he wouldn't be farming an instance of this level." Tom wanted to rush forward and claim this one. With it, he might be able to push to Level 40.

"I'm checking something." Georgia was running her hands along the ground using her Tracking ability differently than before. It almost felt like his tracks were everywhere even though she couldn't see them.

"Fine, stay if you want, but I'm going. Last one in is a rotten egg! If you don't participate in the kill, I'm not giving you a share of the loot." Tom jumped forward.

That man was reckless, but he was also powerful.

Not moving, Georgia kept trying to figure out what she was missing. Something wasn't right.

"It's not safe for you to stay out alone," Larry blubbered.

Even she found him to be insufferable. Yet he was whipped by Tom and would follow the bigger man anywhere and was currently stepping towards the portal himself.

Amy just grinned and walked forward on her own.

Georgia guessed it was better for her to follow along and get credit for the kill, yet something smacked into her forehead. A piece of paper?

The man she'd been stalking appeared before her, a paper stuck to his forehead as he head butted her. She fell back and felt like she kept falling as an older man, in his fifties, appeared before her. He was slightly indistinct, like he wasn't really there.

"Yep. That seems about right." He reached down and grabbed her head, arresting her falling in the endless abyss as if he were a god here. "Since you were going to kill me, don't blame me."

Something wasn't right. Before him, she felt like a speck of dust.

The strength of his hand felt like a behemoth the size of a mountain held her head, then it all vanished.

***

System messages of leveling up spammed the side of my vision. She had been in her 30's, and I had just reset to Level 1.

I peeled the used-up talisman off my forehead and threw it on the ground next to the dead scout who had already started to fade away.

The group that had followed me was of a high enough level that I needed to play to certain strengths. At the F rank, I didn't have any talisman that could directly attack the soul, but I could make a paired talisman that allowed my soul to enter theirs.

Unfortunately, it required direct contact, and it also required a talisman on each of our foreheads. That was harder to establish than I would have liked.

Down in the crevasse, Tom and Amy were currently fighting illusionary sloops. I needed to hurry up before either my talismans ran out, or they started to catch on to the illusion.

Now that I understood their group composition, I jumped down behind Larry. My Sloop-tooth Ax came out into my hand as I swung hard at his neck.

I could tell that the robe he was wearing was a System item, and I wanted to save it if I could, so I aimed high. The sloop teeth bit into his neck and started gushing blood as he turned, wide-eyed to me. He tried to yell, but gurgles were all that emerged around the ax. His allies had no idea.

"Don't worry." I smiled. "You were cowardly enough that I have no desire to cause you pain." A sloop tooth appeared in my hand, and I stabbed it deep into his eye socket to put him down for good.

He had enough vitality that even cutting his throat hadn't killed him immediately. The man really had a coward's healer build. He was all vitality with some intelligence and spirit he got from his class.

But if he didn't want to die, he shouldn't have hunted me.

Larry's body disappeared. Now that he was part of the System, his body was taken by the System when he died.

Though, unlike monsters, he dropped everything on him and even something extra.

I picked up the booklet with a grin. "Healing Hand C," I chuckled.

There was always a chance that a player or a demon would drop one of their skills. Sadly, this healing ability was not able to be used on yourself, which limited my interest in it. I tucked the booklet away for when I found a reliable partner.

I scanned the fight. Tom and Amy were still fighting and yelling at Larry behind them. Soon they would realize he was not sending any more heals their way.

I pulled out two Duggarfin teeth and jumped forward, slashing both of them as illusionary sloops attacked, trying to time my hits with the illusions as best as I could so that they would not realize there was another enemy among them.

Both of their stats were higher than mine, and I was concerned with Tom's class.

[Tom Prener
Level 39
Class: Undying SS
Status: Healthy
Strength 234
Agility: 110
Vitality: 161
Intelligence: 83

Spirit: 64]

He had a troublesome class. With it came multiple skills that would give him strength at the end of his life, and even one to regenerate from near death.

If he wasn't such a dick, I'd have even thought of recruiting him for that class alone.

I didn't remember him in my past life, which meant he must have met his end with these sort of schemes before the Rapture. Otherwise, his class would have made him well known.

This was going to be a little trickier than I had planned.

Chapter 25

Amy was slowing down from the poison, and I was quickly running out of talismans that fueled the formation.

She reached for her spatial ring and then frowned, looking behind her. "Larry? Larry, where the fuck have you gone, you spineless twat. Get out here."

"Tom. Tom!" she called out louder. "Something's wrong. Leave the monsters alone for a second." She coughed into her hand, blood coming up. "I'm poisoned."

"So am I." Tom frowned, realizing that Larry was not healing them.

In his distraction, one of my illusions attacked and he screamed, throwing himself to the side only to touch his body and come away with only illusionary blood. "That didn't hurt. Not really."

Still watching them struggle down below, I bounced the rings in my palm. It was time to surface.

"Ah. You're finally starting to get it," I shouted over the fighting. "The human brain can really add quite a bit if you give it believable visuals."

The illusion around them faded, and they fought themselves at the bottom of the chasm.

"You! Those are my rings." Amy glanced at the jewelry jangling around in my hand.

"No. The second you tried to track and kill me, all of your things were destined to become mine. Unfortunately for you, I don't give second chances." I stood at the top of the chasm with an ax in my hand. "Check your menus. I already poisoned you. It won't be long."

Both of them tried to Inspect me, but I pushed them off.

"Use your gold coins," Tom called out, decisively grabbing a ring that I'd missed. It was on a chain that was hidden under his armor. His fists filled with gold coins as he shoved them into his menu.

Amy also seemed to have her gold in a different ring and did the same, both of them pumping everything into vitality to try and outlast my poison.

"Run right. I'll go left," Tom shouted and bolted away from Amy.

I sighed, having hoped that Tom's rashness would turn into a fight he would easily lose, yet it seemed he was also decisive.

Amy looked lost as Tom rushed off and I jumped to block her. "Please. I..."

"Excuses come easy when you are at the end of your rope. How many people have you killed as they begged." I lunged forward with the Sloop-tooth Ax.

The expression on her face told me everything I needed to know. Amy barely got her spear up to block me, but then she was surprised at my strength, or lack of it.

It seemed my mysteriousness was a little damaged by the strength of my attack.

No matter, they were already split up.

"You aren't that strong." Her eyes lit up with fighting spirit. "Fuck you." She twirled the spear and activated a System ability that turned it into three sharp jabs that I had to dance out of the way to avoid.

"Perhaps not in direct combat," I admitted, and jumped back again as she tried to sweep my legs. "Yet Georgia and Larry died quickly enough."

She charged me, trying to find a soft spot in my gut where she could bury her spear.

I slammed the toothy ax down on her spear, the teeth locking it into place and pinning her weapon against the ground. Then I jumped over it and tackled her directly.

The problem with weapon-based classes like spearwoman was that when you took the weapon away, their strength dropped precipitously.

Unfortunately, she was still decently strong.

Amy hammered a number of small blows into my chest, making my ribs crackle and ache. Yet in a knockdown brawl, I held a very significant advantage.

Blood Boil activated, and I started hitting her with slow, measured attacks aimed to disable her shoulders. She stabbed me in the thigh with a hidden dagger, and I clenched my teeth before I headbutted her to stun her.

"Fuck you. Die." She stabbed me again.

I chuckled. "Didn't even tickle." I started to whale on her, raining blow after blow until her arms stopped working, then her head turned into one big, bruised lump.

Amy coughed out a few teeth, clearly at the end of her rope. "How?"

I stood up, my thigh already healed and showed her the hole in my pants leg. "Regeneration is one of my highest ranked skills. Poor Amy, all alone out in the woods, abandoned by your friends."

She spat at me. "I'm not abandoned. You killed them or scared Tom off."

I shrugged. "It's not my problem that he ran. What I want to know is where are the other instances you've killed people for. There's no information in your ring."

She tried to do something in the System, and I kicked her head.

"I might consider us even if I knew that information." I let my voice trail off.

Amy swallowed, perhaps getting a few teeth caught in her throat as she struggled. "We lived together and kept some of our important things in a safe."

I pulled out Larry's keys and a few letters that were in his ring. It was a mundane thing, but it seemed he'd gotten his mail recently. "Thanks. I have everything I need."

I walked over to our weapons and put my ax away before coming back over with her spear.

I gave it to her. Right in the gut.

"Sorry. I don't leave problems behind." I twisted until the System took her body too. I took everything on the ground and ignored the levels I'd gotten. I was disappointed that she didn't drop any of her skills.

The System giveth and the System taketh away.

Shame, but I couldn't be that lucky.

Now it was time to go track down Tom. I slapped the talismans to my forehead again to get a view of the forest. Tom had suggested that he run back the direction they had come and Amy the opposite direction.

For as reckless as he seemed, he still was ruthlessly trying to survive. I smiled as I locked onto a person moving through the woods.

I found him.

Tom was looking worse for wear, but he kept moving through the forest. The Undying class was a particularly dangerous one. Injuries didn't affect their ability to fight, or in this case, run.

I'd have to be careful. I knew the class's namesake ability, and it would be tricky in a fight.

Rushing in the direction he was moving, I took a shortcut rather than the winding path that they had followed on the way to ambush me. But even with the shortcut, it took me fifteen minutes to catch up to Tom.

I called out to him, "Amy's dead now too. They're all dead. How undying do you feel right about now?" I taunted him, covered in blood and completely healthy. It was only natural for him to believe that I had brutalized Amy and the others.

His head snapped back towards me. "You demon!"

I chuckled. "A very poor choice to compare me to. Compared to a demon, I might as well be a saint. No, Tom. I'm not a demon, it's just that you're no longer a human to me. The second you set out to kill me was the second you became no more than an instance monster to me. Something to be eliminated for me to grow stronger."

"Wait!" Tom screamed. His fear of dying was almost palpable. I wondered if that was part of why he got such a class. "We have millions and millions in the bank. I can give you what the others have saved up, and you can of course keep what you've taken."

I was happy to keep him talking and keep the poison working. After all, when he used Last Stand, I'd need to back off for a time. "Would you have let me off if I begged for my life? I somehow doubt it."

"No. I totally would have. I even advocated that we don't come after you, but Larry, the healer insisted. He was the one in charge and he didn't want to leave any witnesses or someone alive who might know the location of the instance. He wanted it all to himself." Tom dodged behind some trees as if those would save him.

"We both know that's a lie, Tom. Those roles were reversed. I've been watching you this whole time. Tom, tell me, do you believe in second chances?" I asked.

"Of course! Yes. I believe in them." He tried to Inspect me again, only for it to fail.

"Why?" I drew things out, while circling around him.

"Everyone deserves second chances." Tom staggered, the poison was really eating away at him.

I shook my head sadly. "Sure, a second chance when you burn the food or break your favorite sword. But killing? No, Tom. The only way that someone who's made the decision to kill ends up regretting it is when they find themselves on the wrong side of the killing.

"I know your type, Tom. Four of you ganging up on those weaker than you or those who are alone. In a world where that was a way of survival, sure, maybe I'd give you a second chance. But this isn't that world, Tom. You did it for greed." I drew Amy's spear out as if I were going to fight him.

Tom yelled and drew his giant sword, a burst of strength surging through him.

This was the real danger of an Undying. When their backs were against the wall, when it seemed like they were going to die, they were at their strongest.

Tom's body glowed as Last Stand activated, and he screamed as he rushed me. Light seemed to beam out of his eyes and open mouth.

[Tom Prener
Level 39
Class: Undying SS
Status: Wounded, Last Stand, Indomitable Spirit
Strength: 1170
Agility: 550
Vitality: 905

Intelligence: 415
Spirit: 320]

I slapped a talisman on the spear tip before using the spear to deliver it right to Tom and closed my eyes. A light so bright emitted from the tip of the spear that even with my eyes closed it burned.

I rolled to the side as Tom screamed.

My Regeneration was kicking in, and my eyes were quickly recovering. Tom would be less effective with that monstrous Last Stand active. This was what being an SS ranked class meant. He had abilities that completely changed the fight.

Luckily, his Last Stand was still at a low level, and it only multiplied its stats by five. But Indomitable Spirit would stop me from simply crushing his soul.

In the First Demon War and the following War for Supremacy, those with the Undying class became beacons. Of the nine Hell Gates during the First Demon War, one was defended by a single Undying who grew to unstoppable levels. Another was defended by a set of three Undying.

Such a class was the type that little boys and girls would be praying to receive when it was their time to integrate with the System.

I got back to my feet, my eyes healed enough to see Tom's form on the ground, covering his eyes. His entire face looked like he'd been badly sunburnt.

Despite his incredible class, he wouldn't have the opportunity to grow. The class could save itself from desperate situations and grow explosively. Yet Tom wasn't standing at a Hell Gate slaughtering demons.

He had made the mistake of trying to kill me.

The Sloop-tooth Ax appeared in my hand before I dropped it down on the back of Tom's head several times. He collapsed, and I kept going until the System devoured his form.

So much for being Undying.

I wiped my brow. That fight had been closer than I'd have liked.

Glancing around, I found what remained of Amy's spear. The spearhead had completely disappeared, and the talisman had turned the D ranked metal into pure light energy.

I had used a very dangerous talisman that had many uses, but sadly, it didn't work on anything organic. And the flash of light was relative to the rank of the item sacrificed.

If I hadn't used up the spear and its reach to get it closer to Tom than me, I wasn't sure if my Regeneration or Tom's bolstered vitality would have won out.

In the end, it was a game of who recovered first. That was a gamble that I had been willing to make because of my experience with Regeneration.

I rubbed at my still sore eyes and went to pick up the rest of the loot. When I picked up Tom's shirt, I was excited to find a skill book underneath it.

[Last Stand F]

A grin like none other spread across my face. Well, I'll be damned. It seemed the System did like me after all.

I touched the book to my forehead, dissolving it in a flash of light. It wasn't a skill anyone but an Undying should have, and I'd keep it in my back pocket as a last resort.

I stood up as I put Tom's shirt and the rest of his clothes into my ring. No reason to leave evidence. With the instance entrance hidden and too far beyond my current level, I had no more business in these woods.

Fighting with Tom had shown me that I wasn't yet strong enough to stand out. In the dangerous world to come, showing skills or your wealth brought trouble.

I needed to be much stronger, which meant focusing on grinding out instances. We'd have to see what Tom's group had in their home.

My phone appeared in my hand, and I called Gloria.

"What do you want?" she answered.

I chuckled, walking back to my jeep. "There's a car where I am that I need disposed of, as well as an address checked out. They were players, and I think they had locations of points of interest."

"Bodies?" Gloria asked, her tone mellowing. "Are you all right?" she asked after a moment.

"I'm fine. Players don't leave bodies, Gloria. The System giveth and the System taketh. If you've gotten ten levels, it disappears almost instantly." I rattled off the address and told her I'd leave a set of keys in the car while letting her get my phone's location while I got back there.

There were better uses of my time.

Though, Gloria was showing me just how useful it could be to have a group of competent people to use to delegate. Building that out had just become a goal in the near future.

Getting into my jeep, I peeled away from the woods, feeling good about my new skill.

Chapter 26

I woke up in the giant bed feeling oddly lonely. Since coming back in time, I found myself changing, softening ever so slightly. There had been more people around me recently than there had been in a long time.

It took me a minute to roll out of the bed, unused to a bed so big and the creature comforts that came with the present time.

My previous day had ended with a visit to see my mother. Simone had been busy, and Gloria had said that her people were still looking through Tom's belongings, but would save everything for me to scan as well.

When I'd visited, I found that my mother's stats were growing quickly with the poison gone. She was several times stronger than I had expected, and she started to bring me up to speed on being a player. None of the information was new, but it was nice to hear my mother's voice again, so I sat and let her prepare me for returning to the clan.

I stretched as I stood up. Reaching over, I checked my phone.

I had a number of new texts from Bobby and Rodger; it seemed those two were eager to get started.

That would be something for later, for now, I went and took a shower. The daily ritual was calming, and not always available. I had learned not to take simple luxuries for granted. And I would be spending nearly a week farming the D rank dungeon under the quarry with Bobby and Rodger, working to level up.

I got out of the shower and dried off, reflexively checking my stats.

[Name: Bran Heros
Level: 12
Class: Blood Hegemon F
Status: Healthy
Strength: 66
Agility: 54
Vitality: 62
Intelligence: 48
Spirit: 10994

Skills:
Soul Gaze SSS
Soul Resilience S
Blunt Weapon Proficiency F
Endurance E
Throwing Proficiency F
Blood Boil D
Blood Siphon D
Blood Bolt D
Bloodline Collection 4
Regeneration D
Fire Resistance F
Poison Resistance E
Ax Proficiency E
Charge F
Bloodink Quality F
Stealth F
Inscription F
Swim D (Bracer)
Last Stand F]

   I had gained some levels from the four players. With my levels reset, I had gained more free stat points as far as I was concerned. I certainly wasn't going to complain.
   I looked up and saw my reflection, my eyes catching my attention. Stepping closer, I looked at my eyes. For a moment, I thought I'd seen red in my pupil. I stared as I turned my head from side to side, finding that if the light caught my eye just right, my pupil was indeed red.

CHAPTER 26

It was not a complete shock. Many classes could cause physical mutation, those in the S and SS rank in particular. The Undying class were known for getting gray skin at higher levels.

I had half-expected something from the Blood Hegemon, but I had no idea what it would be. My pupils turning red would mark me as someone with a powerful class later.

My phone rang, catching my attention and breaking my staring match with the mirror. Only Simone and Carmen were set to actually ring, so I picked it up quickly.

"Bran," Simone's voice came through the other end. "I was worried I wasn't going to get you before you disappeared again for the week doing Bulletproof Vampire things."

"Just got out of the shower. I'll be out of pocket shortly. Did you get the blood samples you wanted to use to entice me?" I asked.

"Working on it. Snooping around Rick's business is a little harder than I expected, but I have a line on some new girls coming in. I'll do my best to turn you into my knight in shining armor yet."

I chuckled at the thought. "Well, for those ladies, I'm still a man focusing on his own self interests. By the way, did Gloria get you the fob for my place yet?"

"She did. A key already, Bran? This is so sudden. So fast," she teased. "I wanted to wish you well on your trip this week and to remind you that there are people who care for you waiting for you to get back."

The feeling that beat in my chest for a moment was an old familiar one. It was a warmth, the kind that gave a person something worth fighting for. "Well, then I have good news. This weekend, I have a little surprise, the kind of thing that'll ensure that I come back."

"Good. Good," she repeated the word like she was reassuring herself. "Go have fun with the boys. Seems you have Gloria taking care of your interests for you while you are gone?"

"Yep. Feel free to use her if you need her. And the same goes for you. I expect you to be here when I get back. Don't get in too much trouble poking Rick's organization. Especially when your knight in shining armor isn't there to stand between you and his gun," I reminded her of the dangers she had already faced.

She made a kissing noise into the phone. "See you this weekend for a walk through the market again?"

"Yes, though how about you meet me at my place before we go?" I suggested.

"I'll be there," she promised and lingered for a second before saying goodbye.

I put the phone down with a big smile on my face.

Damnit, even if I'd been through love before, when it started to grow, it still made me feel like I was under a hundred again. But I did recognize the feeling. Simone was a hell of a woman, and one of these days, I was going to have to make a more serious move.

Still riding the high from talking to Simone, I texted Bobby and Rodger to be prepared before driving over in my jeep.

Both of them were already ready. Bobby had swapped out his sports car for a big hummer and had the trunk open to a few diving tanks.

I stared at the tanks. "You can use those if you want, but it won't take that long. I'm going to tie you both to me and then make the swim."

"What did you use when you did it the first time?" Bobby asked.

"Empty water bottles," I answered, waving my ring over my body. I stowed some of my belongings and put on a swimsuit. There were twenty swimsuits in my ring at the moment. I was going to wear them rather than torn up boxers. It seemed classier.

Both of the other men stared at me incredulously.

"Spatial rings. They do work." I glanced at Rodger who had a big hiking bag and shook my head. Pulling off an E rank ring I'd gotten from the four adventurers, I tossed it to him. "Put your stuff in that." Then I gave Bobby one too. "Never hurts to be prepared."

The E rank rings, of which I had several now, held three cubic meters. It was difficult to put something as bulky as a car in them, but it was now possible with enough strength.

A player could move something into a ring as quickly as they could actually lift it. This was why one of my rings currently held a motorcycle. It never hurt to have a motorcycle on hand for a quick escape.

I pulled out a length of rope and tied it around my waist.

"Are you sure you can pull us both?" Rodger asked. His bag disappeared into his new ring as he looked it over happily.

"Just make sure it is secure."

Bobby listened and then stuffed one of the oxygen tanks in his new ring before closing up his car. "Alright, ready."

"Let's go then. Down the ladder." I went first, splashing into the water before Rodger and Bobby joined me. "Deep breath," I warned both of them before I shot underwater.

Both ropes went taut as I swam faster than a speedboat, arriving at the instance portal in no time and shoving them both in before letting it suck me in as well.

Rodger fell on the ground of the instance, coughing and sputtering. "Holy shit."

"That's a D rank swim skill for you." I untied the rope around my waist.

"Imagine a D rank running skill." Bobby was more composed and wrung his shirt out, getting to his feet. "So, what are we facing here? I didn't get to Inspect the dungeon."

"Level 22-28 aquatic creatures and then a Level 35 boss. Good news is that if you lure them onto land, they have a long reach but they move terribly slowly." I walked forward until they could see the first sloop.

Both of them had that look that they were staring at their own Inspect readouts.

"That's strong." Rodger took a small step backward.

"I'll kill this one. That will let you both see it in action. Rodger, do you have any ranged abilities?" I asked rather than reveal that I could indeed see that he had one.

"Throwing F and a bow skill," Rodger reported honestly. It seemed Carmen had impressed upon him that I was in charge.

"Good. Then you two will fight the sloops while I rush ahead and deal with something that's farmable in this instance," I told them, stepping towards the first sloop.

I was going to make an impression on both of them as I wore nothing but a swimsuit.

"Don't you need armor or something?" Rodger asked.

I pulled out the Sloop-tooth Ax as I got closer and rushed the last several steps to slam it home on the shark head of the sloop.

It roared and lashed out of its watery pond at me. I screamed back, stabbing it with Duggarfin teeth in one hand and the ax in the other as it threw me back against the wall.

My stats had grown significantly since I'd last fought a sloop head-to-head, not to mention that my class skills had leveled well too.

I put away the Duggarfin teeth and used my left hand for Blood Siphon as I rained blows with the crafted ax with my right hand. In less than a minute, the sloop fell and disappeared into the instance while I stood up.

My wounds quickly healed over between Regeneration and Blood Siphon. The only sign of damage was the blood all over me and my ripped swim trunks, but I took a quick dip in the sloops pool to rinse off, and came back up with a new pair of trunks. At least I got a level out of that fight.

Rodger's eyes shook as he stared at me.

I'd successfully spooked my minder.

"That's a sloop. They are nasty buggers. Do be sure to stay far away because that neck stretches further than you'd think," I cautioned both of them.

Bobby seemed just mildly impressed, but he'd already seen me fight some in the zombie dungeon. "Yeah, neither of us are a tank. You said you are going ahead to something that's farmable?"

"You'll see it when you both catch up," I promised him. "For now, both of you worry about killing these guys."

"That's plenty to worry about," Rodger said, glancing at Bobby who nodded. "We'll meet you when we are done."

"The place only goes one direction. So please do." I crouched, feeling System assistance with the Stealth skill and hurried past the sloops. I'd get experience from the sloop kills and some credit at the end.

At the moment, my main concern was farming as many Duggarfin teeth as I could. Their poison had become almost too useful for me. And it didn't hurt that they were D ranked teeth. From my assessment at the market, they would be by far my best way to make money.

The thought of trying to play stocks had occurred to me, and I remembered a few changes that would come in these last two years. Yet instead of playing with paper money, I was far more focused on earning gold coins. Besides, by the time I gained enough money through my knowledge of the stock market, it would all collapse and a dollar would be worth about as much as fire kindling or toilet paper.

Digital money would be worth nothing.

It had taken less than a few months after the Rapture for the Gold Coin and bartering to be the only forms of payment. The rich billionaires that immediately hid away in their bunker found out the hard way that the way the world worked would never be the same, and they were no longer on top.

A comrade during the Second Demon War had told me a story of finding some giant bunker in Hawaii a year after the Rapture. The whole group wasn't even Level 10, and his guys ripped the armored door off of the bunker and killed them all to eat the food in the bunker.

The people in the bunker had had a huge stockpile of great things from before the Rapture, and his guys were eager for the nostalgia of something as simple as macaroni and cheese.

Billionaires killed for mac and cheese.

I shook my head from my musings as I reached the pool of Duggarfins that surged out of the deep chasm and took out my net.

It was time to farm some fish.

Chapter 27

By the time that Rodger and Bobby caught up to me in the instance, they both had torn pants. I had a feeling that was from slipping and falling on the wet cavern floor as they weren't bloody enough for it to be sloops. Their hair was disheveled, but otherwise looked fine.

And I had been successful in my part. The entire floor of the room was covered in Duggarfins, several deep.

"Oh, you two came."

One Duggarfin snapped at my foot, and I swiftly kicked it away.

"It was getting a little crowded in here. These are Duggarfin. They have poisonous teeth that are D rank weapons because of their ability Sharp Teeth. They'll tear right through you if you let them." I slung the empty net over my shoulder. "Your job is to use your spells or a weapon and kill as many as you can as fast as you can without losing your fingers."

"Where are these all coming from?" Rodger asked.

I stepped into the water. In response, a swarm shot out of the chasm towards me. I threw my net behind the swarm as I jumped out of the water, hauling in my new load.

The Duggarfins thrashed in the net, but as soon as I got them on land, I poured them into a mound and the fish slipped down. A few tried to reach the water, but I killed them swiftly with a few Blood Bolts.

"They are D rank creatures, meaning if you are using F or E rank abilities, you'll rank up fast against them. Yet they are also super weak because these are the individuals of the swarm. What are you waiting for? Get to killing."

After pausing a moment longer, Bobby and Rodger started to slaughter the weak fish as I had pulled new ones up on the shore. Thankfully, the instance absorbed the bodies as the fish died, creating more space for me.

I continued to haul fish up for them to kill. Over the course of the afternoon, the supply began to dry up.

Bobby leaned against the cavern wall, eating his fancy trail bars. "I got my Acid Splash up to E rank."

"I got my Bow Proficiency up to E rank as well," Rodger said, taking out some foil pouches that he quickly started making into a meal. He seemed overjoyed at how easily he was able to take items in and out of his spatial ring.

"Good, good." I had a sandwich and water. "The next section is more sloops like the first. Only the next set of them are a little stronger and have an ability called Stretch, which does exactly what it sounds like it would do for their necks."

"So just keep them at long range." Bobby nodded. "We got the hang of kiting around the ones in the first section. What's after that?"

"A boss. A very big, two-headed sloop in a room that floods."

"Wait, we have to fight one of these in the water?!" Rodger's eyes were horrified. "The only reason we can fight them is because those flippers aren't meant for land."

"Don't worry. I'll handle the boss." I'd rather do it alone so they wouldn't see my Last Stand ability.

"We are being carried," Bobby muttered, flashing me a small smile. "Thank you, Bran."

"Not a problem. I told you both earlier, I just want the Duggarfin teeth and scales, and maybe a nicer portion of the gold," I admitted.

"Twenty-twenty-sixty?" Bobby asked Rodger.

"I don't think I'm in a place to disagree if you want that, young master." Rodger dipped his head towards Bobby.

The mobster waved his hands in front of him. "Don't call me something like that. Keep that for my older brother."

"Nonsense." Rodger shook his head. "Here soon, you'll be able to mop the floor with your brother, and his entire branch of the family business. Your father must know it too; I'd be shocked if he wasn't planning on elevating you."

Bobby looked to me for support.

Sadly, he didn't find the kind he was looking for. "Rodger isn't wrong. I'd bet Uncle Carmen is planning to promote you to his second when Gloria officially steps back."

"She'll step back?" Rodger was surprised.

Bobby answered the question for me, "My father betrothed her to Bran here. She's going to work with Bran to establish a player business related to the family."

Rodger nodded slowly. "Then we should keep moving."

I drained my water to wash down the sandwich. "I'm going to clear the swarm here and then we'll rest. Tomorrow we'll finish the second half and maybe get a good run at the first half before we rest again. It's going to be a month of farming this place to exhaust the instance."

"Not if we speed up," Bobby countered. "If you went ahead and killed the swarm and then the second half while we took care of the first..." He started to do the math in his head. "We could probably do two a day."

I shook my head. "This swarm monster is too valuable to not take advantage of both for leveling skills and these teeth." I pulled one of the teeth out and played with it between my fingers.

"If you say so." Bobby shrugged. "Let's keep going then."

***

While Bobby and Rodger worked on the second round of sloops, I found the hole at the end that led to the boss's chamber. This time, however, it was a little larger. Bobby's big frame had apparently influenced the sizing of this one. It would still be a little tight for him.

I wiggled through and stretched out on the other side.

Last Stand was a potent ability, but it could only be trained through intense life or death situations. Even against the sloop, I hadn't really felt overwhelmed. My Regeneration and Blood Siphon had done enough to keep me on my feet.

Against the sloop-sloop, especially if I tried to fight it in the water, I might be able to push myself enough to activate Last Stand.

I moved through the opening, quickly assessing what was on the other side. The boss was the same as last time, sleeping against the hole on the other end.

I pulled out the Sloop-tooth Ax and charged the boss recklessly. This time, the plan did not involve any measured approach or using talismans. My goal was to fight with my life on the line and be able to activate Last Stand.

The boss woke up a second before my ax met its head. The teeth of the ax bit into one of the heads before I spun to the side dodging the other.

"Going to have to do better." I wove between the necks and slammed my crafted ax into its body several times.

The shark heads slammed into me seconds later, throwing me against a pillar and trying to pin me. I dodged the second head and scraped my ax along its side. I was trying to do as much damage as possible.

The sloop-sloop thrashed at me, one of its heads catching my side and tearing it apart. I didn't even flinch, my ax continuing to gouge out deep wounds in the shark head with the toothed ax.

A moment later, water began flooding into the room, rapidly going up to my knees then my waist. At that point, the sloop-sloop stopped being so direct and started to swim around me in circles, watching and waiting for a point of weakness.

As it swam, streams of blood filled the water, but it didn't seem to care. It was a System-generated monster after all. The blood was more of a graphic addition than a real injury. System monsters weren't real, at least they weren't organic life.

Hell, the way the System ate humans after they died, people started to wonder about humanity's role in the universe.

I pointed at the boss and started firing Blood Bolts. The sloop-sloop came roaring back, its two jaws wide open. I swam straight into its jaw, putting the ax away for a sloop tooth in each hand and let it grind me with its teeth while I punched it with the teeth of its lesser brethren.

The strategy worked.

The boss did enough damage to me that I felt Last Stand start to itch in the back of my mind. I was starting to understand why Tom and the other Undying I'd met in my past life all shared a reckless streak.

I suddenly felt better the more I was getting hurt, like each injury was its own high. The feeling built until a high like none other flooded me, and I grabbed each side of the sloop-sloop's jaws before prying them open like some sort of hero of myth.

Power flooded my limbs as Last Stand took effect, and I punched the teeth into the sloop-sloop's head and dragged it down the side before kicking it hard.

Even underwater, I was able to send the giant fish careening away from me long enough to swim up to the surface for a deep breath before diving back down.

Between Last Stand and the Swim ability, I shot through the water like a rocket, punching into the sloop-sloop's main body and quickly dealing enough damage to destroy the boss.

The boss quickly dissolved into the water.

As the water started to recede, so did the power of Last Stand. The sudden loss of intelligence hit me hard. I felt like I was drunk. My mind was clearly not firing as quickly.

I held onto one of the pillars for support as I had to blink away the disorientation from the rapid shifts in mental stats.

My body felt weak as well, like I'd just been run over by a large monster, but that was just part of the process, and I was more than accustomed to such shifts with being a berserker class called Breaker in my past life. Like Berserk, Last Stand couldn't be used back-to-back.

I could feel a certain kind of exhaustion telling me that the ability wouldn't activate no matter how hurt I got at present. I wasn't sure how long it would take before I could access it again.

Last Stand was truly worth being the signature ability of an SS rank class. That boost in power was like nothing I had experienced.

I sat down, letting Regeneration do its job while the pillars collapsed and gold cascaded down into the room. Bobby and Rodger would take more time to clear the rest of the instance, so I was left with some time to work through the rest of my F ranked inscription materials. These ones, I wouldn't make with my blood. I wanted to be able to sell them.

Quickly, I started working through all of them and lost track of time.

Bobby's head poked out of the hole as he struggled to get through. "Bran, a little help?"

I shrugged and put down my materials, getting up and dragging Bobby out of the hole. "It was smaller when you weren't here. It seems to fit to the largest person in the group."

"Then remind me to put on a few pounds that I'll lose before next time." Bobby shivered looking at the hole, shaking off the claustrophobia.

He clearly did not like tight spaces.

Rodger was a lanky man and pulled himself through without a problem, crawling forward like it was an old past time of his.

"What's this?" The older man's eyes went up as he stared at the mounds of gold coins.

"When you kill a boss, there's some outpour of treasure," Bobby explained and moved over to a pillar. "These look about even. Rodger, you split one with me and Bran can take the other two."

I picked up a quiver from one of the pillars and tossed it to Rodger. "I'd like both of you to speed up. We'll have to clear this instance quite a bit before we exhaust it like the zombie one."

The zombie one had been fresh. This one seemed to have been around for a while before I had stepped into it for the first time. That meant it would need to be cleared more before exhausted.

"Doesn't bother me." Bobby scooped more of the gold into his ring. "We got quite a few levels from it this time. If there's not some hang up on leveling, we could easily get into the 30's." He rubbed his hands together.

I thought about the ripples in the timeline that I was creating.

Bobby was going to be stronger than last time. A lot stronger. And Tom and his group might have killed several other people. I had no way of knowing if those people living would ultimately be good or bad for me and humanity as a whole.

I liked to think I was empowering people that would make a positive difference, but like a butterfly flapping its wings, I might be creating tempests on the other side of the world.

Chapter 28

Bobby, Rodger, and I continued working our way through the instance for the rest of the week, finally leaving on Friday night and piling into our cars.

The first thing I did was call Simone. "Hope you haven't forgotten about me?"

"Who is this again?" she asked playfully. "Oh. Right. That man that I can't seem to stop thinking about who disappears every week. Was this week fruitful?"

"Very." I emphasized the word. "Tomorrow I need to stop by a bank before I go to the market. You can come with me."

"A vampire bank?" she asked, still staying in the dark about players.

"Yep." I had stopped fighting the little game between us. "They sell things on the down low for us. I have many things from this week."

All of the D rank material would sell exceptionally well on the website. D seemed to be the top rank of commonly available materials. There had been one time that I'd seen a B rank item, but by the time I had clicked on it, the site had told me it was already gone.

"Well. I have some blood samples for you to try. I'll get them laid out if you tell me when you'll be by?" That meant she had finished her little espionage mission into Rick's new people.

"I smell a little like fish right now," I warned her.

"This is a hotel; there are plenty of showers. I'll set up the blood in room 104 for you so that you can shower after." She wasn't backing down.

"Fine. Don't say I didn't warn you, though. I'll be there in twenty to thirty minutes. How are you? Did you run into any trouble with your activities?"

"A little, but I called Gloria and she sorted everything out." Simone sounded downright chipper that I was coming soon. "She's really quite competent when I ask for things."

"Are you asking for a lot?" I frowned, wondering how close the two were getting.

"Is that a tinge of jealousy I hear? I am omnivorous when it comes to sex, but you've made it clear that until I run to the other end of the earth, I'm just for you right now," she teased me.

"I'm not that bad." I found myself smiling. "But thank you for understanding."

"One day. A girl can dream," Simone sighed wistfully. "Maybe you'll sweep me off my feet."

"Soon," I promised her. Quickly, I was caring less about her potential future demonification and more about making her mine. "The wards I gave you are up?"

"Yes. And they haven't caught fire like you warned me. So that means no demons have been pushing their way in. By the way, are demons sexy?" Simone asked. "Would one want to work for me?"

"No. Demons aren't sexy, Simone. They reproduce asexually."

"Eww." Simone seemed completely uninterested in hearing more. "That's a shame."

"Yeah. I don't want to imagine the things that sexually inclined demons would have done." I shuddered.

She was quiet on the other end. "You've fought them before?"

"More than I care to admit." I would answer any question she asked, even if she asked me to spill the whole story. So far, it was clear that she wanted limited information, to protect herself.

Which I was just fine to support. Until a person could enter and actually progress in the player world, knowing would just add stress.

"Is... is that what happened to your past lovers? Is that why you had me put wards around my house?"

Damn her intuition.

"Sort of." I got quiet. "I'm going to hurry to the hotel. Take another five minutes off my arrival time." My foot steadily pressed harder down on the gas. "See you soon." I hung up and roared down the highway.

I arrived in under fifteen minutes from the instance and hopped out of the car, rushing to the room and finding it set ajar with the latch in the doorway.

Simone was inside and as attractive as ever, using a dropper to make a small sampler tray of the blood she had gathered. Tonight she wore a silver dress that glittered every time she moved, and her hair was pulled to the side in a messy side bun. One of her toned legs stuck out the slit in the dress.

"Are you going to stare at my ass all night, or are you going to come say hello?" she asked without turning around.

I locked the door behind me and came up behind her in a flash, easily picking her up by her hips.

"Hold on." She scrambled to put down the vial in her hand and the dropper before I pushed her up against the wall and kissed her.

Her lips were soft and slid against mine easily.

She was an amazing kisser; she kissed with her whole body. Her arms wrapped around my head while her chest melted against mine and her hips heated up as she pressed them against me with need.

Damn, I loved kissing this woman.

Her lips drew me deeper into it until all I could think about was just how incredible they were to touch and suck on.

I came up for a breath as she panted.

"Holy crap, you stink," she laughed and batted my chest. "Do not fuck me while you smell like this. Wow. Were you bathing in fish guts?"

"I warned you." Playfully, I wafted some of my smell at her; a week of killing fish would do that to you.

She shuddered. "I was thinking I'd gotten you a room, but you are going to be showering for the next several hours. Also, I'm going to burn this dress."

"Don't. It looks amazing." I let myself greedily drink her in. The front was even sexier than the back.

"I'll get another. It'll be easier than cleaning this one. Let's focus on the blood, and then I'm going to shoo you away into the bathroom." She waved a hand in front of her face. "I'll have a shower ready for you next week."

I ignored her teasing and checked the blood. She had a few drops in each well of a medical tray. Soul Gaze made short work of identifying the blood, yet I found myself gripping the edge of the table hard enough to make it crack.

"Simone... Simone, where did you get these?" I stared at the dozen samples in front of me.

All of them had bloodlines. Most of them were low level, but the odds that any group of twelve people all had bloodlines was so astronomically small that this wasn't a coincidence.

"They were new girls being transported to Rick's place. I paid off the person transporting them so that I could speak to them quickly and get their blood drawn under the excuse of doing a health exam. Bran, what's wrong?"

My eyes raced over the samples, and I pulled back. After I got more levels, I'd take all of these. I was bound to rank up my class again and restart my levels.

I also didn't get any new abilities from repeating levels. I'd like to get more class abilities before I ranked up again. That and leveling them to E or D first would be good. I didn't want to waste the free rank up.

"All of these have bloodlines," I said, returning to Simone's question. "That's not right. Statistically, that's impossible. So that means that for some reason, Rick is collecting girls with bloodlines."

"Could he be like you?" Simone asked.

I shook my head, a much more realistic idea coming to my mind. "No. That's highly unlikely. I'm very rare if not unique. Simone, you need to stay very far away from Rick."

And I needed to get stronger quickly.

There was a greater force behind Rick if he was collecting girls of bloodlines. Some of the clans and sects could be behind the move, but it could also be demons.

"Is it that bad?" she asked.

"There is most certainly something stronger behind him. The girls. Do you know what happens to them? Do they disappear?" I asked.

She winced. "The women in this situation disappear fairly normally. That's why I run this place without trafficking ladies. I want another option to exist. Nothing will ever change if it's just the same scumbags running everything."

"Simone. You must promise me that you won't antagonize Rick. In return, I'll promise you that I will go after him. Hard." I stared at her hard, making sure she could see that I was serious. All joking about me smelling like fish was long gone.

This was deathly serious.

Fuck. This was something she might very well have gotten involved in even if I wasn't here.

I started pacing.

"Bran?" she asked.

"I'm very worried about you. I'm tempted to lock you up in a vault or send you away on a vacation for a few weeks so that I don't have to worry." The more I thought about this situation, the more I realized that this was likely how she had become possessed the first time around.

"I have the tooth you gave me." She watched me.

"Yeah. That might stop some things, but it won't stop this." I rubbed my forehead. "Stay at my place for a few weeks and don't go near Rick again. I know you are trying to help those girls, and they are in enough danger that I'll be right there with you, but I need to prepare."

The more I thought of it, the more I realized she would have tangled with Rick even sooner if I wasn't here. If there was a demon behind him, this was likely how they had either gotten her scent or possessed her in the first place. That meant that a Demon General's soul was here in Vein City right now.

I might even go ask my mother for help. Once she recovered from the poison, she shouldn't be a pushover. Given that she was from the Heros family, I had a feeling that her strength was more akin to an A rank at her level. That would be strong enough to crush Tom at a similar level, even with his Last Stand active and not playing tricks with blinding him.

That was the difference of an A rank.

My mind raced through all the possibilities. My mother might have more resources than she ever let on in my past life. But she also wasn't alive when the first Rapture occurred. It was very likely that she would be tempting enough that a demon would go for her for her bloodline. We were talking about a demon general's soul in play. Even my mother wouldn't stand up to it right now.

"I'll stay at your place and drop it," Simone promised and held my arm. "Are you going to drink the blood? It made you stronger last time."

I shook my head. "That'll cause something to happen that I'm not quite ready to happen." It was tempting, though. "The problem is that I don't know how strong this new enemy is yet. I think there's a demon behind Rick."

"A not-sexy demon," she tried to lighten the atmosphere.

"A very not-sexy demon. They are interested in those with bloodlines. And the people they want do not survive," I warned Simone with a look. "You would be very tempting to them given that your blood is even better than these. Try not to get cut, give blood, or anything for a while." A thought occurred to me. "That girl that Rick was trying to strong arm away from you a few weeks ago… was she one of the ones whose blood I reacted to from the freezer?"

Simone's eyes drifted to the side as she thought through the available information. "Yes. She was one of them."

I rubbed at my forehead. The pieces were starting to come together. And if I had not been around, Rick would have taken that girl. And Simone would have started to try to take him down.

Eventually, the demon behind this would have learned of Simone's bloodline and then possessed her. And that meant Rick could be backed by a future very powerful demon.

My goal at the moment was to delay any awareness of Simone's bloodline for as long as I could. I needed to be stronger. The demon was collecting weak women who weren't even inducted into the System. It likely wasn't strong at this point in time.

Demons split their souls and then sent them out, possessing additional people. Their soul would corrupt the body and turn it into a demon. That was how they spread.

Given that this one was using Rick as a front spoke of its current weakness. The main body would still be decently strong.

I glanced at Simone.

There was another option.

Knowing that she would be possessed by a future demon general, I could use her to lure the demon out of its body and into her. If it were a challenge of the soul, I stood a fairly good chance at beating the demon.

Chapter 29

My weekend went by quickly.

My mother was little help, still in the hospital letting herself recover. She was already several times stronger than me, though, and her stats were still going up. The clans were just that terrifying, and she wasn't even someone important to the Heros Clan.

Yet when I told her I'd found a demon, all she did was tell me to avoid it and anyone it was interested in.

Going to the market again was a bust besides getting more treated paper and a few more ingredients. However, my visit to the bank went well. I sold twenty Duggarfin Teeth and a few Sloop Leathers along with my bundle of inscriptions.

Interestingly, the inscriptions that were selling the best were low rank lightning ones that were apparently used by the bank and other players to generate electricity. Essentially, they were just buying portable chargers...

What a waste.

The cloaking and illusion ones made perfect sense to me, though. And I also got the point of the ones that provided some comfort. But what was the point in saving electricity? People's priorities in this age were just so backwards.

I guessed it didn't matter if that was what they wanted them for. I was mostly interested in the gold they would pay for the inscriptions. Soon I'd find myself with plenty of gold coins for my plans.

I planned to reinvest all of the initial profits into more materials for several cycles until I was satisfied. Most of the coins that I had went right back into the exchange to fund this new venture, along with what I'd gotten from the instance.

Going back into the instance after the weekend, I repeated the cycle for the next two weeks. I stayed inside the instance for a week, and farmed levels and gold coins. Then on the weekend, I offloaded all of my inscriptions into the market before sucking up all of the materials that presented themselves.

Finishing out another week inside the instance, I sat back at a desk amid the broken pillars of the completed boss room, working on my inscriptions while Bobby and Rodger finished the second half of the sloops.

My level had grown quickly to 25, and then slowed down on the climb to 30. But I was determined to see if there was a class skill at 30 that would be worthwhile before taking the blood that Simone had prepared for me.

I could tell that she was getting antsy about the situation with Rick, and so was I. I had gotten materials that would allow her to send me a message with a talisman, even if I was inside an instance.

[Name: Bran Heros
Level: 28
Class: Blood Hegemon F
Status: Healthy
Strength: 82
Agility: 70
Vitality: 78
Intelligence: 64
Spirit: 11010

Skills:
Soul Gaze SSS
Soul Resilience S
Blunt Weapon Proficiency E
Endurance E
Throwing Proficiency F
Blood Boil D
Blood Siphon D
Blood Bolt D
Bloodline Collection 4
Regeneration D

Fire Resistance F
Poison Resistance E
Ax Proficiency E
Charge F
Bloodink Quality F
Stealth F
Inscription E
Swim D (Bracer)
Last Stand F
Blood Hex E
Blood Transfusion E]

    I had received two different abilities with my leveling. One came at Level 20 and another at 25. Though it certainly wasn't guaranteed that I'd get an ability every five levels, it was nice to pick up more for now.

    Blood Hex worked when I put my blood on another creature. I could give the creature a variety of curses. My prior experience in inscriptions played well. Curses and inscriptions were two sides of the same coin.

    As for Blood Transfusion... it was essentially a way to heal. Which was fairly useless for me most of the time. Still, I found a way to level it. I had to prove to Bobby that he could get a resistance if he let me heal him while he poisoned himself with Duggarfin teeth.

    It worked, but he had quit as soon as he had gotten E rank Poison Resistance. Then he called me a mad man. It was probably for the best that he hadn't seen me letting the fish eat parts of my body.

    I worked on my talismans with a hum that a man only made when he was raking in the cash. These were selling well, and I'd earned a reputation on the market.

    A System screen popped up. I glanced at it, doing a double take. I had expected it to be Bobby and Rodger having finished.

[Pink Yuan Bloodline currently being corrupted.
Bloodline will be lost if owner is corrupted.]

I shot to my feet, knocking over the desk. With a wave of my hand, I sucked the desk into my spatial ring before it shattered on the floor. My feet beat across the stone as I rushed towards the hole to squeeze back through to where Bobby and Rodger were working on the sloops.

"Bran!" Bobby shouted. They had a beat-up sloop still chasing them.

I threw my hand forward. A Blood Bolt hit the Sloop before a diagram appeared before my hand, cursing the monster with 'Weaken'. I withdrew Tom's heavy sword from my spatial ring and jumped onto the monster, finishing it in three swings.

"We are getting out of here!" I hit the button on the menu that popped up in front of me and found both of them coming out of the instance behind me.

There was no time to explain the situation. I grabbed them and zipped through the quarry to explode out of the water and run up the ladder with superhuman balance, not even using the hand rails as I tossed them both on the ground and jumped into my jeep.

Bobby was right behind me, getting into the passenger seat. Rodger jumped into the back.

"What's wrong?" Bobby asked.

"Simone is under attack." It was dark enough out that she'd be at her business. My foot hit the gas, accelerating to top speed in seconds as the jeep sprayed mud from the work site behind us.

I slapped a talisman on the dash, making the car harder to notice. Most normal people's eyes would just slip off of it. This talisman was becoming very popular.

"The fucker. We'll kill them." Bobby punched his hands together.

"It was an unwise decision," Rodger echoed with more control.

"It's a demon," I told both of them. "Beings that live in our world and are very dangerous."

"We can still kill them, right?" Bobby asked.

"Think of them as the opposing force to players. Like us, they can level. I don't know what level this one is or how many there are," I explained, continuing to fly down the highway.

Bobby leaned back, nibbling at his thumb. "We are going to the Hotel? Do you think Candy is involved?"

"If one's attacking Simone, it is unlikely that it's being subtle." I continued to hit the gas, desperately hoping I reached Simone in time.

***

Simone played at adjusting the glasses and bottles. Weekdays had become boring, and she lived for the weekends with Bran.

The mysterious man of power had a certain allure to him.

It was obvious from the moment that she saw him that he wasn't what he seemed. The man felt like an old, grizzled veteran that had seen some shit, yet walked in with a body that was like he had just finished growing. That young face had ancient eyes.

The enigma had interested her at first and then even more as she had gotten to know him.

Bran had become a bright spot, and she looked forward to every weekend. She knew he wouldn't describe himself that way, but she saw more inside of him. He cared. He just hid it under a bit of a rough and dark exterior.

She rinsed out the glasses and glanced at one of the napkins that Bran had placed on the bar. His reaction a few weeks ago was troubling, yet she had stayed out of trouble and followed his advice. Instead, she was just minding her business.

He would prepare and deal with whatever came. Bran reeked of reliability. But she could tell that something weighed on him. Sometimes it felt like he was carrying the weight of the world.

She wanted to help, but knew at the same time that she couldn't. The joke about the fountain of youth had sparked

Bran to become more serious to the point that she wondered if she might actually get it one day.

The door to her establishment opened up, and two big men walked in with a cloaked figure behind them.

Immediately, she didn't like the look of the men. Her intuition had always been keen, and those two didn't sit right with her.

"Oh. New customers!" One of her girls had been walking this way and did her job in greeting the three.

As the girl stepped forward, the cloaked figure jerked to a stop as if they'd hit an invisible wall that they started to push. The two men moved forward to snatch the working girl.

"Hands off. If you are looking for something rough, this isn't the place," Simone snapped, her hand falling to her purse and the tooth that Bran had given her.

The cloaked figure shrieked, and Simone saw one of Bran's wards glow before the napkin caught fire.

Her eyes went wide, and she took the dagger, still in the plastic bag, out of her purse. Not hesitating, she moved to stab one of the big men. He blocked the hit with his arm, but the tooth went right through the bag and stabbed into his arm as if it was a block of Jello, not flesh and muscle.

Simone stepped back, taking the tooth with her as a horrible sight unfolded in front of her face.

The man gasped. Black lines raced down his arm, and he fell over, his lips going blue.

"Get her!" the cloaked figure yelled, the sentence ending as it shrieked once more. Another of Bran's napkins caught fire as the demon pushed on the invisible wall in front of it.

The hood on the figure fell back.

Half of the woman's face was covered in a black substance like bubbling tar, and her eyes were just wrong. An inhuman quality filled them, like something out of a horror movie. Her black, clawed hand slammed against the barrier and destroyed another of Bran's napkins.

Simone didn't have time to process the fact that she'd just killed someone as she thrust the tooth at the second man as he tried to grab her. The tooth slid neatly through him before the hostess stand exploded.

Girls and customers were shouting behind Simone, and someone must have pulled a gun because shots rang out and hit the cloaked figure, causing the demon to jerk back before continuing forward.

"All of you shall suffer." The demon produced a red piece of glass that glowed with a swirling inner light that she threw into the center of the room. It shattered, and red wisps shot out in every direction.

Simone watched the wisps. The bits of red seemed to be alive as they sought people out, diving into their heads. Simone watched in horror as one particularly large red wisp hovered like it was watching all of the others and then shifted as if it were evaluating her.

A moment later, it dove right towards her head.

Not knowing what to do, Simone threw the tooth at it to no avail as the red wisp passed right through the tooth, then her hands. She saw the horror that existed in that wisp before it landed on her forehead.

Another of Bran's creations, a card he'd asked her to hold onto, glowed brightly, and a flash went through the entire room, stunning the wisps without a body, causing them to float aimlessly. The people who'd been infected by the red wisps passed out.

Simone, for the first time in a long while, prayed. She prayed for God to help her. Because if demons were real, she hoped so were angels or something else that could save her.

Blinking and trying to clear her head from the sheer panic taking over, she realized she was waking on a bed with Bran standing over her.

Something was wrong with his smile, though.

"Simone. Welcome back. I was worried about you." He pushed himself onto her, but she kicked him back.

Something was wrong.

She trusted her intuition. It had not led her astray yet. And it was currently telling her to run. It was saying to run very far away from the Bran in front of her.

Simone frowned, trying to remember what had just happened before she'd been unconscious, but nothing came. She rolled off the bed before she started to run, fumbling and stumbling, as if someone was shaking the floor underneath her.

"Simone, come back. You're mine, and no one else shall touch you. I will have you!" His voice cracked with something deeper within it. The Bran-lookalike chased after her.

Chapter 30

I threw the door to Simone's establishment open so hard that I broke the hinges off.

As I stepped inside, I spotted people passed out everywhere. Unconscious figures were strewn across all the furniture as if they'd been knocked out mid-panic.

"What's that!" Bobby pointed at a figure that stood with tarry skin that looked like it had bubbled from being burnt.

"Demon," I answered, activating Soul Gaze to see what we were up against.

[~~Amanda Slate~~ Pryyfen
Level: 15
Class: Seeker E
Strength: 143
Agility: 192
Vitality: 151
Intelligence: 193
Spirit: 336

Skills:
Inspect B
Search B
Locate Object B
Tag C
Possession D]

I let out a sigh of relief. This demon was just a seeker. A fairly weak one at that.

CHAPTER 30

My eyes flitted past the seeker to Simone, who was passed out on the floor. I'd have to take care of this demon first so that I could help her. She was likely battling in her soul.

The talisman I'd given her would act on a soul attack and would stun low-level demons. But a soul attack at the level of the demon general that had possessed her before would only be slowed down. The talisman was not strong enough to stop that attack.

The demon tried to Inspect me. I shrugged off the assessment.

"Bobby, Rodger, find everyone in this place and put one of these on their forehead." I gave them both a stack of talismans. Knowing a demon was going to be in my future, I was prepared with Soul Sealing Talismans.

"What about... that?" Bobby pointed to the Seeker.

"Don't worry. I can handle it." I drew the Sloop-tooth Ax from my spatial ring and twirled it in my hand while I quietly put a fist full of Duggarfin teeth in my other hand.

Seekers weren't combatants in the demon army. They had the stats and could wield a weapon, but their purpose was often to be runners for greater demons and expendable forward scouts.

It seemed this one was here in Vein City seeking hosts for a number of demon souls that it had in its possession. There was likely a stronger demon running the show, but this one was manageable.

The Seeker tried to Inspect me again, and when it failed, it turned, trying to grab Simone.

"I don't think so!" I rushed forward, stabbing the demon with the Duggarfin teeth and slamming the ax into its foot. The ax scraped off the hardened skin of the demon, but the teeth punched through its side and poisoned it.

Still, the Seeker was trying to take Simone. She likely had the soul of a demon general in her, and the Seeker was doing its best to recover the general at all cost.

I threw my body on the Seeker, biting my tongue and spitting blood on it before I drew on my spirit's strength to curse the demon. My blood boiled as the curse nearly failed, but the F grade blood imprinted a blindness curse on the demon that would last a minute.

The Seeker thrashed out at me. One of its hands had claws, and I used the ax to hold that arm off as my fistful of Duggarfin teeth continued to slam into its side.

I was pissed off, memories flooding back from years and years of demon fights. I had not expected to encounter a demon so soon when I had first started this journey, but I was certainly experienced in these situations.

Letting out a wild cry, I headbutted the demon in the face.

The dark, boiled skin of a demon was tough, and I bled from the headbutt. Using the blood, I activated my ability and put a low rank curse of weakening on the demon.

The demon twisted, slipping away from the ax as it tore a chunk out of my forearm. Ignoring the pain, I used the blood to curse it again with wracking pain.

"You dare think you can defeat me going all out?!" I roared at the demon, throwing my body like a madman at it, letting my blood flow freely as I cursed it with blood repeatedly.

The demon grew weak and fragile from my repeated curses until I grabbed it by the head, slamming it against the bar until the granite counter cracked. Then I stood up as the demon faded into the world.

I picked up the spatial ring it left behind and pulled out my phone. "Gloria, I need a group to watch the front of Simone's place. She was just attacked. I'm here, but I'm going to be dealing with the aftermath." I didn't wait for a response and hung up before kneeling down to look at Simone.

There was some blood on her, but no injury. I breathed out a sigh of relief and pasted one half of a talisman on Simone's forehead and the other on my own. Taking a deep breath to steady myself, I headbutted her for the two talismans to touch and felt my body fall through the ground.

Simone's soul space was expansive, like a stretching hallway.

Ah.

I could feel it. She was racing away from the demon general, unconsciously stretching the hallway between the two of them and running through branching hallways. Sadly, her soul was far too weak and the demon general was quickly recovering his strength from the stun.

I shattered all of the hallways she'd made, stepping through her soul space in an instant as the demon general caught up to her.

That fucker. He was wearing my face!

I caught the back of his neck, the eyes of my soul glowing like two bright suns as Soul Gaze activated. "Simone. I'm the jealous type. What are you doing playing with this mockery?"

[Bizjub
Class: Void Slayer S
Level: 329
Strength: -
Agility: -
Vitality: -
Intelligence: -
Spirit: 3058]

"Bran!" she shouted. "You're... older and taller."

I remembered that my soul didn't look the same as the body Simone knew. Instead, I resembled me in my past life, looking closer to my late forties and standing at 7'3".

"You called me an old soul the first time we met. You had no idea how close you actually were. Right now we are in your soul, and this demon was attempting to eat you."

"He's lying. Kill him!" the demon shouted in my voice.

I stared at the demon, my Soul Gaze ripping apart the demon's disguise.

What was left was an angry, red creature that only vaguely resembled a human being. The thing was a bipedal with a head, with three arms and a tail that tried to smack me.

I broke the attack with a wave of my hand. A demon general from the first demon wave was not my match in spirit power.

"You!" It struggled in futility against my strength.

I broke several more of its limbs. "Simone, I'm going to explain everything after this is over. Because I have a surprise for you. This thing? It can be your shot at the fountain of youth."

Simone's soul form turned to me in shock. "What do I have to do?"

"Good. We are in your soul. Meaning that you technically can do anything you want. Homefield advantage is huge in matters of the soul. That means you can eat the soul of this demon and steal his power." I pushed the demon down onto the ground. "He was going to feast on your soul and possess your body. Instead, you can take what his soul has to offer, including the power that can keep you younger. It'll do a lot more than that."

"Like make me bulletproof?" Simone asked.

"Soul Absorption Arts are dead. We destroyed every record in this world." Bizjub struggled.

"I hate to tell you, but you failed." I smirked. The arts had come from other worlds during the Second Demon War. "Simone, what you need to do is absorb him. He's nothing but a soul. Think of him like a vapor and breathe him in. Strip him of all his strength."

Bizjub struggled, but I kept him pinned.

Simone had to be the one to kill him for this to work. And she would benefit greatly from this demon. Soul-eating arts could take a skill at low levels, and at high levels, you could even take a demon's strength.

Though, they weren't for the faint of heart.

She sat down and stared at the demon soul as I kept him pinned on the ground. Taking a deep breath, she pulled. It took a moment, but soon the demon began to pull apart like he was made of smoke and funnel into her mouth.

"Good. Good. This isn't your real body. It's a soul, so you don't have lungs to fill. Just keep breathing in until he's completely gone." I broke more of Bizjub's body and hurried behind Simone to put a hand to her back, injecting some of my spirit into her to crush parts of Bizjub's soul that he tried to reform so that he could attack her from within. There was no way she could take a soul of this strength on her own.

Simone kept going, trusting me to handle anything else around her.

Taking in another soul was a rather simple art, but there were a few tricks, like being able to neutralize the other person during it or avoiding the pitfall of them attacking you from within.

I was here to guide Simone. "You're doing great. He's almost gone."

She took one last huge breath in, draining the rest of the demon into her. "I feel bloated."

"It's going to take a bit to digest him, if you will." Sending several more spikes into her spirit, I destroyed all of Bizjub's presence from the power inside of her. "You might sleep for a while. I need to return to my body now so that I can take care of the rest of your girls and make sure you stay safe."

"There was one in..." She paused, reading my face. "Oh. Right. Well, then I'll just sit here bloated until I wake up next to you. You will be there, right?"

"Yes. As soon as I take care of the rest of the people at your place, I'm taking you back to my apartment and putting you in my bed where I can watch over you." I kissed her forehead. "When you wake up, I'll tell you everything. I'll explain it all and help you adapt. I promise."

She nodded. "Alright, take care of my girls. You... you handled that demon like he was nothing." She stared up at me. "I'm glad you came, that you came to save me when I needed you most."

"Don't worry, I said I was going to handle it. Besides, I've fought much worse." I kissed her again and pulled out of her soul. She'd recover faster if my giant spirit presence wasn't weighing down on her.

"Bran?" Gloria had already arrived and was sitting on a couch not far from me. "I didn't want to separate you two."

"Good job." I stood up and dusted off my pants. Time flowed strangely in soul spaces. "A demon attacked here. They shattered an object full of demon souls that are trying to invade the bodies of everyone who has passed out. I've done some measures to stall them, but I need to clear them out. I used the one in Simone's body to turn her into a player."

Gloria swallowed. "She's a player now?"

"Will be when she wakes up," I answered.

"What about the rest of them? Are all her girls about to become players?" Gloria glanced around the room at the girls that were now laid out on cots and blankets to keep them comfortable.

"No. The rest won't be so easy. I'll see if Bobby can't turn Candy into one. It requires a level of trust to guide them through the process. For the rest, I'll enter their souls and crush the demon," I said.

Gloria hesitated for a moment. "Could you turn me into a player with one?"

I stared at her for a long second. "You want me to inject a demon into you and let you kill it so that you can become a player?"

"If Bobby's girl can do it, then so can I," Gloria countered.

I thought for a long moment. "Fine. Only you, though."

I could probably catch one and stuff it in my soul to carry it over. But that wasn't something I was going to do repeatedly. Going into someone's soul required a lot of force, and then for them to even listen to my soul-eating arts, it required trust.

"Let me get started on crushing these demons." I pasted a talisman to my forehead and one to a girl on the floor before I headbutted her.

A few seconds later I stood back up, having hurried through the process. These weak souls weren't worth me eating.

"She's good. Move her over to a place to recover, and get your people to keep bringing me other ones. Also, find and bring over Bobby so that I can explain to him and you at the same time how this goes."

Chapter 31

The night had been exhausting.

The last thing I remembered was Rodger helping me bring Simone back to my place and passing out with her in bed.

I woke up to a feeling of pleasurable warmth between my legs.

"Oh," Simone moaned, and a pair of glowing, green eyes pierced my own as I opened them in the darkness of night. "I've been waiting for this."

She ran her tongue along the base of my shaft like one would savor their favorite ice cream flavor. I groaned and pressed my head into my pillow. Her tongue was incredible, pushing firmly against the head and swirling around it with dexterity.

"Simone." I reached down and grabbed her hair, running my fingers through it and curling them to get a grip. "Don't stop." I held her lips to my cock.

"Oh, I won't. You know, I liked you quite a bit, but there is such a thing as being worried about physical compatibility." A warm hand curled around my shaft and pumped it with languid strokes. "Thankfully, we don't have to worry. You have more than enough to satisfy me."

Her tongue played with the tip, flicking it repeatedly before peppering it with kisses and leaving little patches of saliva all over. I bucked against her lips, wanting to be in their warmth.

It had been a while since I had been with a woman, and she was teasing me. Her pouty lips enfolded the head, and my abs tensed before her wet, silky tongue started to play over it as she bobbed over me.

I gently rocked her head. "Gods."

She was using a gentle suction. Her pillowy lips were sealed tight around the shaft, running up and down it while her fingers played delicately at the base.

"Even bigger?" she moaned around it. "Oh, please." She licked it. "I'm going to love this."

Her glowing, green eyes pinched slightly as the pressure increased, and she started to slowly pump the base with firm, steady strokes.

"That's it. Take it deeper." I rocked her head down deeper, feeling my head tickle at the entrance to her throat.

Her eyes stared at me amusingly as if I'd just issued a challenge.

A tight, wet warmth engulfed my top slowly as she continued to stare at me while two fingers pinched in a ring started to pump the base as quickly as she could.

She swallowed around me, continuing to bob, this time with far more pressure and quick, slick motions back and forth.

I wasn't pushing her down anymore. I was holding on. "Simone, fuck. I'm going to cum."

She increased the pressure of the suction again like she was going to suck it out of me.

And she did.

My hips bucked, and I pumped my seed down her throat as she let out satisfied coos and slowly drew my cock out of her mouth.

"Damn. I feel like an idiot for waiting if it was going to be like that." I told her, shuddering as she licked the sensitive head again.

"You'll be able to go another round, right?" She licked it again, using her pillowy lips to tease my head before her hand cupped the head, rubbing in small circles.

I chuckled. "Simone, you have awoken a beast. I can go all night."

In response, she gave me a smile as she leaned down and swallowed my cock again. This time, there was no gentle build up. She worked it amazingly, yet I was so over-sensitive that I balled my sheets with my fists. She had to lean on my pelvis to keep it down on the bed as she gave me the most mind-blowing blowjob of my life.

It left me gasping on the bed.

"Don't tell me you are already defeated?" She crawled on top of me, and I could only make out her outline in the dark and those glowing, green eyes.

"Not a chance." I grabbed her hips, my stiff member already recovering.

"Good. Because I have to thank you for today. Thank you so many times." She slid back, her thighs already moist from giving me head. "I know you don't want me to call you a hero, but it's pretty tempting."

"Maybe for you. I could rush into danger to save you. It wouldn't be so bad to be your hero," I answered honestly, feeling the lips of her labia running along my cock.

"No. When demons came, I prayed." Simone's voice became a whisper. "It was you who came to dispel my demons." She shifted forward quickly, catching the tip in her folds and then sank back onto me.

I ran my hands along the smooth skin of her tight ass and along her toned thighs, brushing the inner side.

Simone hummed as my hand explored her. "Yes." She rocked slowly. "I want you to feel good. That's the best part of sex, making your partner moan, groan, and beg for more." Her hips rolled as her sex squeezed me.

"Things are going to change." I let out a breath as she rolled her hips again.

"I know, but I get to know more now. Perhaps I'll get to stick around more too?" she asked, squeezing me into her once again.

"Sex aside, I already wanted to tell you everything after you were initiated. You have the screens?"

"Yes, but be quiet." She placed a finger over my lips as she started to settle into a languid rhythm that drove me crazy.

She wasn't quite moving fast enough to set me off, and I wanted to thrust up into her, drive her against a wall for more. But she put her hands on my chest and closed her eyes, her hips curling and pumping over me.

"I want to savor tonight."

"There will be many more nights," I promised.

"Oh. I know there will be. I'm going to make sure of it. Sit up a little?" Simone asked.

I put an arm around her waist and pulled myself back towards the headrest, squishing the pillow into the small of my back for support.

She leaned on me, her breasts pressing against my chest and her breath tickling into my ear. "So many more nights." She sank herself down on me slowly whispering, "You're not going to get rid of me."

"I never wanted to." I kissed her cheek and held her slim waist against me. "Oh, that feels great." She was like a vice made of liquid silk, squeezing my cock as she rode me slowly. "But I need more."

"This?" she asked, picking up the pace. "Or this?" She picked it up further. "Or maybe this." She started to ride me at breakneck speeds. "Cum for me. Fill me up," she started to whisper sweet nothings into my ear.

They weren't words but soft coos and encouraging moans as her sex soaked my balls.

I held her hips, grunting as she expertly brought me to the peak and then slowed down. "Don't you dare."

"Give it to me," she whispered.

I threw her to the side, rolling with her and pinning her hips to the bed before I started pistoning into her.

"Yes!" she let out a loud shout.

I barely heard her over my desire, and crushed our hips together with wet slaps until I had my release. A moment after, I looked down, realization hitting me. "I didn't make you come."

"Oh, I did." She hooked her legs behind me and pulled me down on top of her, peppering my neck with soft kisses. "I have an admission to make."

"What's that?" I played her game.

"I came more than you." She licked my neck. "I love sex, and I orgasm easily. So the fun is making my partner wild." She pulled at my hips with her legs pushing me in slightly before pulling me out. "I want you to enjoy me and come back for more."

"That's not going to be a problem." I kissed her.

"But Gloria?" she asked, a hint of vulnerability in her tone.

"You don't need to worry." I shifted slightly to get my knees in a better position. "You won't be left behind. Besides, I don't think I'll ever get enough of this." I thrust into her, my cock twitching with readiness for another round. "There are things we'll need to prep—" I was stopped by a kiss as she squeezed my hips forward again.

I wasn't stupid enough to keep talking and started railing her again before picking her up and flipping her over on the bed. This time, I took her from behind and then against the wall.

Afterwards, we moved out into the kitchen for a juice break only for her to wind up bent over the counter and begging for more.

***

At some point in the night, we must have fallen asleep because I woke up to a blonde woman with familiar green eyes going down on me. She closed her eyes again and focused.

I was stunned.

The strangest part of the moment was that she was wearing a nun's veil and the sexiest habit I'd ever seen. The woman's face was innocent as she dutifully performed her blow job like she was worshiping my cock.

"Simone?" I asked, my voice shuddering as a pair of familiar lips made me cum as she pulled her lips off to answer.

My seed sprayed all over her face as she shifted like she was trying to get it evenly across both cheeks.

"Morning. I was just performing my daily supplication. Though, I'm a greedy woman who might need it more than once a day." She licked at the cum on her face.

I had so many questions. Rather than ask, I activated Soul Gaze and pierced the illusion wrapped around her. Using my ability, I saw the Simone I knew, but with a younger face.

"Gloria showed up a few minutes ago and thought I'd wake you." Simone stood and twirled around.

The veil had more cloth to it than the rest of her outfit. It somehow hung loosely, but was so thin and pulled tight that it was beyond sexy, not to mention it showed off the sheer, thigh-high stockings that squeezed her thighs.

"A wonderful wake up. Here I thought I was going to be answering your questions this morning, yet I find myself with more than enough of my own." I blinked and shifted Soul Gaze to check her character sheet. My jaw fell open. "Wow."

Simone had a big smirk on her face. "That's the kind of reaction a woman wants to hear."

"Enjoying that shot from the fountain of youth I see," I teased her, trying to regain my footing.

"Yes, I am. I didn't sleep last night. After I got enough of your cuddles, I went and browsed the internet to understand how video games work a little better. It seems like I'm living one now?" she asked.

I was still staring at her stats.

[Simone Sweet
Level: 68
Class: Lilim Saint SSS
Status: Overjoyed, aroused
Strength: 284
Agility: 284
Vitality: 282
Intelligence: 287
Spirit: 386

Skills:
Soul Absorption Art F
Radiant Insight C
Disguise A
Lilith's Gaze F
Blessing of Lilim F
Lilim's Whisper F
Saint's Mercy F
Bastion of Athena F

Sanctified Bonds F
Veil of Netherlight F
Wracking Pain F
Soothing Kiss F
Heartbreaker F
Pink Yuan Bloodline A (Unawakened)(Claimed)]

The more I read, the further my brows rose.

"I mean this as politely as possible, Simone. I'm a little jealous of your abilities." She was an SSS rank class! That meant she got twenty stat points per level. Plus she had multiple class specific abilities that I'd never seen before and had to drill into to get a better understanding.

About the only thing that hadn't caught me off guard was her level. Given that I let her get full credit for the demon general, I wasn't surprised that it had given her so many levels. It seemed she had absorbed a small part of its spirit power and a skill too.

But to add an SSS rank class to that for the stat points... Simone certainly had far greater potential than I expected.

"So, that means I'm strong?" she asked, squinting at me and activating Lilith's Gaze, which was an improved Inspection.

I instinctively pushed it aside.

"Because I can see Gloria's stats and she's just normal for now, waiting on you for guidance. But I can't see yours." She squinted again.

"You don't have to squint to see it. Just focus on the ability," I joked. "I'll explain everything in a moment. Let me get some clothes so that I can go over this with you and Gloria at the same time."

I needed a moment to wrap my head around some of her abilities.

Disguise had clearly come from the demon general, which was how she was appearing as she did this morning and why it was already at A rank.

As for Radiant Insight, that was an ability I had only vague knowledge of from my past life. A phoenix clan that assisted our world in the second demon war had it. I could only assume it was an innate skill that came from her Yuan Bloodline. Still, it did explain a few things.

As for the rest of her abilities, they were likely tied to her class which appeared to focus on healing, with a few unique abilities.

I couldn't believe she had the vaunted Bastion of Athena. It was a healer ability for the mind, protecting it from the horrors of battle and war. More people lost the ability to fight because of a deteriorated mental state than anything else in the First Demon War.

That ability alone would make Simone a precious treasure, but with everything else, she was priceless.

Chapter 32

I sat at the breakfast table as Gloria gave me a prepared plate, which was a lovely meat stuffed omelet.

"You cook?" I asked her, slightly surprised.

"No. I just think eating out of Styrofoam is depressing." She sipped her coffee. "So..." Her eyes shifted to Simone who was happily pretending to be a slutty nun. "Things changed."

Simone had picked her class based on her intuition skill and a few internet searches last night.

"Yes, they did. Simone told me you haven't picked your class yet." I started eating as Simone sat down next to me and started eating her own meal.

"No. I asked Bobby, and he said you were the expert. I have twenty-seven options." She glanced at a menu that I couldn't see.

"That's not a bad number. The classes are all ranked. A being the highest and S above that, with SS and SSS even above that," I explained quickly.

"I have one SS," she reported.

I stopped eating and squinted at her. Were both of these girls going to be ridiculous? "What's the class?"

"Twilight Flamecaller," she reported.

"Impossible. In order to have that class, you have to have the bloodline of..." I trailed off, staring at her hair. "Fuck. That's not dyed, is it?" I tried to figure out how I had not put the pieces together earlier.

I thought her hair was just a trendy dye because Bobby didn't have the bloodline, but perhaps it came from Gloria's mother, meaning it ran in the Nester blood. Her Mother was the original Nester family member. Carmen had inherited the Nester family when she had died from cancer.

"Yeah. My mother and brothers dye theirs to be dark. Mine never dyed well, though. It took tons of bleach to get rid of the color so that I could turn it into anything else." She played with her hair. "Finally I just gave up."

"It's probably because the blood runs stronger through you. Prick your finger, please," I told her.

Simone chuckled. "He's not a vampire. He swears." She seemed to be in a fantastic mood. Somehow, all of this seemed to have taken a weight off her shoulders rather than add to her burdens.

Gloria pulled a pocket knife from her jacket and pricked her finger without a problem. A little bead of blood welled up, and I wanted to throw myself across the table to get a taste of it.

[Gloria Nester's Blood
Magnamalo Bloodline S (Unawakened)]

"This isn't even fair," I groaned. "Yeah. You have the bloodline of the Magnamalo."

Both ladies blinked at me.

"It's a big, ancient monster, kind of like a bulky sabertooth tiger but with huge spiny blades on its shoulder, and sort of a fleshy flower around its head," I explained, fanning my hands by the side of my head, trying to keep myself under control.

"Why the fuck is that in my blood?" Gloria looked at the drop accusingly.

"That goes into the long history of our world and the universe at large." I sat back. "Take the Twilight Flamecaller. It's a fantastic class. And a class with SS rank will serve you very well."

Gloria tapped the air in front of her before she groaned and held her stomach.

"That's your body adjusting." I used Soul Gaze on her.

[Gloria Nester
Level: 17
Class: Twilight Flamecaller SS
Status: Confused, Jealous
Strength: 48

Agility: 42
Vitality: 51
Intelligence: 62
Spirit: 49

Skills:
Inspect F
Flame Mastery F
Twilight Ember F
Twilight Shroud F
Fireball F
Magic Resistance F
Tough Skin F
Magnamalo Bloodline S (Unawakened)(Unclaimed)]

"That sucked," Gloria groaned and took another sip of her coffee. "Will that happen all the time?"

"Only when you gain a large portion of stats compared to your current ones at once," I explained. "Your level caught up once you picked your class and boosted those stats. Congratulations. Now you could pick up a football and charge through an entire defensive line. Also, you are bulletproof."

"Really?" she asked.

"Yeah. Though Simone can get shot, she'd basically just shrug it off with her vitality," I explained.

Both girls were looking critically at each other with their Inspection.

"Holy crap. She's strong." Gloria was looking at Simone's sheet with wide eyes.

"She's unbelievably lucky." I shook my head. "The demon that tried to possess her was very high level. That's how she's jumped so far ahead."

Simone held her head high before her brows furrowed. She dipped her head to me. "Thank you again."

"Don't mention it. I'm the jealous type, and someone laid a hand on my woman." I played it off as not a big deal, but doing all that jumping into people's souls yesterday had even tired me.

"What class are you?" Gloria asked.

I paused, debating if I should share. "This all has to stay secret. You can't even tell your family," I warned her.

I leaned back, trying to figure out how to explain the pieces I was willing to share. Though, I'd made up my mind; I'd tell Simone privately about my past life later. We weren't going anywhere.

"Once you saw her bloodline, you were hooked. She's not going anywhere," Simone said. That intuition of hers was terrifying. "Just tell her." She turned to Gloria. "Sorry, he saw that S rank bloodline and I'm pretty sure he's never going to let you go now." She patted her sympathetically.

Simone was being far more playful.

"My class is Blood Hegemon. Unlike both of you, it doesn't have a clear ranking. Instead, it improves its rank with the more bloodlines I collect," I told them both.

"Oh. Totally not a vampire." Simone rolled her eyes. "What does it do?"

"Melee fighter with healing and curses," I told them both. "If something hurts me, my blood can hurt them."

"That's a mildly horrifying way to fight." Gloria stared at me like she was seeing me in a new light.

"It helps that I heal quickly," I added to neither of their satisfaction. "Anyway. Now you are both players. This weekend, when we go to the market, use your Inspect ability and only that ability to scan everything. Also, there are things called instances where we can enter to kill monsters." I glanced at Gloria. "Anything from that apartment?"

"Yes. I had a few guys work on their laptops and iPads to get all of their correspondence and information. Tom was aware of three active instances." Gloria pulled out her phone and texted me an image. "They also had a lot of funds. We are talking on the order of nine figures. My people are working to siphon that all off." She was largely in charge of money laundering for the Nesters; it would be easy enough for her.

"Good. That'll be more than I could even spend. They tried to kill me," I said, checking my phone. "Everything they had is now forfeit. Okay, not bad. Bobby and Rodger still need a little help with the instance we've been doing. Add in these three, and we can start to build a force."

"Cancel the plan to host the F rank instance?" Gloria asked.

"No. We can use it for recruitment. We will find some desperate and willing players through those that show up." I nodded to myself.

"What about the rest of my girls?" Simone asked.

"I cleared the demons from them. Bobby helped Candy become a player like I did for both of you. Next I want to secure the girls from Rick's operation. Wait, I'm getting ahead of myself again. Do you both have any questions?"

"Am I a demon now?" Simone asked. "Lilim is a demon thing, yet I'm a saint too. There's..." She touched the side of her head. "I think I'm growing horns."

"Probably." I pointed at Gloria. "Her hair is about to get very purple, and she's going to have fangs I think."

"Wait, what?!" Gloria yelled loudly, her hands going up to the top of her head immediately.

"It's a powerful class. My eyes are turning red. Powerful classes change your appearance as well. Anyway, no, you aren't a demon. Think of it this way, every world has different classes. The cultures during their early stages are reflected through the classes offered. There's a girl in my clan who gets the Medusa class. She's not a monster, but she's going to have some wicked hair. The System for each world learns from that."

"They are alive?" Simone asked.

"No. People have compared them to the AIs that are starting to come out. They might be able to replicate a lot of things, but they certainly aren't capable of thought. Instead, they can send messages, create classes because of the unique inputs for each," I tried my best to explain what I had grown to understand.

"Then why did the System give me this bloodline?" Gloria asked.

"That goes way back to the birth of this world. Many great beasts died when the worlds were born. They found the demons to keep them from infecting each world. In the process, their blood was integrated into the world and randomly appeared in the population. The bloodlines are then passed down through children," I continued to explain.

Simone rubbed at her face. "So this world is young?"

"It's an egg. Right now, there's a shell around it preventing anything from coming in or out. When that shell shatters, everyone in this world gets to become part of the System."

Gloria nodded. "But there are already demons here."

I sighed. "Exactly the problem. They are ramping up in activity in preparation for when the egg cracks. This world is…" I shook my head, that was a problem for later.

Simone squinted at me. "How do you know all of this?"

I met her eyes. "My family is the Heros Family. We go all the way back to Ancient Greece. The other four of the five families are the same as us, all from ancient parts of the world. We were sent into hiding to protect ourselves so that we could rise up when the world's egg hatches, and defeat the demons."

It wasn't a full lie, but I would tell Simone more later.

"Understood." Gloria crossed her arms. "I'll get some people started on the Rick angle, and then step into one of these instances and get some experience. We need to see how this all works." She spoke to Simone, "If you don't mind, I'm going to go. Thank you for all the information, Bran."

"No problem. Tell your father anything but about my abilities. Eventually, I'll be stronger than Simone because I'll have collected enough bloodlines. The best way then to go after me will be to kill those whose bloodlines I've collected." I met her eyes, telling her silently that included her.

"Why not take mine now?"

"Because every time it upgrades, it resets my level. I want to push it higher before the next reset. I will have your blood eventually." I gave her a leveled look, letting her know there was no other option.

Gloria nodded and grabbed her coat, throwing it over her shoulder before walking out.

Simone sat patiently to my side, only tracing small lines on my leg. "You lied to her."

"I lived another life," I came out with the full truth. "Before this one."

"How long?" Simone asked.

"A little more than five hundred years." I watched her reaction.

Simone stared into the middle distance, several things seemed to occur to her. "You've been through a lot. I saw your soul, that was the you from then... This doesn't go smoothly, does it?"

"No. In a little less than two years, it's all going to go to shit. This world was nearly a breeding ground for demons that would hatch so that they could launch a renewed wave of terror across multiple worlds. We are going to have to fight to save this world and contain the demon threat," I said simply.

Simone stared into my eyes. "If you are doing things differently than last time. Then... you weren't here helping me last time, were you?"

My gaze softened, and I took her hand. "It doesn't matter. I'm here now, and they won't touch you."

"That demon general... last time. Did it get me?" She swallowed.

I nodded slowly. "When I recognized who you were, I purposefully kept you close to try and stop the general. To take a piece from the Demon Lord would be big. Yet the more I got to know you, the more I wanted *you* and not to take a piece from the Demon Lord."

She hugged my side. "Thank you. Bran, you saved me. You saved my soul. In this life I'll do whatever you need." She was terrified, realizing what she'd avoided. Yet she was strangely calm as she held onto me.

"Too late, Simone. You are already mine." I pinched her side and pulled her into my lap. "After last night, I'm going to enjoy you forever."

She smiled and wiggled in my lap. "Oh, is that so?"

My lips found hers, and the table scooted as I pressed her down on top of it. "Yes, it is."

"Then feast, my Bran, my hero." She touched my face softly before giving me a tender kiss that picked up in heat. "Thank you for telling me the truth." She hooked her ankles behind my waist and rubbed me against her hips as she let out a breathy moan. "Because I am never letting you and that fat cock of yours get away, Bran."

The plates fell off of the table as we nearly broke it and moved on to the shower and then back to the bed.

Chapter 33

It turned out that having Simone in my apartment meant it was substantially more difficult to want to leave. We only made it out by noon because I didn't have much in the way of food besides the sandwiches in my spatial ring.

And Simone refused to eat those.

"So, I can store things in this?" Simone walked with one arm linked around mine, the other admiring the new ring on her finger.

"Try it when we aren't in public. As long as you can lift an object, you can put it in the ring," I explained.

"Pretty sure I can lift a lot of things. Your fridge can also fly," she snickered. I officially needed a new fridge.

"Yeah, do your best to not rip the door off their hinges or crush people. It takes some adjustment when your stats jump as much as yours have," I warned her. "Which is why we are taking you to one of these new instances. I need to try it out, work on a few of my own skills, and you need something that is supposed to be broken to punch."

"I'm not particularly a violent woman. I've been working to make sex work safer for a decade," Simone reminded me.

"You are now strong enough to make Rick and anyone else who even thinks of running a dirty brothel regret their decision until everyone else looks at them and decides it isn't worth it to even try. Simone, you are about to hold a very real amount of power both in the mundane and player world." I leveled a look at her.

She shrugged. "I'll stick to my convictions while I stick to you. I have a feeling being with you will allow me to make the changes I want to see in the world. Where's this instance?"

I reached my jeep and got in. "Not far. This one is in the city. A player named Tom killed the people that knew about it to monopolize the resource."

"Asshole," Simone snorted and got in the passenger seat. "Wait, if we go now, are those sandwiches all we are going to have to eat?"

"Uhh... yes?" I hazarded.

"Let's stop at a grocery store on the way. Seriously, Bran, after the apocalypse, did you not learn to cook for yourself?" Simone chided me.

"I did, but there wasn't mayonnaise anymore." I blinked at her in full honesty.

***

Simone and I reached the instance. It was in the basement of an old, condemned apartment complex.

"Spooky." Simone walked out behind me. "This is an instance?"

"Level 21, E rank. Should be super easy for you," I told her.

"For me?" Simone pointed at herself with a surprised expression. "I'm the healer. From what I've read about video games, that means I'll stay back here." She pointed at her feet. "You go up there, by the monster." She pointed off into the distance, making a slight shooing motion.

"Come on." I grabbed her arm and dragged her forward. She was still in her blonde, sexy nun disguise. She had refused to take it off. "Are you going to keep that disguise?"

"It suits me. Or would you prefer something like this?" She turned into a buxom latex clad redhead.

"I like you. The Simone I've been having drinks with," I told her.

"Awe. I wanted to try out a few things." She turned back into the blonde nun. It seemed that it was a personal favorite.

"See that?" I pointed to the bug-like creature made of vines in front of us. "Use Heartbreaker on it."

"Fine." Simone squared up and drew a pink magical heart in front of her, with each hand doing one half.

When the ability finished, it flashed for a moment before a giant pink laser blasted out from the center like it was a beam from the Death Star. The insect, which was made of vines, was missing half of its form after the blast and fell over before dissolving into the instance.

"Oh. That wasn't so bad." Simone clapped.

"Yeah. Not so bad." I frowned, staring at the spot where the insect had been. Why the heck didn't I have an ability like that? I could only blame myself for selecting the ?? Rank class. Perhaps if I had gone with a SS rank mage I'd be able to outdo her at the moment.

Stepping up, I picked up a red flower from the monster.

[Blood Bloom E]

My brows went up. Jackpot!

"Is that good?" Simone seemed to see my excitement.

"It's the main herb for a bloodline awakening potion," I explained. "It might not work on your bloodlines, but for the girls that Rick has and the ones in your employ, it will work wonderfully." I stuffed the flower in my ring.

"Will it make them part of the System?" Simone asked.

"Nope. But even the F rank bloodlines will gain enough stats to be Olympic athletes," I explained. "Bloodlines are very powerful. We'll have to farm this instance quite a bit."

Simone wasn't going to be the only one growing stronger, though. Fighting the demon souls had leveled me as well. Sadly, none of those demons had been anywhere near as strong as the demon general.

Yet I had gained enough levels to shift my focus to Level 40 and a new skill that I wanted to rank up.

I cut my arm, and blood flowed down into my hand as [Crimson Blade] activated, making a pristine blood-red longsword. It was a little larger than normal, but I had the strength to use larger swords in a single hand.

Simone saw me cut myself, and her hands wove a small pink spell form that drained into my arm, healing the cut as soon as the sword was done. "Can't you make that without hurting yourself?"

"I'm also trying to train my Regeneration. Besides, I'm not Gloria with her Thick Skin." I huffed just thinking about it. Gloria was going to be a walking tank while torching everything around her. Somehow, it fit the mobster.

"Well, take my healing and like it." Simone poured more unnecessary healing into me.

I started out at a slow jog and burst into a run as I saw the next plant bug. One by one, I started clearing them out, giving every other one to Simone to blast apart with a single shot.

She weaseled out of using a weapon to fight several times, explaining that she would stick to magic and healing anyway.

"You changed a little, you know that?" I pointed out as I picked up more flowers. Simone laser cannoned an entire group of the bugs.

Then again, she was three times their level and a far higher rank.

"Of course I did." She scanned around us. "I almost had my soul eaten by a demon, and a guy I was fairly infatuated with came and saved me. There are layers to that, Bran. Layers that got peeled off along with apparently a decade of aging." She flashed, and the disguise was gone. "Bran, if I walked into my hotel right now, someone would ask me if Simone was my mother."

"Older sister perhaps," I argued.

"Point stands." She glared at me and returned to her blonde priestess disguise. "I feel like a new person. One that you lifted out of her former life. A lot of worries have fallen away. Someone gets hurt around me? I can just wave that away. My own mortality? That's now questionable—you were over five hundred years old and looked middle-aged."

I wrapped an arm around her shoulders. "Well, if you have any questions, I'm here for you."

She went up on her tiptoes and grabbed my face to plant a lingering kiss on my lips. "That's the best part. I got this man who's both very helpful and very loving."

"Loving?" I frowned. That wasn't normally a word that was used to describe me. A little crazy, sure.

"In your own way." She sighed. "Now, I have other decisions to make. Like, what to do with my business? It seems that I'll be busy with this new life, and if you are going to head back to your clan, then I'm coming with you. So I might just end up giving it to the Nesters with the caveat that if I come back and there's forced labor, I'll blow them all up." Simone frowned at the end of her statement. "Then am I better than scum like Rick if I just threaten people?"

I squeezed her tight to break that spiral of thoughts. "Simone, other people have forced their moralities and principles on you your entire life. Now you are strong enough to turn the table. In a very weird way, it's just how humanity has operated for a long time. You are nothing like Rick. He took people's wills away. I never want to hear you compare yourself to him again."

She saw another group of plant bugs and waved her hands to create another beam of pink destruction that wiped them out. "So, you didn't fight me on going with you to your clan." She decided to focus on a singular aspect.

"You'll need to meet my mother before that. I worry about taking you, yet I'm smart enough to know you'll make things more difficult than I care for if I try to stop you," I joked.

Simone patted my cheek. "It wouldn't be that bad, but I might not be very helpful if any of these girls we rescue turn out to be hidden treasures."

"I'm going to pass on that. My thoughts were more in line with using any money we get from Rick and what I've gotten from Tom to set up a business for them to work at and prepare for the coming days. Since it's clear that my abilities require them to be alive, then I am invested in preparing for their survival," I said.

Simone teased my cheek. "You big softie."

"Literally no one has ever called me that. I used to break demon armies," I huffed.

Simone shrugged. "Maybe that was just to protect yourself. As much as you saved me, I'm determined to save you."

I raised an eyebrow, not aware that I needed saving. "Fine. Whatever keeps you at my side."

She pressed herself to said side. "I'm not going anywhere. So, your mother. What kind of woman is she? In your past life, she would have died, right?"

"Yes. I have fond memories of being raised by her. Yet the woman I woke up felt colder than I remembered." It had been a long time. I stared off into the distance as we continued to walk through the instance.

Simone took the lead and just blasted away any monsters that appeared.

I had gotten my Crimson Blade to E rank. It was unlikely I would be able to push it to D in this instance.

"She raised you alone?" Simone pushed.

"Yeah." That had just been the way of things.

"Do you know who your father is?" She was practically prying this out with a crowbar at this point. "He had to be really tall—your soul was giant."

"No. Just that it was an arranged marriage between my mother from the clan. She avoids him. That much is clear. When I joined the clan in my last life, much of those who would have known were gone. The War for Supremacy hit all the clans and sects hard," I told her. "The Heros Clan nearly didn't survive, and we certainly weren't a power after it."

We had managed to anger the 'Clan Killer' as the man became known. Thorin Aegir, outcast from the Borrson Clan and one of the most feared men in the world at the time. He had a paired class and bloodline like Gloria. Along with the knowledge of the Borrson Clan, he had advanced incredibly fast.

My mind went to the time he had left me nearly dead and my Regeneration had evolved to save me.

"That's the part where as soon as the demon threat was gone, everyone killed each other to try and come out on top?" Simone had gotten the quick and dirty version of my five hundred-year past life.

"Pretty much." I pointed ahead of us. There was a wide-open space with more giant plant bugs, and one that was the biggest we'd seen yet. "Once we kill everything in this room, we move onto the next. You've been firing off your ability, but I'd like to see you get up close and personal with a few of these. If you get hurt, I can heal you."

"With your blood." She wrinkled her nose. "Okay, let me do this. But we aren't over discussing your family," she called over her shoulder as she walked up to the first group and threw a completely novice punch with her whole body.

Of course, her skill in punching didn't matter as much as her massive strength stat.

The plant bug exploded from her punch, and she stared at her fist for a second as the other two in the group jumped on her. Then she moved at the last second, avoiding both of them and destroying them with a few sharp kicks.

"I thought these were hard?" she called out.

"For Gloria or Bobby, they would indeed take some effort. For you? No, you've cheated, and things won't be hard for you for a while." I sighed. "Come on. Let's go visit my mother, get Gloria, and deal with Rick."

Chapter 34

I stopped by the bank on the way to introduce Simone to my mother.

"Wicked cosplay." The young greeter glanced at Simone, his eyes struggling to pull away from her.

I ignored him. There was no malice in his gaze.

"Right this way, Mr. Bran." The account manager smiled tightly at me, his Inspect slipping off me once again as I batted it away. A moment later, he looked at Simone who was still being a nun and following me almost devoutly.

His jaw almost hit the floor.

"Ah. She's not quite as adept at hiding her stats," I replied calmly as we walked inside.

"I am far less experienced," Simone echoed, following me. "Though, I endeavor to learn more from Bran."

"Ah. That makes sense." The man's smile was tight as he tried to recover.

Simone's level and stats told a story that he wouldn't fully understand unless he also saw her skills and that they were all unpracticed.

"When you feel the tickle of an Inspect coming at you, just mentally push it away." I turned to the manager. "Try it again on her."

"Yes, sir." He focused on Simone who continued to look like a demure young lady. "I don't see anything now."

"Well done, Simone," I encouraged her. It would be a little easier if she wasn't so glaringly talented. Though, she could only avoid the Inspect for people with weaker spirits and low-ranking Inspect skills.

"When they see my strength, they know yours is unfathomable," Simone intoned.

I grunted, not saying what I wanted to say in front of the manager. "Funds from my recent sales?"

"Ah. Yes. You've taken over the inscription market." He turned his computer to face me. "90,128 gold coins are in your account at present."

I relaxed a little. Not a bad amount for the work I had done. I had been getting a little over a thousand gold coins per run with Bobby and Rodger, then funneling that all into inscriptions and turning around three times the profit for several weeks.

"For the USD, I have an account I'd like to merge with mine." I handed him a card that Gloria had given me. The money from Tom and the other three had been 'cleaned' and put within the account.

"You can do that online." The manager studied me as if wondering why I didn't do something so simple.

I stared at him and pushed the card further forward. My attempt to do it online had failed. It was just easier to make him complete the move.

"Oh, I mean. Of course." He gave a strained smile. "We also have some of your recent orders here and the funds taken out." He fished through his drawers and handed me a small spatial ring.

Sadly, this one wasn't for me to keep. It was just how they transferred items around.

I took it and emptied the inscription ingredients into one of my own spatial rings. There were a few bloodroots mixed in as well. They were criminally cheap in the store. Enough of those and I could actually start upgrading some weaker bloodlines.

"Wonderful. Here's a stack of inscriptions." I placed them in front of the manager. The stack of paper was about two feet high. "If there are any questions about the function, please let me know."

"Ah. I did have a special request." The manager pulled something from his drawer. "One of the higher ups at the bank noticed that you seem to be quite proficient with inscriptions and wanted me to pass this along."

I took the sealed letter and threw it into my spatial ring for later. "Wonderful doing business with the bank as always. Is there a chance for me to withdraw all of my coins?"

The manager smiled. "Absolutely no problem." He moved to do as I asked.

"It's fine. Not right now. Is there a limit on how much I can take at once?"

"Ah. We ask for some time to move the funds around if you withdraw more than a million in one go." He smiled.

I nodded. Clearly, they were doing quite a bit of business. Soon I wasn't going to be able to expand my inscription business any further. Then again, special requests like the one I had just received were likely to be far more lucrative.

"Perfect." I stood and held my arm out.

Simone daintily held it. "Good day to you." She bowed to the manager and walked out with me.

"You are being a little cheeky. 'Unfathomable'," I snorted as we left the bank.

Simone chuckled. "Did you see his face? He's terrified of the mysterious Mr. Bran. Do they not know your last name?"

"No. I'd rather not lean on the Heros Clan just yet. I'm going to head there and have to pretend to be uninitiated actually." That was going to be a pain, but doable.

"Will I have to be uninitiated too?" she asked.

"We'll see what my mother recommends. In my past life, I went through the external rites for my clan. Though, I know something about the family rites and I'll need to be Level 1, but thankfully, I can fix that. The big problem is that you are a little too eye-catching." I looked at Simone out of the corner of my eyes as we headed to the hospital.

"Me?" She batted her lashes. "Should I disguise myself as an ugly hag?"

"Your bloodline and class might be too tempting for some of the old men in my clan." I gritted my teeth. "My mother would know better, though."

"I'm excited to meet her." Simone pulled me ahead to the hospital. The people we passed often paused to stare at us.

But in the hospital, people were too busy to stop and stare, leaving us be as we made our way to my mother's room.

She was still in bed, watching TV as I entered.

"You're back... and you brought company." My mother stared at Simone, clearly using her Inspect to get a better picture of her strength.

I did the same to check on my mother.

[Elle Heros
Level: 38
Class: Swordmaster A
Status: Tired
Strength: 351
Agility: 474
Vitality: 212
Intelligence: 251
Spirit: 190
...]

My mother was well within the range of an A rank fighter for her level. And she had a B rank bloodline.

"This is Simone," I introduced her, a little surprised that Simone had decided to continue wearing her blonde saint disguise to meet my mother.

"She's newly initiated? Very weak for an SSS Rank," my mother commented dryly. "But she's got plenty of potential."

Simone stepped up to my mother. "Bran saved my life, and I'm determined to be useful. I hoped to return to the clan with him."

"Impossible," my mother cut her off. "Bran already made things difficult for himself by becoming a player. You will just give one of those old geezers a reason to harass him until they can pry you out of his grasp. You aren't a boon for Bran right now—you're fresh meat in a forest full of predators."

"Mother." I stepped in, not liking the tone she was using with Simone.

"And you, show me your stats." My mother frowned at me.

I resisted another attempt. "How about this?"

This time, she Inspected me, and I carefully wove what I did and didn't want to display for her to make a convincing lie.

[Bran Heros
Level: 40
Class: -
Status: Healthy]

My mother squinted. "Your spirit is high enough to manipulate what I can see? You still messed up the level."

"I will fix it before I go back to the clan." I was planning on using the bloodlines that we'd get soon to reset my level. "And I can whip up a few talismans with Simone's help to disguise my class and hers."

"She's still a little too pretty," my mother commented, turning to Simone. "Accept a Slave Seal from Bran and you might not get taken away. We'd need to make your class much less appealing too."

Simone hesitated at the mention of Slave Seal, until a look of determination filled her face. "If that's what's required to stand by his side, then do it. Do it now."

"I'm not interested in slaves," I sighed. Slave Seals were a stupid tool. If you couldn't ensure loyalty without one, you really weren't fit to command someone. Not to mention that there was a way out of them anyway.

"It's for her too. That way, no one tries to run off with her," my mother coached.

I glanced at Simone. "Give me a drop of your blood." I held out my palm.

She took out a dagger she'd gotten from the E rank dungeon and pricked her finger, dropping a drop of blood in my palm.

I added one of my own and quickly made a very complex Slave Seal. "Here. See this loop? You and you alone can tug on it and it'll come undone."

The two drops of blood had been stretched out into a tangled knot that I held out to her.

Simone raised an eyebrow and poked the loop I'd mentioned. "Okay."

"Now eat it," I told her.

All the while, my mother watched me curiously. "Who taught you all of this?"

Simone took the Slave Seal and swallowed it with a grimace, a band appearing on her throat for a moment before disappearing.

I had been prepared for my mother to question my knowledge. "A book. I found it on a corpse by an instance. It detailed many inscriptions."

She clearly didn't entirely believe me, but she didn't pursue her questioning. "You have three months before we return to the clan."

"I came tonight to show you Simone and tell you that we were attacked by a demon. The demon had a gem full of souls and tried to possess a large number of people. I'm going after the organization behind the demon." There was no point in being anything but direct with my mother at this juncture.

My mother nodded and pushed aside the sheets. "Fine. If you are going to be that stubborn, I'll come."

She waved a hand in front of her and a ring I'd never seen before was now on one of her fingers. She quickly swapped out her hospital gown for a pair of simple jeans and white shirt. Then she walked up to me and pinched my cheek. "Stop acting all grown up, I—"

"You almost died, mom. That ages people. I've watched you lie in that bed and wither away without fighting." I slapped her hand away. "Don't be cute with me."

In another life, I had watched her die. Die without reaching out to the clan or my father who was clearly still alive, and now was alive.

"Here's the address." I handed her a sheet of paper. "I'll see you at eight." Turning, I grabbed Simone and marched out of the hospital.

My mother stood behind us, stunned as I marched out.

Part of me wanted so badly to reconnect with her. Yet instead of the loving mother I remembered, I had found a woman resigned to her fate. I'd spent hundreds of years fighting, and I had trouble being around anybody not willing to fight back.

"Simone, what does your intuition tell you?" I asked.

My partner sighed. "She's terrified of her own family. Not you, the clan. In your past life, what was her status?"

"Nothing special. If anything, she was just a pretty woman that was average for the clan. They married her away, likely for my father's bloodline," I told her what I knew. "My grandfather is kind of an asshole."

"You learned from your past life?" she asked.

"No. I've met him before, but never again after my mother passed." I didn't want to get into that history.

"How does the clan get your father's bloodline?" she asked.

"Me. My Heros Bloodline overpowers any other that might be in me, and it gets added to the whole. It's just how our bloodline works. Basically, they just keep mixing it with others through arranged marriages and kids. As soon as I was born, my mother's use to the clan dried up." I grimaced.

"She doesn't resent you, though. If anything, I think a large part of her fear is you heading back to the clan. She doesn't want you to go." Simone's intuition was working overtime, but I appreciated her ability to read people.

"Too bad. There's too much value there for me to back out now. But for now, I have some work to do before we go after Rick's organization tonight. We're bringing Gloria and Bobby. Now remove that damned Slave Seal."

"I think it's nice." She touched her neck where the black line would be if I used Inspect.

"I'm not sleeping with someone under a Slave Seal," I told her.

It disappeared in an instant as she used the trick I showed her to break it.

Chapter 35

[Name: Bran Heros
　Level: 40
Class: Blood Hegemon F
Status: Healthy
Strength: 94
Agility: 82
Vitality: 90
Intelligence: 76
Spirit: 11022

Skills:
Soul Gaze SSS
Soul Resilience S
Blunt Weapon Proficiency E
Endurance E
Throwing Proficiency F
Blood Boil D
Blood Siphon D
Blood Bolt D
Bloodline Collection 4
Regeneration D
Fire Resistance F
Poison Resistance E
Ax Proficiency E
Charge F
Bloodink Quality F
Stealth F
Inscription E
Swim D (Bracer)

Last Stand F
Blood Hex E
Blood Transfusion E
Crimson Blade E
Crimson Barrier F]

My progress was coming along steadily. And the demons had proven useful for leveling. My newest ability wasn't as exciting as I had hoped, but as I was gaining allies, it seemed appropriate.

Being able to sacrifice my health for a barrier to protect myself and others would allow me to keep them safe. I'd just have to heal the health I used for that ability, or have Simone heal me in return.

I was looking over my stats while Gloria pulled up in a black SUV and piled out with Bobby, Rodger, and even Candy.

Simone handed me another chicken tender that I was eating while we waited.

"Welcome. We are waiting for one more." I took a bite of my chicken.

Gloria was clearly the one in charge of the little group. "Who's that?"

"His mother," Simone answered. "She's a little cold, but she means well."

"Did you get the items I asked you for?" I looked at Gloria.

"Yeah. I don't understand why I'm getting you cooking equipment, or are you getting Halloween decorations?" Gloria seemed a little miffed about buying me big cast iron cauldrons.

I smiled at her. "No. It's for you. You have flame mastery, which means you can help me cook up some food."

Bobby chuckled. "He's going to make a woman out of you yet."

The mob boss snapped her fingers, and purple flames shot out from her hand to torch me.

Simone snorted, and Veil of Netherlight appeared between Gloria and me, blocking the flames.

"He could have healed from that," Gloria growled.

"That might have singed his clothes." Simone handed me more chicken. "I like that shirt."

For a second, I thought I was going to get to train my Fire Resistance. It seemed that Gloria was still looking for a reason to pick a fight with me.

"Alchemy," I clarified. "Not food. But if you want to make me something, I won't complain. Some sort of fire control spell is needed as part of the qualifications. That's why I can't do it myself—trust me I've tried."

"Oh?" The fact that her specific skills were needed caught Gloria's attention. "Like those expensive potions that I see in the market?"

"The very same ones." I nodded along with her. "Though, I want something you won't find there. We are going to pick up a lot of ladies with bloodlines that aren't awakened. For the lower ranking ones, I want to be able to awaken them."

Simone glanced at me. "What about the higher rank ones?"

"I don't have the ingredients I need for those," I admitted. "But the low-rank ones, even if they aren't initiated in the System, they'll gain enough strength that they'd be far and above a normal person. After this is all done, I'm going to get them to work for me. Don't worry, though, I have a plan for your two bloodlines. But that will require a trip to my clan." The Heros Clan had plenty of resources for bloodlines.

A lone figure was walking towards us, and I stood up.

"Welcome, mother," I greeted her.

She watched me and turned to the industrial area that we were overlooking. "Down there?"

"Third building." I pointed at a particular one. "At least, that's what we know about the human who runs the operation. We want to pull out all the women he has with bloodlines while we are at it."

She nodded. "I'll take the back. You can go from the front." My mother was far more serious than I remembered, and launched herself into the night, holding onto her sword.

"Will she be fine?" Bobby asked.

"Oh, I think she has more tricks than me right now." I stared after her figure, remembering Simone's thoughts that she was terrified of the clan. "Follow me. I don't think she's going to be patient."

Putting the rest of my meal into a spatial ring, I started out at a jog down to the warehouse. Unlike a normal place where you'd expect guards and thugs, it was quiet on the outside.

Yet I trusted Gloria and Simone's research and went in guns blazing. Blood Boil made me swell slightly and blood came out of my palm to make a Blood Blade just before I smashed in the door.

A few voices shouted from inside, but Gloria's purple flames rolled in around me and burnt two of them to cinders in seconds. The mobster walked in confidently, her coat trailing off her shoulders.

Simone came next, while Bobby and Candy brought up the rear.

Someone had given Candy a sword and a shield. I glanced at the weapons, but decided to ignore them for the moment. I was more interested in the scene before me.

The center of the warehouse was dominated by several bubbling vats and heavy machinery. Yet the rest of the warehouse was cages, endless cages lining the walls, and several dozen people. There was a constant clamor from some of them, while others had fallen silent at our appearance.

"Disgusting," Bobby sneered.

I wasn't even moved by the sight, moving forward at a quick pace. I had unfortunately seen worse. Scanning around, I spotted a figure on a walkway above the vats.

"Kill anyone not in a cage," I told my group and rushed up to the catwalk to confront the figure.

Bobby burst into action, throwing out splashes of acid on figures that swarmed them. Gloria threw out dark flames that tossed people aside as Simone let giant pink beams rip dozens of them apart.

[~~Carl Vinder~~ Graz'grave
Level: 92
Class: Abyssal Sorcerer A
Status: Corrupted
Strength: 320
Agility: 230
Vitality: 409
Intelligence: 517

Spirit: 601

Skills:
Inspect A
Possession A
Abyssal Roots D
Seed of Destruction D
Darkness D
Dark Rot D
Unending Agony C
Shadow Fish Bloodline S Awakened]

If I had to guess, this demon was in charge, mostly because he had an S ranked bloodline. Even if he worked for the general, demons were selfish creatures. He would have taken the best for himself. His Inspect slid off of me.

I felt like I was back in my last life, facing off against a demon several times more powerful than me with my sword in hand.

"A troublesome boy," he regarded me.

The man was well on his way to being fully corrupted. His entire body was covered in what looked like burnt, black skin, and a pair of claws extended on either hand.

"I will deal with you and then that Heros woman that showed up tonight." He raised a hand, and dark, inky black tendrils shot from around him to drill into me.

Their progress slowed as Simone's Veil of Netherlight appeared to block them. Sadly, her ability was only F rank, and even then, she was outclassed by the demon's stats.

Her protective bubble shattered.

But she had bought me a little time. Jumping over the tendrils and using them as footholds, I jumped towards the demon. I had fought Abyssal Sorcerers on many occasions. This brought me back.

The demon pointed a lazy claw at me, and his ability Unending Agony shot through my body. For a moment, it was complete and utter torture, my world narrowing down to just the demon as I fought through the pain.

Then a golden shell seemed to wrap itself around my mind. Simone's Bastion of Athena sheltered my mind from the demon's ability.

I landed next to the demon, my crimson longsword blurred as I worked through the forms of the old sword art that I'd mastered in a previous life. They came to me in a burst of introspection. I suddenly remembered years of my life spent working on my sword, like muscle memory.

An old Orak named Thetis had come to our world during the Second Demon War and taken me in as his apprentice. The pale giant had been a brutal mentor.

Shattered Blade Arts was a brutal way of fighting, perfect for my previous class of Breaker. It was a style filled with heavy swings for me to overpower my opponent.

Yet the one in front of me outclassed me in stats at the moment.

I used a lesser-used form for this situation, my blade coming at the demon in sweeping blows that didn't fully commit and allowed me to alter the strike as needed.

The demon blocked my blade with his claws, but I didn't let up.

Suddenly, a swell of strength filled my back as Simone used Lilim's Whisper. [Sword Proficiency F] Appeared at the edge of my vision as I pressed the demon back.

The demon's claws gouged out a section of my chest, and I felt the tickle of his Dark Rot ability seep into me and try to sap my strength. Simone's Saint's Mercy joined my Regeneration in fighting off the damage.

"You aren't my match, demon," I growled, pushing forward with my sword once again.

His strikes found my sword in his way, deflecting his claws, and even his Abyssal Roots were pushed aside by another Veil of Netherlight. Simone put this veil at an angle to deflect rather than try to push back the attacks head on.

Simone was getting better quickly.

I hadn't found a reason to use Shattered Sword Arts before now, and without System assistance, it felt sluggish. Yet my world faded away to memories of my past practice.

My footwork was immaculate, honed into my soul with thousands of hours of performing them in sand and bog to perfection. Each stroke had been swung well over a million times.

[Sword Proficiency E]
[Sword Proficiency D]

The demon was less able to block my attacks. The System shrouded my movements and my attacks like a mantle of power as I pushed forward.

Meanwhile, Simone's abilities pushed to counter the demon.

The demon tried to switch its focus to my woman to weaken me through my support, but I stepped up in the demon's face, forcing it to focus on me or die.

"You don't have time to look away." My sword pushed him back.

[Sword Proficiency C]

The next stroke cut right through the demon's hand. The panic on its face only encouraged me. It was realizing that I was not only a match for it, but I might also just win this fight.

I was best against a more humanoid opponent, especially a demon. I had needed to be in order to survive. And I would be damned if this demon stopped my plans.

The demon threw Darkness over Simone and me.

Soul Gaze made my eyes shine bright, even in the magical darkness, preventing me from pausing for even a second. My sword didn't stop. The E rank weapon, however, wasn't able to withstand the attack, and my sword broke in half.

The demon staggered back out of the darkness. As it spotted my broken sword, it swelled with confidence as it pointed at me again.

"Die, strange human." A small bead of coiling green and black magic appeared at the tip of its finger.

I didn't back down, swinging my broken blade over my head and waiting for his strike. Seed of Destruction was a powerful ability, but it required more time than I'd given him so far in the fight.

Instead, I waited, letting him build up the ability.

"Bran!" Simone screamed.

"Don't help," I told her, my focus was entirely on my sword form. The broken blade wouldn't hamper me one bit.

My mind faded from the current setting on the catwalk of the warehouse.

Instead, it drifted off to the far-gone battlefields. I could almost smell the smoke and the scent of blood so heavy in the air that I could taste the coppery tang.

Although, it was also entirely possible I was tasting my own blood.

One arm hung limp at my side, and I held my broken sword high above my head.

Thetis had watched as I had squared off against a ten-foot-tall demon Juggernaut that had mowed through our forces. People I had drunk with just the night before had died in the fortress around me. The Juggernaut over Level 2000 had laughed at my broken sword and rushed me, with a spiked shield powered by several powerful abilities.

That had been my moment. I had planned to master the Shattered Blade Art. Thetis wouldn't help. He believed that one only became stronger through adversity. The Shattered Blade Arts was precisely about drawing out power in a life-or-death moment.

Back in the warehouse, power gathered at the tip of the blade. In the memory of fighting the Juggernaut, the same thing had happened. The only difference was it was red in the past, and gold in the present.

My eyes opened in both memory and reality as I swung down.

The light gathering at the broken edge shot out, filling the remainder of the blade with light as I swung down into the Juggernaut and at the oncoming blast of Seed of Destruction at the same time.

For a moment, my life flashed between past and present until I couldn't tell which it was.

[Sword Proficiency Upgrades to Sword Mastery Upgrades to Shattered Sword Art SSS]

I jumped a whole two evolutions of Sword Proficiency.

[Learned Sword Force F]

A series of rank ups appeared in front of me.

[Sword Force SSS Upgrades to Sword Will ???]
[??? Learned]
[Error! System Recalibrating]

The flood of System messages devolved into utter junk.
I didn't have time to worry about what the System was going to do with this move. I needed to focus on execution.
My sword continued its current path, cutting right through the lower ranked ability of the demon, blowing it away and piercing right through the demon with such force that the entirety of his being was blown away.
At the same time, a thin, gold light traced from the top of the warehouse down through the foundation and cut a razor thin slice through half of the building in front of me, right down an empty row between pallet racks in front of me.
The boom from the single slash was deafening, yet I didn't mind it at all.
I saw the Juggernaut from my past life fall in two, while the demon here ceased to exist. The catwalk ended in twisted metal a few inches from my feet. The rest of it was nowhere to be found.

[Recalibration Failed]
[Forced Rollback]

It felt like my entire being, down to my spirit was being crushed, and I stumbled back, grabbing the railing and coughing blood as it dripped out of my ears and eyes.
"Bran!" Simone rushed up to me, throwing healing at me as she scrambled up the steps.
"Get away from him." My mother landed on the railing next to me, a sword pointed at my face. "Where is my son?"

Chapter 36

"Going through something at the moment, mom. Maybe give me a minute." I coughed more blood up as the System tried to reconcile my latest technique.

Regeneration and Simone's abilities were doing their best, but the System's forceful rollback had nearly killed me. It seemed some of my skills from my past life were still with me, just not something I should force.

"My son was nearly in tears over playing his last baseball game not that long ago. I was in that hospital long enough for you to become a player, maybe to even become a little jaded and bitter. I was certainly not in there long enough for you to learn inscription, nor for you to master a sword art. I'll say it again. Where. Is. My. Son." She held her sword to my neck.

I chuckled, meeting her eyes with deadly calm. "You were in that bed for far longer for me. Long enough for me to nearly die hundreds of times. Long enough for an Orak to take me in and teach me the sword, when my own mother was a swordmaster."

"All of the races save for humans were wiped off this world," my mother stated, yet she seemed to find something in my eyes. "But you aren't lying."

"How can you be so sure?" I asked.

"Even if you become a thousand years old, you are my son. I changed your diapers and taught you how to ride a bike. I know your expressions."

"No. You pretty much let the hill teach me how to ride a bike," I shot back.

Her eyes narrowed slightly before she let go of whatever worry she had, and snorted, shaking her head. "I'll help you overcome that disastrous sword art. It fights with the assumption that you are stronger than your opponent. The Borrson Clan and their brutish berserkers might get away with an art like that, but you should wield something more flexible."

I snorted. "Those brutes? I wasn't even aware they could find the pointy end of a sword. That's why they stuck to big hammers and axes—far less confusing."

My mother shook her head again. "You shouldn't know any of that information."

"Yet I do. Doesn't change the fact that I'm your son. As for returning to the clan, just know that I plan to elevate my status and yours along with me," I promised her. "Grandpa is going to be so pissed when we hop to another branch and leave him behind."

"That would... never mind. I assume you know what's required for that to happen." She glanced at Simone in a slightly different light. "I'll leave you to that. What are your plans for this place?"

Despite my strangeness, my mother accepted my new abilities quite quickly. I was sure she had seen all kinds of strange occurrences through the clans and players, but it was still touching that she trusted me.

Although, telling me she'd taught me to ride a bike was a test. Luckily, my response was in line with my past complaints.

With my mother no longer pointing a blade at my neck, I used the railing to haul myself to my feet and look out. Gloria and Bobby had held their own, though Bobby was hovering over a Candy who seemed to be freaking out and covered in blood.

"Situation, Gloria?" I asked the mobster.

"That guy seemed to be the only one who was very strong," she answered, a pile of charred corpses around her, her purple flames still flickered on several of them while piles of clothes denoting players or demons had disappeared.

My mother stared at her. "Unique flames and purple hair. Bloodline?"

"S rank," I told her.

"Going to bring her to the clan?"

"No. I'm going to keep her here to implement our plans. These people will need a place." I glanced around the room.

There were dozens of people still in cages. Some of them were worse for wear.

"Simone, I need you to make sure you are using Inspect before you let anyone out of a cage. There are a few who are already lost." I spotted a young girl in a cage near her that was already a demon.

My words seemed to trigger the girl, who jumped out of the cage that apparently wasn't locked, rushing for Simone.

My lover turned and rocked the demon back into the cage with a punch that contained more force than her frame would suggest she was capable of giving. "Is there anything we can do to save her?"

"No. She's already lost."

Simone made a pained expression as she drew a pink heart in front of her and a laser beam vanished the demon. "These things are disgusting."

"You can say that again." I stared down at the vats below me.

"Since you seem to know too much, what's in the vats?" my mother asked.

"Alchemical mixtures," I answered, jumping down from the catwalk and nimbly landing on the edge of one. I stuck my finger in to taste it.

[Alchemical Mixture - Incomplete]

I tasted Bloodroot, Bell Blossom, and Purple Grass.

Getting an idea of what they were doing, I went to the controls for the vats. There were some applications of modern-day equipment.

Alchemical recipes that I was used to would say things like 'boil until the mixture gives off a sweet smell, then reduce heat and add ingredients.' We did not have many thermometers a dozen years after the Rapture.

So reading the procedure that the vats were programmed to complete didn't entirely make sense, but I could make some educated guesses.

"Hey, mom, can you search the place for a crate of Bitter Luan Seeds?" I asked her, staring at the panel and tapping a few buttons to try and see where it was in the process. "Gloria, come here and get your first lesson in alchemy."

"You know alchemy too?" my mother asked, her eyes narrowing.

"No. I've just watched it a few too many times. If they have those seeds, then there's a good chance that they beat me to the punch on something." I looked at Bobby who was still comforting Candy and then saw Rodger. "Ransack the place. I want anything of value. Leave Simone to opening the cages."

She had a softer touch and Bastion of Athena to help any of the people deal with their present situation. It couldn't be understated how much easier releasing them would go if she could keep them calm.

Gloria came over to where I was looking at the screen. Her arms were crossed under her breasts in an almost unconscious gesture. I was fairly sure she wasn't pushing those up on purpose for me.

Her coat hung over her shoulders, trailing behind her. "What's this?"

"The vats are being used as large cauldrons. If they are making what I think, my mother will find the seeds. The trouble will be that I don't exactly know the right quantities for a batch this size. You'll have to crush the seeds and add the powder slowly once the vats reach this set point." It had a clear curve for the temperature mapped out and the current progress. I just had to hope the demons knew what they were doing.

"Okay, and then what?" she asked.

"Cool it down. If there's a setting on here for that step, I don't see it," I answered, staring at the bright screen.

"Here." Gloria pointed to a button and opened up a new menu. "It's even labeled."

"Oh. Well then, I'll leave the panel to you. Add about three buckets full to each vat." I picked up a nearby bucket and held it out for her.

"Crushed or uncrushed bucket?" she asked.

"Crushed." I wasn't entirely sure, but that seemed about right for the amount of liquid in the vats. "It should cool to a dark pink syrup consistency."

Gloria nodded. "Then what do we do?"

"We'll bottle it up for later." I glanced at the vats. "This will make quite a bit. Enough to serve us for a while. How'd your first fight go?"

"Fine. It wasn't my first fight. I'm not a stranger to violence." Gloria seemed a little annoyed at me asking after her.

"As my fiancée, I need to check on these things," I told her. "That, and I can heal you if you took any damage."

"They didn't break my skin." She showed me a spot where her skirt was ripped, but there was no wound.

I smirked. "You feel strange about that?"

She glanced away from me. "I shot myself a few times. It didn't do anything, it... it makes me feel like I'm no longer human."

I regarded her and nodded. "You aren't. Now you're a player. Things like laundering money or running thugs isn't going to pay nearly as much as growing stronger as a player. This brew, if we can finish it, is for awakening bloodlines. We'll awaken the ones for the people here, and you'll need to employ them."

"To be the thugs you said won't pay?" she asked.

"I don't care what you make them do. Have them push paper in an office for all I care. What I care about is that they stay safe and we engender some trust and goodwill with them. Unless I find an artifact, they won't become players for almost two years," I told Gloria as my mother landed next to me and dropped two large crates down.

Then she pulled out an industrial plastic barrel.

"Those are the seeds, and this was with them." She kicked the barrel lightly.

I twisted off the cap of the barrel and pulled a spoon out of my spatial ring to dip into it before pulling it out. "Hmm." It was a red, tar-like substance.

[Refined Earth Blood S]

This was rare stuff, refined from thousands of barrels of oil, almost impossible to do at scale after the Rapture.

I licked a drop of it, but it did nothing for my class. Shame, not that I had expected it. "Don't suppose they left a recipe book around here?" I asked.

"Someone had to have instructions to program the vats." Gloria opened the cabinet by the computer and started rifling through the heavy manuals.

"You two deal with that." I glanced over at Simone who was getting more people out of the cages.

I was not very familiar with technology anymore, and Gloria was plenty capable. Honestly, she was proving smarter than I had given her credit for being initially.

I hurried over to Simone, sweeping the cages with my Soul Gaze to make sure there weren't any more hidden demons. "How is everyone?" I asked.

"In poor shape," Simone was honest, while talking down one of the women and getting her to head into the shipping office space. "I'm trying to get them all to sit down so that we can talk to them at once." She put a vial of blood in her spatial ring.

I raised an eyebrow.

"What? I'm looking after you while I do this too." She grinned. "Going to make you so powerful that you just kick the demon's butts before they become a problem."

I smiled and planted a kiss on her cheek. "You really deserve a class with Saint in it."

"Damn right." Simone opened another cage. "Come on out. We are going to help you get back on your feet, if you'd please wait in the shipping office." She guided the shell-shocked lady out and towards the direction she had indicated.

Bobby was back on his feet. He and Candy seemed to be mirroring Simone now. Helping people out seemed to be helping Candy through the trauma.

I ended up scratching the back of my head. Having capable people around me was leaving me with idle hands. Rather than sit around, I went into the shipping office to see already a dozen women looking up at me as I entered.

CHAPTER 36

"Hello." I waved. "I'm Bran. In a few minutes once we get everyone in here, we'll talk about what happens next. I'm sure some of you have lost your visas or passports or whatever. That won't be a problem. We'll find you work."

Seeing all of these hopeless faces reminded me of refugees in my past life. Someone had once said that what they actually wanted was a way to contribute, along with guaranteed safety.

"In fact, I'm looking for employees for a new business. Everyone will be new and need training anyway, so if any of you are interested we can talk later. For now, please enjoy some food." I started to pull all of the food and water out of my spatial ring. I had stored several weeks' worth of sustenance for myself.

Quickly, one then another took a bottle of water and a sandwich. More came in and saw the food and water with others already eating, and took up what was offered.

I was slowly on my way to building trust with these people, and I was starting to learn I could use some help in carrying out my plans.

Chapter 37

Simone sat to my side with Bobby and Candy while I stood in front of the fifty or so people that we had rescued from the demon.

"That's it. We'll get you all set up in Simone's hotel for the short term. Gloria, who's back there checking over those industrial vats, is one of the heirs to the Nester Crime family. They rule Vein City. So when I say you can work in the city without a problem with your lost visas, I have the power to make that happen," I finished my spiel.

"What about our families?" One woman raised her hand.

"If you want them brought here, I can get that arranged." I gave Bobby a look. "We'll even get them a job, just like you."

That statement seemed to cause a ripple of murmurs through the crowd before me.

Simone was off to the side. She'd managed to get blood drawn from all of those we had rescued and was arranging the vials and quietly making a tray of blood drops.

"What will we be doing?" another asked.

"I'm not entirely sure yet. We'll probably ask that you attend some therapy and some self-defense classes. After a situation like this, the self-defense classes can be quite empowering." It would also serve as a nice way to quietly prepare them for the Rapture. "Gloria has a number of businesses under her control, and I have an idea or two that I'm starting up as well."

The demons had clearly found a way to sift through the population for those with bloodlines. If we could mimic their approach, maybe we could do it and recruit those people.

Unlike the clans, I'd be looking through the entire mundane population.

"Any more questions?" They were surprisingly quiet. I figured the questions would come after they got comfortable. "Great, Bobby and Candy here will take you outside. There are a number of vans pulling up to help you get situated in the hotel."

I stepped to the side and let Bobby and Candy take over. My attention was far more fixed on Simone. "What did you tell them?"

"That we'll do a health screening. Which we will. Help me carry these? I don't think they should see what you are about to do." Simone lifted the tray carefully, and I grabbed the vials.

"Who says I'm going to do that now?" I teased.

"Me." Simone grinned. "I want you to be stronger. Though, when you fought that demon, it was like you were someone else, someone a lot more like the man I saw in your eyes when you first walked into the brothel."

"The sword brought up memories." I shook them off again. "What do you have for me, then? I'm ready to reset my stats. But the trick is I want to do it again right before I go to the clan."

"Then we'll save Gloria for then, and try to find some others." Simone put the tray down now that we were out from the others.

Rick's corpse was left in the room we stood inside. He had been dead for several days by the looks of the body.

Simone's voice drew me away from the view. "We have fifty-three blood samples for you. Twelve F, twenty-three E, ten D, five C and three B," she presented them proudly to me.

I smiled and shook my head before I started to sample each of the blood drops.

"So, are you going to add them all to your harem?" Simone asked.

I choked on the drop I was taking just then. "No. Fuck no." I wiped at my mouth. "They are in a terrible situation. Pushing them that way does nothing good for either of us."

"Some of them are quite pretty," Simone offered.

"There are plenty of pretty women in the world, Simone. No offense to them, but if they got themselves in a situation like this, they are lacking in a particular type of competency that I find vital in a relationship." I paused as she stared at me for clarification. "Survival, Simone. The ability to survive and thrive in the present day at the very least."

"That's not entirely fair. Most of them have probably had very difficult lives," she argued.

"Trust me. It's only going to get harder, which is why we need to quietly prepare them. We'll keep close tabs on the B rank ones, though." I finished all of the blood samples, feeling a shift inside of me. I braced myself against the wall as my insides decided to rearrange themselves.

Between the instance with Simone and the demon here, I had hit Level 41 before all of the blood samples.

[Name: Bran Heros
Level: 1
Class: Blood Hegemon D
Status: Healthy
Strength: 157
Agility: 145
Vitality: 153
Intelligence: 140
Spirit: 11085

Skills:
Soul Gaze SSS
Soul Resilience S
Blunt Weapon Proficiency E
Endurance E
Throwing Proficiency F
Blood Boil B
Blood Siphon B
Blood Bolt B
Bloodline Collection 57
Regeneration B
Fire Resistance F
Poison Resistance E
Ax Proficiency E

Charge F
Bloodink Quality D
Stealth F
Inscription E
Swim D (Bracer)
Last Stand F
Blood Hex C
Blood Transfusion C
Blood Blade C
Crimson Barrier D
Sword Proficiency C]

Simone used her Lilith's Gaze on me, and I didn't push it aside, showing her everything. The blood samples had jumped my class by two ranks, as well as given me 311 stat points.

"Oh! Your Regeneration is B. One more and you'll be able to restore limbs," Simone said, recalling what I'd told her about the ability.

I chuckled. "If only it was that easy. I don't think my class will break the barrier to A rank. A rank and the S ranks usually have a hidden requirement to advance into."

Thankfully, I knew them for many skills like Regeneration. For something like weapon proficiency, a player had to actually learn the sword and start working towards an actual style. It was the same requirement to upgrade a weapon proficiency to a weapon mastery then eventually to a System recognized mastery of the style.

Though, the skill would fall back to F rank as a result. That was the difference between coming to a fight with a knife versus a sword.

As for Regeneration, I'd have to give it some exercise before I tried to find a suitable opponent to bring it to A rank.

"As for Regeneration, as long as I don't lose a limb or my head, I'll heal now. I could even get my heart ripped out and it would grow back," I chuckled.

Simone gave a look that asked how I knew that fun fact.

"Either way, I am certainly much stronger. I might not be a match for your stats right now, but my higher-level skills make up for it easily." I gave her a look. "You did great back there."

"Of course I did." Simone smirked. "What would you do without your favorite woman?" She hooked her arm in mine as if to say that I was going to be stuck with her.

I kissed her deeply, wrapping my arm around her waist and lifting her slightly off the ground.

In return, she wrapped her legs around me and started to grind her hip against mine. "You know how to give me a reward?" she whispered.

"My mother is quite literally in the other room." I hooked a thumb over my shoulder, hoping that would calm her down.

"That only means you have to keep me quiet. Isn't it exciting?" Simone nibbled at my neck.

I threw her over my shoulder as she started laughing as we left the room to go back out into the warehouse proper to check on Gloria and my mother. "You'll be punished for that later," I promised her.

Simone only laughed more as I hauled her back out. She had really loosened up with the change into being a player.

Gloria looked up from her work to raise an eyebrow at me and Simone. "Don't think I've ever heard her laugh like that before."

"Life with him has a way of bringing out the better in me." Simone squirmed and adroitly left my grasp to land on the ground, her sexy saint outfit falling back into place. "How're the potions?" she asked Gloria.

I checked the mobster as Simone asked. She'd grown to Level 25 already.

"Coming along. The program has an optional last step. I wanted Bran to see if it was something we were going to do." Gloria finished crushing more of the pink seeds and poured them into the vat before going back to the panel and tapping on it a few times. She showed me the optional portion.

I rubbed at my chin. "That's not part of the potion that I know, so I suspect it's tied to our new ingredient."

There wasn't a lot of the ingredient considering the size of the vats. Even with the programming in place for the vats, getting this quantity of ingredients again would be astronomically difficult at the moment.

"Pour the whole thing into one of the vats and run the optional program at the end." I decided to risk a quarter of the products. "The other three vats will give plenty for us. One vat will probably be enough to awaken all of their bloodlines." I hooked a thumb over my shoulder. "The other two we'll store for use later as we try to build out this force."

"And what, pray tell, will we be doing with this force?" Gloria looked away from her task to raise an eyebrow at me.

"Give them work, even if it's just pushing papers in a building you use for money laundering," I told her. "Fold them in somewhere and make them feel like they are contributing. That's how you help them. Make them feel like they are a part of something. It'll help keep away the gloom of what happened to them. Secondly, I want them to get some combat instruction. Enough that they learn to control their new strength and won't freak out should something happen."

My mother had been silently listening at the side. "I can assist with that. Otherwise, you awaken their bloodlines and one of them might just break whatever instructor you send their way. But you talk as if the prophecy is going to come true soon."

"Prophecy?" Gloria asked.

"The Five Clans all have the same prophecy," I told her. "One day soon, the world will emerge into the universe. Everyone on this planet will become a player, and demons will contest us for the world, claiming it as theirs."

"Roughly," my mother agreed. "The Heros Clan has been preparing for over three thousand years and has been in hiding a little over two thousand. Almost every generation has said it will happen in their lifetime." She studied me.

I shrugged. "Then what's the harm in preparing? Besides, I'm collecting people of bloodlines."

"Low-ranked bloodlines," my mother added and saw Gloria's brow pinch down into a frown. "B rank will get 100 stats. A rank will get 200. The difference is that most A rank bloodlines have a potential evolution to S rank or higher. S rank, 500 stats. SS rank? A thousand. SSS Rank gets two thousand."

"The higher level they are, the less that would matter," Gloria countered.

"You won't hit the higher levels without a foundation." My mother was fairly stuck in the clan's way of thinking. I'd known plenty of people who had excelled without powerful bloodlines. Though, they were the exception.

Two thousand free stat points was a huge boon.

"Then give those with the low bloodlines a foundation," I told her. "Because I am confident that the clan's prophecy is coming, and I want a force of my own in Vein City to deal with it when it comes."

"It seems things are calm here. I'll leave you to your plans." My mother turned and left just as quickly as she'd come.

"She's a little prickly," Gloria commented.

I stared at the mobster. "You're one to talk."

"I was forced into an engagement with you. I wasn't happy." Gloria turned to me.

"Wasn't?" Simone picked up on the past tense. "That means you are now?"

"Bran is giving me new things to work on." Gloria patted the machine in front of her. "Now, if I could start to work on Alchemy and maybe continue to level my abilities, it would be a different story."

"You can rank up your abilities by sparring with someone stronger than you," I added. "Tomorrow, you pick the place, and we'll give you a workout. Simone, you should come too. We can give your healing abilities something to do."

Simone looped her arm in mine. "Until then... Maybe you can help me scratch an itch while Gloria finishes up the potions."

Gloria waved her hand. "Go find a room, you two."

Chapter 38

Simone woke me up in what was becoming a new normal again. "Ah." She wiped at her slightly swollen lips. "Thank you for the meal."

"You are insatiable." I got up, thanking the System and the world for giving me Regeneration as an early class skill. This was a pretty glorious way to wake up.

"Only for you." Simone winked. "Gloria called. She was up late last night finishing the potion. You should give her a reward."

"What about the test vat? Did she learn anything?" I asked.

"She told me that she'd bring you a portion of it to see what you thought." Simone rolled off the bed and straightened her clothes.

To my surprise, the sexy saintess outfit was no longer an illusion, but actually real. Someone actually sold things like that.

"What's on the agenda for today?" Simone asked.

"I need your help in making a few talismans. Now that my Bloodink has grown more powerful, I can manage a few new ones," I explained. "Then we'll check in on our new employees and check on that special request I got from the bank." The sealed card appeared in my hand as I tore it open and began reading.

"What is it?" Simone came around my side to read it over my shoulder, not that I was hiding anything from her.

"As I thought. A higher up in the bank used their influence to contact me." I read through the request. Even if a business promised anonymity, that never seemed to stop those at the top. "The request is overly vague, but they want me to identify some sort of inscription for them." I tapped the card in my hand a few times. "We'll go this afternoon."

"What if it's a trap?" Simone seemed more worried than me.

"He'd be an idiot to try and trap me." With my Bloodink jumping to D rank, the number of talismans that I could make had multiplied several fold. Trying to trap me would be a terrible idea. "If it all goes well, then I'd like to see if we can't improve Gloria's strength some. There's a B rank instance I located. That's my final goal before heading back to the clan."

"Already thinking of that?" Simone asked.

"Three months isn't actually a lot of time. We'll probably need an entire month to clear out that B rank instance. Getting the people we rescued set up, finding more, and hammering away on gaining gold is a lot to take on. I think it will feel short in the end." I sat down at the table and pulled out some inscriptions before patting my lap. "I need to borrow your Disguise ability."

"What for?" She sat down in my lap, familiar with it.

"We are going to use it to hide some of my stat sheet qualities. When I enter the clan, I'd like to be able to let others Inspect me and see what I want them to see. First off, we need to change my class." I pricked my finger and then dabbed it on her nail, using her to help me make the inscription.

Her A rank Disguise would make this much better.

"So, you need me to hide your class. Do I get to choose what it will say?" There was a growing smile on her face as she asked the question.

I had a bad feeling about going along with her request, but her smile was hard to turn down.

"It needs to be strong enough to be respected but not so strong that I get a giant bullseye on my back. It should be an S rank." I narrowed my eyes on her.

"Oh it'll be S rank." Simone got more of my blood on her nail. "This is my one condition for helping you."

***

Gloria walked in an hour later and Inspected me. It seemed that she was getting used to using the ability as much as she could.

Her eyes opened wide when she got something from it. "Wait. What? You're… you're… a vampire?"

Simone almost fell out of her chair laughing.

I sighed. "Yes. An S rank Vampire class." It had been her one condition for helping me make dozens of talismans.

"I thought you weren't a vampire." Gloria sat down at the counter next to me. The woman had her signature coat over her shoulders though she had high-waisted leather pants that pinched her waist while a loose blouse tried and failed to hide her large chest. "Done staring?"

"You're my fiancée. Isn't it good if I'm able to appreciate your figure?" I shot back.

She sighed and pulled a potion out of her spatial ring, placing it on the counter in front of me. "Tell me what this does."

[Potion of Blood Bursting SS]

I let out a whistle. "Damn. I had no idea that Earth Blood and an additional step would make such a difference. Do you have the other one?"

She put a second potion on the counter. "This one is fairly self-explanatory. I have fifty-three of them set aside for one of my men to bring to the hotel on your word."

[Blood Awakening Potion C]

I nodded. "Just make it part of their orientation when you give them jobs. We might still get a runner or two until then. Let them run if they do."

"I already sent a few people to make sure the B ranks are comfortable. Simone said they were important," Gloria explained.

Pausing, I stared her in the eyes so that she knew I meant the words I was about to say. "Thank you. That will help me greatly. As for the first potion, it's quite simple. Awakening a higher-level bloodline is harder. It has a chance to upgrade the bloodline while awakening it. This thing"—I pointed to the upper-level potion—"would quite literally get you, me, the entire Nester Enterprise, and all of Veil City wiped off the map if one of the clans learn you have one of them. Now imagine the hell that would break loose if you revealed you had an entire vat. How many did you bottle?"

Gloria looked at the bottle again. "It boiled down more with the final step. So about twenty-five."

"Great. Who knows about them?"

"Just you and me. I haven't shown them to Bobby yet."

"Yeah. Don't do that. In fact, save one for yourself, one for Simone, and put the rest in a ring. Then hide that ring." I took off one of my F rank spatial rings. "Use this."

She didn't hesitate, putting a second potion on the counter and putting the rest into the other spatial ring before handing it to me. "Do you know a place to keep this safe?"

I took out some inscription paper and bit my thumb, starting to work an intricate spatial lock on the ring.

"What's that?"

"Spatial Lock talisman. I write a knot formation, and it has to be written exactly backwards in order to unlock it. But it also stays in a fixed location." I finished the talisman, picked up the ring, and put it next to the fridge before slapping the talisman to it, and the ring was sucked into a void and disappeared. "There. Even if someone finds that, they won't get it. Well, technically, they can. But if they are strong enough to get it, then we really don't want to be standing in their way."

Gloria poked the potion in front of her as Simone came out from the bedroom with a towel over her hair.

"I'm clean! Time to get dirty again. Oh, Gloria," she laughed.

Gloria shook her head. "What did you do to her? It's like she's a different person."

"I think she had more pressure on her than anyone realized." I smiled at the woman that Simone had transformed into. "Simone, Gloria brought you a present. It's a way to upgrade and awaken your bloodline."

"Will it give you more stats?" Simone's first question was about me.

"Unknown," I answered. "You two should drink it together. Is there still any hot water?"

"Yeah. I don't think your shower runs out." Simone picked up the potion and uncorked it, waiting for Gloria, who was far more suspicious of the potion.

"Might be better for you to take off your clothes first, Gloria." I rubbed under my nose.

"What about her?" She pointed to Simone who was in a dress.

"She's naked. She's just wearing an illusion. Well, the towel is real." I looked at her with Soul Gaze and Simone gave me a mischievous grin.

"Fine. Don't make an excuse to come peek," Gloria angrily muttered and got up to walk into the bedroom.

Simone pouted. "Here, I'm all for peeking, but we should respect boundaries. How bad is this going to be?"

"I'm asking you both to drink it at the same time because I think if you see what it does to her, you'll make me force it down you." I gave a smile that didn't quite reach my eyes.

There was some truth to it. And I wasn't sure I would be able to force Simone. Simone was still twice as strong as me.

Both of these girls were lucky freaks of nature and were only going to get stronger from this. If only potions like this would work on the Heros bloodline.

But making them both stronger would benefit me in the end. It would also help in clearing the instances that we'd acquired. The next period would be farming them as best as we could.

"Ready," Gloria called from the bedroom.

"Do it in the bathroom," I told Simone and walked behind her. "Also, lay down as soon as you take it."

Simone shuddered and hurried into the bedroom to collect Gloria and bring her to the bathroom attached.

I stopped short of the door until I heard the bathroom door close and then walked in, going right up to the bathroom door and leaning against it. "If you need me, shout," I told her.

"We'll be fine. I'm tougher than you think," Simone said, and I heard the noise of a cork pop before someone gulped.

"This isn't so bad," Simone called back before she let out a blood curdling scream.

Gloria was far more subdued, letting out an angry moan and her body hitting the floor.

The Blood Burst potion was brutal. In order to evolve a bloodline, it required stimulating the bloodline to the max before ejecting all of the weaker blood.

Right now, both of my ladies were bleeding out of everywhere, even the pores of their skin.

I pressed my head to the door, feeling an almost physical pain as I heard Simone's screams.

"Bran!" Simone screamed out, and I nearly tore the door open to rush in.

I snatched her naked body off the floor as she thrashed, and I held her close as she coughed blood, more blood running out of her eyes.

"I'm here. It won't last much longer. Use Bastion of Athena on yourself," I told her, cursing myself for not thinking of the ability earlier.

I didn't dare use my abilities on her; the blood transfusion might interact with what was already happening with her body.

The blood that came out of her was thick and dark, drying quickly. Simone stopped crying, but she held onto me and shook as her body purged the impurities.

"I'm sorry." I stroked her hair. "It is rough. I know."

"You've done it?" Simone asked.

"No. It doesn't work with Heros blood," I told her. "But I've been in this position before." I held her tightly and pecked her forehead, ignoring the blood getting all over me.

Gloria had dragged herself to a sitting position, still jerking as she watched me with Simone. I didn't think there was any anger in her gaze, just a strange look of pain.

Reaching out, I grabbed her and pulled her next to Simone, holding them both in my arms.

"I'm fine," Gloria said through gritted teeth.

"Sure," I replied. "This is for me. I can't bear seeing you both this way."

Thankfully, the potion's effects were short lived, and a glance with Soul Gaze showed me that it was effective on both of them.

They were understandably exhausted, so I picked them both up, one in each arm and brought them over to the giant shower, placing them on the bench and taking a wash cloth in hand to carefully clean them both.

I touched every inch of both of them, but it wasn't sexual. It was filled with the tender care of taking care of someone who had just gone through something rough.

Gloria didn't even balk as I got into every crack and crevice.

"Damn," Simone eked out. "That was so much worse than when I got a ton of stats at once."

"Well, we did get that too," Gloria said, staring into the middle distance, clearly looking at her character sheet. "A thousand stats. What's a Magnamalo Queen?"

"Something clearly badass." Simone smirked. "It sounds better than Blushing Phoenix. Though, I'll take it. I jumped two ranks. SS and another shit ton of stats." She slowly shook her head.

"Good," I encouraged both of them. "The goal from here on out is to get both of you strong enough to join me in a Level 87 B rank dungeon."

"Did you get stats from me?" Simone asked.

I quickly checked into my bloodline collection, and interestingly enough, I had not gained Simone's change.

[Pink Yuan Bird Bloodline - Upgraded, refresh required]

"Nope, but we'll save that for later when I'm ready to join the clan. You two are now my secret weapon to ensure that I can reset my level."

Chapter 39

I arrived at the bank that the letter had indicated was where I would meet my customer.

"Hello, Valued Customer." A greeter smiled at me, and his eyes wandered to the two women behind me.

I didn't blame him. They were a little extra radiant after awakening their bloodlines. "Here's my account number. I have a meeting with someone high up at the bank here, though I didn't get his actual title."

The man walked over to a computer and typed in my account before his demeanor shifted to something a little more rigid. "Sir, right this way. We have a special lobby for members of your distinction."

He quickly led the three of us up to the second floor where there was a swanky lobby. This one even had fresh bakery goods sitting out and a coffee bar.

"Please make yourself at home. The account manager for you has been alerted."

Gloria seemed right at home as she walked over to the coffee bar to make herself something, snatching up several different cookies on a plate.

I stared at those cookies and then at her waspish waist.

"What?" Gloria took a bite of a cookie and liked it, adding another of that type to her plate.

"That you have a sweet tooth wasn't even on my bingo card. Was it on yours?" I asked Simone, who was joining Gloria in going through the pastries, though she went for a muffin.

"We don't really put on weight anymore, right?" Simone said, stuffing half the muffin in her mouth. "Do you realize how much I have to deny myself to look the way I do?" She chewed the muffin.

"I've always loved sweets." Gloria took another big bite of the cookie and then picked up a brownie.

A handsome man of indeterminable age chuckled as he walked up to us. "It is a perk of being a player. Our vitality and strength work well to keep us at our prime. If you eat too much, then it just seems to melt off." He glanced at the two ladies, clearly Inspecting them. His face showed mild surprise before he turned to me.

I only let him see my first name and the fake class. "Pleasure to meet you, Vincent."

I didn't need my Inspection to recognize a hero from the First Demon War, yet I wanted to see what I was dealing with.

[Vincent Jear
Level: 38
Class: Golden Fist A
Status: Amicable
Strength: 1218
Agility: 920
Vitality: 1519
Intelligence: 832
Spirit: 291
...]

His brow furrowed at his failure to Inspect me. He had an upgraded 'Appraisal', but it wasn't enough.

"I keep my cards close, Vincent. I'm assuming you have a need for my talents."

My coffee gained a packet of sugar, and I sat down in the lobby to have this conversation. No one else seemed to be present on the entire floor.

Vincent had a good-natured smile. His age was a little hard to pick out, probably because he was far older than he looked. Despite his broad shoulders and muscular figure, he had a baby face and two ancient eyes set into them.

The man was a legend. He was someone who quite literally turned money into power, standing before the nearest Hell

Gate to Vein City and holding the front. He became a beacon for the Free Player Alliance afterwards.

But that had led the clans to make an example of him. They had slaughtered him, before hanging his head in the center of Vein City. It was good to be strong, but oftentimes, standing out too much only got a player hammered down. It was part of why I kept my cards close.

"Strange that we haven't met before, Bran. Those of us who are old enough seem to run into each other eventually."

"I've been idle for some time." I shrugged, not giving him much and letting him think I had far greater depth than I would normally. "These two are learning from me at present; they have quite the talent."

He glanced at both of them again and nodded. "They do."

"Gloria Nester here is actually training to be an alchemist. I don't particularly have much luck with fire, but I know how to make many things. As for Simone, well, with her potential, one can never go wrong. She will be a powerful healer." I gestured to the two ladies who were indulging their sweet teeth. "So, what does a man like you need from a simple inscriptionist?"

Vincent pulled out two of my inscriptions from his spatial ring. "You made both of these?"

"Indeed. Rather simple inscriptions." I smiled at him.

"Yes, they are. I've had a few experts in most fields work for me." He tapped the two. "One of them is widely considered one of the best inscriptionists in the world. Even the clans seek out his help. He took one look at your work and nearly fell out of his chair. According to him, this was the work of a supreme master, one that might even eclipse him."

My lips curled even a little further. "What an honest man to say there's someone better than him."

Vincent almost winced. "That's the problem. He's quite prideful. To hear him say such a thing told me that he was far outstripped by you. There was a problem I had given him, and he was unable to solve it, so I would like to offer it to you."

Thinking back to the past, I tried to puzzle out what he was going to ask me to do. Though he was a hero in Vein City briefly, my interaction with him had been minimal.

Rumors swirled with the stink of a smear campaign led by the clans after he had died. Lots of accusations were made about mishandling money to become as strong as he was.

"Well then. I do enjoy a puzzle." My smile was so wide that my eyes pinched closed.

Vincent was old school and pulled out a photo for me to see.

I was prepared for many things and ready to keep my cool, but what was on the photo made me lean far forward to double check the details.

"A Vault of Pandora," I breathed.

The man smiled. "I heard they were called Vaults of Archimedes. Some call them man-made instances, or perhaps man took over an old instance."

My smile was stiff—he was completely wrong. The Vault in front of me was nothing other than a trap.

"You want me to open it?" I had seen one of these before, though it was at the bottom of the Indian Ocean at present. That one, I'd opened after studying it for a few months.

"We'd like to hold an event from the FPA to allow everyone into them. From what we've been able to gather, the space inside of it is absolutely massive. There are records of one in the past where it tested those who entered and gave great strength to the victor." The man seemed excited to explore it and search for treasures.

"Really, people went into one before?" I was absolutely sure they didn't come back out. Or if they did, they were not the same people who went into it.

"Yes. It's said that's how the Sect of Heaven's Fist rose to the prominent position they hold today." He smiled fondly, likely thinking of what he could do with such a power.

Yet he missed the blood drain from my face. Unknowingly, he had just placed a missing puzzle piece in front of me.

The Sect of Heaven's Fist was a breeding ground for demons. The whole sect was compromised. Promising youngsters were sent from the clans or lesser sects, and it wouldn't be until the end of the War for Supremacy that they would strike while the clans were weak and begin the Second Demon War.

By the time the information came to light decades later, it was apparent that the sect had been demons for almost as long as the clans had been in hiding.

If they had uncovered a vault... it made a certain sort of sense. These things were giant demon-made artifacts to hide their presence from Ancient Beasts and the System itself.

I rubbed at my forehead. "The means to open one... I'd have to examine it in person as well as consult my records. I do know that I have texts discussing the opening of a previous one. I do not believe it was Heaven's Fist, though."

I was sure it wasn't. The one I had experienced in a past life was deep under the ocean, unearthed with a giant tectonic shift as part of a successful Hell Gate.

Right now, I was unfortunately too weak to deal with what he had put in front of me like I would have liked. Ideally, I'd be able to go in there and crush the demon souls that lay within before they possessed everyone.

Picking up the photo, I took a closer look.

In truth, my mind was also running a mile a minute trying to piece together several other events with this piece of knowledge. Vincent had fought the demons in the First Demon War. It was unlikely that he'd unlocked it and entered it in my past life.

Which meant... the clans might have killed him to keep its existence a secret. Did those old men delve into this, and did they figure out the truth? Or could this have been a piece in the background of the War for Supremacy?

Either way, it was a bomb that I could defuse.

"That is more promising than I'd hoped." Vincent sat back. "I won't share the location with you until you have some confidence in undoing the seal." He threw out several folders of photos and information.

"I'll need a photo with it under the moonlight. If you can bring someone with keen senses of mana, they might be able to see more under the moonlight than pictures can produce." I decided this was also an opportunity to take advantage of this man. "There will likely be a list of rare ingredients needed to unseal this. It will require a mix of alchemy and inscription if it is like the one I've read about before. Then there is also the factor of my cost."

"On success, I ca—"

"You are using my time by simply presenting this puzzle to me and asking me to research it. Half will be paid up front, or I won't begin work," I told him sharply, glancing up at the man with five hundred years of doubt in people.

Vincent cleared his throat. My gaze had an effect on him. "Of course." He pulled out a pen and clicked it as he thumbed a pad of paper to a new page and scribbled a number down and slid it over to me.

I lazily picked it up, staring at the number. One million. That was a lot of gold coins. I almost thought he was trying to pay me in mundane currency, but he put coins at the end. Paying me in anything but gold coins for this work would be an insult.

Yet I couldn't show an ounce of excitement over this quantity. "That's fine, I guess. When I have time to work on this project, I'll contact you to see if you've taken the additional photos. It is of some interest."

He tore off another strip of paper and slid it to me. "I'm very interested in this happening quickly."

I looked at the three million number with a little more excitement. "There are other projects happening. I can promise to have something by the end of the year." I would need to go through the clan's rites to get the kind of power that I'd like to handle the Vault.

"Half a year," Vincent said to himself. "We've waited far longer than that. Another half a year is nothing. I'll have someone get the photos at the next full moon, and a wizard to inspect it at the same time."

"Good. Good." I nodded sagely.

The vault itself was made of complex and powerful inscriptions. Yet the locking mechanism was something that was made to be undone from the outside. I was fairly confident that if my Bloodink got to B rank, I could pop it open with ease.

"Then when you deliver those notes, I will expect the first half of the payment," I told him, getting to my feet and waving the two sugar fiends to follow me.

Really, who would have pegged Gloria as someone with a sweet tooth?

"Bran, about tha—" Simone started, but I held up a hand.

"We're going to an instance to train Gloria. We can talk there." I wanted to be completely safe from prying ears.

Chapter 40

"It's a trap," I told them as soon as we stepped into another of Tom's instances.

This one was an F rank, Level 40. It should work well for farming some quick levels for Gloria and me, though the loot would be abysmal. The others I had found on the map were low level, perfect for working Bobby, Rodger, and Candy through. Not so much of a challenge for the two lucky ladies.

"That Vault he wants into is more like a seed filled with demon souls. It'll test people, kill a lot of them, and then those who rise above get stuffed with a demon soul when they are worn down and tired."

Simone gasped. "Those poor people."

"Are probably dicks anyway." I shrugged. "The problem is that they'll then be poised to backstab organizations at vital moments. This is a big chance to set the demons back."

Gloria was a few steps ahead of us, her purple flames harassing the first monster group made up of three F rank rats. "So your goal is to go after these demons?" she asked.

"Mostly. That and to take over the world!" I laughed maniacally. "To have the power to stop the demons that are seeded into this world already, I'd have to unite several powers that control the player world. So, yes, rule the world. Though, I'm not much of a leader beyond being the one to be at the front of a battle line and take on the biggest guy the other side has."

"So you'll just crack heads on your way to get there?" she asked.

"No. I'll probably only crack a few heads before I find someone like you who can help me actually piece things together successfully into an organization. You're smart, and

I could really use your type of experience, Gloria." I stared her down. "That's why I didn't stop your father when he foisted this engagement upon us."

She narrowed her eyes and was probably trying to be a little intimidating with the purple flames dancing behind her on the dying rats. "That's why?"

"Yep. Honestly, I knew very little about you. All I knew was that you were competent enough to be rattling at the cage your father had imposed on your business," I explained while Simone put out a blanket on the ground.

The instance was actually rather quaint, if you ignored the rats. It was warm and sunny out in a field.

"Since then, there's only been more to like. You are beautiful, and honestly, more competent than I expected. The bloodline is an extra plus." I smiled at her.

Gloria struck a beautiful figure that she did her best to make imposing with the coat over her shoulders. "Thank you." She eyed me. "You still need to take this seriously." She glanced at Simone.

"Simone stays. Obviously," I reminded her. "The Heros Clan encourages all men of the clan to sleep around, preferably with women of potent bloodlines."

Gloria made a face. "That... why?"

"It's how our bloodlines works. You have a kid, and the Heros bloodline wins out, every time. It absorbs the other potential bloodline and sort of adds it to the primordial soup that our bloodline has become," I explained.

"Sounds a lot like your class." Gloria nodded.

"I agree. It's part of the reason the class caught my attention. Blood is powerful, doubly so for someone of the Heros Clan. I don't want to bring a kid into the mess of a world that's on the horizon, though. Yet, I digress. I have been taking this quite seriously, Gloria. I went out of my way to make you a player, which involved some risk for me to carry a demon soul into yours and then disable it so that you could kill it. When the opportunity arose to help your bloodline, I took it. When I had the opportunity to make you stronger, even stronger than me, I took it."

She narrowed her eyes on me. "You've used me as an errand boy."

"Yeah. You have some rough edges, Gloria. I might remind you, when we first met, it was because you were planning to kill your father. Make no mistake, I'm leading this family of mine. Your help is invaluable, but will you resent me the same as you have your father?" I pushed her. It was probably time that we had this conversation and came to an understanding.

Gloria paused as the rats melted back into the instance. "You think I'd try and kill you?"

"Possibly." I shrugged.

"No." She shook her head. "You've opened too many doors for me already." She paused as if thinking about something that this conversation finally made her face. "I appreciate what you've done for me."

"But...?" I led her forward.

Her eyes flickered to Simone.

Ah. She really couldn't get over monogamy. "I'm going to add more ladies most likely. Not just for beautiful women to have sex with either. That's just a plus. I need people who are competent and can assist me with my plans."

"You have to have a relationship with them?" Gloria asked.

"Not all of them. But I've long outlived the concept of monogamy. If you are going to be part of this family, it's going to be more than two of us, more than three of us. Because the world is about to get so harsh that two people standing alone against it are going to get rolled over."

"Again, you keep speaking like you know the future," Gloria scowled.

I leaned back, watching her. "Because I do. I lived it once before. This time, I'm doing things differently."

I had decided it was time I worked to pull Gloria closer. Telling someone a secret was a powerful way to gain trust, by showing your own hand. That, and beating around the bush with her was going to just slow down progress on my plans.

She was a smart woman. Her first reaction was to look at Simone, who was carefree. "She was supposed to die... I was too?"

"Yes to both." I nodded.

Her mind continued to race. "You also told him about my bomb." It dawned on her, making her shake her head. "Here I'd been obsessed with finding the leak. There was no leak."

"Sorry. I needed to gain Carmen's trust. In my past life, I worked for him. I know him well enough to know that I can work with him," I explained.

"So you told him that you know the future, proved it with my bomb. My father's always been a man of very fine principles. Then... you asked for his help and he gave you me." She pieced everything together quickly.

Simone cleared her throat. "He was pretty much prepared to turn you into a work horse. That was until he discovered you actually had potential between your bloodline and class. After that, when he spoke to me of his plans, they always included improving you as a player."

I glanced at Simone, but I didn't correct her. "So, what will you do, Gloria? Ready to take your engagement seriously? If we are honest, between the spatial ring, the alchemy knowledge, and the access to instances, I've given you quite the engagement present."

Both women winced.

"What?" I asked Simone.

"Not romantic at all," she sighed.

Gloria shook her head, not so much angry as disappointed. "If you want me to take this engagement seriously, you are going to have to get down on one knee."

I stared at her. "Really?" That sounded more princess than mobster, but I guess she had already defied my expectations several times.

Gloria just stared at me.

I cleared my throat, ready to get down on one knee, but Simone grabbed me and shook her head.

"Not now. Make a thing of it, and you'd better have a very expensive ring," Simone warned me.

Gloria heard her. "I'm a size six."

I glanced at her waist. She seemed smaller than that.

"Ring size," she practically growled at me.

"I know," I shot back. "Now why don't you spar with Simone while I work on clearing this dungeon."

CHAPTER 40

Clearing a dungeon was far more comfortable than the conversation we were having on jewelry. I whipped my hand to the side and a sword of blood hardened into a pristine blade.

"Don't overdo it," Simone warned me.

I moved forward, wanting to kill some rats and relieve some stress.

***

Simone finished laying down the blanket and sat on it as Bran wandered off slightly angry and likely going to use monsters for therapy. She thought about using Bastion of Athena to see if it would help but left it alone.

"Might want to put that away if we are going to fight," Gloria told her.

Simone glanced at the other woman. "No, I don't think you'll touch it. If you can singe it, I'll put it away and deal with you seriously."

Veil of Netherlight became a bubble around her as Gloria took the challenge and poured purple fire over her ability. Gloria frowned, pushing more fire onto the barrier.

"Right now, we are both E rank with these abilities, yet I have more than twice your stats." Simone brushed her hair off her shoulder as the other woman tried harder to pop her ability. "What do you think of Bran?"

"Huh?" Gloria huffed and threw her arms to the side as purple flames split from the ground and tried to go underneath Simone's blanket.

Veil of Netherlight, however, guarded her from every angle. According to Bran, it was an extremely powerful anti-magic protection. Using it against Gloria, especially while annoying her, served to train both of their abilities well while also proving to be immensely satisfying.

Bran had said that, when training, a player needed to fight similar rank skills or higher rank skills to see any real progress.

"Bran is extremely skilled in selective things," Simone said.

"Alchemy, inscription, and killing things." Gloria threw her hands forward again, trying to wear out Simone's barrier. "So what?"

"He's terrible at a decent number of things. You should see him and the internet. It's like a cat and water. Right now, he's put a giant task on his shoulders. He wants to save humanity from an onslaught of demons that will come in a little less than two years," Simone laid the situation out for Gloria since she didn't ask.

The mob princess paused. "Really?"

"Yep. A sort of protective layer around this world is going to crack, and nine 'Hell Gates' as he called them are going to open up. Apparently, world to world travel is difficult, but these have been set up ahead of time. The second this world is open, demons will storm it in an attempt to possess every human on this planet." Simone had gotten most of the story from the Rapture to the First Demon War out of Bran. It wasn't exactly the most romantic of pillow talks, yet she knew being someone to share his past life with was important.

"That sounds... bad." Gloria paused. "He lived through that?"

"That and several more disasters to come. It sounded like at the end there was one final bastion of humanity. When that cracked, he hatched a desperate plan to send only his soul back to this time," Simone informed her as she dusted off her gown and stood amid more purple flame. "He needs our help."

Gloria tilted her head. "He's..." She glanced off in the distance where he was tearing apart rats like a mad man. "He's strong."

"Physically, spiritually, and yes, he knows a lot." Simone nodded. "Yet he's alone. So very alone. It sounds like he's been that way for a long time. He needs our help to fill in the gaps where he's not an expert. That means forming an organization that's larger than just one man to shoulder the burden he's placed upon himself."

Gloria stopped sending fire over Simone. "So? Why are you all in on this then? To save the world?"

Simone shook her head. "Do you know why I made a brothel?"

"So you could roll in the money?" Gloria huffed.

Simone darted forward, stepping up into Gloria's face before the other woman could react, her fist lagging only a second before it hit Gloria in the cheek and deformed it for a second before blasting the other woman back and causing her to roll through the field.

"Fuck, your face is hard." Simone shook out her hand and healed herself before waving her hand and healing the woman who'd stopped rolling on the ground. "No. I thought years ago that I could make a non-exploitive alternative to the sex industry. I thought that I could change things."

Gloria laughed at her. "So you were like one of those mom-and-pop toy stores that started making things out of recycled plastic?"

Anger surged through Simone again. She kicked the other woman in the ribs, sending her flying until she hit the edge of the instance which glowed briefly before rebounding her back to Simone's feet. Then she healed Gloria.

"That was a rude comparison, but apt. It didn't work, but I kept trying. It certainly made a difference for some women, but not really enough to matter in the grand scheme of the world."

"That's where your class came from?" Gloria asked, still panting from being punted. "Also, you are freakishly strong for your size."

"Thank you. I work out a lot." Simone smiled down at Gloria. "There's a new opportunity for me and for you. Bran is, with or without us, going to make a sizable impact on the world. I want to help him, both because I've found myself enamored with the man and his struggles, and because it will give me an opportunity to make a greater impact in helping women than ever before." She held a hand down to help Gloria get up.

Gloria blinked up at her and took the hand. "So what do you want from me?"

Simone lifted her up and placed her back on her feet. "To help fill in the gaps along with me. Bran needs a reason to do things beyond 'save humanity'. It's a lofty goal, but I think it'll tire out before he gets to the end. Help me help him keep going. Find your own goals in all of this, and for the love of god, send me a few images of rings you like because we both know Bran is going to pick out something awful."

Gloria snorted. "You aren't half bad."

"Neither are you, once you get past the bossy princess." Simone smiled as purple fire engulfed her. Thankfully, she was prepared enough, and another veil wrapped around her. "Really? I thought we were having a moment?"

"We were, but you said that if I burnt your blanket that you'd take this seriously." Gloria pointed behind her where the flames had passed by and the corner of the blanket was now on fire. "It seems you were too focused on what was in front of you."

Simone narrowed her eyes at the taller woman. The two of them would get along just fine, but she was going to teach Gloria a lesson in trying to outsmart her.

Chapter 41

Tom's additional instances and the others from the map sped my plan up beautifully. The next month passed by quickly. We split into various groups and worked down the instances. Well, except for the B rank instance.

We were getting closer to being able to consider running the B rank instance, which was progress I could not have hoped to achieve on my own.

Stat-wise, Simone and I could compare. The problem was that stats alone wouldn't be enough to get through the instance. Everything in that instance would have B rank abilities. And if any of those skills were defensive, we were screwed. Maybe if we had enough gear, we could power through, but the gear we had gotten was weak against a B rank.

And we had all come together more through our time in the instances. Even Gloria had mellowed out, becoming much more fun to be around. But my focus at the moment was Simone, who had told me in quite simple terms that it was time to go shopping.

I had tried to suggest a little more time in the instances, but she had replied, 'If you don't stop killing monsters and take me shopping, I'm going to start healing the monsters.'

So, I was now dressed up far nicer than I had ever looked in my previous life. A part of me was dressing up just to impress Simone.

My pants were neatly pressed and my shirt was something new I'd picked up that fit my growing frame better. Becoming a player had added a little more around my shoulders.

"You look incredible." Simone met me at the mall. She wasn't wearing an illusion this time.

Her bangs were pulled back over the horns that had been growing around her head like an ivory crown. Rather than her saintess outfit, she was dressed in a floral-print summer dress that squeezed at her chest before becoming so loose that it blew with the breeze around her thighs.

It was a simple, yet immaculate piece.

Suddenly, I remembered why we couldn't just leave home together. Grabbing her by the waist, I gave her a taste of how I was feeling, lifting her up slightly so that I could kiss her lips.

Simone dove in head first, wrapping her arms around my neck and holding on while our tongues battled in public for a moment. "Now, put me down. We should get going before we draw a giant crowd."

A pair of teens had stopped to gawk, and when I glanced their way, they ducked their heads and hurried on like they suddenly had something very important to do very far away.

I chuckled. "You just made me too excited."

"Glad I can still have that effect on you." She hung off my arm as we walked into the mall, buffeted by cool air when the sliding doors opened.

A few kids that I might have known from high school pointed at me, but honestly, I couldn't remember that part of my life very well.

"What are we buying?" I asked, focusing back on Simone.

"Nothing in particular. Just shopping," Simone replied cryptically.

I'd normally take it as a woman being… well… a woman. Yet Simone seemed to be a rather goal-oriented person. She had something specific in mind, but I was happy to go along with her.

We deserved a break. And all the money in my bank would be worthless eventually. If she wanted something nice, I was fine to buy it for her.

"Well then, I'm going to love seeing what you pick out." I went along with it.

Simone gave me a big grin, and we started to walk through the mall as she commented on stores. "Oh by the way, Gloria said all of the bloodline holders stuck around and are doing well at their new jobs. A few of them brought their families over, and we of course drew their blood."

"Oh? That's great." I felt a little guilty as I realized I had forgotten to keep asking about the people we had saved. The instances had taken all of my attention.

Simone gently guided us into an intimate wear store. There was a small group of men, the bag holder types, who waited around the front of the store as if going deeper would embarrass them.

I rolled my eyes. It was just underwear, sexy underwear even. I was a big fan of this type of store. Rather than stop at the entrance with them, I walked inside with Simone.

"Glad to hear they are doing well. Have we found how the demons were finding the bloodlines?" I pulled her to a stop at some particularly fitting garments. Red was always interesting, doubly so when it made her green eyes pop even more.

She hooked a finger over a set and carried it with her as we continued shopping. She picked out a few more, and some were clearly not her size, but rather Gloria's.

What I found odd were the white, almost bridal style ones that she gravitated towards. I found myself holding a growing stack of lingerie as she casually walked around, snatching various pieces.

"Some luck, but not much. We need you to do some verification later this weekend." She brought us over to the changing booths and didn't let go of my arm as she pulled me in with her. "I need a second opinion," she answered my raised eyebrow as I put down the stack of garments.

I held my arms up. "Happy to, just wondered if that attendant was about to try and stop us."

"What? It's not like you aren't a perfect gentleman." She winked and threw her sundress off in a single motion before hanging it on the side. Underneath the dress was a matching set that was a soft yellow embroidered with orange flowers.

As quickly as she removed her dress, the bra and panties she was wearing soon found themselves hanging up as she pulled the top one off of the stack and held it up to herself for a moment before tossing it to the side.

This continued for several sets until she found a strappy black one she liked enough to put on. She twirled in front of the mirror before turning to me. "Do you like it?"

"I love you in anything," I replied smoothly.

She rolled her eyes. "Unhelpful smooth talk."

While those were the words she said, I got a kiss for my answer, so I was fairly certain I had gotten the answer right.

"Now help me take it off." She turned her back to me.

I raised an eyebrow.

"It's part of the test. Take it off like you're going to devour me." She blushed and leaned against the wall as if she was shy. We both knew she wasn't.

My hands easily slid under the multiple straps and peeled her out of it as I pressed her to the wall and kissed her.

She delighted in my touch, running her fingers through my hair and indulging in the kiss for a moment before she put her hands on my chest. "We have more to try on and then more stores after this."

I felt a smidgen of disappointment. A certain part of my anatomy had jumped to conclusions and was ready to drag her home.

She continued to try on a number of sets before coming down to two sets and debating between them. "Which one do you think is better?"

Both were white and fairly simple. One played with sheer fabric to tantalize, while the other specialized in loose, silky fabric.

"I think they are both great." I did not know the correct answer, but I knew enough that the wrong one could be disastrous.

Simone rolled her eyes and waved her hand.

I felt the System assist her, and an illusion settled over the booth before she sat me down on the bench and opened my legs.

"Then we'll just have to test it." She stripped out of the one she was wearing and hung it to the side before an illusion of the sheer one settled over her. "Don't want to get the real one messy... yet."

She then unzipped my pants and pulled out my cock. Her finger ran over the sensitive head.

"We'll let him decide. This one?" She rubbed herself against me in the one illusion before it switched. "Or this one?" She went to the silky one and did the same gesture.

I twitched happily in her hand and pulled her mouth closer. "Maybe this one." After watching her try on all the outfits, I was more than ready to thrust right up into her.

Simone kissed the tip, her tongue coming out and playing with the shaft for a moment as she carefully paid attention to every inch of it.

"I guess you deserve a reward for all your work," she whispered before she started giving it sloppy kisses. She completely ignored the wet noises sounding in the dressing room, and the possibility of getting caught was driving me wild.

"We both know you love this just as much as I do. Admit it." Experience with Simone told me she would make any excuse to give me a blowjob. She loved giving them, and not just as a prelude to the main event. It was often that I'd find she'd had her own orgasm while pleasuring me.

Simone continued to give me sloppy wet kisses. "I do." She licked me balls to tip. "There's something wonderful about it." She locked eyes with me.

I let out the smallest of groans, trying to muffle it so that others wouldn't hear.

She shook her head with me in her mouth before coming off, pressing a demure finger to her lips. "No noises."

Giving me a wicked smile, she leaned down and swallowed me deep, sucking on me. I had to grab onto the horns hidden in her hair as I tried to slow her down. Jolts of pleasure raced up my spine, and I wanted to grunt, moan, or cry out, but I held the noises.

She smiled around my cock as she watched me struggling to stay quiet, and that only encouraged her as she redoubled her efforts to force me to break my silence. Her eyelids closed halfway, and she fell into her own enjoyment as she poured pleasure over me.

"Simone," I whispered a soft moan.

She shook her head, lapping at my shaft before pushing herself onto it further and taking me into her throat. She held onto my hips as she slammed it down again and again.

At this point, I was twitching like mad in her throat, my cock begging for more. The tension of trying to stay quiet was having the secondary effect of preventing me from cumming.

Simone smiled, only going harder until my vision started to spot with the strain. Her slippery throat coaxed my cock deeper into pleasure as she expertly drew every inch of me in and out of her.

If giving blowjobs was a ranked skill, Simone would certainly be SS if not far above.

I held onto her horns as she upped her game once again, pulling me out of her throat only for her tongue to slather love over the head and take it back into her slick depths in deep thrusts.

She grinned up at me, daring me not to make a sound as she used an ability. Soothing Kiss was meant to help those in pain by filling them with enough pleasure that the wounded would fall asleep. She activated the skill, and I was flooded with pleasure. I couldn't help but let out a gasping moan as I erupted into her mouth.

Simone suckled on me a little more, making sure she had gotten every drop of my seed, and stood up with a very satisfied smile on her face. "I think I'll just get them both."

"Of course." I had no strength left to resist. In post-nut clarity, I knew that she had just wanted to do this the whole time. Trying on the outfits was a ruse, and I had no problem with that fact.

She quickly organized the garments into what she was going to buy for herself, for Gloria, and what she was going to put back. Oddly enough, everything that she had tried on, she was going to buy.

Simone was humming happily as I recovered from the incredible blowjob.

"Alright." I felt like my legs weren't made of jelly anymore and stood. "Let's move on."

"Yep. We just need to buy these." She was almost skipping. The only reason she wasn't was that she was attached to my arm.

Given the rather ridiculous funds at my disposal, both Simone and Gloria had cards to my account. It would be impossible to spend all of it before the Rapture, and there was no point in hoarding it. Even then, Simone asked for my card, delighting in me buying. Simone checked out as I stood confidently behind her.

One attendant kept staring at us, but I wasn't bothered. She was mostly staring at Simone with a mix of awe and envy.

We walked out, and the very stuffed bag of undergarments disappeared into her spatial ring as soon as we were out of sight. I almost asked where to next, but then I decided to be surprised. Simone hung off my arm as we walked and commented on the stores as we walked.

It was a fairly relaxing day for us. We had all gotten better at the instances, and as a result, fighting the monsters had gotten easier, but strolling the mall with Simone was a new pleasure I hadn't realized I needed.

Chapter 42

Simone and I made three more shopping diversions, which included four blow jobs and a cone of ice cream, before Simone stopped at a jewelry store.

"Jewelry?" I asked. "I didn't peg you for someone who likes jewelry. You normally just wear a single statement necklace."

Simone turned to regard me. "You can tell me what type of jewelry I wear, but can't tell that I really want you to get me a specific kind of jewelry?"

It only took me a moment to understand.

Right, I was supposed to get Gloria a ring. Of course I should get Simone one. Taking charge, I pulled her into the store.

I spotted the dolled-up saleswoman and threw down my Black Platinum credit card on the counter. So far, the card had been recognized by a few of the higher-end stores, and the saleswomen had reacted by giving Simone plenty of attention.

"I'm buying a few rings. I'm particularly interested in engagement rings."

The saleswoman almost snatched up the card, but instead gave me her most helpful smile and was very alert. "Wonderful. We have a whole engagement section, if you'll follow me."

I picked up the card and mirrored her on the other side of the displays, pulling Simone along with me. "So. I imagine you'd like something that is simple yet makes a statement?"

Simone raised an eyebrow. "Sometimes, you are brilliant; other times, you are so dense."

I shrugged. "When I have a target or a goal in mind, I am fairly good at achieving it. Everything else…" I trailed off, knowing that I often had tunnel vision.

"At least you know." Simone stopped before the four counters that wrapped around a big mirror. She tucked some of her hair behind her ears as she leaned over to look into them.

"Are you helping pick out your own ring?" the woman asked.

"And for another," Simone answered offhandedly.

I expected the woman to react, but she was completely stoic.

"I've heard it all," she answered my look.

"Great. Then I'm getting two. Hers'll be a statement diamond, big with a bright gold band, maybe a small few just to make the center one look bigger." I pointed at Simone. "As for the other, I need white gold and gaudy. Like, a giant stone in the center and then we can play 'how many diamonds can be put on a tiny ring' with the rest of the metal."

Simone chuckled at my description, but she didn't correct me.

"What? She's a total princess at times." I had gotten to know Gloria better over the last month. We'd even gone on a few dates.

In and out, she was a mafia princess.

She had a rough exterior, and she also had extravagant expectations when it came to material goods. She refused to drive anything but a Rolls-Royce, and her personal Rolls-Royce was black, armored, and had gold trim.

When it came to getting her a ring, about the only thing better than this would be if there was a decent black metal.

The saleswoman, smelling an easy sale, pulled out several trays and collected the rings before slotting them in a smaller show tray. "These are our simple, yet tasteful lines."

By tasteful, she meant stones big enough to hit someone and do some damage.

Simone played with the rings for a moment, trying a few on and wiggling her finger while she admired them.

I now understood why I had been brought shopping. I didn't have to ask, nor did I mind. Instead, I looked the rings over, checking as she tried different looks.

They were all rings to me, but I carefully watched Simone's expression as she tried each.

When she put the final ring of her set down, I picked the third one. "This one. Put it in a box for me. And then I will also take this one." I picked the most expensive looking one for Gloria.

"She'll love it," Simone added.

"Uh huh. Did she have one picked out for you before you took me on this date?" I asked.

"What?" Simone playfully put her hand on her chest.

I shook my head at her antics. "Box them both up, and while we're at it, I'll just buy this whole display." I waved my hand over the four cases.

The woman froze. "All of them?"

"You know what? We'll buy the whole store." I waved my hand around, feeling quite happy with both her and Simone's reaction.

I had always wanted to do something like this. And I had more money than I could spend. Why not fuck around? Besides, now I had anniversary presents well into the future. Fine jewelry like this wouldn't exist very long past the Rapture.

Sitting around and scraping gold into beautiful designs was a lost art. Because those that did that were quickly possessed and died.

The saleswoman didn't ask again, scurrying off with my card and whispering to the other woman on the floor who immediately stopped helping the couple that was just browsing.

"It will be just a moment as we settle up," she called out. "Boxing all of it will..."

I waved my hand over the glass and the contents disappeared. "Magic trick." I winked at her. "Don't tell anyone, though."

The two ladies gasped and looked at each other before my credit card, and decided to ignore it for the sale they were about to get.

Simone rolled her eyes, but she hung onto my arm and the two rings that were boxed as I quickly vanished the entire store. Both sales women were quickly working the checkout counter.

I had a very smug smile on my face as I leaned on an empty display. "So, I'll have Gloria pick us up and take us to Velluto Rosso?" I took the two ring boxes from Simone and put them in a storage ring.

"That's a place she reserves for celebrations and special events," Simone said and waved down at herself. "I am not dressed for it."

"If you tell Gloria that's where we're going, she'll take thirty minutes to get ready herself. There's a makeup place down the row that offers walk-in makeovers, and I know you have at least one dress that would work that you've bought today," I countered.

"I need makeup?" Simone pretended to be aghast.

"Your lipstick could use a touch up." I grinned at her, feeling more than a little cocky.

She planted a kiss on my cheek. "Stall Gloria if she comes early." Simone hurried away.

"This'll be on the card?" the saleswoman asked with a tension like she was barely staying on her feet after the sale. I had a feeling her commissions were going to make her year.

"Don't talk about prices, just put it through." I sounded bored and pulled out my phone, thumbing through to find Gloria's number. I was about to give her a call, when I thought of something I had to do first. So instead, I swiped a few lines down and called someone else.

"Bran?" Carmen's rough voice came over the phone.

"Hi, Carmen. You at the location on 18th street? I have something I need to ask in person. It'll be short," I told him.

"I am. Someone will let you in back. How long?" he asked.

I glanced around. "Probably less than ten minutes."

He spoke to someone with the phone covered before coming back to the conversation with me. "I'll be ready." Then he hung up.

Carmen was often a man of few words, at least until you got half a bottle in him.

I glanced at the giddy saleswoman offering me my card back and nodded to her in thanks before heading out. Simone would be busy for a while, and there was no reason to call Gloria until I'd finished my chat with Carmen.

Taking off at a steady jog, I knew the way to Carmen's fake office. I had to keep my speed in check lest someone take too much notice. It was an easy pace for me, yet would rival a seasoned marathon runner.

Stopping at his office, a big man at the front desk spotted me and silently buzzed me into the back room. Carmen was alone, having shooed out his prior appointment before I even got there.

"Well, Bran?" He got up and walked over to the liquor cabinet. "What'll it be?"

"I'll take your selection, something a little sweet would be nice today," I told him.

Carmen hummed. "Good news then. For me or you?"

"Going to get right down to it. I'd like to take your engagement to Gloria a little more seriously. Would you be willing to give me your blessing?" I asked him.

He paused mid-selection of whiskey and turned to look me over again. "It would be my honor to give you my blessing, Bran." He nodded his head and reached into the back of the cabinet for a blue bottle whose label had faded. "This calls for something special."

I didn't recall that bottle from my past life with him. "Oh." That caught me a little by surprise.

"Bran. The things you shared with me when we first met, they caught me fairly off guard. Not just because you shouldn't know them, but because of what they signified to me. It would seem, in that life, I took you under my wing and was preparing you, to an extent, to take over some of my territory." Carmen slowly poured two glasses.

"You treated me right, sir. I became pretty thick with Bobby, and the two of us worked closely with you," I told him.

Carmen shook his head slightly and handed me one of the glasses. The liquid was thick and had an oaky aroma. "No. When you told me all of those things along with Gloria's... actions. My first thought was that the me of that life probably regretted he didn't have a daughter to bring you into the family fully." He clinked his glass to mine.

I stood there dumbly. "What?"

"The things you told me. In your previous life, I trusted you like a son. This time, I am able to make amends and do it right. Welcome to the family." He took a sip, and I mimicked him as each of his words hit me like a maul to the chest.

My vision blurred slightly and I had to blink away the strange wetness in my eyes. "Thank you. That... that means a lot. I always respected the hell out of you, and you did right by me. You might have a few less scars right now, but I still see much of the same man before me." I raised my glass to him. "To family."

"Family," he echoed and joined me in a sip. "Gloria has actually come by a few times and heaped praises on you. To think that the players needed so much money cleaned. But I guess these gold coins are funny assets."

He had a few on his desk that he picked up and played with. "They disappear from the books when people use them, so they need to do some clever accounting. You had a good eye helping her get into that area. It's been a lot of business. Her other two brothers have noticed the shift, though."

I hid my surprise with another sip of the thick whiskey that most certainly had a little honey in it. Gloria must have worked something out with Vincent. But what surprised me more was that she gave me credit when talking to her father. "She's full of surprises."

"That she is. And becoming strong. You've been running her and Bobby through a gauntlet. They've both reported their gains. Gloria has far outstripped Bobby, but won't tell me entirely why." Carmen played with one of the coins and sipped his drink. "You both are allowed your secrets, but I wanted to say thank you. She's thriving in a way that I didn't know she needed."

"To be honest, you just have to put a challenge in front of her and watch her tear it down. She's a remarkable woman." I realized how much my tune had changed since the last time I had talked in front of her to Carmen. The day he had proposed the engagement, I had been a little harsh.

"Glad to see the two of you are working things out. I hope you got her a nice ring. My baby girl is a little spoiled." Carmen grinned as he took another drink.

"Bought out a whole jewelry store just to be safe." I half-joked and the older man laughed. For a moment, it hit me just how much happier I might have made Carmen in this life. "Though, I think I'm going to strike while the iron is hot and invite her to Velluto Rosso tonight."

Carmen nodded and picked up the phone. "Consider the place yours for the night. And you have my blessing." He started dialing while I texted Gloria.

Chapter 43

Gloria's Rolls-Royce rolled up, her driver pulling up next to the curb. She rolled down the back window. "Get in."

"Nice to see you too," I greeted her and went around the side to get in the roomy back seat. It always struck me as odd that there were two distinct seats with a fixed console in the middle. It was as if the middle seat was an affront to comfort.

But the lack of a middle seat made no difference to me. I was a big enough man that the middle seat wasn't ever really an option.

"When were you going to tell me about your deal with Vincent?" I prodded her, adjusting my suit that I'd swapped into at Carmen's office.

She coughed into her hand. "Driver, we're picking up Simone next," she said, only for the car to pull smoothly back into traffic. "Is that why we are going to Velluto?" she asked.

"No, just happened to get a compliment from your father when I visited him for something else. Why hide it?"

"It isn't profitable yet," Gloria scowled. "That man is incredible with numbers, but I'll pull it out of the red in another week or so, and then it will actually be a nice fount of gold coins for us."

I reached over and patted her arm. "Well done."

The mafia princess blushed a little at my touch. We hadn't gone far, but we had grown closer. I was starting to understand the woman far more.

But the original deal her father made did get in the way of anything more at the moment. Somehow it seemed to form a mental block, like it was forced and not by choice. Our engagement needed to be replaced with one we both agreed to enter into.

It was a little backwards, but it was the position that we were in.

"Yeah. Well, I don't really need to show off to my father; I'm sure you could use the extra credit," Gloria defended her actions, but she didn't meet my eyes. "That and you've given me a lot lately. It's only natural that I try not to be too deep in your debt."

While she was looking away, I took the chance to give her a once over. The mafia princess wore a white coat over her shoulders, a dark red dress, and stockings that seemed to go on forever. Gloria had glorious legs.

She turned back sharply. "What have you been up to today? Simone said she was stealing you but refused to tell me what for?"

"Shopping," I deadpanned. "Do you realize how stuffed my spatial rings are at present?"

My current inventory issues were partly my own fault for buying out an entire jewelry store, but I left that part unsaid.

"I'm sure it was brutal for you." Gloria rolled her eyes. "Simone and you are disgustingly sweet together."

"I thought you had a sweet tooth," I teased her.

Gloria sighed, and I didn't miss the hint of jealousy within the sound. "Doesn't matter."

"It does," I corrected her. "But that's fine. We'll pick her up and head to Velluto Rosso to celebrate. Your father cleared the place out for us after I told him the good news."

"He cleared it out?" Gloria sat up straighter. "You aren't going to tell me why until we're there, are you?"

"Nope. Oh look, there's Simone." I pointed at the mall as a beautiful version of the woman I was growing very attached to came up to the car as it pulled up. I rolled down the window. "Wow, I came for a beautiful woman, but I think I'm going to have to wrap you up and take you home before other men have wild ideas."

"Thank you." Simone batted her lashes at me, and went around to the front seat.

Makeup could really work wonders. Simone was already a ten, and the subtle additions she had made somehow elevated her to an eleven. She wore a new dress, a silver number like the one she'd threatened to burn after I had come back from the sloop instance. It was perfect for the special night.

"Good thing the place is all ours," Gloria said.

"All ours?" Simone looked back at me, surprised.

"I went to Carmen before I called Gloria. He quite liked what I had in mind," I told her cryptically.

"Oh. OH!" Simone covered her mouth with both hands as if something very important occurred to her. "I'm so happy you did that. That's going to make it a thousand times better for both of you. You have to tell me about it later."

"Wait, she knows?" Gloria pointed an accusing finger at Simone.

"She lives with me. Hard to keep a secret from her." I shrugged, not even trying to hide the disparity.

"I also wake him up in an extra special way every morning." Simone smiled angelically back at both of us.

"I'm aware," Gloria sighed.

She hadn't much appreciated being nearby when it happened after resting in the instances. But Simone did not care one bit. And after today, I had a feeling she would care even less. It might even excite her.

"We should get business out of the way before we get to the good stuff," I said to both girls. "Gloria is washing money for the North Trust Bank now. Player gold coins go missing because people use them. The bank needs some of that money cleared up, and Gloria is helping in return for coins."

Simone nodded. "That'll be a wonderful earner for us. Thank you, Gloria. Now it's my turn. We've got the girls settled. They are doing well, and their bloodlines are awakened. The B ranks are getting extra special attention; Rodger and your mother are helping them train. Rodger apparently has some pretty serious background, even if mundane."

"We have some of their family coming in. All of the family member's blood is being sampled for testing on arrival, and a few drops left over," Gloria added in. "It'll be saved until you are ready to return to your clan so that we are sure you have the ability to pop over to a higher rank and reset your level."

I chuckled. For a Level 1, I was going to blow them away. I knew from history that the clan had an instance under their control that they kept open for their newly initiated. The only trick was that if anyone too high level entered, they could disrupt the mechanism that kept it from collapsing. Even if I could fool people, the System would cut through any disguise. I needed to actually be Level 1.

The thought of cleaning house inside the instance made me rub my hands together and smile.

"Perfect. Going to have fun with that one," I said. "My inscriptions are dominating the market through North Trust. I'm pulling in about fifty thousand gold coins a week. I tried a few new ones, but the market wasn't very confident in them. So, it's stopped growing. Unless I start introducing some new talismans, which I'm not sure I want in the hands of the general populace, I'm stalled there."

"I used the vats and the recipes you gave me. Using a pot and a thermometer, I got the rough temperatures mapped out and a technician working on programming it into the vats," Gloria informed me.

"Good. We could pump out some of those healing potions. How do costs look?" I asked.

"Given that I'm not trying to grow mundane money and just trying to spend it all in the next two years... good. We could probably make fifty percent margins on gold coins if we sell at market rate," she reported.

I leaned back. "Two years to make as much as we can," I looked out the window, my mind starting to wander back to old memories.

"About that." Gloria pulled out a tablet. "Are there things we have now that become expensive after it all goes to shit?"

"Medical supplies are pretty important for about half a year until healing potions completely replace all of that. Camping gear always moved well," I said, thinking back to the beginning of it all.

"What about bunkers?" Gloria asked.

"They are a trap," I said. "You have to keep moving and keep engaging in the world or you fall behind. That said... two years... would that be long enough to build a fortified estate? One with its own water source and preferably amid woods so that we can expand from there." A home base would be invaluable, especially if we could have running water and perhaps a few creature comforts to attract people.

"With how much money we have to blow, we could get a lot done. West side of the city?"

"North," I answered quickly. "The Hellgate opens to the west, and we don't want to be too close to that."

"Could we stop it from opening?" Simone asked.

I hesitated. "That's a fairly large shift from what I know. Having the locations of each of the Hellgates is a decently large advantage right now. But when the rapture happens, they will become glaringly obvious. There's a giant red beam that comes up from each of them and they terraform the land around the beam. A Hellgate is a danger, but also one of the best growth opportunities we'll have before the War for Supremacy."

"Where the hidden powers of Earth duke it out for who's on top." Gloria shook her head. "In my day, there was a thing called respecting territory," she mimicked some old mob boss.

"No one gives a shit. As soon as people realize they can kill other people for their gold and gain levels, things get messy. Fairly sure the War for Supremacy was just some greedy old men in the clans and sects trying to gobble up more personal power."

I stared out the window, the scenery changing from the modern city scape to one filled with rubble, tall buildings had mostly fallen, and shorter squat buildings had been built out of the scraps. The streets were splattered with blood, but no bodies. The System didn't leave any.

"Bran." Simone reached behind and took my hand. "It's okay. We'll stop the worst from happening."

I shook my head out of the memories. "Right, focus on what we can do now. Gaining all of this gold is good, but I don't know how much more we can reinvest and keep our plans moving along. I have a few more recipes we can work into the alchemy market, but we should start using the gold to improve ourselves before we head into the B rank instance. Holding onto too much of it could be more trouble than it is worth."

Gloria nodded along, the car pulling up to Velluto Rosso just in time for us to cease business talk.

"We pried Bran out of the instances for a few days, let's enjoy this." Simone hopped out, and I had to hurry to catch her arm before she ran into the fancy Italian restaurant. Then I moved around the side to open Gloria's door.

"If you'd join me." I held my other arm for her.

Gloria rolled her eyes and took my other arm. "You're going to make so many men jealous if you walk around with both of us."

I grinned. "That's the best part," I teased.

"Don't get too many more when you go to the clan," Gloria warned before glancing at Simone meaningfully.

"That's my job," she said. "He won't be wanting at least."

I shook my head at their antics. The two of them were getting along well, at least. "When I head to the clan, there are many plans in place, but not girls. There's still plenty of time, and the three of us need to get through the B rank instance."

"How hard is it going to be?" Simone asked.

"1600-2000 stats on the monsters probably," I told her.

Simone let out a soft whistle. "That's not too bad." She still seemed nervous about those numbers.

"You might be able to match their stats, but their skills will all be B rank or close. Not to mention, we have no idea what we are walking into."

The hostess for the restaurant didn't even ask us a question. The moment we stepped inside, she stood alert and hurried to lead us deeper into the place to a lovely booth that was raised slightly above the rest.

"Time for business is done. Now it's time for pleasure," I smiled as the hostess came and bought several bottles of expensive champagne. "Before we get to that, though, allow me to start this off right."

Chapter 44

I had run through different ways to propose in my head.

I knew that I could do it one at a time, and that might even be the smarter option, but I knew both of them were going to follow me in the future and there was no reason to separate them now.

Kneeling down before both of them as they started to take a seat at the table, I pulled two ring boxes out of my spatial ring.

Not giving myself time to chicken out, I started talking.

"Simone, you are lovely. From the moment I met you, I realized you were special, and the longer I've spent with you, the more I've come to know that I only saw the tip of the iceberg then.

"Gloria, we got off to a rocky start. This whole relationship was forced upon both of us, but this is an opportunity to stop any future moments from being forced upon us. I want them to be what we have chosen. Your talents and mind continue to impress me, I truly want you at my side for what is to come.

"Both of you, would you marry me?" I opened the boxes, sure that I had them held out to the right woman.

Simone jumped up and snatched my hand before pausing and waiting for Gloria. The other woman seemed a little hesitant with the double proposal, but cleared her throat and stepped up, taking my other hand.

"Yes," they said together.

I stood up, grabbing both of the lovely ladies around the waist and kissing Simone deeply before switching to Gloria and giving her a peck on the cheek. "Then let me get these rings on you both."

Simone accepted the ring with another kiss and a promise deep in her eyes that made my cock twitch.

Gloria took her ring with a soft smile. "That wasn't half bad. Two at once, though..."

"That's my life right now." I sat down on the booth, arranging myself in the middle so they could each take one of my sides.

Simone chose to press herself to me while Gloria sat familiarly close, but not on top of me. The mafia princess was a proud woman, after all.

Both of them were breathtaking, and I was a lucky man.

Though I'd been a little harsh with Gloria at first, now that she was truly mine, I was going to spoil her like the princess she deserved to be.

I looked up from the two of them to see our waiter. The poor young man had dropped his notepad and was staring with his mouth open. We made eye contact, and he snapped to attention, snatching up his pad and coming over in a hurry.

"Congratulations." His tone held no small amount of awe. "Then we are celebrating tonight? I'm told your meal, no matter the expense, has already been comped."

"Grand. I think if you get one of those ready"—I motioned to the bottles of champagne—"I'd love to pop it. Otherwise, just bring us a spread of your appetizers." There was no reason to be shy with spending. When Carmen said all expenses were paid, he expected you to treat yourself.

The waiter picked up one of the bottles on ice and handed it to me before laying out three glasses. I ripped off the cork to a satisfying pop and started pouring before it fizzed over. There was no sense in wasting perfectly good champagne.

"Bran, you aren't going to put any teeth in this?" Simone asked, though the question sounded like it had a very preferred answer.

"Of course not." I smiled. "Champagne is for flavor, not getting drunk. Now, if only they brought me some whiskey..." I trailed off, pouring them both glasses and holding mine out in front of me. "To two wonderful women."

"To a man that quite literally saved my soul." Simone blushed and lifted her glass next to mine.

Gloria joined us. "To the three of us and what we'll build together."

We all clinked glasses and took a moment to bask in the dry, yet sweet champagne. In the time we'd spent together in the instances, all of us had grown quite comfortable.

The server came out and brought an array of appetizers that we picked through.

Simone covered her mouth after gushing over the roasted goat cheese and tomato sauce dip. "I got you something, Bran. You'd said before that you liked to paint; surely, it would have been difficult to get pigments where you'd been." She put out an easel that had a big tray in the front of it loaded with high quality paints.

"Thank you; this is lovely." I kissed her cheek. It was the thought that mattered, and she wanted to make sure I could do something I enjoyed. It was a plus that using it would make me think of her extra calming exercise in painting.

Gloria took a sip of her champagne and held her hand out, clearly with something in it for me.

I put my hand under hers, and she dropped a car key in my hand. Seeing the logo on it, I had a good idea of what it was.

"Gloria!" Simone huffed. "We had a limit! Five hundred."

The mafia princess blinked, as if something occurred to her that hadn't before. "Oh."

"She thought you meant five hundred thousand," I chuckled and muttered under my breath. "Spoiled princess." The keys, however, disappeared into my spatial ring.

Simone shook her head and forgot about it with another scoop of creamy sauce with steaming bread.

"Both presents are incredible." I nodded to Simone. "I told Gloria that you can charge an electric car with certain abilities or talismans. Lightning is a common enough element, so in my hands, this bad boy can go as far as I want for free."

"I figured you'd just do something with talismans. It's not armored or anything," Gloria clarified. "I couldn't get that in the budget."

"The budget you blew past." Simone's voice rang with the slightest tinge of bitterness, but I could tell she was already moving past it. "So, Gloria. Now that you've accepted the engagement, are you going to move in with us?"

Simone had fully moved into my place, which now had part of the patio converted into a yoga area. Even if she wasn't teaching classes anymore, she said it still helped with flexibility.

I wasn't complaining. Breakfast had a new and improved view as far as I was concerned.

Gloria fidgeted with the diamond encrusted ring of her finger. "I'll have someone come by and drop off my things tomorrow morning. Tonight, I'll come home with the two of you, but I'm fairly sure that Simone will want your attention tonight." Gloria smirked.

Simone's hand petted my thigh with promises. "That's fine. I don't think we should force the two of you to that stage yet. Have you even kissed on the lips?"

"Nope," I answered. "Which is why I think I need to take Gloria on a few more dates."

"Preferably ones that don't involve monsters," Gloria added. "I do have plans with my older brother coming up, though."

I raised an eyebrow at her, knowing that meeting up with her brother was likely not a very amicable meeting. "Know that if anyone takes any aggression towards you, I will put them down."

She kissed my cheek. "You'll fit right in with the rest of the Nesters. Yes, I wouldn't mind showing you off a little. My brothers can be a little rough around the edges."

"I know it. Though, it isn't like you need me to defend yourself," I chuckled. Of the three of us, Gloria was the one who was naturally bulletproof now. I'd shrug them off with Regeneration, but they'd make me bleed.

"It's about appearances. That, and I'd like them to not know I can shrug off a bomb or bullet until I really need to." Gloria was still playing games with her two brothers.

I knew the Nester family encouraged some level of competition amongst the siblings. Bobby had largely been left out, and in my past life, the two older brothers nearly killed each other a few times. Taking Gloria out of the picture had likely turned it from an indirect to a direct conflict.

"Then it's a date. We do need to keep pushing ourselves and preparing for the B rank instance, though. That'll be in a month and a half. Hopefully, we can push ourselves up to that level by then," I said. Her taking me at her side had a fairly large meaning in the Nester Family. It was a sign of me being part of the family.

"We've made a lot of progress," Simone jumped in, clearly wanting to shift the mood back to celebratory. "Tonight is about enjoying ourselves." She waved for the waiter. "He'll take a glass of some very expensive whiskey, neat."

"Trying to get me drunk?" I teased as she threw two Duggarfin teeth onto the table in preparation.

I looked at the teeth. She was definitely going to try and get me drunk.

"What about your brothel?" I asked her.

"I'm managing it now," Gloria spoke up.

"And if I find a single woman there against her will..." Simone trailed off, the threat evident.

"My girl has her instructions. Something like that happens and everyone associated with it hits the curb the next second. Two strikes and she won't have to worry about it anymore." Gloria was oddly threatening while she sipped her champagne.

I found that answer damn sexy. Competent women were my catnip, and a little violence was just the way of the world.

The waiter brought over an expensive glass of whiskey that Simone added the teeth into and started stirring.

"Anything else I can get you all?" The waiter fidgeted a bit.

"Steak." Gloria grinned. "Let's do six of your best filets. Medium rare."

"Is that for all of us, or is your bloodline part pig?" Simone teased.

"Ha." Gloria let out a humorless chuckle. "That's for us, unless you'd come here asking for something else? It's on my father, so why not get the best?"

"I'd like two of those medium well, please," Simone said, and the waiter looked at me.

"Add two to that order and make them rare," I put in my order.

Gloria slid a vial across the table to Simone, their eyes doing some silent communication.

I Inspected it.

[Sweet Spider Venom C]

"Oh?" I asked, seeing the name and getting a little curious.

"What? We've both been working on our Poison Resistance as well," Gloria added. "We just don't have Regeneration to make the process anywhere near as quick. I thought I'd use you as a guinea pig. See what poisons were more palatable? It might be a good venture once the Rapture hits. We could sell ranked alcohol, and it's an exercise for my alchemy."

Simone added a few drops and got the whiskey up to D rank before handing it to me. "Bottoms up, Bran. We are celebrating tonight."

The D ranked whiskey started hitting me hard as the girls fawned on me. At some point, we ordered a second round of steaks and plenty more drinks.

The waiter was impressed with us in multiple ways by the end of the night.

Feeling pretty amazing and more relaxed than usual, I swept Gloria up as we left the restaurant, carrying Gloria back to the Rolls-Royce.

The three of us managed our way back to my place where Simone quickly tucked Gloria into one of the guest rooms and then pulled me away to have me all to herself.

Chapter 45

I rode next to Gloria.

We had spent another week of grinding through the available instances. Though between our group and Bobby's, we were running them down to exhaustion.

"Ah. Here are some coins." Gloria handed me a F rank spatial ring.

I took a peek inside and tapped the ring to my character menu before dumping all the gold into vitality. "This is ten percent?"

"We'll push everything down to the bare minimum we can operate before you head to your clan. I'll have the extra talismans to sell for a few months until you get back." Gloria was fantastic at managing the business.

I touched our rings together and handed over a giant stack of the talismans for her to manage. She now had people going to and from the bank daily. I was also trying to stay further away from Victor.

He'd gotten me all the extra photos that I'd asked for, and I was dreading the Vault of Pandora. It represented a ticking time bomb.

From everything I could piece together from my memories, he didn't crack the vault open before the Rapture. Yet I'd made a few waves in this life, and I worried one of them would ripple all the way to that Vault.

I could only hope that what I was doing would make a difference in the right direction. The ladies with bloodlines were learning quickly, and a few of them had really taken to self-defense after the trauma that they had endured. They were happy to not be as vulnerable anymore.

One of the B rank girls was the one driving Gloria and I at the moment.

"Ms. Nester, we're here." The woman pulled the car to a slow stop. "Do you need me to come in?" She was pretty in a plain sort of way. Her long, brown hair was pulled up under a drivers cap and she wore a pressed suit jacket with a matching pencil skirt.

"No, thank you. Just stay with the car. Feel free to stop anyone if they try anything." Gloria unfolded her legs and got out of the car. Today she was making a statement in a deep purple dress with a white coat hanging off her shoulders.

The driver's eyes were glued to me. "I never got a chance, but some of the girls have been asking me to say this if I met you." She dipped her head to me. "Thank you for saving us."

"It wasn't all me." I never liked being treated as a hero. It was off brand. I could be a selfish ass when the moment required, but I did genuinely want better for humanity if it could be accomplished without sacrificing those I cared about.

"The others dealt with the small fries. None of us would have left that place if you didn't kill the demon. We saw your strength." Her eyes nearly glowed with fervor.

"Well, thank you. I hope in the future you all will continue to help Gloria. She manages a lot for me." I used Soul Gaze on the woman.

[Jenny ~~Mur-~~ Mul Branova
Class: N/A
Level: N/A
Status: Healthy, Awe, Embarrassed, Inspired
Strength: 32
Agility: 59
Vitality: 28
Intelligence: 29
Spirit: 29
Skills:
Awakened Bloodline of The Long-Eared Fox B]

"It's our pleasure." Jenny beamed at me.

I paused, wondering about her last name. I had seen a crossed out name like that before . It meant that she'd changed it, and her self-identity of her previous last name was still fading. "That last name?"

Her eyes went wide and she blushed. "Uh. Well... You see..." she stuttered.

"It's okay. I can see you changed your last name." I didn't think her eyes could get wider, and I was very wrong.

"You can see that I changed my name?! We saw you cut the warehouse in half and obliterate the demon. Then the saintess told us she worshiped you..." Jenny dipped her head. "If it's alright with you, some of us whose family's sold us wanted to take on a new name. It's..." She had trouble meeting my eyes. "Mul Branova. One of the others came up with the idea."

I wasn't an expert on names. "I can't help but notice my name seems to be part of that."

"The saintess said you didn't love your last name and we..." Jenny was not the most confident speaker. "Mul is supposed to mean 'follower of' or... um... 'devotee of', and Branova was a slight mash up with the Italian 'nova' with your name. We assumed with your relationship with Nesters, you might be Italian."

"My family has their roots in Greece actually," I clarified, slightly amused at the woman's stumbling. She could probably break a linebacker over her knee now, but despite that jump in her strength, she was still rather shy.

"That makes sense." She rambled.

"So that means your new name means... Devotee of Bran... new?"

Jenny's face was bright red at this point. "New Devotees of Bran." She hid her face behind her hair.

I paused for a moment, processing the information.

"Um, then, as one of my Devotees and the first to introduce herself, why don't I give you a gift." Reaching into my spatial rings, I looked for something appropriate.

There were all sorts of materials, talismans, weapons, and armors inside my inventory. Many of them had lost their use to me, especially those at the F and E rank. Yet for Jenny, it would be a potent tool.

Talismans were out. She might be able to learn to activate a few of them, but it would be difficult. Materials wouldn't do her much good.

I wanted to keep her around, especially since she was a B rank bloodline, so I pulled out an E ranked shirt that I'd found in one of the instances. It was a dark forest-green.

Given it was an E rank, she'd be completely unaffected from small arms fire and would shrug off even a few unranked physical attacks even from a System player.

She took the shirt with a strange look.

"Watch this." I pulled out a gun from my spatial ring, put the shirt up against her and fired twice.

Jenny twitched and closed her eyes but then opened them to look at the front of the shirt. "It felt like you tapped me."

"The shirt's magic." I went with the simplest explanation. "No gun or knife is going to get through it. A tank shell would only kill you because the shirt doesn't cover enough. The shirt would survive, though."

Gloria was now giving me a tired look, likely from firing off gunshots right outside the meeting place with her brother.

Jenny quickly started stripping, and I looked away. She was already shy enough.

"Thank you so much."

"Just do your best, okay?" I encouraged her.

In a past life, I'd had more than a few new recruits join forces at the front of whatever war. Often, they became obsessed with the rumors and stories that swirled around me, beginning to idolize me.

Jenny felt like another one of them. The best thing to do was give them the tools they needed to survive. Whether that be some armor, training, or perhaps a little courage. Warriors weren't produced no matter how much you invested in them. They were forged through survival. Nudging the odds of their survival was the best way to make a new warrior.

At least, that was my experience.

"Done?" Gloria raised an eyebrow.

"What? Did you know they changed their last name?" I asked her.

"Eighteen of them." Gloria was one step ahead of me. "It weirded me out a little when their last names started changing with Inspect, but soon we got to the root of what was happening. Now, we need to get in before my brother can worry too much about those gunshots."

Yep, I confirmed that she had not liked the added noise at all.

"I was just proving a point to Jenny here." I glanced over my shoulder. Jenny had the shirt on—bless the System magic that made it fit both her and me—and was putting her suit jacket on over it.

"Thank you again." She bowed to me. "I'll keep the car safe. Enjoy your meeting."

Gloria narrowed her eyes on me.

I shrugged. "She's going to protect you. I want her to be as good at her job as she can be." I caught up to Gloria who had stopped several yards away.

"Fine." Gloria grabbed my arm and held onto it. "So, what happened to my brother?"

"The oldest?" That was the one we were meeting. "He died charging into demon lines during the First Demon War." I waffled my hand. "Overall, he was so-so at the whole player concept. He stayed back too much and became a little under-leveled compared to those who worked for him. In the end, Bobby said he was trying to prove a point to those that ran with him and overestimated himself."

Gloria nodded slowly. "Doesn't surprise me. Of the two, Michael's the schemer, sitting back and playing games. Orvin is much more direct. Not as much as Bobby, but he'd yell at you rather than hide snakes in your bed. After experiencing the System for myself, I can understand how those who make other people do the work for them don't thrive."

"There are some, like Victor, who do well at hanging in the back. Yet Victor is the type to try and remain neutral so that he's available to everyone. His only problem in the past life was that he stuck out too much," I said.

"The clans didn't have a bone to pick with him?" Gloria asked as we walked up into the brightly lit warehouse.

Ahead of us was another group with a broad-shouldered man I had seen before. Previously, I'd thought he was going gray early, but now I realized he too probably had a bloodline like Gloria. He dyed it heavily, but a little gray still poked through.

"No. They might have discovered his Vault, but he firmly stayed neutral so that he could just be a bank." My eyes raked over the people present, Soul Gaze active.

I held my reaction in check when each of the four men with Michael came back as low-level players with stats that had certainly seen plenty of gold coins.

They reminded me of a certain assassin.

Gloria glanced at me, likely seeing the same.

Four Inspects bounced off me as I swatted them away harshly, and Gloria's eyes lost focus for a second as she worked to do the same. These guys had put all their points into the three physical stats, not that I blamed them. Those were the most effective at present. Some of the uses of Spirit wouldn't be known for a while.

Michael's four men frowned behind him, but the man himself didn't notice. "Sister! I'm so glad you trust me to show up with just one guard."

"I let you have four." Gloria smiled. "I know how you sometimes struggle to feel safe." She briefly gave him a hug. "This is Bran. He's the new fiancé that our father found for me."

"Pleasure." I stepped forward with my hand out. According to custom, as a bodyguard I was a moot and not part of the conversation, yet being Gloria's fiancé elevated me enough that I could join in.

Michael adjusted to my new status quickly, his smile only a touch stiff. "Wonderful. I'm glad our father found someone to put up with her," he laughed. There was no malice in his tone, yet I was pretty sure it was there.

He really was the kind of guy to hide snakes in a person's bed.

"No guards then?" Michael smiled. "I'm glad my little sister trusts me so much." He waved his hand, and the four men with him grabbed some fold-out chairs and a desk to place them down between the two. "Yet, we need to talk. Some of your men have been operating in my territory, and we need a resolution. Father's territory is absolute."

Michael sat down on one side. I pulled out a chair for Gloria and scooted her in while I smiled at the four players, making it obvious that I was looking at their stats with a smile.

CHAPTER 45

I had been training nicely with Gloria and Simone; the four of them weren't nearly as threatening as they believed.

Chapter 46

Gloria rolled her eyes. "Really, Michael? I don't have time for this. Just make whichever little underling of yours duke it out. Why are the two of us here for something so mundane?"

"These things need to be handled without bloodshed so that the family appears united," I rubbed Gloria's shoulders and answered before Michael could, putting him on the back foot.

Both of them knew this game, yet I'd been working for the mob longer than they had been alive.

"Your fiancé seems to know it better than you." Michael smiled as he tried to drive a wedge between us.

Gloria smiled, surprising her brother as she pulled me down and gave me the first real kiss we'd shared, though it was brief. "He's remarkable in so many ways. When I say that father found him, I was covering for father. In truth, Bran here cornered both me and father in a single move, forcing the engagement. I respect my fiancé deeply, and he's welcome to add his input at any time." She played with the diamond-encrusted engagement ring fondly.

I knew part of this was an act, yet the best acts had to have enough truth to them to sell the fake parts.

"Interesting. Should I be having the conversation with you... Bran, was it?" Michael smiled.

"That would be improper. Maybe once Gloria and I wed next year, I can assist her more directly. Until then, I'm not family." I put my hands squarely on Gloria's shoulders, indicating through the gesture that she had my full support.

We were a united front against anything Michael threw at us.

"Then what were those gunshots?" he asked, tilting his head.

"I was proving a point to Gloria and her driver." I shrugged, staring at the four players behind Michael pointedly before returning to Michael. "Say, where did these four come from? Gloria, do they remind you of someone? Like that guy you brought with you to 'protect' you from me?"

"The one you summarily killed to prove a point?" Gloria asked. "I'd nearly forgotten about him. Poor man didn't know what he was walking into." She shook her head sadly. "Though, I do enjoy my new guards. They are a touch better."

The four behind Michael shifted professionally, but I could tell they were signaling each other. That told me all I needed to know. They were connected to the assassin that Gloria had brought with her.

Given the assassin's class, it was easy to make assumptions, but he might have just been an ear for Michael.

"These? They are my most loyal men. Incredible what some proper training can accomplish." He smirked.

I was trying to dredge through my memories. With my spirit, they were still crisp, but I had never paid much attention to Michael. In the First Demon War, he was distant from me, and as one of Carmen's sons, he had a sizable force.

Yet I was trying to remember if there was anything out of place with their power. Because in front of me now was not something I'd expected.

While I might have made a few ripples, the first player he had sticking to Gloria was well before any of my ripples should have gotten to him. Meaning that in the past life, Michael had players around him as well.

I played through the bits of facts I knew. He did end up sucking up most of Gloria's territory after her death.

However, if he had these players and then he fought with Orvin as much as I remember, why didn't he have an overwhelming advantage?

"Everything okay?" Michael asked me, pulling me from my thoughts. "Curious what they went through?" He didn't look back at the bodyguards once during this exchange, like he had full confidence in their loyalty.

I reminded myself that I was dealing with someone who'd put snakes in a person's bed. It was highly possible he was playing a game in the dark.

I stopped teasing out the 'why' for everything, and instead focused on what was in front of me at present. Michael had players, but he wasn't one himself. That was manageable.

"Very much so." I played right into Michael's comment. "They are much stronger than they look. Which is saying something since each of them looks like a bodybuilder."

"They don't look very tough at all," Gloria laughed as she stared at them. "Hey, brother, how about we solve this with a simple fight? Let's iron out how much you think was lost, and we'll bet that amount on a quick fight?"

Michael was clearly fighting down a giant smile, having thought he already won. "Sure. Will you be fighting, sister?"

Gloria laughed. "No, your men wouldn't stand a chance. I'll let Bran fight one of them. You okay with that, dear?" She looked over her shoulder at me like a doting wife.

"Perfectly. Do you want me to fight all four at once?" I laughed.

Michael's smile shifted to a strange frown. He glanced slightly at one of his men. At the same time, I met the man's gaze and put the full force of my bloodlust in my eyes.

The man was frozen like a statue while Michael tried to check with him.

"Michael? What's wrong? Here, I'll even make it easier. Bran, give me your gun, and we can make it one on four." Gloria held out her hand.

I reached like I was pulling something out of my pants and handed a gun to her that she laid on the table. "Here you go. Happy to have a little fun. Come on, guys."

Michael's brow was pressed into an intense frown before it rose up and he laughed. "You almost had me, sister. Careful, boys. My father engaged him to her. Don't hurt him too much or we might not survive the repercussions of their bluffing." He had a big smile on his face as if he'd figured out a puzzle.

Sometimes those who schemed the most couldn't see the most obvious answer. I was going to break his men. We hadn't been idle recently, and I'd had some nice gains.

[Name: Bran Heros
Level: 44
Class: Blood Hegemon D
Status: Healthy
Strength: 200
Agility: 189
Vitality: 263
Intelligence: 184
Spirit: 11129
Skills:
Soul Gaze SSS
Soul Resilience S
Blunt Weapon Proficiency D
Endurance D
Throwing Proficiency F
Blood Boil B
Blood Siphon B
Blood Bolt B
Bloodline Collection 57
Regeneration B
Fire Resistance E
Poison Resistance D
Ax Proficiency E
Charge E
Bloodink Quality D
Stealth E
Inscription C
Swim D (Bracer)
Last Stand F
Blood Hex C
Blood Transfusion C
Crimson Blade C
Crimson Barrier D
Sword Proficiency C
Frozen Resistance F]

Rolling my shoulders, I got ready for a fight.

"Ah. Bran sometimes gets a little carried away," Gloria added. "I can't promise that your men will make it out alive."

I chuckled. The woman was going to take a pound of flesh from Michael. All of these men were similar to the assassin.

Their highest stat being around 100. Not to mention, their skills were trash.

"They are tougher than they look." Michael's eyes squinted in satisfaction. "Your fiancée had good instincts. Line up and fight him. And remember, leave him alive." Michael shifted his attention back to Gloria. "I know you've just stepped into the world of players, sister. Your interests in North Trust Bank have damaged my own, and I'm going to show you that the depth of that world is greater than you know. Break him, boys." Michael snapped his fingers, and all four of his men jumped at me.

Gloria threw her head back in genuine laughter, so uncontrolled that she almost fell back in her chair.

If Michael had any regrets, it was too late.

His first man pulled a knife and came at me. I sidestepped his attack, grabbed his arm, and used his momentum to swing him back around into the other three.

It was almost comical the way I bowled over the four men.

"Wait!" Michael jumped to his feet.

"Sit back down." Gloria kicked the table between them hard enough to catch him in the hips and slam him back down into his chair.

I laughed and finished the first man by slamming him to the hard concrete floor, my foot cracking his head as if it were an egg hitting the sidewalk.

"You weren't aiming for me, but my woman?!" I grabbed the next man, throttling him by the neck and wrenching it free of the rest of his spine with a well-practiced motion.

"You see, dear brother." Gloria's words had a little venom to them. "Bran is very much the jealous type. You should have seen what he did to your man you had following me."

"Stall them! Men! Attack!" Michael screamed and threw himself to the side as gunfire erupted from all over the warehouse. The mobster was crawling on the floor amid the bright flashes.

Gloria was fine. Her Tough Skin was E rank. She just looked annoyed with crossed arms as bullets ripped her dress and pinged off her body. My vitality was high enough that unranked bullets only pushed in about half an inch before stopping, only for my Regeneration to push them back out immediately.

I completely ignored the gunfire, focusing on the last two players. A blade of hardened blood appeared in my hand as I moved supernaturally swiftly and cut them both down before looking up to focus on the men firing.

A good number of them were players, but they were fairly weak.

"Are you going to let him run away?" I had to shout to ask Gloria.

She stood like a statue amid the gunfire. "I can't kill him, Bran. Family rules. We have to take him in alive."

I waved my hand. Blood Bolts formed quickly, and I returned fire at the shooters. But my shots were more effective. The Blood Bolts removed limbs and punched right through crates and then the person hiding behind them.

"That's a pain. Wonder why he's not a player," I muttered, trudging through the gunfire for the crawling mobster and putting my foot on his back. He stopped like I was weighing him down with a car while I made a Crimson Barrier to block all of the bullets. It had the nice effect of muting the sound.

"Hey, why aren't you a player too?" I asked the man in question, not caring at all for the fight that was about to start outside the barrier.

Purple flames suddenly shot through the warehouse, finding the shooters who weren't even fleeing despite our overwhelming advantage, and turning them to ash. The powerful flames barely even stopped, passing like a wave and turning them all into smoldering piles.

Michael's eyes were wide. "Wh— My sources said that you just became initiated a month or so ago. How can either of you be so powerful!?"

"Let's talk about those sources." I bent down over him, taking a talisman out of my spatial ring and peeling the back off of it. "Did you know that stickers are sort of amazing? I missed things as simple as stickers. Simone got these for me."

"Huh?" he asked stupidly.

I put a matching sticker to my forehead, "Don't worry. This'll be over in a second. Gloria said I couldn't kill you, but trust me. This might be worse." I headbutted the man.

Michael looked left and right, trying to understand where he was when I appeared next to him and grabbed his shoulder, slamming him down to his knees.

"Here you are an ant, and I am a god. You are going to tell me what I want to know." There was no condition, no threat. Because here, with the vast difference between our Spirit stats, there was no need for me to even treat him as a relevant factor to what was about to happen.

Chapter 47

I stood up and dusted myself off as Michael lay on the floor, a trail of drool coming out of his mouth.

Gloria had her phone to her ear. "Yes, Daddy. Bran just came to. I have to go." She hung up. "Is he going to be okay?"

"He'll recover over the next few days. Can't say he'll be the same, but he should be able to answer any questions Carmen has. Might shit himself every time he sees me, though," I answered with a shrug.

"Having experienced your spirit once myself, I don't blame him. Are all people in the future that strong?" she asked.

I scratched my cheek. "Eh. A fair amount of players progress to 10k in their top stat. Spirit was always my lowest."

Gloria's eye twitched. "Lowest."

"Yeah. Only need so much when you learn some soul arts to help you too. When someone fights you in your soul, there is a serious home-field advantage. After the Rapture, there are some additional ways to get stats too," I said.

Gloria narrowed her eyes. "What did they call you, in your past life?"

"Ah..." I sighed and shook my head. "It doesn't quite come off right."

"No. What was it?" Gloria had a smirk as she poked me.

"The Wandering King," I sighed. The name almost bothered me as much as being called a Hero. I didn't like being a king. Unlike the others who had gained such titles, I refused to rule a set of land.

Oh System, that might change this time around. I almost shuddered before remembering that I could shove the task of managing that onto Gloria and Simone.

"Anyway," I changed the topic. "Your brother has several items of great value. He actually has a Cursed Awakening Artifact, as well as a journal from your mother that will prove very useful. It seems there were some players in the Nester family tree. Let's go check on Jenny first. What do we need to do with your brother, and you were on the phone with Uncle Carmen?"

"We should stick around for him to arrive. It's going to be a family matter, and he'll want to hear your take on everything," Gloria said.

I bit the inside of my lip. "It's very important to get both the artifact and the journal. I'm not sure what conditions he has set up should something happen to him."

"Can we send Jenny?" Gloria asked.

"Too risky. He's got a couple guys..." I trailed off as we both stared at each other. "Simone?"

"She's got a spa day," Gloria said.

I winced. Simone had made quite the point of the self care moment. "It would be faster if I went anyways." From the information I'd extracted from Michael, nothing he had in place could stop me.

"Have Jenny drive you. I'll be here." Gloria pulled her chair up off the ground and sat on it, crossing her legs.

I nodded and took off at a jog that could beat an Olympic sprinter, rushing towards Jenny and the car. Leaving Gloria behind was fine. Michael had brought his strongest men with him. There was only one danger back at his mansion, and with my spirit, she'd be trivial.

"Sir." Jenny shot up from where she was leaning on the car, four big guys sleeping on the ground by her. "Sounded like there was some trouble." She glanced at my chest where a little blood was on my shirt.

"I'm fine. The rest of those idiots aren't. I need you to rush up to the north side. There's a mansion—I'll guide you."

Jenny didn't ask about Gloria or request any more details. She simply hopped behind the wheel and hit the gas hard enough for the frame of the car to thump.

It wasn't until we were on the highway that she asked what was on her mind. "Sir. Those men..."

"Michael's men. It seems he was already secretly working on some angles of business and keeping it from the rest of the Nester Family. Gloria and I started entering into a similar business, and it seems he thought he could cut our work off." I had learned much from Michael's soul.

So much more made sense after understanding his plans.

"The Miss is okay?" Jenny asked.

"Perfectly fine," I said. "It takes a lot to hurt Gloria. She's got thick skin. And I heal unnaturally fast."

Jenny nodded. "I took those men out like they were children. Will... will I be like either of you?"

"One day. We are preparing you and the others for that day because it's going to get rough." I was honest with her; honesty built loyalty.

Jenny gripped the steering wheel, a little flash of determination in her eyes that showed even through the rear-view mirror. "Understood, sir."

She was flying down the highway, using her supernatural reactions to weave between cars. No one would be stupid enough to pull over Gloria's personal car.

"Take this exit." I pointed up ahead.

Jenny wove over several lanes of traffic and had to slow to a stop behind another car at a red light.

I was fairly sure she would have blown the light if it wasn't for the other car. "Two lights, then a right followed by a left," I gave her instructions and let her floor the gas pedal as soon as the light turned green. "When I get there, you just need to stay in the car and keep it running."

"Will you be coming out in a rush?" she asked.

"I'll have a person or two with me and a few items. Doubt there'll be anyone in there alive after I'm done." Michael had complete control over the players under his organization and had left them a number of orders. They wouldn't take kindly to me entering his mansion. "Just protect Gloria's car. I do not want to deal with a pissed off Gloria if it gets damaged."

Jenny drove down the streets as I pointed out turns until she came to a decently isolated mansion with a guard house at the front gate.

I opened the car door and jumped out, rushing the guards. I threw myself through the bullet-proof glass and summoned a blood-red sword that ended both of the players. Their bodies disappeared moments later.

Jenny, for her part, didn't do more than stick her head out the window. "It might be a faster departure if you open the gate for me so that I can pick you up at the house."

I checked, but neither of the men had spatial rings. It seemed, for whatever reason, that he didn't have many rings to go around.

"Head on in after me." I pushed a big button to open the gates and nearly tore the door off its hinges as I flat out sprinted down the long drive to the sprawling mansion.

For a brief moment, I wondered if Gloria had a place as large as the mansion in front of me.

That thought was shattered as a large caliber bullet hit me in the chest and made me cough. Several red dots covered me as gunfire started to rain down on me.

I gathered my feet underneath me in a large stride and shot up through a window on the second story, crashing in next to two shooters and ending them swiftly.

They weren't why I had come, but I wasn't one to allow somebody to fire bullets into my body.

Men appeared as soon as I entered. Most of them were a touch superhuman, having stats in the forties and fifties. Against mundane forces, these men were very effective. Yet, in the world of players, they were far too weak.

Blood Bolts rained out of my hand in return for any gunfire and left them dead.

I rushed through the place for Michael's wing where he kept his most precious items. The man was beyond paranoid, and because he hadn't become a player, he couldn't use spatial rings.

Thus, his artifact was in a false back of a safe.

His room was grand beyond belief. To make matters worse, there were a dozen women lounging around who snapped to their feet as soon as I entered.

I immediately judged him, because unlike his goons, he hadn't helped these women grow stronger at all. It was clear he was afraid of them being stronger than him, even under the effects of the Cursed Artifact.

"Stop!" several of the women screamed and tried to forcibly halt my progress.

I pushed my way through them to the safe in the back of the room, a pretty, black metallic thing hidden from his view by a self-portrait.

I rolled my eyes and punched right through his face in the painting and dented the safe. My sword made short work of the safe door, and the painting fell aside with the metal door, as if both were made of flimsy canvas.

"Stop!" One of his slave harem jumped forward, pulling the pins out of several grenades at once and throwing herself at me.

My eyes went wide, not for my own sake, but because this bastard forced these women into suicide.

Grabbing her, I flung her to the ground and threw the grenades to the side. All of the women were clinging to me to try and stop me, making it easy for Crimson Barrier to pull blood from my arms and spring up around all of us.

The explosion knocked down the wall and made parts of the ceiling sprinkle down on me.

Another woman tried to grab the artifact and run, but I stopped her and wrenched it out of her hand. It was a small, gold- and blue-banded object in the shape of a shepherd's crook, called a Pharaohs Crook.

[Pharaoh's Crook - System Artifact

The holder of this item may bless another with access to the System at the cost of their freedom. Those initiated through this artifact cannot resist the commands of the one who used it on them.]

The artifact was a disgusting object. One that I hated holding in my hands.

I knew too many who would abuse this type of power easily. It was the reason I'd rushed here. It could not fall into the wrong hands.

The crook disappeared into my spatial ring along with the diary as the women seemed to lose their steam in trying to stop me. Their orders must have been about protecting this object. With it now in my hands, they weren't being compelled.

So much of Michael's past life made sense now. If he had a force that he'd made with this, the Rapture was about the worst thing to ever happen to him. As soon as the Rapture hit, this item became useless. Anyone that could be initiated already was initiated, which meant his ability to compel new recruits went away.

Also, much like how people could work their way around Slave Seals, this artifact could be tricked as well. If a person could convince themselves of a different meaning in his words, they could change their actions.

The concept was similar to people who were slaves and managed the mental gymnastics to convince themselves that the best way to 'protect' their master was to kill them. Worse, once that person finished such mental gymnastics, the Slave Seal would *force* them to try and kill their master.

I shuddered at the horror all of that produced.

Michael in his past life must have lost too many of his slaves and been forced to the front in an effort to hold onto the rest of the people he'd gathered that he couldn't control. That, or a particular someone had managed to subvert his control and get to him.

I ripped open the bookshelf which was really a door to a safe room.

Down a flight of stairs, a young man looked up at me and spoke with an almost physical force. "Leave and kill yourself."

My spirit automatically fought back against the mental intrusion, and the man coughed up blood.

[Jasper Franz
Level: 10
Class: Mesmer S
...]

"Leave and go kill yourself!" Jasper screamed, activating his ability again, only to groan and fall over in more pain.

"You have orders to do that, and you can't fight them." I knelt down next to him. "It's not going to work on me at all. And you should know that Michael is dead. Once he's dead, does his order still hold? How about this? I have complete control over Michael, thus my words are his. Stop yelling at me, get up and follow me." There wasn't a ton of time to put him back to rights. I'd do that later.

Jasper froze, his eyes working through the problem before he stopped screaming at me and groaned as he stood to follow me.

The man was treated very well. His little hide-away was well stocked. Then again, he was Michael's prized jewel.

Chapter 48

Jenny was eyeing Jasper in the mirror as we drove. "Who's he?"

"Someone to look after for a while." I glanced at the young man, not knowing him from the past life. But if he were ever able to slip Michael's control, I didn't doubt he'd send the man rushing headlong into a suicide of a battle. "Jasper, you are free to do as you wish, but I ask that you refrain from using your abilities on anyone around me."

"Yes, sir," the young man answered. He had to be maybe sixteen, so he wasn't much younger than me, but I understood that I didn't act like an eighteen-year-old.

I rubbed the top of his head. "Don't worry. We are going to meet with a few people after this. You'll see Michael, but he won't be in any condition to talk, so you are going to have to answer a few questions for him. You are going to be completely honest, alright?"

"Do you have some control over him?" Jenny asked.

"Unfortunately," I replied. "Michael had a tool to give people power. None of these tools give it for free. The best extract some sort of price for granting the power, but something material that can be paid. Others, like this one, extract the price from the person getting the power. This one gives control over that person to the one who used it on them," I explained with a sigh.

"But they get power?" Jenny asked. "So if you used it on me, I'd just have to do what you said?"

"Yes..." I hesitated, staring at the back of her head with a slight sense of unease. "Though, these things are tricky. I'll explain later. Rather than a boon, I'd consider them cursed."

Jenny nodded. "Understood, sir. We are almost there."

She pulled up to the warehouse that now had a dozen black SUVs and some big men guarding them. Stopping the car, she jumped out of her seat and rushed around the side far faster than a human should be able to move in order to let me out.

"Thank you." I dipped my head and got out of the car, pulling Jasper along with me.

"Bran. Hold on a moment." One of the men turned and whispered into a microphone. "Alright, come on. Who's the kid?"

"Michael's hostage—had to go collect him." I explained.

The big man had probably seen some shit, but he made an ugly face at the word hostage. He spoke into his microphone again, and I was already moving past.

"Watch the car, Jenny. We'll be back." I walked into the warehouse with Jasper in tow.

"Bran." Gloria noticed me first. She was sitting at the same table as before, a hospital bed now next to it and three doctors hovering around Michael.

Carmen was there as well. Next to him was Bobby and Carmen's second son Orvin. "Bran." Carmen nodded to me. "I think we need to hear a full accounting of this."

"Great, I can explain everything in a minute. Anyone who doesn't need to hear player information needs to leave." I put Jasper in a chair as several of them looked at the young man strangely. "Michael will be fine. I put him in that state. It was a harsh move, but I was in a hurry. He'll be fine in a few days when his spirit stabilizes."

Several of the doctors turned to me with a frown before turning to Carmen.

"Out. Everyone who's not family, out. Bran, and I assume your young charge, stay," Carmen demanded, and everyone couldn't have left fast enough.

"Well, first off. This is Jasper. Jasper, can you tell Orvin there to start jumping up and down and hooting like a monkey?" I asked the boy.

"Orvin, start jumping up and down, hooting like a monkey," the boy reiterated.

"Wha—?" Orvin was about to counter with something, but whatever he was about to say was lost as he started hooting and jumping up and down, going the extra mile by scratching at his armpits.

"Tell him to stop and forget that happened," I told Jasper.

"Stop, forget that happened." Jasper's voice rang with power.

Orvin stopped, blinking several times. "I'm not going to hoot like a monkey. Father, who the fuck is this?"

Carmen and Gloria were not paying attention to Orvin in the slightest, all of their attention was now on Jasper.

"That demonstration..." Carmen looked like he had an itchy trigger finger.

"Michael had this boy under his control. Supernaturally so," I answered the unspoken question. "Those types of control are tricky, and I've superseded Michael at present."

Orvin wasn't done. "Nothing happened, though."

"It did," Gloria said quietly. "You don't remember because he told you to forget what happened." She focused back on me with a very serious look on her face. "Bran, can you ask him if... if..."

"Jasper," I cut her off. "Have you used your powers on Gloria?"

"Twice," he said, looking down at his hands. "Once for Terrance, and the other for... for..." He glanced at Carmen and the words spilled out. "To kill Mr. Nester."

Carmen closed his eyes. "Bran. Explain it all."

I threw down the old diary from my spatial ring. "You see, it seems your late wife passed a few items on to her oldest son. Among them, a diary from one of their ancestors that talked about a special item that could give people screens that popped up in front of them and supernatural powers."

Gloria sat up straight. "You said it was a cursed artifact."

"It is. It basically makes those who get initiated into slaves," I growled. "Which is why I'm not going to let any of you have the artifact."

Carmen's eyes narrowed, but he relaxed slightly. "That's fine. So, Michael has been initiating men and slowly trying to take over the family? Boy, have you used your power on me?"

The boy shook his head. "No. He... he couldn't get me close enough to you." Jasper trembled before Carmen.

"I'm going to have to work on him a little to untie some of the knots," I explained. "Then he can work on his own."

"A power like that, though..." Carmen trailed off, seeing the boy not as a resource but as a large liability.

"It won't affect Gloria or me. Our spirit is much higher than his. I could seal some of his skills..." I trailed off. It was really down to the kid to either use his abilities for good or to hang himself when eventually the world was full of powerful people who would crush him the second he used it on someone he shouldn't.

"Please seal that mind control for now," Carmen told me without hesitation.

I stared at Jasper. Then I pricked his finger before pricking my own and turning my blood into a D grade ink. I made a quick talisman that I then pasted to his head.

It dissolved instantly.

"There. The skills Hypnotize and Mesmerize are sealed. Sorry, kid." I rubbed the top of his head. "Continue to answer any question that Carmen asks you."

The head of the local mafia continued to question the boy about what Michael had been up to. Jasper had quite a few answers. Michael had used him to manipulate a large number of people. He had recruited people that were then made slaves through the artifact.

Carmen even dug into some questions that had never occurred to me about local politicians, growing quite concerned when he learned the depths of Michael's schemes.

Eventually, Carmen wiped his face and shook his head. "To think he did all of that."

The most affected by the answers was Gloria. Her face was pale yet relieved at the same time. Michael had used Jasper to plant the idea to kill Carmen in her head.

I decided to capitalize on her innocence. "Uncle Nester. Since we found the bottom of Gloria's supposed betrayal, perhaps there's no need to punish her," I put a hand on her shoulder.

The man leaned back taking in my question. "Of course. Gloria, I will no longer force you to marry Bran. I forgive you, my daughter." He hadn't referred to her by familial terms since the incident.

I reached down and took the ring off Gloria's stunned finger.

"Wait." She tried to snatch it from my hand, but I pulled it back and got down on one knee.

"Gloria, will you marry me?" I proposed to her a second time right away. "He just took away any force on this, and I want another answer now that the weight of your father's words aren't on you."

She pulled me up and kissed me once before slipping the ring back on her finger, admiring it once again. "I wouldn't part with a ring this lovely."

I grinned like a fool and nodded, allowing the mafia princess her stubbornness to pretend it was about the ring and not about me.

"Fair enough." I stood behind her. "Then I'm sure Gloria has told you what happened when we arrived here..." I went into my own telling of the story, followed by my race to Michael's mansion and back.

***

At the end of my retelling, Carmen solemnly stood up and had someone wheel Michael out of the warehouse as he left with his son. Carmen took Jasper with him to answer some additional questions. I gave him full control of the young man; now that Jasper's powers were sealed, he wasn't much of a danger, and I knew Carmen would take good care of him.

My larger concern was what he'd do to Michael.

I left with Gloria, and we rode in the back of her car. "Where are we going?" I asked.

Jenny glanced at Gloria, and the mobster sighed. "To our little budding company. Jenny and some of the ladies have been begging to meet you again. And I thought you'd like to see that they are all doing well. Are you really not going to use that artifact?"

I sighed. "With so much of the System, it's about perception. Say I used this on Jenny up there. She'd become initiated and able to grow much stronger," I spoke loud enough that she could hear me too. "Yet my words would be a compulsion to her. You can twist them and sort of free yourself, but that compulsion never really goes away, just redirected. So, they will forever be under a mental binding. It is a curse."

"I already work for you and Mrs. Nester. Would it be that much different?" Jenny asked.

"Yes. So much different." I rubbed at my forehead. "Imagine that I told you to stop hurrying at some random point in your life. Then later I got frustrated at you driving slowly because you quite literally couldn't hurry and told you to go faster. Now you are stuck doing everything as fast as you can."

"Oh." Jenny didn't sound convinced.

"Could you make it easier on them?" Gloria asked.

"Maybe. Why do we need to initiate her and the others, though?" I asked. "It isn't like I have a ton of instances for them to run in order to up their stats."

"Well, when you go to your clan, these instances are going to be idle, and Bobby can't do them all," Gloria answered thoughtfully. "We could use some hands in clearing the lower ones."

"We'd be happy to help, Sir Bran," Jenny spoke up quickly from the front.

I sighed. "Let's see the other girls and explain to them, and see their reaction. I'll explain it better then." Certainly some of the women wouldn't be so eager.

Chapter 49

I was wrong. So very wrong that I was trying to figure out a graceful way to bow out of the room quickly as I sat in a small conference room with all of them.

There were twenty-one Mul Branova girls in the group, three more than even Jenny realized.

I had offered them more power at the cost of having to listen to my commands and many of them were quick to accept the terms.

"Why don't you try it on Jenny first?" Pattie urged me.

I rubbed my face.

Gloria was with me too, giving me a look as if asking why I was being so reluctant when they were so willing.

"Fine," I gave in.

There would be a little reprogramming I could do, and then I'd have to be careful about what I asked and clear the slate often. My biggest concern was potentially seeding a ton of resentment that would backfire.

Yet they were so demanding that it would almost work the opposite if I kept denying them. At some point in this life, I realized that I was just one man and needed a team. Actually, I needed even more than a team. I needed an organization.

"Let's go over what's about to happen." I looked out at the twenty-one Mul Branova women in the conference room. "There is a thing called 'The System'. It's a power of this world that gives you strength beyond that of human capabilities. It works very straightforwardly, though much of it is a reflection of our beliefs."

"What does that mean?" Jenny asked.

"Classes are an easy example. Things of this world's legend will appear as classes, but the same classes might not exist on other worlds. Say there's someone with a Medusa class; it's a powerful SSS Rank class. It's a mirror of what we believe Medusa to be, turning it and the person who uses it into the myth," I did my best to explain. "The compulsion this will put on you will do something similar. It's a reflection of what you think I mean when I give you an order. So that's on me to be specific, and you need to work to not misunderstand."

Jenny nodded. "What's SSS Rank?" It seemed she was the voice of the Mul Branova ladies.

Gloria stepped in and gave them all a quick primer while I pulled out the crook and played with it briefly to see if there was anything I could do with it. Artifacts were rather useless after the Rapture, so I hadn't done much with them before, but three attempts at changing its properties with talismans all failed.

By the time I finished the third, they were all staring at me waiting.

"Jenny, come here." I raised the crook. It quickly grew to a size that I could hook it around her neck while checking on her with Soul Gaze

She waited patiently as the crook tightened slightly and flashed, making her eyes glow.

"Alright, now tell me your class options and we—" I froze as I saw her class change. For once, I was completely speechless. "Wha-?" I tried but couldn't finish the thought.

Gloria burst out laughing as she read the class at the same time.

Jenny blushed. "You said it was a reflection of our beliefs. Let this be a testament to them. Even the System recognizes my feelings." She turned to the rest of the girls. "It gave me the class, New Devotee of Bran."

The rest of the Mul Branova girls started clamoring, asking her a dozen questions each.

I wanted to hide my head in the floor. Why was something like this already occurring in the System?

[Jenny Mul Branova
Level: 1
Class: New Devotee of Bran SS
Status: Elated, excited, devoted
Strength: 44

Agility: 101
Vitality: 40
Intelligence: 41
Spirit: 41
Skills:
Awakened Bloodline of The Long-Eared Fox B
Blessing of Bran F
Power of Blood F]

The System even had a skill with my name! Jenny had said it was a show of their devotion, but this was too much.

Were these ladies really this devoted? It seemed impossible to me. Yet they were at the very bottom of their life, and I had dredged them up, given them power, stability, and more.

It wasn't unlike several sects, mafias and other organizations used such methods as the foundation of loyalty for their members.

"Me next." Katie was in front of me, almost putting the crook around her own neck, but it needed me to initiate it so that it grew.

Which, it did.

A moment later, she became initiated, picking the same class as Jenny immediately. As soon as it was done, she began gabbing with the other woman as the two of them quickly started to sort out everyone and form a line so that they could one by one become New Devotees of Bran.

I tried to find an excuse in their statuses, but they were all genuine in their desire to get initiated this way.

Beyond the silly class name, it was ridiculous that every one of them was getting an SS class! And the starter abilities had my attention as well.

[Blessing of Bran F - Increased Defense against physical and magical attacks, those attacks that do penetrate Bran's Blessing will heal at an amplified pace.

'Bran's greatest desire is for those who follow him to survive.']

It was a named skill, and one with flavor text! It was practically Tough Skin and Regeneration in one. Honestly, I was a little jealous. Why didn't I have a skill like this if it was my own blessing?

And the other skill, Power of Blood, gave me an even greater headache.

[Power of Blood F - Increases benefits from bloodlines and other blood related abilities. May be increased by drinking the blood of Bran's enemies.]

"Wow." Simone appeared next to me. "Are you sure you aren't a vampire? Because it looks to me like you are making more vampires."

"What are you doing here?" I asked, working through the last of the Mul Branova women waiting to be initiated.

"Gloria called me. She's a little worried." Simone's eyes grazed over the women that I was initiating.

"What for?" I was genuinely confused. "She was goading me into this."

"Yeah, well, she's growing concerned that so many ladies are joining you right now. Maybe you should tell her how you felt about my Slave Seal," Simone told me.

I wasn't an idiot. After a moment, I puzzled it out and let out a bold laugh. "Where's Gloria?" I finished up the last of the Mul Branova girls. "I'll be right back."

Getting up, I left them to settle into their new reality, though I was careful not to give them any orders.

Gloria had stepped out of the office room and was talking to someone on the phone. She put it down when I came out. "Bran. I see we are making an army."

Rather than answer her, I grabbed her cheeks and pressed my lips to hers. "Gloria, don't feel jealous. Those girls just lost out on any chance to be with me. Now that I've initiated them like this, I could never in good conscience be with them romantically."

Simone laughed at my side. "Bran isn't going to make them into a harem or anything. Think of it this way, Bran only really wants Generals and Queens. That's you and me, while he gets to be the Hegemon above it all. Those girls are lieutenants at best."

Gloria was blushing from the kiss, but her face softened slightly at Simone's words. "Tell them that." She put the phone away. "A bunch of them already are asking if he needs an assistant or a driver."

"A driver might not be bad," I said. "But they are just a driver then. There's a bigger problem we need to tackle first. A little undoing of the logic for what I just gave them. I need to frame it in a way that's a little distant."

Simone had a wicked smile. "I have an idea. Follow my lead?"

I squinted at her, but shrugged. Simone hadn't led me wrong, and she wasn't going to. "Fine."

"This way." Simone swayed her hips back and forth, taking one of my arms, while I used the other to hook around Gloria's waist and bring her too.

Back in the conference room, the Mul Branova ladies were still giddy with their new situation but became quiet at my entrance.

"Jenny." Simone pointed to her. "Why don't you lead this group? Amanda, you are getting promoted to Bran's driver." She quickly settled that question.

Amanda was the other B ranked bloodline that had joined the Mul Branova girls, and she pumped her fist at the news. It would be good to keep the other high value bloodlines safe, so I didn't argue.

"Alright, all of you understand that if Bran gives you a direct order, it's going to become a compulsion. Rather than think of him as your master, let's realize he blessed you with this power and he's a greater being than you fully understand. Even the System has shown your devotion and that he's something greater," Simone continued elegantly as my frown deepened.

I didn't like where this was going.

"Thus, please listen to Bran's ten commandments. They are his iron-clad desires for you and shall be your guiding light." She dipped her head in reverence and gave me the floor.

I did not like being on the spot. And I was never good at inspirational speeches. 'Kill Demons and Live' was the entirety of the speech I'd given before the final battle of the second demon war. Through retelling after the fact, it had somehow become an hour-long impassioned speech. I never really lived that one down with some of the veterans.

Yet, I did have some fairly rigid principles that I felt like I could use at the moment. "First and foremost, you must survive above all else. You are no good to yourselves or me dead."

They all nodded, and many of them started to talk about the Blessing of Bran.

"Second, you are to enrich your lives through joy, learning, and passions," I continued, trying to stay general enough that the words would help them lead good lives and would anchor the compulsion to vague terms they could all have quite a bit of freedom in. "Third, cooperation with each other is beautiful. Fourth... uh..."

They were all staring at me with wide eyes.

"Fourth, treasure what is important to you." Fuck, that was generic. Oh well, let's continue down that path. "Fifth, face your fears and conquer them, of course with number one being more important."

"Six, kill and dismantle demonic operations where you can. Seven, do what's right rather than what's convenient. Eight, live your life by your own principles..." I was struggling, and turned to Simone with slight annoyance that I was going to have to come up with ten of these. "Nine, true strength is controlling your temper and protecting those weaker than you. Ten, be happy."

Okay, I might have phoned it in that last one.

Yet, it didn't matter. The Mul Branova girls were clapping excitedly. Fuck why do speeches always end up this way? The words had sounded stupid to me, but they seemed pleased.

"You heard it from Bran himself." Simone leaned on me. "Those ten shall be above all else that he says in the future. Those are your guiding commandments. Everything else is just words."

She was placing these high up in their sense of the control that I now held over them. In the same breath, she was downgrading everything else I said. As far as reprogramming the control, it was a fairly good method. Even if I felt a little awkward being revered by them. I'd balked at being a King before, and now Simone was going to try and make me a deity.

I had almost made the last three the same 'kill demons' commandments. As far as I was concerned, it really was our top focus. But I'd gotten a little inspiration towards the end.

Gloria stepped forward to get the womens' attention. "We'll be changing up some of your work now. There are places with monsters that you can kill to grow stronger. You'll be on the company clock, so what you earn inside will be given to us. There are also plenty of other women like you who've been taken advantage of and could be rescued by Bran. Let's find and protect them like Bran would want."

A few of the women looked to Jenny, who seemed to be the leader as she raised her hand to be called on.

I nodded to her. "Yes, Jenny?"

"Why can't we Inspect you?" she asked. "We want to know more. It seems that we..." She looked around. "We all have bloodlines, but Gloria said they were rare. Not to mention, it seems that your power has something to do with blood?"

"Go on." Simone nudged me. "If you can't show yourself to your devotees, then who can you show yourself to?"

I sighed. "Please do not reveal my secrets," I told them, making sure to phrase it as a request and not an order.

"Never!" Jenny said in a hurry, and the rest all nodded as I stopped resisting their Inspect and bared all of my stats and skills before them, including the new skill.

[Worshiped F - The power of those who believe in you makes you stronger. +20 to all stats.]

I shook my head as they all stared into the middle distance at the screen in front of them and started to poke at my skills and see new ones and whisper.

"That spirit...

"Soul Gaze? SSS?"

"Is his spirit some divine come to a mortal shell?"

Simone smiled and swayed against me as they all whispered, and stupid rumors began to form.

I sighed. I needed to go kill something. That always cheered me up.

Chapter 50

I woke up to Simone's soft lips wrapped around my cock. "Damn, this will never get old."

Her lips and tongue worked me to a peak with the skill and knowledge that only a familiar lover could as I popped in her mouth and she sucked me clean before coming off.

"I hope not." She ran a finger down my length. "It's great seeing your sleeping face as you squirm a little before you wake up."

"Succubus," I teased her, grabbing her waist to pull her down on top of me and kissing along her neck.

"We don't have time. Gloria is already ready," Simone moaned.

I fished a finger down under those saintess robes of hers. "So? Let the princess wait on me for a change."

"Bran!" Simone cried as my finger found her paradise soaked and plunged straight in, curling my finger in a come-hither gesture and hitting her sensitive spot that I was very familiar with by now.

I stroked it with one finger while an arm was wrapped around her waist, and I continued to kiss up and down her neck. Simone didn't last long. She never did, which was half the fun. There was nothing greater than giving your partner pleasure.

Rolling a panting Simone off of me, I got up to get dressed.

"Tease," she mumbled, pulling herself together. "That's just a taste."

"Takes one to know one," I shot back and was dressed for the day. "Isn't Gloria waiting?"

"Oh. Now it matters." She rolled her eyes and got off the bed, letting her robes fall back into place with a few small tugs and reaching the door first to open it up.

Gloria had moved into our apartment and was sipping orange juice at the table with a laptop now open. "When I heard Simone, I thought I might as well settle in."

We had all settled into a routine. Yet, today was going to be different.

"Is everything ready?" I asked, stealing a piece of toast from the toaster and putting some butter on it as I sat down and took a bite.

"The Order of Bran—"

"Please stop calling it that," I groaned.

"The Order," Gloria shortened it with a smirk, "has taken over three of the instances and found twenty more bloodline holders. Though, the highest is a C rank."

Both women wanted me to collect their bloodlines before we went into the B rank instance. Yet I needed to be able to rank up my class again before heading back to the clan. The clan had an instance as part of the rites for new members that would actually be a problem if my level were anything but 1.

I could fake my sheet, but not so well that I could fool the System.

"Gold?" I pushed us forward in the conversation before either of them could start to argue.

"With the gold you got from Vincent, and everything we've earned, I pulled our operations down to the bare minimum. We have 2.7 million gold coins." Gloria laid down a D rank ring that was likely stuffed to the brim.

"Are we going to use them now?" Simone asked.

"No. We aren't sure what we're facing in the B ranked instance. Waiting half a day won't hurt. What if both of you need to boost your spirit to survive it, and instead we'd already spent it all on strength?" I asked.

"We'll probably be putting it all in your vitality anyway." Gloria smirked. "Since you'll be the one up front."

I was also the only one of us with B rank abilities. The leveling up of my class boosting my class skills was a strong tool. Though, in the B rank instance, they should be able to push theirs higher.

Perhaps I'd find the trigger to ranking mine to A for the class abilities. Then there were those that I already knew, like Regeneration.

"You two better put in the work then." I finished my toast. "Let's go. I'm all packed, and waiting isn't helping any of us." I snatched up the ring full of gold coins and started heading out.

Simone was right behind me and Gloria just threw her laptop in her spatial ring to keep up with us.

At the parking garage, two women leaned against a pair of decked out Rolls-Royce cars. Jenny was chatting with Amanda. The two leggy women were getting their fair share of stares as people left for work.

"Bran." Both of them stopped leaning on the cars and stood up straight as soon as I entered. I thanked my lucky stars that they didn't call me anything strange.

"You're going away for that trip today, sir?" Amanda opened the door of my car while Jenny opened Gloria's, both of them staring at each other in almost defiance as to who would take us.

"We'll take both cars," I told them, sliding into my car. "Though I'm not sure when exactly we'll be back."

"Don't worry. We'll be waiting," Amanda reassured me with a sharp nod and coiled her blonde hair up under her driver's cap before she got in the car.

***

The drive and the trek up to the B rank instance wasn't difficult at all for us. I half-expected Gloria to break a heel, but she managed to deftly avoid twisting her ankle.

"Where is it?" Simone asked as I paused by the chasm.

I threw a rock, hitting a critical talisman and breaking it around the instance portal.

Simone's eyes went wide. "You hid it?"

[Level 87 B Ranked Unstable Forest Instance
24/12 Charges]

"Being double the charges can't be good," Gloria noticed immediately.

"No. It's very unstable, which is part of why we need to deal with it." I didn't hesitate and walked up to the portal, letting it suck me in.

The women were only a step or two behind me as we found ourselves walking out of the chasm in the forest to what looked like the same forest we'd just been in, only there was a layer of mist over the ground. It wasn't broad daylight like we'd left; instead, it was low light, as if it were dawn or dusk.

"I don't see any monsters." Gloria just had to poke the System with her words.

There was a titanic bird cry in the distance, and trees groaned as a giant walked among them.

Gloria handed me the spatial ring with all of the gold. Each stat could be leveled independently of the others but increased with each purchase. "Use it all."

I looked at both of them, hesitating for a second.

"I'm already the strongest." Simone smiled. "But I'm going to hang back and be healing you."

Gloria shrugged. "While you are gone, I'm going to be skimming off the top and working on my own stats. With Michael gone, and me taking more business from Vincent, I might even be stronger than you when you get back from your clan." She goaded me.

I knew her statement was a lie, but both of them wanted me to be stronger. If we were fighting giants, I needed more vitality, and dumped one and a half million gold coins into it. My stat rang up until it grew 315 points. Then I dumped the rest into strength, gaining 263 in that stat.

Part of my heart bled knowing how much harder it was going to be to progress those with gold in the future. The first go was always the most satisfying.

"He looks tougher." Simone pinched me. "Feels a little sturdier too."

I rolled my eyes at her antics, checking my stat block.
[Name: Bran Heros
Level: 52
Class: Blood Hegemon D
Status: Healthy

Strength: 491
Agility: 217
Vitality: 606
Intelligence: 212
Spirit: 11157
...]

I was still going to be weak compared to a B rank monster at Level 87. As if to prove me right, one walked through the trees for me to use Soul Gaze on.

[Mistwalker Behemoth B
Level: 87
Strength: 623
Agility: 291
Vitality: 721
Intelligence: 145
Spirit: 2
Skills:
Stealth B
Smash B
Mist Wall B
Misty Step B
Night Vision C
Crush B]

Its glowing eyes turned towards us. The thing was some giant tree monster covered in moss and shrouded in a thin layer of mist as it kicked more up with each stride. It had to be four stories tall.

"I don't think its Stealth is working," Simone added, reading the same stats.

"Who said it was using it?" I challenged her, flicking my hand to the side. A blade of hardened blood sprang out of my wrist.

The behemoth moved our direction in large strides, and I rushed forward to meet it, Blood Bolts flying out of my hand.

I ran up right within range and activated Crimson Barrier. The thin layer of red barely did anything as the behemoth smashed right through the barrier with a kick, and I crossed my arms in front of me before its foot continued into me.

Its wooden foot broke both of my arms and sent me skidding backwards.

Purple flames flew over me as Gloria tried to burn the behemoth. Simone's healing washed over me and assisted my Regeneration in knitting my arms back together.

"That's not so bad," Simone tried to downplay it. She hadn't reacted so well the first time that she'd seen such extensive regeneration.

I shrugged off the broken arms and wiped at my mouth. "No biggie. Let's keep going."

My blood sword started chopping at the behemoth's foot, scraping and cutting at it while Gloria did her best to burn a hole in its chest. Simone occasionally threw out big pink beams to help Gloria.

The Mistwalker tried to punch down at me, but I activated Blood Boil and jumped on its arm, weaving my sword along it as I raced up to its face, slashing away at every inch of exposed wood on the monster on my way up.

Unfortunately, what goes up must come down.

It managed to smack me against its neck, like someone swatting a mosquito. My body ached from the strike.

I dug my sword into the monster and held on, using my sword to ride back down to the ground, leaving a jagged cut in its bark from the neck down to the shin.

"Keep going, Bran!" Simone cheered.

The behemoth kicked at me, but I rolled just under it and hurried away to draw it further from both of my women.

As I moved, the monster used an ability. It had used Misty Step, if I had to guess. The entire behemoth vanished in a puff of mist, only to appear over me, a foot crashing down.

I had no time to react beyond bracing with my sword and stomping into the ground as the behemoth tried to crush me. I managed to brace myself enough, but I was stuck underneath its foot.

"Hold on, Bran!" Gloria shouted, pouring more purple fire over the behemoth.

The monster flashed as I felt the System assist it in its next attack.

Crush activated, and the weight on me easily tripled. I felt my arms snap before the foot fell down onto my shoulders;

the force of the B ranked ability was going to turn me into a pancake.

Simone was attempting to heal me like crazy, and while my body was both becoming liquified and healed, I had a moment to try to decide the next step.

My shoulders cracked and then healed over as disks slipped in my spine from the weights and everything felt like it was going to crumble. Blood poured down from my hairline, and I met Simone's eyes. "Stop healing me."

She gasped, but she did as I asked, and the foot glowed again as the behemoth activated Crush again and stomped me into the forest floor.

Chapter 51

Gloria stopped her attacks as she watched the behemoth crush Bran into the ground. Her eyes were wide, and she snapped at Simone.

"Why'd you stop healing him!" Gloria screamed with everything she had until her voice went raw.

That man had swept in, upended her life, and then piece by piece put it back together. She was Family again. She was in the lead for the younger generation of Nester. And every day, she was growing more powerful both in wealth and personal power.

Yeah, Bran could be a little rough around the edges, but he was always there when it mattered. Not to mention, he understood her family in a way that few men ever would. He understood who she was as both a woman and a member of the mafia. Incredibly, he respected both equally.

Seeing him crushed broke a piece of her.

Simone, however, was completely calm, which only made Gloria more angry.

"Have you forgotten? Our man is not someone who gives up." Simone laughed. "He went back in time only after the entire world fell. Being stepped on by a giant? That's training."

Sure enough, a deep roar of rage came from under the behemoth's foot as Bran surged back up his eyes glowing.

[Bran Heros
Level: 52
Class: Blood Hegemon D
Status: Broken Bones, Bleeding, Last Stand, Excited
Strength: 2455
Agility: 1085

Vitality: 3030
Intelligence: 1060
Spirit: 55785]

He looked worse for wear, but Gloria held her chest and sighed.

She shouldn't have doubted him. The brute of a man was probably just trying to rank up some stupid skill. She huffed and made a purple Fireball, hurling it at the stupid giant tree that had tried to crush her man.

Simone stood to the side with a giant smile on her face as Bran threw the behemoth onto its side and went into a rage smashing it repeatedly with his fists. "He's really something."

"Something, alright. Nearly gave me a heart attack," Gloria huffed.

Simone raised an eyebrow. "What was that? You're head over heels for him?"

"Not a chance. He's just a good partner. It would be a lot of work to replace him." Gloria tried to flip her hair and forgot it was still up.

Simone laughed and made a heart in the air before blasting off another giant pink beam. "Well, let's let him have some fun here and stay back until he calms down. I think he has it under control, but this is the first time he's using this skill around anyone else."

***

I came down from Last Stand, staggering as the body disappeared under me. I felt drunk with the drop in intelligence.

"Need a hand?" Simone asked.

"Please. Brain. Hurt," I grunted.

She was at my side in an instant, giving me her shoulder. "You were incredible. Did you rank up the skill?"

"Not that time. But I bet I'm close if I keep it up," I chuckled.

"Then we'll do it like that again? You almost made Gloria die from heartbreak," Simone said.

"That's not at all how it happened," Gloria refuted. "If he dies, we are both done for too. I was just worried about what would happen." She wasn't convincing at all. "So... you're doing that again?"

"Not yet." I held my head as it cleared back up. "It won't activate again if I'm immediately in danger. I need to rest."

"How does that work?" Simone asked.

"Not sure. Some people think it's a safety feature built into the System. Like if I yo-yoed in and out of that ability several times, I might seriously hurt myself. It multiplies my stats by five, but it also wrecks me when I come down from it." I sat down with Simone's help as Gloria picked up the loot.

"Moss. All of that for some moss? And some Gold, of course. Three hundred from a single monster." She let out a slow whistle. "Not bad. How many of these do you think are in here?" She seemed ready to vent out some of her stress.

"Not a clue." I pulled out a bottle of water and started drinking. "This place could only be a square mile, or it could be huge. There's no way to know."

"If you need a break, then we are all going to rest," Simone decided for the group, sitting down next to me. "So, Bran. Tell us about the clans."

I raised an eyebrow at her, but there wasn't much else to do while I rested. Simone was good at that. She picked her moments excellently. "There are five. Borrson Clan are the Viking gods; they all have the bloodlines of Titans and Giants in their veins. Some of them get huge. As a result, a lot of them don't fit in with the present world and live off in Antarctica, far to the North in Canada or several islands. The Borrson Clan is quite possibly the most physically imposing of the clans, not to mention that they have a level of resistance to magic and physical damage. In the end, they stop a demon gate that the rest of the world didn't know existed in the Arctic."

"How big are we talking?" Gloria asked, glancing over where the behemoth had disappeared.

"I think the biggest I've seen was like sixteen feet tall," I told her. "But as they say, the bigger they are, the harder they fall."

Simone chuckled. "So. A clan of giant Nordic gods, a clan of the Greek gods and heroes. What's next? Egyptian gods?"

"Check. They're the Ennead Clan. Summoners, necromancers, and bestial warriors," I explained.

"How do necromancers work if corpses disappear?" Simone asked.

"They just raise them out of the ground. It's more of a summon than using actual corpses," I explained. "Think of it like a death-themed summoner. All of the clans used to not be in hiding and were full of players."

"I can't believe they stayed strong through it all," Gloria shook her head. "The Nesters have certainly had their ups and downs."

"They have not entirely avoided internal turmoil. The Wukong Clan used to be the Yudi Clan. There was a bit of a rebellious child of the family that took over. They all go through phases, but come out stronger for it." I shook my head thinking of clan politics as being good. In the middle of it, the conflicts could be rough.

"So, who's on top?" Simone asked.

"One I haven't talked about yet. Kailash Clan—they have an old man known as Shiva who is currently the strongest human on Earth." I sighed thinking of the battle between him and the Demon Lord. His subsequent death was a blow that nearly caused the loss of the First Demon War. "Enough history lesson. We don't have to worry about any of them for now except the Heros Clan."

"Well, what about them then?" Simone prodded.

"Are we going to play twenty questions and drill me for more?" I dusted off my pants. I couldn't use Last Stand again, but I was ready to do more exploring in the instance and better understand it. And exploring sounded like much more fun than getting into a history lesson on my family.

"You're fairly tight-lipped about your clan," Gloria added, putting her hands on my shoulders to stop me from running off. "We are just worried."

"Clan business is complicated, and we have a month here. I'm sure you can get it out of me before we are done, but we need to keep going. We could have done the last one without Last Stand," I said.

"Just heal you through all that while we pound it down?" Simone asked for clarification.

"Pretty much. I could have toughed it out and not needed to boost my strength to ridiculous levels to finish that faster. That thing was tough, though."

"What if the next one is even harder?" Gloria asked.

"Then stay very quiet and back away," I teased and got up, starting to move through the forest. Most places didn't just have big one-off monsters.

Though, it seemed that this instance was going to be a forest of giants based on the distant bird call and the Mistwalker Behemoth that we'd already seen. The mist was thick, but thankfully, what moved in this forest was loud, stomping and breaking branches as it moved.

There was another Mistwalker we spotted and avoided, only to find a pack of smaller creatures. Smaller, though, was relative to the Mistwalkers. Each of these monsters was sixteen feet tall.

[Shellback Giant B
Level: 82
Strength: 523
Agility: 421
Vitality: 521
Intelligence: 151
Spirit: 2
Skills:
Hard Shell B
Anger B
Blunt Weapon Mastery B
Protect B]

The bald Shellback Giants each dragged a big club behind them and had a dark black carapace on their back.

"Guessing backstabbing isn't going to work too well," Simone murmured.

"That weapon mastery... are you going to be okay, Bran?" Gloria asked.

I flicked my hand to the side, drawing out another blade made of blood. My health dipped slightly, but I felt Regeneration restore the lost blood. "Are you kidding me? What better chance to work on my weapon mastery? Simone, just keep me alive. Gloria, at some point, you are going to use one of these to work on your Tough Skin."

The mobster's face went pale.

"I'll help Simone heal you," I offered.

"That doesn't make it better. I'm not really up for getting hit." Gloria looked down at her unblemished skin.

"Getting hit now in a controlled environment is far better than getting hit when we aren't there to help you. Besides, I'm going to be leaving for the clan, and I don't want to have to worry about you." I grabbed her hand, and the princess melted.

"Fine." Gloria gritted her teeth and glared at the giants. "Not yet though. Let me get a little stronger so that they don't just instantly smear me on the ground. I'll cover you while you go in." She waved her hand, and a purple fireball appeared at the ready.

I got up, charging into the pack of five giants. Blood Bolts splashed out on them, and then the blood twisted into hexes, slowing all of them down. They were still fast, clubs swung from every direction, and I let myself be driven back by the first and recovered in time to rush up the last one.

My feet pounded up the club and to the giant's shoulder as my blade danced at his face. I bit my thumb to draw a diagram on its forehead before flipping off as a black sphere of darkness wrapped around it and it started swinging wildly.

"You'll be last," I promised that giant and used Crimson Barrier to block several swings, sliding under a giant as the barrier shattered and cleaving into its legs. It was time to play with my new ability.

I let part of my blade break off in the giant's wounds, activating Sanguine Locking. My spirit crushed the resistance from the giant, and it froze. All of its blood was now held in my control.

The other three were pissed now, Anger activating and their faces turned red as they sped up their clubs, swinging with a precision and deftness that defied their size. I parried one, only for my blade to break and reform with another use of my blood.

Three should be safe enough.

I spread my foot across the ground focusing in and breathing steadily, with my sword out before I charged amidst the three giants.

Clubs rained down on me like hail in a storm. My sword broke more often than I would have liked as my other hand used Blood Siphon to sustain myself along with Regeneration and Simone's heals.

Instead, I fought three on one to push myself and force myself to focus on my sword work. This was something I'd done more than once; pushing my body to the limits was part of being in the System. Shedding a little blood didn't bother me; it was only a little red water leaving my body.

A club shattered my sword and another caught me in the side, breaking half my ribs and ejecting me from the circle of giants.

"Bran?" Simone called out. Both women were waiting for me to say it was time for them to let loose.

I wiped some blood from my mouth as the giants rushed me. "Five more minutes. I'm having a little fun." Shooting to my feet, I summoned another blade and roared as I rushed back into the fray.

This was the life that I was familiar with. Fighting with the purpose of growing stronger.

Gloria's voice drifted over the combat. "He's insane. I can't watch this."

Chapter 52

"Just let it hit you." I coached.

We had spent three days in the instance and still hadn't run out of monsters to fight. Then again, I was using each one as an opportunity to train.

A Shellback Giant was frozen by my Sanguine Locking at present and was standing in front of Gloria who had changed out into a purple bikini with rhinestones so she would not get blood on her clothes.

"Wait, is it going to hurt?" she asked.

"Yes. Probably a lot." I had a wet towel and was scrubbing blood off my face, while Simone stood ready to keep Gloria alive. "Releasing it in 3...2...1..."

Almost a second later, Gloria went flying behind me, and I locked the monster back down to turn to her while Simone was healing her.

"See? That wasn't even so bad. If you squared your stance, though, you wouldn't have gone flying so badly." I tore off a piece of my sandwich.

There was a veritable horde of sandwiches in my spatial rings. I was going to get a bunch of rings and save food from this era—they wouldn't go bad in the void of a spatial ring.

Gloria got up with a groan. "My skill didn't level up."

"It's going to take a few hits," I lied. It was going to take a lot more than a few. "Wanna take one of the clubs we got earlier and hit it a few times to feel better?" I held out one of the giant's clubs that magically resized to fit us.

"We aren't all brutes," Simone said, but Gloria charged up and snatched the club out of my hand before screaming and smacking the frozen giant. The mafia princess was tougher than Simone thought sometimes.

It would be good practice; she'd probably get some blunt weapon proficiency if she kept it up.

"No, Simone, we aren't all saints. Some of us would rather push through life with a little anger than simply trying to make it a better place." I smiled at her. "Don't change, though."

I unfroze the giant without giving Gloria warning. She dodged the first strike before the second sent her flying, and Simone sighed.

"Warn me!" Gloria shouted.

"Real life doesn't come with warning. Get back up there, Gloria. Also, nice swimsuit. Is all your stuff studded?" I asked as I unfroze the giant again, and she jumped off the ground where Simone was healing her to fight it again.

"Is this how you learned to fight?" Simone asked.

"Me? No. There wasn't anyone there to heal me or stop the monsters." My gaze shifted to the distance as I froze the monster after it hit Gloria. "After the Rapture, demons started attacking Vein City within a week. Yet it was the low-level monsters that started appearing everywhere that caused mass panic. I went into it with a baseball bat and enough anger at a world that had done me dirty that I wasn't sure if I really cared if I lost."

Simone put a hand on mine while she healed Gloria. "I'm so sorry, Bran."

"It's fine. I made something of the situation." I had made peace with that life long ago.

"Getting a title like 'The Wandering King' does not sound like you loved it." Simone glared at me. "This time, we'll be here for you, and the Mul Branova girls will become a force. You'll have to make a base around Vein City and protect it along with them." She had a big smug smile on her face.

I poked her nose. "Don't get too cocky. Be happy that you don't have any physical skills to level. Oh wait, let me see." I reached under her saintess outfit, but she escaped my grasp, dancing away.

CHAPTER 52

***

Gloria had a club over her shoulder as we walked.

We'd run out of monsters, it seemed. Her clothes had been changed out yet again.

Gloria had way too many coats in her ring. So far, I swore I'd seen at least forty different jackets hanging off her shoulders.

I shuddered at the cost of all those designer coats.

This instance was quite large, and we'd cleared everything that I could spot. There was a large hill that we were climbing up to see if we could spot the boss.

"We haven't seen that bird yet," Simone said as we neared the top. Her words were almost prophetic as a huge shadow fell over us.

"You had to say that." Gloria shielded her eyes as a giant bird was flying down as if from the sun. "I'm going to clobber that bird."

The monster's wings continued to expand as it grew closer and closer. I couldn't quite tell how far away it was with the sun behind it.

Yet Soul Gaze helped me there.

[Giant Eating Roc B
Level: 95
Strength: 923
Agility: 921
Vitality: 921
Intelligence: 151
Spirit: 2
Skills:
Rain of Feathers B
Drop B
Flying B
Keen Sight B
Tempest Wing B
Swallow B
Digest B
Bloodline of the Golden Roc SS]

"I think we killed all its food," I said. "Now it's hungry."

"Oh no. I'm not getting fucking eaten." Gloria shook her head. "I can get smashed around by giants, but I'm not letting that bird eat me."

"Too bad." I shrugged. "You could probably level your magic resistance by exposing it to acid. Get ready. This thing might stay in the air; avoid those claws at all costs." I ran to the very top and waved my sword at it as I fired off Blood Bolts.

In return, the Roc focused on me and swooped down with a more direct goal.

As it grew closer, I began to realize the massive size of the beast. That bloodline on it made it far harder than it needed to be too. Yet all of those facts only made it more intriguing for me.

Simone fired off her Heartbreaker, and pink beams thumped as they shot through the air while Gloria was throwing fireballs like fast pitches. All of our attacks looked like bugs on a windshield as they splashed on the Roc's massive size, looking inconsequential.

It swooped down fast with its talons out for me.

I threw myself off the hill as my women continued to pelt it with magic and twisted the blood from Blood Bolt into hexes to make it more susceptible to magical attacks. This fight was going to be a slog if I couldn't get up there and fight it.

The bird finished its first pass and spun around midair, flapping its wings.

Simone went flying, and Gloria jumped up to snag her, a barrier of purple flames protecting them both as she landed half way down the hill.

I held onto the rocks, letting the wind rip at my skin. It was so powerful that it actually ripped and tore the clothes off my back before tearing at my skin.

A leaf in this wind became a dagger while a twig became a spear.

I was so busy hunkering down in the wind that I didn't see the colossal bird move until its talons were wrapping around me, piercing into my thigh and shoulders.

"That's not good." I let go to keep it from ripping my arms off.

It took off like a jet, my legs flopping back with the force of its ascension.

Curling in on myself, I did my best to withstand the Roc's flight. The thing was seriously fast, and I tried to reach out to the talon, my arm blowing back anytime it caught wind.

I managed to get a bloody hand on its talon and cast Blood Bolt from point blank range, my blood spilling all over the Roc's feet before it started to race up, forming a D rank curse that wrapped all over one of its feet while another ability soaked into its other leg.

"Sorry, buddy, you shouldn't have picked me up." I activated a curse of heaviness on one of its legs while the other was primed for Sanguine Locking.

In its panic, it dropped me, but it clearly used the System ability because the weight on me as I fell was abnormal, my body racing down to the crown of the hill that I was just on.

Throwing out Crimson Barrier at the last second, the barrier shattered with my fall, barely soaking the damage before my body slammed into the hill hard enough to make a crater.

Rather than worry about my current state, I smiled up at the Roc as it plummeted to the ground, mowing down a line of trees. I quickly activated my Sanguine Locking.

"You picked up the wrong one," I groaned, feeling Last Stand activate.

Even with the increased stats, I had trouble pulling myself out of the crater. But as I made it to the surface, I spotted the Roc struggling to get back into the air with two numb feet. It was a B rank monster, with incredible stats. My D rank Sanguine Locking wasn't as effective as it had been on the giants. And there hadn't been a chance for me to focus and exert my spirit.

My spirit pushed down on it as I focused and locked up more of its body as my Regeneration healed me enough to make a sword and pull myself to my feet.

"Gloria, get out here. It's time to roast a giant chicken!"

"If I get near that, it's going to eat me," Gloria said and threw a splash of purple fire at the Roc from a distance.

"More training for me." I dragged myself forward. With each step I was gaining strength. Last Stand was still with me as I passed my normal strength and found myself rushing forward with my sword to carve myself a piece of the damned bird.

How dare it drop me from so high up!

Simone started blasting pink beams into the Roc's head. Gloria's flames wrapped around one of the wings, starting to cook the feathers.

It struggled against my locking, but a bit of focus from my spirit and it stopped. Only then, it seemed it was out of options and it shed its feathers in what was essentially a storm of giant swords that swirled all around it.

"Protect yourselves!" I used Crimson Barrier on instinct before smiling and putting my sword forward, using the chaotic swirl of deadly feathers as sword practice, taking a step forward with each strike to get in range of the downed boss so that I could work to finish the fight.

Eventually, the feathers fell to the ground, and it had nothing left as we worked for another ten minutes to put it down.

The boss's body sank into the ground, disappearing into the instance as that central hill cracked and an avalanche of gold coins spilled out along with a few pieces of loot.

I jumped forward, snatching the boss's drops before they were buried.

"What'd you get?" Simone asked, looking at my hands.

I held out the short sword and the skill book.

[Sword of the Falling Feather B]

[Drop B]

[Sonic Cry Skillbook]

Simone looked at it. "Is it any good?"

"It stuns people you target around you," I informed her. "I'd have you take it; you could use some better protection." I glanced at Gloria for her opinion and she just shrugged.

"Is the sword for dropping on people from high up?" she asked.

"You can use Drop yourself when falling; it would protect you and cause you to land with high damage. I'll keep that for next time I get picked up and thrown down a mile in the sky. Besides... the best loot is here." I waved at the huge pile of gold. "Somewhere in there are two B rank spatial rings. That means twenty cubic meters of storage space."

Gloria's eyes lit up, and she started to suck up the gold with her other rings in search of the spatial rings.

"Not going looking for it?" I asked Simone.

"Why? I'll give it to you and stay close. That way you can carry my stuff." Simone gave me a sweet smile. "Besides, there should be one more item, right?"

She moved the gold near our feet aside and picked up a Nun's Veil.

I swore the System loved her far too much. If I didn't know better, I'd have thought it sent me back just to save these unlucky ladies.

[Veil of the Saint B

Grants Saint's Sanctuary B when worn]

[Saint's Sanctuary - Monsters will not attack the user as long as they remain non-confrontational]

My eye twitched as she put it on and batted her lashes at me.

"It looks great, doesn't it? Also, now I can't attack anything." She paused. "I hope *that* doesn't count as an attack." Simone gave me a sultry wink.

Chapter 53

We left the instance and set up Gloria's giant tent with multiple rooms and talismans pasted on the outside so that people and animals would be forced to avoid it.

The second everything was set up, Simone had me set up a 'shower' talisman. It was one for clean water, but strapped to a tree limb; it was good for a cold shower, and we took turns cleaning ourselves.

I enjoyed being able to make such simple quality of life talismans with nothing more than my blood. Typically, this one would have required a water attributed F rank item and the means to make ink. That was not necessarily expensive, but most players did not have that readily at their disposal. I was able to pull a water attributed F rank bloodline to the surface and create the bloodink.

Scrubbing myself clean, I wandered back to the tent, slipping in and falling face first into the bed. Sleep sounded so good.

"Bran?" Simone slipped in next to me and rolled me over so that she could snuggle in with a few kisses for an apology. "So, when are you going to fuck Gloria?" She wiggled into my arms, my slowly growing member pressing between her tight bubble butt cheeks.

I grunted. "When she's ready."

"She's not that kind of girl," Simone said, slowly stroking me. "You're going to need to take her. Preferably hard and fast."

"These walls are thin." They were curtains.

Simone turned around in my arms, and I felt less tired than before when she kissed at my neck and down my chest. "Hmm. Then you should be quiet."

With both of us freshly cleaned, I could smell Simone's scent again, and my erection continued to wake me up more. I tried to hold onto her, but it was futile. The woman slipped down, kissing down my stomach to my cock and began to smother it in loving kisses.

"It's been too long. He wouldn't take you out with all the danger around," she complained to my member before swallowing it whole without preamble.

I grabbed onto her veil, feeling her horns beneath. They started above and behind her ears, curling just around her skull and coming together at the front to point up.

When she was going down on me, they made fantastic handlebars. My fingers curled around them, and I didn't hold back, thrusting her down so that I was buried in her throat and let her work her magic.

Simone's warm, wet mouth loved me with every inch. She somehow managed to squeeze pleasure from every inch of my cock until I was bucking and dumping my first load of the night down her throat in just a minute.

"Ah." She wiped her plump lips. "I've missed that. You have too. You didn't last long at all. Have I gotten you too used to multiple times a day that a few days without and you're overflowing? Well, we better fix that." She went right back down on me.

I was so sensitive that I wasn't guiding her but holding on as Simone blew me three times in a row. She came off with a sigh and went for round four, but I snatched her waist and pulled her up so that she was sitting in my lap.

"You know, if you keep this up, I won't need anyone else." I ran my hands through her hair.

She slipped her hip up and sank down over me while I held her thin waist. "You say the sweetest things. I think you should fuck Gloria, though. She's good for you and for us."

Simone squeezed her abs as she rolled her hips, sliding me in and out in small strokes. Her pussy squeezed me with slick pulls at each motion as she put her arms over my shoulder and smiled at me.

"Yeah? I'm having a hard time thinking about other women at the moment." I twitched inside of her as she rolled into one of her frequent orgasms.

Simone only let out a small gasp and rested her head on me, continuing to rock me inside of her. "I love you, Bran."

"I love you too, Simone, which is why I'm going to defy my mother. When you come with me to the clan, you are coming as my wife." I held her writhing waist as she continued to slide me in and out of her silken vice.

"In that case, Gloria can wait. But you should do her before you leave," Simone nodded her head to emphasize the point.

"Worried she's going to run away?" I chuckled.

"No. I think she'd chase you." Simone squeezed my cock tight and leaned on me breathing heavily as she gave me incredibly tight strokes.

"You're incredible." I meant that in multiple ways. Both the present moment, her encouragement of me, and all the reasons that I did love her.

"Of course I am. I'm a saint." She kissed me softly as she came again and sank down on me. Her quivering sex set me off, and I painted her insides.

"Are you sure you aren't a succubus in disguise?" I asked.

"No way." She gave me a look of pure innocence with her hands clasped in front of herself. "Does this look like anything other than a saint?" She spoiled the moment by doing kegels on me while she spoke.

I flipped her over, pushing her back onto the bed and driving myself deep inside of her. Thoughts of sleep were completely gone. "I love you. Let me show you how much."

We had a month together before I'd have to head to the clan and we'd have to tighten up how we acted. Not to mention, I was going to be gone within the clan performing the rites. While I knew some of what was coming, part of it had forever been outside my grasp as an outsider to the clan.

"I'm not going anywhere." Simone splayed herself out on the bed gasping as I ravaged her.

***

After Simone performed her morning supplication, we found Gloria set up outside with a desk, a strange device, and her laptop.

"What's that?" I asked.

"Satellite internet." She typed away. "Things are all on track. Do you two feel better?"

"Sex always helps with stress," Simone answered.

Gloria shrugged, and I wasn't sure if she disagreed or didn't care. "So, are we going in search of anything or are we going back in?"

"Have Amanda or Jenny get these items and leave them in a bag at the chasm." I handed her a list.

She glanced over the sheet and nodded, quickly starting to type it up. "How long will it take to clear this?"

I stared at the instance. "I think we could get it down to a day each run. That would give us a little less than a week of buffer to sort things out before I head to the clan."

"And less training." Gloria perked up, closing her laptop. "Let's leave the stuff out. Jenny will drop your things in there."

I put a ring on a loop, hanging it by the tent entrance. It was full of items we'd gotten but were just going to sell. "Add that to their list of things to do. They can sell or use it. Those B rank clubs will sell like hotcakes so we should jack the prices high at the start."

"Is it good to arm everyone out there?" Gloria asked.

I shrugged. "It doesn't hurt to make everyone stronger for the Demon War. Most people are decent. Those that aren't... Well, they'll find out the hard way that they made a poor choice if they go after any of our people. Their first directive is to survive, and I hope they tell me if anyone went after them."

Simone went down by the instance portal and waited. "So, this is the part where you start telling us more about the Heros Clan."

"There's probably a lot of politics going on in it," Gloria added. "So you should tell us everything. Maybe we can pick out some insights that you might not have?"

I stared at both of them and sighed. "The Heros Clan is split. There are three main factions that control the bulk of the clan, as well as hundreds of outer branches. My family comes from one of the outer branches..."

***

I had gone over everything I knew from the Heros Clan with Simone and Gloria multiple times the past few weeks, as well as countless details about Vein City and the upcoming events that I remembered.

Both of them had gotten into intense discussions about what their change in fates would do for the world, as well as laying their thanks at my feet for what I'd done to help them. They asked to tell the Mul Branova girls what I'd done for them, and I refused.

Those girls worshiped me enough. It seemed that several more had joined their ranks, based on the fact that my Worshiped skill had changed.

Jenny and Amanda visited weekly, giving us an update of the Order as well as dropping off a ring full of outfits for Gloria and whatever I asked for the week before.

I played with several inscriptions and combined them into a more functional shower for Simone, to which we had to delay the next instance for half a day as she showed me just how much she enjoyed the improvements.

Overall, our lives were progressing much in line with my desires.

In short order, we found ourselves clearing out the instance for the final time. The Roc died as gold poured down the hill, and I picked up a vial from its corpse.

[Blood Essence of the Golden Roc SS]

I hissed. Why was an SS rank item dropping from a B rank instance? Ever since I saw it on the boss, I had the inkling of an idea that maybe I'd get some sort of loot related to the blood. But this was too much.

Blood Essence was the crux of a bloodline. With this, I could actually transplant it to someone else.

At that thought, my mind drifted to women I'd known in my past life, but then I shunted that aside. They weren't the women I'd once loved. It would be incredibly weird if I sought them out.

They didn't know who I was and it would be very one-sided. Hopefully, I'd ease the burden enough of the

First Demon War that they wouldn't become the hardened women I remembered.

Tucking the vial into my spatial ring, I looked over my shoulder at Gloria and Simone. All three of us had grown greatly in this instance.

Simone was almost Level 100. There was usually a powerful ability at that threshold. Gloria was Level 94 and I was 90. Many of our skills had grown to B rank against the B rank monsters and the repeated use of our healing abilities.

"Oh." Gloria pulled a coat from the gold and threw it over her shoulders as the designer one disappeared. "More fur than I usually go for, but very nice," as she pet the white fur coat.

"It's B rank. Not much is going to punch through it," Simone said, picking through the gold for the other two items. "A pair of... stones?"

"Communication stones, B rank," I said, seeing them. "They are synced such that you can activate them and talk between them. You could be literally on different worlds and they work. Hold onto those."

We cleared the rest of the hill, and it seemed that the stones had counted as two items, but I wasn't upset. With me leaving soon, Gloria would take one and I'd take the other so that we could stay in contact and plan.

I might be in the clan for a while. It was a big, tangled knot, and the more I'd talked with the two of them, the more they wanted me to use the clan for its people rather than a resource piggy bank to break.

And I had to admit, the thought was quite tempting.

Yet new plans were required now that we had a growing force. The Mul Branova group had grown to thirty-eight while we'd been training. Also, Bobby and Rodger had grown to Level 40 alongside Jenny and Amanda, who had somehow become the leaders of the group.

I didn't understand why they were still our drivers, but if they wanted the job, I'd allow it.

"Four days to settle everything up, Simone. Then we head to the clan," I told her and hit the button to exit the instance.

Chapter 54

[Name: Bran Heros
　　Level: 90
Class: Blood Hegemon D
Status: Healthy
Strength: 539
Agility: 265
Vitality: 654
Intelligence: 260
Spirit: 11205
Skills:
Soul Gaze SSS
Soul Resilience S
Blunt Weapon Proficiency C
Endurance B
Throwing Proficiency E
Blood Boil B
Blood Siphon B
Blood Bolt B
Bloodline Collection 57
Regeneration B
Fire Resistance F
Poison Resistance C
Ax Proficiency D
Charge B
Bloodink Quality D
Stealth D
Inscription C
Swim D (Bracer)
Last Stand E

CHAPTER 54

Blood Hex B
Blood Transfusion B
Blood Blade B
Crimson Barrier D
Sword Proficiency A
Worshiped F
Sanguine Locking E]

I finished looking at my stats as I opened the door to my mother's place. "Mom?"

"Here," she called out from deeper inside.

I walked into the place, seeing boxes everywhere and my mother in jeans and a T-shirt wiping her forehead.

"It doesn't matter if you are powerful. Packing is an exercise in patience," she taped up a box.

I waved my hand over the boxes and everything else in the room, sucking them into a D rank ring. "Here, this should be easier."

She frowned at the ring and then her eyes danced over the others. "B rank?" She spotted the nicest ring on my finger.

"Level 87." I spoke of the instance. "It's where I've been lately," I said, not offering more. "We moving?"

"I'm not renewing the lease now that we are going back to the clan," she said. "This was mostly a place to hide."

"Hide from who?" I pushed her.

She shrugged. "People. My life is more complex than you likely understand, Bran. Also…" She threw the ring back at me and used her own. "I pack in boxes as a way to clear things out. I have my own rings."

Hers was an A rank ring.

Damn. My mother certainly had much more than I realized in my past life.

"Why'd you come back early?" she asked.

"Checking in. I depleted the B rank instance and thought I'd swing by, but it seems that wasn't necessary. Tell me, what do you know of the current clan?" I had regaled Simone and Gloria with what I knew of the future, but the present was still a little hidden for me.

"It's a mess. Besides a bunch of old men wanting more bloodlines added to the pool, it is just resources." She sounded a little upset.

"Like you, like me? From what I've been able to understand of grandfather, my father must have had a decent bloodline to sell you off," I tried to probe her for more intel.

She stopped and gave me an unamused glare. "I loved your father, and we had you, but circumstances were complicated. He couldn't stick around and still can't be around me. Now, are you going to help me, or play twenty questions?"

I shrugged. "Why not both?"

She glared at me but went back to packing.

I started to clean out some drawers while continuing to poke my mother for some of the current affairs of the clan. She wasn't very knowledgeable, claiming that she hadn't been back in a while.

Given her low level and general apathy for the clan, it seemed she wasn't lying.

After spending the afternoon helping her pack everything into boxes, I bid her a good day and headed out. There was still more for me to do before it was time to go to the clan.

I passed one of the girls from the Order on my way. "Please let me know if anything happens in the next few days."

"Of course, sir." She nodded sharply and continued her post of watching my mother's apartment.

Amanda jumped to open the door to my car. "Where to, sir?"

"Carmen has a dinner for us tonight," I said, getting in. "Let's go get me a nice suit. The girls are going to dress up for it as well."

***

I pulled at the new suit as I got out of the car at Velluto's.

"You look fantastic, sir," Amanda said. Jenny was already at the restaurant, leaning against Gloria's car. "Yes, you do. When can you swing by and induct the new ladies? We are growing."

Jenny pulled out a few vials from a spatial ring, and Amanda hurried over to collect them and bring them to me.

I waved them into my ring. "I won't use their blood until after. Are you two doing okay?"

"Better than okay, sir." Amanda bowed her head. "We have far more than we could ever dream. This is… this is incredible. Thank you from the bottom of my heart."

"Each of us is making at least 200k working for Gloria. Some of us are roommates. Others are buying nice apartments by the park. All of us are planning to move into the compound that recently broke ground eventually," Jenny added more detail.

I nodded. "Gloria has you guys managing that?"

"Not me." Jenny rubbed at her nose. "I keep busy with the Order, and Amanda here is a training nut who's quickly running out of partners."

Amanda blushed. "I'm the first line of defense if someone comes for Bran while we are traveling."

I patted the top of her head. "Thanks. I can handle myself though, you know."

"Of course, sir!" Amanda hastened to correct herself. "I only—"

"Don't worry. That strength will come in handy in the near future. Keep building it," I told her. "Please try and relax around me more, though."

Eventually, she wouldn't be my driver, but perhaps she could be a lieutenant.

"Yes, sir. Please don't bother with us much longer. I'm sure the rest are waiting on you," she said.

I regarded both of them for a second, and then pulled out two B rank clubs for them and set them down. "Gifts, from me."

Jenny snatched hers. "B rank!" Her eyes glowed.

"Keep it in reserve for now, but it'll crush what you hit like tin cans if you need to," I told them both. "And while you two are both working, please keep an eye out for some of the devotees who might prefer crafting over fighting." Building an army was one thing, but I also needed people crafting potions, armor, weapons and more.

It seemed that the Devotee class was very much a generalist class; it raised stats significantly and increased survival. I'd have to find some skill books that I could cobble together into a working Alchemist. That would be my first priority.

Gloria was quickly growing too precious to sit behind a cauldron all day.

"Will do, sir," Amanda said and gestured for me to continue into the restaurant.

I let them wait by the cars and walked into Velluto's.

The place was just as I remembered it, except that Carmen was sitting at the head of a table with Orvin, Bobby, Candy, Gloria, Simone, and a very pale Michael that was wearing a bib full of drool. Jasper hovered at Carmen's side and had filled out a little.

"You look well, Jasper," I said as I came up on the empty chair between Gloria and Simone. My two ladies were an absolute feast for the eyes. With the arrangement, it seemed that I was being accepted as part of the family already.

"Thank you, Bran. Carmen has been taking great care of me." He dipped his head.

I knew Carmen's character well enough to know that was the truth. After what Michael did to the young man, Carmen would want to make amends. It seemed he was well on his way.

As for Michael, he wasn't dead, but he wasn't much better off.

"He has his lucid moments," Carmen said, seeing me stare at Michael. "And they are getting more common."

"I must have been rougher than I thought." I sat down. "Then again, I'm not used to doing such things on non-players."

"His spirit stat has been recovering," Bobby said. "I think he'll come back to himself in a few weeks."

Carmen almost looked sad at that fact. Then again, he could delay acting while Michael was like this. "I'm told that you've all made great strides." Carmen motioned for drinks to be brought out. "It is about time that we celebrate the explosive growth of the Nesters."

Once we all had a drink in hand, he raised his glass high. "To Family. May we be stronger together."

"Family," we all echoed, clinking out glasses and taking a sip.

Even Carmen drank, which meant any business would be light from this point on. The focus was celebration and pleasure.

"Money is pouring in from Gloria," Bobby said with a nod towards her in congratulations.

"Yes, my team is taking great care. I've been stuck in an instance with Bran who is a merciless trainer," Gloria said, taking another sip and enjoying the fine whiskey for a moment.

"Better harsh training than harsh reality," Carmen intoned. "I can't see. Jasper, how is everyone's strengths?"

The young man looked over the table. "All of them could have individually crushed Michael's whole operation now."

I doubted he really had a sense for what was required of that, but he wasn't wrong. Even Bobby and Candy had grown quite strong. It was clear he was being sweet on his girl, almost like he was resisting hugging her while she sat next to him.

Seeing Candy as a Level 42 paladin sitting among the mafia family was interesting, to say the least.

"We are still a long way from being a force in the player world," I cautioned everyone. "But we are progressing nicely."

"Gold coins from working with North Trust have gone a long way," Gloria said.

"The cash too," Orvin agreed, trying not to be the odd man out. "We're making big progress with that influx."

"Spend it all," Carmen said. "In the next year and a half, spend everything. We want goods, factories, shelter, and power. I want the Nester Family to be completely self-sufficient by the end of the next year and a half."

I nodded. He had tried to scrape something together like that after the rapture, but global supply lines were one of the first things to fail in the new world. "Gas only has a six-month shelf life. Solar can be spotty, and wind sticks out too far. Geothermal on the other hand... perfect for heating in the winter and harder to disrupt."

"Orvin, have fun with it. Use redundancies." Carmen shrugged. "We are preparing to be independent of the city and the world. You used to love those prepper videos."

"Before I learned that you can't really do that," his son sighed. "Let me dig into it. Can we really use all the savings?"

"All of it. There won't be a point to money in banks," Gloria said.

Orvin shook his head like he didn't want to believe it. Yet I knew for this conversation to happen, Carmen had already informed all of them of what we would be up against.

I sipped my whiskey; this wasn't too serious of a topic to drink. There were no actual plans being laid, just conversation around them.

Gloria put a little poison in my drink and stirred it for me before putting a weaker poison into her own. Even while celebrating, we were pushing ourselves. It was part of what let me know Gloria was the kind of woman I could rely on to continue to evolve next to me.

"So, tell me about the instance," Candy reignited the conversation. The blonde had her hair straight and back, with bubblegum pink lipstick on.

"It was full of giants," Simone laughed. "Four stories tall that stepped on Bran like he was a bug."

"He got squished more than a few times," Gloria added. "Though, most of those times he came back out swinging. People have had some names for him, but in my opinion, he should be called The Cockroach King, because he seems to survive everything. He survives poison, getting smashed by B rank giants with clubs. The boss is even a giant Roc that picked him up and dropped him from like a mile in the air. No matter what, he just gets back up, dusts all the blood off of him and keeps going."

By the end, she was staring into my eyes. There wasn't anything but hope that I'd continue to be almost immortal to her.

I might have pushed Gloria hard in the instance, but I was fairly sure that after seeing me really train, she had a new appreciation for how hard I was to kill. That, and she was really starting to hope that I stuck around.

Leaning over, I kissed her on the lips. "Well, players grow by surviving the hard parts. At least, that's how I've always done it."

Gloria's hand snuck under the table and played with my thighs as she pretended that nothing was happening. "Well, at least now I'm very durable."

Chapter 55

Jenny and Amanda drove us back and dropped us off.

We'd exercised our Poison Resistance, but after some heals from Simone and my own Regeneration, the buzz didn't last long. Instead, I held both women by the waist as we walked into the grand apartment.

"Going to miss this place." Simone pulled me down for a sensual kiss.

"We have a few more days," I said, knowing that they were going to be packed with preparations. We had plenty of work on top of everything the Nester Family was doing to make a safe haven for after the Rapture.

Gloria turned my chin and gave me a slow kiss as she sucked on my lips. Simone's hands wormed their way around my belt. I knew if I let her, I'd be out of these pants in seconds. Yet Gloria had been giving me signals tonight at dinner, some that I really didn't want to ignore.

Simone continued to tease me, but my pants stayed on.

"Since tonight has been so lovely…" Gloria trailed off and slipped out of my grasp before dropping her coat and then her dress as she walked towards the bedroom, stopping in the doorway to look over her shoulder. "Are you just going to stare, or are you going to come?" She crooked a finger before slipping into the bedroom.

Simone had my pants off a moment later. She kissed me as she stripped off my jacket and shirt in no time.

"One of these days, I'm going to be in there with both of you," she whispered a promise. "But tonight, I think Gloria is feeling a little like she wants to lock you down before you leave." Simone finished undressing me, her hands wandering over my chest, and she kissed me again. "Go get her. Don't keep her waiting."

I gave Simone one last kiss, swearing to keep this woman, and heading to the bedroom, passing Gloria's coat, dress, and even her bra.

Gloria let out a sigh as I came in as if I'd taken too long, or she was relieved.

I wasn't quite sure which. She could be tricky like that.

But that didn't matter. She was gorgeous, and I stopped to take her in. She had let down her silvery purple hair, and it cascaded down one of her shoulders as she leaned back on the headboard. Her plump red lips curled at the edges in a wicked smile as she enjoyed my reaction.

As for what she was wearing, it wasn't much. Just stockings, heels, and jewelry.

"Come here," she beckoned, trying to remain in control.

I nearly laughed at her thinking she'd hold control, but I was happy to play along for the time being.

I came up to her, my cock already standing proud as Simone had stripped me down before I came in. "Hope you weren't looking forward to the unwrapping." I had to crawl onto the bed to reach her.

She took my face and brought me in for a kiss.

I scooted closer, sucking on her lips as my hand found her long thighs and cupped her tight butt. Then I explored, moving up her thin waist and finally taking her gloriously round breasts in my hand.

Gloria sighed as we broke the kiss. "You have soft hands for how rough you are."

I rubbed over her nipples, playing with them. "Oh, they can be plenty rough." I ran my hands through her hair and got like I was going to stand up and fuck her face.

She shook her head. "That's not going in my mouth."

"No?" I asked.

"Nope." The mafia princess smirked. "You are going down on me. Once you're done down there, you can have your fun." She grabbed my hair and used her full strength to push me down.

"You are going to regret this," I chuckled, only fighting her a little until she couldn't see the smirk on my face. I knew this type.

With a flick of my fingers, I ripped her panties right off and gave her slit a long, savoring lick. By the end of our time together, she was going to be begging for my cock.

"That's it," she sighed and relaxed against the headboard.

I pulled her thighs apart to give me room to work, and my tongue expertly drew out moans from her as I began to play along her folds, dipping inside to taste her rich desire and then teased at her pearl for just a moment before returning to the rest of it.

"Oh," she moaned and tried to pull me back to playing with her clit.

Yet I was fleeting in staying there, instead stimulating her elsewhere only to give it just enough attention to whet her appetite.

"More." She was more forceful in trying to get me to return to the spot she wanted.

I let her push me back and slowly played my tongue over it in lazy figure eights. "That?"

"More." She bucked, pushing my face into it.

I never stopped, just slowly teasing it, suckling on it. All the while, Gloria's ridged poise cracked and melted as she wanted me to finish her.

"You want me to do something like this?" I lashed it with my tongue, causing Gloria to tense up, sucking in a sharp breath of air, but then I stopped. "Yes or no?"

"Yes. More damnit," she moaned, but it wasn't pleading enough for me.

"Oh?" I licked it. "I think I want something in return. How about you beg me for my cock? Hmm?" My tongue touched the spot she wanted, and I waited.

"Give me your cock," she said without much real heat to the statement.

I chuckled and gave her just as much effort in a slow lick. "More, you should be out of breath, begging me for it." I loved princess types. More importantly, I liked to make them beg.

Gloria rolled her eyes. "Give it to me, big man. Stuff me full."

This time was a good fake, I'd give her that, and kissed her pearl, my tongue swirling it in my mouth just enough for her to gasp and let it out before she finished.

"Damnit, Bran, fuck me. Stuff me with that giant cock of yours. Take me. Please!" She put enough into the ask to satisfy me this time.

"Well, if you insist." I flipped her off the headboard and pressed her face into the bed before I shoved it deep inside of her. All in one fluid motion.

"Wai— I— Ooh Ohh." She melted into the bed as I pressed her into it, my finger finding her clit and driving her to completion as I did just what she asked for.

"Feel good." I held her hips and drove myself as deep as I could. This woman needed a good fucking if she thought that the only time she was going to get to feel good was when I went down on her.

Gloria was gasping as she orgasmed under me, and I wasn't stopping, driving her sensitivity into overdrive.

"This—" She was cut off as I slapped her rear, making her squeeze tighter around me.

"Better, tighter," I demanded, riding her into the bed as she came undone a second time, squeezing me through the orgasm and her juices overflowing down my balls.

"Good girl," I rewarded her, reaching around and playing with her clit with one hand while the other lifted her off the bed, using her own weight to drive myself as deep as I could go.

Now that the System was in play, there were more positions we could do that required the kind of strength that humans couldn't have.

Gloria reached behind her with both arms, trying to hold onto me as I thrust so hard that I bounced her on me. She fell down on my cock, pleasurably impaled over and over.

"How's that? Beg me for my cock." I stopped for a moment to let her catch her breath.

Gloria was panting, her eyes a little glazed over. "That... that is incredible. This is sex?"

I chuckled. "This is great sex, the best sex you'll ever have." I bounced her again. "Beg for it."

"I want your— no, I need your cock, give it to me."

There was a raspy need in her voice that satisfied me enough to kiss her as I started to bounce her on me, her ass pressing against my pelvis and my hand moving up to play with her chest as we both started to sweat.

"These are incredible." I played with her breasts, feeling her necklace bounce against my hands and jingle slightly amid the wet slapping of flesh every time I drove myself deep inside of her.

Gloria lost herself, begging for my cock as I switched and laid her out on the desk and made her scream.

Then I brought her over to the bed, making her hold on and bend over as I put one leg over my shoulder and speared into her. I pounded into her until she shook so hard she lost her grip and still begged me for more.

I lifted her up again, holding her in front of the mirror so that we both faced it, and she held onto my arms while I rammed into her from behind.

Her makeup had started to run with the sweat, yet she was so much more beautiful, nearly drooling with pleasure, singing a sweet chorus of moans, begging me for more.

"Yes. More. Deeeeeper," she cried out as I buried myself deep and sprayed into her. "I'm so full," she cried out, rocking on me.

I chuckled and held her chin so that she watched herself. "That's much better. Don't you think?"

She caught my finger and sucked on it. "Delightful. I didn't know sex could be so... good isn't enough. Mind blowing," she breathed the last word.

I pulled her off with a wet noise as we finally uncoupled. "So, how about sucking me as a thank you?"

She smiled, pressing her rear against me such that her sex rode on the base of my cock and her hand curled around the head. "No," she said pointedly with a big smirk. "But I'll give you a handjob. My first." She rubbed her thumb along the ridge. "And I'll let you cum on any part of me you want."

"Your throat," I answered quickly.

She rolled her eyes, but there was a smile in them. "Try again." It might have worked in the throws of everything, but the princess part of her personality was reemerging.

"Your ass." I knew that face and tits wasn't likely to get me anywhere.

She started to pump and stroke my cock while she turned and kissed me. That left my hands free to play with her marvelous breasts and elicit a few moans from her while we kissed.

"Bran," she said, breaking the kiss and looking me in the eyes. "I hope you know that if you don't come back from the clan as soon as you are able, I'm going to hunt you and this down." She gave my cock a squeeze before returning to pumping it.

"I'm eager to get back." My hands played along her soft undersides of her breasts while tension built up in my hips. "Maybe if I do this enough, I'll get you down on your knees."

"You wish," she scoffed and hurried up what she was doing. "Warn me when, so I can shift. Maybe next time, you'll earn a single kiss on it from me, but it'll take much more to get me to kneel before you."

I smiled at the challenge and grunted as I felt the peak coming.

She gave me a few more pumps and slid off of my cock, leaning against the mirror as I blew my load over her ass.

I looked up to see her smiling as she watched me in the mirror, only for the smile to vanish into a smirk. "I need a shower, maybe two."

"Three." I smiled back. "Definitely three. We might get dirty again a few more times." I picked her up and carried her off to the giant bathroom attached to the master bedroom.

Chapter 56

Gloria and I were close to being ready for my departure. Gloria had joined me in bed the last several nights, but refused to submit in truth. Though, I think I was able to awaken a new joy for sex in her.

I was currently initiating the rest of the new Mul Branova ladies as well as handing out potions to help them awaken their bloodlines. I humored them as they reported some rather mundane work.

They were expanding and supporting Gloria with anything that came remotely close to the player world.

"Sir." Amanda came up to me. "I got a call from the one watching your mother. She said a big man, Level 68, just pushed his way into the building." She showed me her phone; it was a picture of a man I knew very well.

I nearly tipped my chair over. "When did this happen?"

"Just now. I'll get the car ready." She rushed out, and I was right on her heels.

Thorin Aegir. He was a powerful man in my past life. In fact, some credited him for the end to the War for Supremacy. After all, he had charged into the Heros Clan because they had killed his woman, and had torn the head off the patriarch and several of the elders before leaving alive.

After that show with all the pressures on the clan, it had collapsed into a smoldering pile of what it once had been. The clan had survived in a much lesser sense and was no longer considered one of the top powers of the world.

Yet Thorin still earned the nickname 'Clan Killer'. The man was an outcast from the Borrson Clan. He had the bloodline of a Steel Titan along with a powerful coordinated class.

Was he tracking down some lead related to the clan? He had to be in conflict with them at least in minor ways before he had resorted to killing the patriarch.

I threw myself into the car behind Amanda as she took off.

"Should our person on the ground try to intervene?" Amanda asked.

"No. She can't stop him." Even if it was years earlier than when he earned the 'Clan Killer' title, he was powerful. The Mul Branova ladies wouldn't hold a candle to him.

"You know him?" Amanda asked.

"He's strong. Very strong," I warned her. "Let me go in alone, but keep the car on. I might have to extract my mother." Could this be part of his problem with the Heros clan?

"Understood." She peeled out, her foot most assuredly plastered to the floor of the car as she raced through traffic as if everyone else was at a standstill.

This was not good. Thorin was half the reason I wasn't going to invest too heavily in my own clan. It seemed that they had too many enemies, and strengthening them too much might create more ripples than I could account for and manage.

Not to mention, their infighting spilt out to other forces more than once.

Yet here was Thorin 'Clan Killer' Aegir. If I wasn't careful, he was going to kill my mother, which would mean I'd have to kill him.

Thoughts of him being the poisoner, or someone sent by the poisoner, flickered through my mind. I had too many useless 'what if's' that I couldn't act on and not enough information at present.

So when Amanda's tires screeched to a halt in front of the apartment building, I threw myself out, rushing up the stairs to face the situation head on.

I raced up the steps and broke my mother's door off its hinges.

She was cornered in the kitchen with Thorin looming over her.

"You touch her and I'll fucking kill you." I had a handful of Duggarfin teeth in one hand and a B rank club in the other.

Thorin was no fucking joke. The man, player status aside, was seven-five, and like all the Borrson, was just big in about every aspect. A lot of them were like me in my previous life and continued to grow well past adulthood.

[Thorin Borrson Aegir
Level: 68
Class: Iron Viking SS
Status: Amorous, Confused, Angry
Strength: 1832
Agility: 391
Vitality: 1632
Intelligence: 421
Spirit: 856
Skills:
Bloodline of the Steel Titan SS (Awakened)
Titan Physique S
Steel Physique S
Hard Skin A
Fire Resistance A
Poison Immunity C
Electrical Immunity A
Shadow Immunity F
Frost Immunity D
Viking Frenzy A
Ax Mastery S
Titanic Strength B
...]

The abilities just kept going. The man was strong.

Like nearly all the Borrson Clan, he had a berserker class. Yet he had a paired class and bloodline that would give him an innate advantage in his growth.

Thankfully, he wasn't nearly as strong as the one time I had fought him in my past life; he was as strong as many of the old men in the clans. Though, it was that fight where I had evolved my Regeneration the first time.

I would have to play this carefully, but I should be able to escape this with my mother and myself alive thanks to Last Stand.

"And who are you? Some minder from the clan?" Thorin's voice was a deep resonating bass as he drew an ax from his spatial ring, ready to kill us both.

"Stop it, both of you." My mother's voice cracked with the force that only a mother or a lover could have.

To my utter astonishment, Thorin put away the ax and scratched the back of his head. "Dear, he came at me."

"Dear? DEAR?!" I repeated the word. In my whole five hundred years of life, I wasn't as shocked as I was right now. "Mom, why is he calling you 'Dear'?!" I demanded answers even as a potential one was squashed down in the back of my head.

No way.

Thorin was... big like me... a berserker, like me... Now that I really looked at him, he was a little bigger around than I was in my past life, but the face... there was a passing resemblance.

I pulled out a chair and sat down on it with a thunk as the Duggarfin teeth and the club disappeared into my spatial rings. "Don't tell me."

"Bran. Meet your father. Thor, meet Bran, your son," my mother sighed as if this was basic knowledge.

I realized I had it all wrong when I had first arrived. She certainly didn't look helpless right now.

"Thor, you aren't supposed to be here," she said sternly, glaring at the giant of a man.

"Well... you see..." Thorin stumbled over himself to try and make an excuse.

I sat in the kitchen dumbfounded as my mother cowed Thorin 'The mother fucking Clan Killer' Aegis, the founder of the Aegis Clan, and one of the most feared men on earth for over a hundred years.

Had I gone back in time, or into a parallel universe where things had become opposites?

"You were in the hospital. I saw the payments," Thorin argued, but even then he sounded weak.

"You said you didn't track that account," my mother scolded him, yet there wasn't much heat behind it, like she'd already guessed as much. "Anyway, as you can see, I'm out now and doing fine."

"If you used that, then you were in trouble," Thorin huffed.

"You took how long to get here?" My mother pursed her lips in rebuttal.

They were arguing like a married couple. They *were* a married couple. I had to remind myself.

This whole situation had me reeling. The ramifications!

If he was married to my mother... then... did he attack the Heros Clan because he perceived her death as their fault? Maybe someone inside the clan was responsible for the poisoning.

Either way, if my mother didn't die, then the final act of the War for Supremacy would never be kicked off, or at least, not as it had happened in my past life.

I rubbed my forehead. Shit, this was more than a butterfly flap. I had just made a giant shift in the future. Possibly so much that the value of my 'future' knowledge would decrease quite a bit.

"You know how it is, I can't fly," Thorin complained.

"Why can't you fly?" I asked mechanically.

"He weighs like five tons," my mother said, answering my question. "It's the titan physique, more than a few of the Borrson's get it, and it makes them ultra dense both physically and mentally, like the fact that he shouldn't be here." She poked the large deadly man in her kitchen.

I knew of the titan physique, but I hadn't thought about it in terms of modern travel.

"Which is why he probably had to take a freight ship here and walk most of the way." My mother was not happy. "We shouldn't be seen together, even if you are outcast from your family. You have a titan bloodline, and they'd kill you and Bran knowing that you passed it to the Heros."

"I have the Heros Bloodline," I corrected my mother, glancing at Thorin and realizing that with the strength of his bloodline, I should have had a titan bloodline. Yet my Heros blood had overridden it.

"Same thing." She waved my comment away.

"You were in the hospital. How could I stay away?" Thorin stomped and shook the apartment. "Those bastards could have easily cured you."

My mother patted the air to calm him and stop Thorin from collapsing the building on us all. "There was no obligation, and I'm not entering instances to pay them tithe for the express purpose of staying off their radar."

"Then what is he!?" Thorin waved at me.

"My son, who's about to go through clan rites and is smarter than you are giving him credit for." My mother sighed. It seemed that my father was a handful. "Bran, now would be a great time to show off that head of yours."

"Thorin." My voice sounded just as exhausted as I felt. "You're my father." Yet rather than focus on the present, my mind was swimming through my past life, reevaluating everything I had experienced.

Did he know in my past life? Is that why he didn't finish me in that fight? I had thought he had taken me for dead before my Regeneration upgraded and I survived just barely.

But if he knew? I was having multiple headaches at once.

"Yes, we've established that Bran," my mother sighed. "Clan Rites, remember."

"Yeah. We are leaving tomorrow." I breathed and pulled myself together. Rather than worry about everything, I'd use this opportunity. "I'll be returning here afterwards with mom. So, if you want to hide out until we are back, I have a fortress being built outside the city."

Thorin raised an eyebrow. "A fortress? But you are just being initiated?"

He tried to Inspect me, and I pushed it aside. His brow furrowed and he closed the gap between me and him in an instant, hitting me in the gut hard enough to surprise me and shatter my concentration. In that moment, he had long enough to Inspect me without my resisting.

"Ah. You've been initiated." He dropped me.

I puked blood on the floor. "What the fuck."

A good half of my ribs were cracked, and I was fairly sure he just popped my spleen. Holy shit, that was a punch. Thankfully, such pain barely phased me, and I could just put on an act, which wasn't hard with the actual damage done. I was able to weave what they saw, but I showed them enough of the truth.

"Don't try and hide from me." He bent down over me. "Oh, Regeneration. That's a good one. Sadly, I don't get hurt enough to train it. You should be thanking your old man for helping you."

"Thank you." My voice dripped with sarcasm.

My mother had her head tilted as she had managed to Inspect me during that moment too. "We both have health potions. You weren't in any danger. That class... Vampire?"

"Very low rank for the name. Something's wrong," Thorin agreed. "And that spirit, incredible over four thousand. Soul Eating Arts? There are records of those in our clan, but no practices."

"He's been hunting demons in the city," my mother said. "Now we know why. He's eating them."

Thorin wrinkled his nose. "Needs to work on his physical stats with that dedication. He might be able to get a physique after he awakens his bloodline. I'll get someone at the clan to sneak me something appropriate once he's back and we know what it is."

"Thank you, Thorin, though his sword skills seem to be coming along." My mother clicked her tongue. "I bet it's still that brutish form. You ought to fight with an ax if you want to fight like this idiot." She hooked a thumb at Thorin.

I peeled myself off the ground, my organs healing and ribs settling back into place. "Well, thank you both for caring."

"Still, you can't go to the clan. The Rites require Level 1," Thorin said.

I glanced at him and smiled before taking out several vials of blood and sampling them each. I could not help but do the big reveal at that moment.

My stats exploded as I ingested Simone and Gloria's bloodline along with the rest of the new Mul Branova girls. "Don't worry. I just need to hide that I'm already initiated for a little while."

My class ranked up twice. Clearly Simone and Gloria's blood had a profound effect.

"Tricks are stupid in front of absolute power. You need to grow stronger," Thorin said, glancing at my mother. "You will be back, or I'll hunt you down again."

"We will be back." My mother put a hand on my shoulder. "Won't we, Bran?"

"Of course. I promise not to cause too much trouble in the clan." I smiled, lying through my teeth.

My mind was swirling, which was not the state I had hoped for as I headed off to my clan for the first time.

If Thorin wasn't going to crush the clan, then my plans needed to change and change quickly.

My return had already made greater waves than I had ever imagined. I would just have to become strong enough to weather them head on.

[Name: Bran Heros
Level: 1
Class: Blood Hegemon B
Status: Healthy
Strength: 655
Agility: 381
Vitality: 770
Intelligence: 376
Spirit: 11321
Skills:
Soul Gaze SSS
Soul Resilience S
Blunt Weapon Proficiency C
Endurance B
Throwing Proficiency E
Blood Boil B
Blood Siphon B
Blood Bolt B
Bloodline Collection 86
Regeneration B
Fire Resistance F
Poison Resistance C
Ax Proficiency D
Charge B
Bloodink Quality D
Stealth D
Inscription C
Swim D (Bracer)
Last Stand E

Blood Hex B
Blood Transfusion B
Blood Blade B
Crimson Barrier D
Sword Proficiency A
Worshiped F
Sanguine Locking E]

Afterword

Well, that was a fun one. I had been sitting on wanting to do a regression/returner for a while. Bran's character is fun too, everyone likes someone who's competent and ready to curb stomp someone to get what they want.

I actually was fairly obsessed with writing this one. Finished Ard's Oath 3 about a week late and then turned around and wrote this giant in like 3 weeks. The shorter chapters were somehow super motivational. It was like when you stay up reading 'oh just another chapter' except this was writing because I could bang one out in an hour. Excited to continue this series, not planning on making it a super long one, but obviously it has potential.

There are three covers made for the book and I'm excited to watch Bran muck about in the clan in the next book. Anyway, thank you everyone for supporting me having fun and reading my work!

Please, if you enjoyed the book, leave a review.

Review Returner's Defiance

I have a few places you can stay up to date on my latest.

Monthly Newsletter

Facebook Page

Patreon

Also By

Legendary Rule:
Ajax Demos finds himself lost in society. Graduating shortly after artificial intelligence is allowed to enter the workforce; he can't get his career off the ground. But when one opportunity closes, another opens. Ajax gets a chance to play a brand new Immersive Reality game. Things aren't as they seem. Mega Corps hover over what appears to be a simple game. However, what he does in the game seems to effect his body outside.
But that isn't going to make Ajax pause when he finally might just get that shot at becoming a professional gamer. Join Ajax and Company as they enter the world of Legendary Rule.

Series Page

A Mage's Cultivation – Complete Series
In a world where mages and monster grow from cultivating mana. Isaac joins the class of humans known as mages who absorb mana to grow more powerful. To become a mage he must bind a mana beast to himself to access and control mana. But when his mana beast is far more human than he expected; Isaac struggles with the budding relationship between the two of them as he prepares to enter his first dungeon.
Unfortunately for Isaac, he doesn't have time to ponder the questions of his relationship with Aurora. Because his sleepy town of Locksprings is in for a rude awakening, and he has to decide which side of the war he is going to stand on.

Series Page

The First Immortal – Complete Series

Darius Yigg was a wanderer, someone who's never quite found his place in the world, but maybe he's not supposed to be here...Ripped from our world, Dar finds himself in his past life's world, where his destiny was cut short. Reignited, the wick of Dar's destiny burns again with the hope of him saving Grandterra.

To do that, he'll have to do something no other human of Grandterra has done before, walk the dao path. That path requires mastering and controlling attributes of the world and merging them to greater and greater entities. In theory, if he progressed far enough, he could control all of reality and rival a god.

He won't be in this alone. As a beacon of hope for the world, those from the ancient races will rally around Dar to stave off the growing Devil horde.

Series Page

Saving Supervillains – Complete Series

A former villain is living a quiet life, hidden among the masses. Miles has one big secret: he might just be the most powerful super in existence.

Those days are behind him. But when a wounded young lady unable to control her superpower needs his help, she shatters his boring life, pulling him into the one place he least expected to be—the Bureau of Superheroes.

Now Miles has an opportunity to change the place he has always criticized as women flock to him, creating both opportunity and disaster.

He is about to do the strangest thing a Deputy Director of the Bureau has ever done: start saving Supervillains.

Series Page

Dragon's Justice

Have you ever felt like there was something inside of you pushing your actions? A dormant beast, so to speak. I know it sounds crazy.

But, that's the best way I could describe how I've felt for a long time. I thought it was normal, some animal part of the human brain that lingered from evolution. But this is the story of how I learned I wasn't exactly human, and there was a world underneath our own where all the things that go bump in the night live. And that my beast was very real indeed.

Of course, my first steps into this new unknown world are full of problems. I didn't know the rules, landing me on the wrong side of a werewolf pack and in a duel to the death with a smug elf.

But, at least, I have a few new friends in the form of a dark elf vampiress and a kitsune assassin as I try to figure out just what I am and, more importantly, learn to control it.

Series Page

Dungeon Diving

The Dungeon is a place of magic and mystery, a vast branching, underground labyrinth that has changed the world and the people who dare to enter its depths. Those who brave its challenges are rewarded with wealth, fame, and powerful classes that set them apart from the rest.

Ken was determined to follow the footsteps of his family and become one of the greatest adventurers the world has ever known. He knows that the only way to do that is to get into one of the esteemed Dungeon colleges, where the most promising young adventurers gather.

Despite doing fantastic on the entrance exam, when his class is revealed, everyone turns their backs on him, all except for one.

The most powerful adventurer, Crimson, invites him to the one college he never thought he'd enter. Haylon, an all girls college.

Ken sets out to put together a party and master the skills he'll need to brave the Dungeon's endless dangers. But he soon discovers that the path ahead is far more perilous than he could have ever imagined.

Series Page

There are of course a number of communities where you can find similar books.
https://www.facebook.com/groups/haremlit
https://www.facebook.com/groups/HaremGamelit
And other non-harem specific communities for Cultivation and LitRPG.
https://www.facebook.com/groups/WesternWuxia
https://www.facebook.com/groups/LitRPGsociety
https://www.facebook.com/groups/cultivationnovels